Exile
Steph Macca

Contents

Triggers and Warnings

- Assault (physical)

- Blackmail

- Blood/gore

- Bodily Fluids

- Bribery

- Broken bones

- Caskets

- Child abuse/neglect (off page back story)

- Choking

- Corruption

- Death

- Decapitation

- Drugs

- DVP

- Fire/arson (including physical harm)

- Funerals

- Group scenes

- Guns/shooting

- Inhumane experiments

- Isolation

- Kidnapping

- Knives/shivs

- Loss of a family member

- Masks

- Medical neglect (off page back story)

- Mental Illness Discussions

- Mind games

- Morgues

- Murder

- Permanent markings

- Removal of body parts

- Scars due to trauma

- Sexual assault (off page back story and recollection, including mention of injuries)

- Stabbing

- Starvation

- Suicide

- Swearing

- Torture

- Unethical behavior from professionals

- Violence

- Weapons

Run, little killer.

We like to chase our prize before we claim it.

Recap from Ravage

"I suppose I should congratulate you," he jeers. "Welcome to the family, daughter-in-law."

Avery breathes in sharply. "What?"

Grey looks at me, a flash of panic in his eyes. A guard has him in a headlock, crushing his throat, but that's not what he's afraid of.

"You're married now," my father says sternly. "And apparently, a shareholder in Lilydale. You'll have to excuse me for not being more *delighted*."

She squeezes my arm, falling quiet. I can sense the dots connecting, her eyes darting over to Christopher—probably realizing that the piece of paper he had her sign this morning was a marriage license.

I should have told her, but I didn't want to ruin our little bubble of happiness. I didn't want to put that weight on her shoulders just yet.

My mother really thought of everything—including a clause in the trust that stipulated any shares in a company or organization tied to her inheritance must be partially distributed to my spouse... *from the majority shareholder.*

It was a safeguarding measure. If I was still the majority holder, a small percentage would go to my wife as marital compensation. But in our case, where I no longer held the majority, the clause was designed to protect *my* interests in the inheritance—meaning my father lost a fraction to ensure an equitable split since I'm the sole beneficiary. It's like my mother knew this was a possibility. If he hadn't forced my hand by making me sign over two percent, Avery's small marital percentage would have come from me, making him the majority shareholder even if our combined shares equaled more. But now, our marriage has tipped the scales—*all because of his greedy actions.*

Her five percent share has reduced his to forty-six... allowing me to take back the power with my forty-nine.

Sure, he can have Elsher try to sign off to say I'm not mentally capable, but thanks to Christopher's psychiatric assessment, I've been deemed mentally sound to enter into marriage—at least for today. Plus, he officiated our license, with his freshly ordained credentials off the internet—meaning my father can't strong-arm or bribe an outsider official to say it wasn't legal. We might end up in a stalemate, but we'll be able to stop them dipping their greedy fingers into the fund. The injunction request has already been filed with the marriage license, so for now, we've managed to stop them.

It also means that if he kills me, Avery gets everything.

And he is fucking livid.

"Put the gun down," I say, my voice low.

I never should have let Avery come with me. Grey and Theo struggle against the guards, eyes dark with anger as they fight to get to her, sensing the rising danger. We have to play it sensibly here—one wrong move...

"Arthur," he turns, looking at the other man. "What would you like to do here?"

I'm horribly aware that we are outnumbered. None of the guards seem confident enough to side with me, not while my father and Arthur have the upper hand—and certainly not while he's pointing a gun in our direction.

"Send the birthday boy down to solitary confinement," Arthur replies. "And the other two as well. They can go in together—we'll bend the rules just this once since it's a *special* occasion."

He motions for the guards to step forward, and as soon as one of them lays a hand on me, I snap. There's no way I'm leaving Avery alone with these assholes. I turn around and swing at the guard, punching him square in the face. Another makes a grab for Avery, pulling her away from me and I see *fucking red*.

They aren't taking her away from me—away from *us*.

I lunge forward, breaking his wrist with a loud snap, forcing him to let go of her. More swarm toward me, trying to take me down in pairs, and I slam my body into them, sending them backwards onto the ground.

Behind me, I hear the commotion as Grey and Theo lash out at the guards again, trying to break free from their holds.

Someone manages to get my arm behind my back, but Avery throws her bodyweight into him, tipping him off balance. In my peripheral vision, I see her throw a punch, managing to get a guard in the nose.

That's my fucking wife.

Smiling, I move onto the next guard closest to me, splattering him against the wall with a loud sickening crack before he drops, motionless.

A roar of voices startles everyone, our heads whipping in unison to the end of the corridor to find the members of *Cirque des Morts* charging down, led by Byrone at the front of the pack. The distraction gives Christopher a moment of leverage, throwing his guard across the hallway. He falls into Arthur, the older man losing his footing as he lands heavily on the ground.

"Get up!" I hear my father yell, urgently.

Immediately, I look for Avery, reaching under a guard's arm to grab her wrist. I kick the guard hard in the kneecap, feeling it break under my foot. When he goes down, I yank her to me, Avery smashing into my chest. Her gray eyes peer up at me in panic, and I'd give anything to take that fear away—to get her out of here safely.

A few guards stumble backwards, trying to move out of the way as my people slam into them. They go flying past me, falling like dominos. I grip Avery in my tight hold, spinning her around just as the sound of a gunshot rings out.

Someone yells, followed by eerie silence as I twist my head to find my father on the ground, knocked over by a guard. The gun is still in his hand, and I quickly scan my eyes over everyone—Avery, Grey, Theo, Christopher, Byrone... trying to figure out where the shot landed.

I breathe a sigh of relief when they all look fine, surveying the carcasses on the ground.

"Damon..." Avery whispers, and I turn quickly to look at her.

Her hands are outstretched, palms up, and my heart stops at the sight of them covered in blood. My gaze darts to her face, finding tears in her eyes as she stares at me wide-eyed and panicked.

"Fuck!" I hear Grey yell, but it's muffled by a ringing in my ears.

A chill runs through me and I glance down, spotting droplets of blood dripping around me onto the floor. That's when it hits me...

I'm the one that's been shot.

"Damon!" Avery screams, pain shooting through me as my legs give out and I hit the ground.

My vision starts to go hazy, darkness creeping around the edges. The last thing I see before it all goes black is Avery and Grey leaning over me, frantically mouthing my name.

Prologue

Damon

I always said that if people saw me as the villain, then I'd be their fucking villain. And secretly, a part of me loved it. Most people want to be admired, loved. Why bother with that when you can be feared and respected?

I pride myself on knowing everything, always being in control. Ever since I was dragged into Lilydale, a violation and mockery of my mother's legacy, I vowed to seek retribution and revenge on my father.

The end goal has always stayed the same—*kill him*. It was only fair... an eye for an eye, subjecting him to the same fate as Lily Emerson-Dale.

When they started pumping the facility full of patients, a second, albeit equally important goal, emerged—*save them*. I couldn't save my mother but I could try to save them from my father. And bringing him down at the same time? It was a win-win situation.

It was obvious from the first *real* patient after me to arrive that these people were not criminals; they were victims, let down by society and the people who were meant to protect them. And now, they were under the control of my father and his lapdogs. I swore from that day that I would take back control in every way and shape imaginable. After all, my father's sole purpose in life, aside from accumulating wealth, was to keep me chained and exercise his obsessive need for power over me. It was only fitting that I would take back that control and power from inside the one place he dared not to enter. It's the perfect resolution and ending—a full circle moment. The great Alexander Dale created Lilydale to cage me and exert dominance, only for me to beat him at his own game.

In his mind, we are nothing but beneath him. He only surrounds himself with people he deems worthy of his presence. In other words, fellow chauvinistic assholes like Arthur Whittingham.

I knew he couldn't resist a power struggle. Any opportunity to strike me down he will take without hesitation. But I had the upper hand since he was afraid to spend more than fifteen minutes inside the walls of the Lilydale Foundation Center, scared he'd be swallowed up by the demons he harbored there and suffocate to a slow death. After all, don't they generally say that people live and breathe their own worst fears and guilt? While the rest of the world might see him as some kind of community hero, he's a spineless bastard haunted by the ghosts of his past actions. Everywhere he looks, everywhere he goes, he sees them. It's easy to pretend they aren't real. Except when one of his ghosts is still very much alive, angry, hunting him down.

Me.

He's terrified of meeting the same fate as his wife and losing everything. And well, he should be. Because his day of retribution is coming.

Over time, we grew in strength inside Lilydale. Everything went according to plan—*my* plan—and in my mind, I had prepared for every possible scenario.

But what I never expected was to end up *here*.

In violence and corruption, I found an unexpected peace. An inferno of flames in an otherwise dark abyss—someone to dance with my demons.

My control started to slip, but for once, I didn't mind. Because it was taken by someone I never saw coming.

For the first time since my mother died, I experienced *love* again—even if I didn't want it. Her vibrant light choked me, wrapping around my black heart like barbed wire, ripping me apart, until finally, she cracked me wide open.

In my own personal hell, I found *her*.

Avery.

For the first time, someone saw me as more than their savior. More than a leader and someone to fear.

She wanted to save... *me*.

So now, it's only fitting that I should *die* for her.

Chapter 1

Grey

Warm blood seeps down my knuckles, cascading like a waterfall along my wrist and landing somewhere on the floor. But despite the obvious pain I should be feeling from repeatedly punching the metal door in my room, I feel absolutely nothing except unbridled rage and the aberrant, uncomfortable sensation of panic.

Along with the fresh, copper scented blood that's freely flowing from my split skin, there's sticky, dried patches of murky red on the palms of my hands. And it kills me to know it's not mine.

It's Deadman's. No—I can't call him that right now.

I slam my foot against the door, changing tactics. Except for the loud banging, it achieves nothing, other than sending a shooting pain through my leg. I don't care though. I have to get out of this fucking room. The irony isn't lost on me that I've spent the majority of my time in Lilydale being able to come and go as I please from this cell, and suddenly, when I need to leave it the most, I'm trapped.

Mental images of Avery and Damon are firmly implanted in my mind, burning a hole in my fleeting sanity—if there was any left to destroy before the events of today. They replay over and over, and I just know Avery's hands are covered in Damon's blood as well.

Her small, pale hands were frantically pumping Damon's chest, trying to perform CPR before the guards grabbed both of us and ripped us away from Damon's gunmetal pallor, still frame. The fuckers tasered me after I swung at one of them. The last thing I remember before my mind blanked out temporarily is Avery shouting at the top of her lungs—repeatedly calling out mine and Damon's names, before suddenly Theo's was added into the mix with a new air of frenzy. I could make out her threats and pleas, doing everything she possibly could to get control of the situation.

But what even is control? We had it for so long, used to being able to roam freely, making the guards bend to our will. Now... that apparently no longer exists.

We were forcibly pulled apart in the hallway and shoved back into our own rooms. And for the first time, I couldn't get back out.

That old cunt must have shut down the building's entire system, blocking our ability to override their efforts and open doors, even with Byrone and Jillian's talents. They frisked me before throwing me into my personal prison box, confiscating my staff access card and cell phone. And because of that, I have no doubt they did the same to the others too. No contact, no exit, no way of knowing what is happening in that hallway.

Fuck. I have no idea if Avery is okay or if Damon is still alive. Not to mention our other members who joined the fight before all hell broke loose.

There's a blinding madness inside me and I can't seem to get a grip on it. I've always been good at wielding my anger, being in control of it instead of the other way around. But now I'm a prisoner to my own emotions, spiraling more and more as the minutes pass without freedom or updates.

I keep punching and kicking the metal door non-stop, desperate to break it down or find some reprieve—even if that means seeking out pain to stop me from losing my shit.

The last time I blacked out beyond saving, I came to in a pool of blood—one of my favorite places to be, only second to being buried inside Avery. My father was dead underneath me, unrecognizable, nothing more than a mangled corpse reflecting my built-up rage that had finally imploded and exploded into violence. It took me five whole minutes before it dawned on me that the dizziness I was feeling was due to my own blood loss, my neck slashed open and red liquid drenching my shirt.

A neighbor had heard everything and when paramedics and cops arrived at our front door, that was the end of the ordeal. I blacked out again, waking up handcuffed to a hospital bed.

I relive the pool of blood often in my dreams. Which is how I know that the amount of blood that surrounded Damon is serious—life threatening even. He was left bleeding out on the floor, and when Avery was dragged away toward the female dorms, I didn't see anyone else step in to continue CPR administrations. Every rational part of me is trying to prepare for the worst. People don't survive that—not often. I should know. I've spent all my time in Lilydale perfecting my craft, learning the limits to draw out suffering if need be. And although Damon has one hell of a stubborn-ass nature, not even he is immune to the finality of death.

Fuck! How did things get this far?

We didn't just stir the pot with our little matrimonial surprise—we blew everything into a million tiny pieces. Alexander and Arthur will be out for blood now. Literally. Vultures like them scavenge and hunt ruins, picking up the leftover pieces for their own personal gain.

Now Avery is defenseless and alone, a sitting target—and fuck, I don't even know if my best friend is still alive. Alexander would be more than happy to watch his son die on the floor of Lilydale on his birthday. Arthur too. Especially with them now knowing that Avery is Damon's legal heir and she's within reach for the kill—an easy target they seem all too keen on taking out. Alexander will stop at nothing to reclaim what he believes he is entitled to. She's just an obstacle in his obsession, in enemy territory while we're wounded and caged inside their prison cells. He'll want her out of the way as soon as possible.

I have to get out of this fucking room. Now.

In the distance, I can hear the sound of sirens surrounding Lilydale. I'm not surprised—this is one situation that they can't sweep under the rug. They can't exactly claim it was a suicide or some other bullshit story when multiple witnesses saw the smoking gun in Alexander's hand. Not only that, but guards are dead too. I know because I killed a few myself, the sweet sounds of bones cracking under my weight as their blood spilled onto the floor.

Death is inevitable in Lilydale—a hazard of the job. It's probably listed as a risk in their job description.

They will blame the deaths on us—the unruly, mentally deranged patients. As for Alexander, with money comes influence and power, and they will believe his and Arthur's word against ours.

"It was an accident. It was self-defense. My hand slipped because they were attacking us. We had no choice—it was life or death. I tripped over. I was pushed. He was coming for me."

I need Damon to be okay. He can't be dead. I refuse to believe that he's gone.

Even though I saw his eyes close, his breathing falter and skin turn a shade of pewter, there's no way he is dead. It was supposed to be the other way around—Damon was meant to kill Alexander. Fuck, if there's a God out there, he can take me. I'll gladly give up my life if it means saving Damon and Avery. Theo too. At least if he's around, Avery will be protected. I know he'd give his life for her as well.

We had finally gained the upper hand, surprising them with our wildcard move. Agreeing to let Damon marry Avery was the most humbling experience ever. I wanted it to be me marrying her one day, somewhere far away from this hellhole. I have no idea how that would have worked, or if marriage would even be on the cards with our interesting situation, but it was a reverie nonetheless. I wanted to tie her to me in every way possible, short of infusing our bodies together like some fucked-up version of Frankenstein. We could have played *rock paper scissors* to decide who gets to marry her, even if I'd be awfully tempted to chop off their hands to win by default.

Regardless, the impromptu marriage was our only chance, the loophole we needed over Alexander. I'd do anything to keep her safe and to fuck Lilydale's financial leverage into the ground—even giving up the chance to marry her myself. Having them all with me, that's the only thing that's important. We're a family now. And maybe it was our opportunity to also get out of this hellhole. We could use Damon and Avery's positions as shareholders to fight back legally, expose Lilydale for the corrupt empire that it is. But apparently, Alexander felt as strongly about it as we did—just the other end of the emotional spectrum.

All the lights are out, and with the sun now sitting somewhere on the other side of the building, the looming darkness that approaches does nothing to calm me. With every second that passes, it's a second more they have to potentially hurt Avery. It's more time to make sure Damon is well and truly dead, to wipe out the only person who is capable of freeing us from their corral.

How the fuck do I get this damn door open?!

Surely, a building would have to have some kind of emergency switch. In the event of a power outage or fire, there would legally have to be a way for people to escape otherwise it would be a building code violation. Even if Arthur has blacked out the whole building—electricity, access pad settings, and security measures—there has to be a back-up.

I hope Byrone is working on it. And Jillian too. Maybe they can find a way to override their security, infiltrate the systems and turn the power back on. Then, they just have to unlock the doors—just for a split second—like they have done so many times before. Hopefully their devices have enough battery charge.

We're relying on too many *hopes* and *maybes* for my liking.

Byrone was there—he knows what went down. He is as loyal as they come, so I know they are working on doing something. Someone would have gotten a message to Jillian, or she put two and two together like the smart cookie I know she is. Right now, they are our only hope unless something happens or changes.

There's no doubt in my mind that Arthur's IT people are fighting our advances, but we can't afford to fail here. I need to get to Avery and Damon.

A sickening crunch reaches my ears when I punch the door again, and this time, the pain does manage to catch me by pleasant surprise. I stumble back slightly, clutching my fist. Looking down, it's easy to tell that through the blood one of my knuckles is probably broken. I'll just switch hands. I can punch just as well with my non-dominant one—Ambidextrous overachiever of vengeance.

As I start to pound the door with my other fist, it takes me a second to realize some of the banging I'm hearing back isn't an echo of my own actions. Pausing, I listen, eyes narrowing as the door rattles in front of me. Someone is on the other side and whoever it is, they are kicking it equally as hard.

"Who's there?" I question with a raised voice.

There's no response, and immediately I'm back on edge. Turning around, I try to find something I can use to slam into the door. Everything is bolted down, but before I can figure out Plan B, the lights suddenly flicker on.

Low, deep humming confirms that power is now surging through the building, my heart hammering in my chest. Quickly, I rush back to the door, slamming my foot into it as whoever is on the other side does the same.

Come on, Byrone...

Seconds tick by, torturing me as our window of opportunity grows smaller and smaller. Bile threatens to rise up my throat as I wait, throwing my whole weight into the door for good measure. And to make it hurt.

Just as quickly, the lights turn off again, sending me back into growing darkness—but not before the sweet sound of a click grabs my attention.

Just in time. Good fucking job, guys.

The metal door creaks open ever so slightly, and I lunge for it, my fingers prying themselves into the tiny gap as I yank it toward me. It swings open forcefully, a body barreling into the room and colliding with me.

"Christopher?" I murmur in disbelief, glancing over him as he pants heavily, business shirt disheveled and hair a mess.

He straightens up, running a hand down his lower face in relief—which I instantly notice has no traces of blood unlike mine. Besides his hair and clothes being unkempt, he's oddly clean, not at all reflective of the bloodbath that just went down.

"We don't have much time. Come on," he says, jerking his head in a gesture for me to follow him into the corridor.

There's no need to tell me twice. I'm out the door a second later, hot on his heels.

If they think it was a massacre before, they haven't seen anything yet.

Chapter 2

Avery

I stare at my palms with wide eyes, doing my best not to hyperventilate. High school was such a blur but it's strange the little bits of knowledge that reappear when you least expect it.

The day Miss Callaghan taught us about body anatomy and hematology, I was nursing bruised ribs after my father kicked me the night before. Until now, all I remembered from that day was how exhausting it was trying to breathe normally. In and out, controlled breaths, inhaling tiny sips of air through my dried lips while she rambled on about the human body. I thought I wasn't paying attention to her words, but somehow, my brain filed away some of the information for later use. I just wish it wasn't relevant for right now.

The human body has roughly one and a half gallons of blood.

Once, I spilled a carton of milk at home. That was roughly half a gallon. The mess sent me sliding on my hands and knees all over the kitchen floor while I hastily tried to clean it up before my father noticed—he always did though. It seemed like a lot of milk at the time, but now, my mind is splicing together that image with what I witnessed today, and suddenly, it feels like I saw more blood than milk.

How much blood can you lose before you are beyond saving?

Everything happened so quickly. In my almost disillusioned state, I barely had time to take notice of my surroundings.

But here I am.

It all looks so different—like a dystopian world, bereft and full of regret.

I must resemble a living nightmare for the *normal* people that linger nearby. They think I don't see their terrified eyes and hear their whispered words... but I do. I don't blame them for being afraid. I'm scared too.

Sitting here, covered in blood, it feels like I've come full circle in life. Once again to my horror, I find myself at the hospital, tainted and covered in the ending existence of someone else.

Except this time, it's different.

I'm covered in my husband's blood.

My husband.

The words are still foreign to me. There was barely any time to register my shock when that bomb was detonated. It took every ounce of strength not to show the disbelief and confusion that flooded my entire body when I found out I was married. All I knew was that I had to hide my reaction from Alexander.

I'm married to Damon.

The man who haunted my nightmares *and* my daydreams. The one who, not too long ago, made me fear for my life. Who promised me nothing but pain and suffering.

Married to the very one who saved me from a fate worse than death.

And now, I'm sitting here, covered in his blood after he took a bullet from his own father to protect me. I want to kill him... lovingly, of course. He should have let me take the hit. We need him.

The patients need him.

Cirque des Morts needs him.

How did I end up here? And for a second time in a year nonetheless.

Realistically, I know the answer to that on a surface level. After we were dragged away from Damon, kicking and screaming, I found myself back in my room. But a short while later, the door opened, leaving me face to face with a barely composed Dr. Smith and two police officers.

At first, they took me to his office—a sight that will be forever ingrained in my soul. The corridor still showcased our earlier fight; blood splattered all over the walls and floor, and dead bodies flat on the ground surrounded by uniformed officials. You'd think *that* would be the worst sight. But nothing could prepare me for the crimson pool in the middle of the walkway. Damon's physical presence may have been gone from the spot, but in my mind, I could still see him lying on the floor. His pale skin, ragged breathing. My hands trembled as I tried to pump his chest, repeating his name over and over as I begged him to wake back up before rough hands tore me away.

I couldn't let him die. Even the dead bodies surrounding us couldn't distract me from the pool of blood I knew was his.

Lilydale promised to save me, even when I adamantly believed I was beyond salvation. But in a strange turn of events, I was saved.

By Grey. By Theo. And by Damon.

There's no life for me if those three aren't in it. Damon is the glue that holds us together—the foundation of support while Grey and Theo are my pillars of strength.

It turns out Dr. Smith is quick on his feet. When the police and paramedics arrived at Lilydale, they started triaging staff and patients, escorting those who needed medical attention to the hospital. Even if Dr. Markel was a skilled surgeon and not hyperfixated on lullabies, he'd be out of his depth with what just happened. Too many dead and injured for one man to handle.

From what I could make out as I was escorted in handcuffs from Dr. Smith's office to the entrance, Alexander and Whittingham were too busy chatting to detectives, getting their story straight. They don't care about the welfare of the patients or staff, so it was up to Dr. Smith to jump in, directing first responders to people he thought needed medical attention. But he knows as well as I do that I wasn't injured. For once, I caught on quickly to his tactic and stupid riddles, playing along. I was covered in blood, making it unclear whether or not I had any wounds, so I used that to my advantage.

It gave me the opportunity to temporarily get out of Lilydale, away from the disaster that was going down. It's ironic really—especially after Dr. Smith tried so hard to get me out of the facility after Sam's death and accidentally framed me for murder. At least this time he got it right...

I didn't want to leave Grey and Theo behind, but after catching a glimpse of Damon's lifeless frame being hoisted into a separate ambulance, I knew where I needed to be. That man did not just save me to be left alone and unprotected. I suspect that was Dr. Smith's motive too, as well as attempting to get me away from Alexander and Whitface. My new father-in-law wanted to kill me—and not in the hilarious in-law fashion that people joke about. Actually *murder me*—and his own son.

The only consolation was that I saw all the dead bodies in the hallway when I was escorted to Dr. Smith's office. If Damon was being taken to the hospital, that had to mean something. It has to mean he was still breathing or had a fighting chance. Otherwise, they would have left him on the cold floor with the other bodies...

Right?

Perhaps I can use our marriage as leverage somehow at the hospital. Maybe that was what Dr. Smith was also hinting at me to do. I'm not sure—all I know is he was trying to get me out of there while detectives scoured the corridors, taking photographs and placing those bright yellow numbers where dead bodies lay fallen.

In Lilydale, our marriage probably means nothing except for currency and a weapon of war, but to the outside world, to the hospital... Maybe it holds power.

Of course, I'm still a criminal in the eyes of the law and very much a suspect who was directly involved in the events of today. I may not have held a gun, but I can bet my life that Whitface wouldn't hesitate to throw me under the bus. They will spin the narrative, blaming us for the events that went down. Especially Damon when he can't defend himself.

When I arrived at the hospital, Damon was nowhere to be seen. I was taken, still handcuffed, to a tiny room near the ER. Apparently, they have a special room for people like us. A small, isolated white room where law enforcement can keep me away from the general public like I'm a dangerous monster. It's adjacent from the waiting area, people staring through the open door at my bloodied frame with horrified looks.

Cuffed and chained like an animal, covered in a sickening amount of blood, it's easy to see they think I killed someone. If only they knew that the real monsters were the ones in expensive suits, living among them. Soulless creatures who would rather kill their own blood than risk losing a single cent from their beloved bank accounts.

I've never been a patient person. I'm my own worst enemy. Every second that passes, the voices in my head chant my unspoken fears, threatening to send me into permanent madness.

I don't know what's worse really: being here, clueless and wondering if Damon has taken his last breath. Or being away from Grey and Theo, wondering if they have been hurt by the aristocratic madmen who call themselves doctors and businessmen. After all, wouldn't Alexander and Arthur want to make sure they are silenced? The police will be asking questions while the media flocks to the Lilydale grounds, eagerly frothing at the mouth and demanding their next front page story.

Money can't buy our silence. But a bullet can.

"Can you loosen the handcuffs?" I ask the cop stationed at the door.

He glances lazily over his shoulder at me, chewing gum. "No."

He practically reeks of arrogance and superiority even though he's probably only a handful of years older than me. His murky blue eyes spoke volumes when he first laid eyes on me at Lilydale. He sneered at my frame, not bothering to be gentle when he cuffed me. Even the product in his hair smells expensive, the wax ensuring every single black hair remains in place while dealing with us. I know officers don't get paid much, so there's no doubt in my mind that he's some kind of nepo baby, using his trust fund in his free time while wielding power at work to feel as important as his wealth proclaims him to be.

"It's hurting me," I say quietly, attempting to draw a fraction of humanity from him. The silver cuffs bang against the table as I jiggle them, showing him how tight they are pressed against my wrists which are turning a light shade of purple.

"Tough shit," he mumbles, laughing to his colleague.

"Loosen the fucking cuffs," I snap in frustration, losing my cool.

His work companion, a slightly older woman in her late twenties, doesn't seem to share his amusement. She doesn't quite roll her eyes at him, but they do flare for a moment. He laughs enough for the both of them though, drawing more attention from waiting patients as he ignores me.

I hate it.

Finally, a nurse stops in front of them, holding a manila folder in her hands.

"You can bring her into the consultation room," she says softly, glancing over Captain Asshole's shoulder to smile at me.

Her aging skin is flawless, and on a better day, I'd ask for her skincare routine. But I just lock eyes with her hazel ones, offering a small smile back.

"Fineee," the asshole scoffs, as if inconvenienced by doing his damn job. If he was doing it properly, he'd be at Lilydale, arresting the real villains.

Stalking over to me, he's rough again, making sure to slam my hands into the table as he uncuffs me from the metal link that's securing me to the bolted-down furniture. Before he can readjust the cuffs to tighten them again, the female officer chimes in.

"Leave them off, Harry. She's a patient, for God sake."

"She's a criminal, Emma. Probably shot up half that hall-way."

The nurse steps into the room, making her way over to me. "I'll take her from here, Officer. Why don't you go get a coffee?"

Harry—Captain Asshole—looks between us for a brief second, unfazed at being dismissed. If anything, he looks overjoyed. "Alrighty then."

Who the hell says *alrighty* these days? Loser.

When the two cops disappear down the corridor, the nurse turns to face me, tucking a piece of sandy blonde hair behind her ear.

"Hi, sweetheart. I'm Alyssa. You can come with me."

Her still-soft tone instantly soothes me, which is a mile-stone achievement in itself. The demons plaguing my mind don't vanish, but her presence does ease some of the tension in my muscles.

Following her through large double doors into the ER, I'm taken to another small room. No table this time—I'm treated like a human—Alyssa gesturing for me to sit on the bed as she flicks the curtain closed to give us a bit of privacy.

I start trying to think of an excuse for being here, an injury that I can pretend needs treatment. But I'm frozen... because the truth is the only thing that hurts is my heart. Damon protected me, keeping me out of the line of fire.

Against his own flesh and blood.

I want nothing more than to find him, to ask how he's doing, but I can't.

Surprisingly, she doesn't ask where it hurts, her wrinkled hands flicking open the folder again. Her eyes scan over something, a frown tugging at her lips. Finally, she glances up at me, a tight smile appearing.

"You might not remember me, Avery. But I remember you."

Chapter 3

Grey

"You better start talking," I growl quietly at Christopher, taking in his frazzled expression. Ha—some psychiatrist he is. Aren't they supposed to be calm and composed in an emergency? I guess, bloodied knuckles aside, maybe I could have a career as a doctor.

Likes blood—check.

Remains *somewhat* calm in an emergency—check.

Able to remove limbs—*double check.*

At least he had the foresight to hold the Westwood main door open with a stack of books before the power went out. But then again, the real question is, "How did you get into the male dorms without power?"

He pauses in front of the main hall doors, glancing over at me. "I triggered the emergency switch."

"Right," I drawl out slowly. "And why is this not an option for our rooms?"

Christopher raises an eyebrow, silently answering the question.

"Of course. There's no emergency exit for the *prison* cells," I mutter, unsurprised.

A few detectives come round the corner from the staff room corridor, pausing as they spot us. The good doctor raises his hand casually, gesturing toward me.

"This patient is with me."

Somehow, they buy his bullshit excuse, continuing on their merry way, but not before sneaking a few disapproving glances at my hands. They don't stop to ask questions, and when they are out of earshot, I narrow my eyes at Christopher. "Weren't you fired?"

"Temporarily on hold," he responds dryly.

"Right. Next question: Where are they?" I ask sternly, getting straight to the point. I need to know where those assholes are so I can get *them* to the point as well—the sharp pointed end of my trusty shiv, that is.

Rounding on me with lightning speed, Christopher draws to full height. "Listen to me, Grey. This is serious. You can't go barreling into Arthur's office and start murdering him and Alexander. Not only will the cops shoot you before you lay a hand on them, but you'll implicate the rest of us too. The place is swarming with first responders."

My eyebrow twitches at the use of *us*, but I only say, "I'm pretty quick, you know."

An exhausted look crosses his face as his sudden burst of energy depletes. "Damon has been taken to hospital. Avery too."

"Are they okay?" I ask quickly, momentarily putting a pause in my plans to rip Arthur and Alexander apart limb from limb and count all their organs by hand.

His face scrunches up with devastation, and for a brief second, true colors begin to reveal themselves. He cares about his cousin—that's an interesting development. But I shouldn't be shocked really. After all, he's a pain in our ass but he's an enemy of Arthur's, which means he's an ally of ours. The thought is almost laughable, but at this point, we need all the help we can get.

"I don't know," he mutters quietly. "Damon's in pretty bad shape. Avery is fine but I told the paramedics she needed to be properly assessed off the premises by hospital staff."

"Smart man."

Christopher looks taken aback by the mild compliment. Hopefully he latches onto it in his mind because I doubt there will be more where that came from.

Getting Avery away from this mess is both a blessing and a necessity. While Alexander and Arthur are here, dealing with the fallout, she's safe. And with Damon.

It's a slight comfort knowing he's getting proper medical attention but... not everyone can be saved.

I can't think like that though. It's Damon—you can't kill evil that easily. Alexander has proved that theory and Damon is twice the man—and force of nature—that he'll ever be. They share the same blood. We're all cut from the same cloth—our modus operandi is just different.

"I was in the corridor being questioned by detectives when the paramedics took him. His condition isn't good, Grey. I think you need to be prepared."

My face remains expressionless as I nod. "He'll be fine," I say blankly. "Plus he has Avery with him."

"I understand that. But she's not a doctor—"

"No, but she's his everything, Christopher. *She's* his reason to live, to fight. Just like she's mine. He *has* to be okay. There's no other option here."

More officers walk past and he motions toward the library with a dip of his head, indicating privacy. Slipping through the doors, it's empty and I try not to let sweet memories drown me. I might be relieved that Avery is away from this damn forsaken place, but she's also away from *me*. I can't protect her from here. And the only two people in this world that can keep me calm are not with me. It's a double-edged sword.

"Alexander will go after her," Christopher finally murmurs with a sigh, leaning his palms on the table's edge. "This isn't over."

"All the more reason to let me end his miserable existence now," I muse. "I know Damon made me promise that he could do it, but I think under the circumstances, he'll forgive me."

Everything is still shrouded in darkness. Surely, Arthur will have to relent and put the power back on soon. The officers will be getting suspicious, but not only that, Dorothea's body is probably thawing out downstairs. She already resembled the living dead in her alive state, so I wouldn't rule out the possibility that she comes back for revenge on the old cunt. What a plot twist that would be.

Christopher paces away from the table, leaning against the nearest bookshelf as his leg bounces nervously. "We need to anticipate their next move. And we should do it now, while authorities are on site. It will give us time to prepare."

"How the hell do we prepare when we can't communicate with each other? They took our cells and I doubt Byrone and Jillian have access to their systems without the power being on."

He nods. "I'll work on getting the power restored. From what I've overheard, they are currently using the morgue to house the deceased until the coroners are able to transport everyone. It's running on a separate back-up generator."

Gotta keep those bodies frozen.

"How many dead?" I ask.

"At least half a dozen—mostly guards."

"Mostly?" I ask cautiously, not enjoying the turn this conversation has taken.

Christopher purses his lips into a tight smile, as if the simple action might keep me from losing my shit. That's how I know it's bad—we've lost someone.

"Leighton Pierce. I believe he was a friend of yours."

A deep sigh of regret leaves me, chest tightening for a moment. "How?" I demand, rubbing my temple.

He clears his throat, probably catching on that no facial gesture or calming words will soften the incoming blow. "One of the guards pinned him down too hard. We'll have to wait for the official autopsy results but I'd say blunt force trauma—possible asphyxiation."

"Those fucking cunts," I snap, shoving him into the bookcase as I storm past toward the library doors.

There's no stopping me this time though. All Christopher can do is hastily catch up before I reach the door that leads to the foyer outside Arthur's office. It's propped open with heavy weights, and the usual guards are nowhere in sight. Officers are standing around the foyer, giving me suspicious, narrowed glances as I rush toward the man in his office.

Christopher manages to catch me just before I barrel through the doors, gripping my arm tightly as he gives the officers a firm look. "He's with me," he says again sternly, flashing his staff card.

On the other side of the door, Arthur hears the commotion, lifting his head. He pauses his conversation with a scowl, glancing around at the detectives in his office and fucking Alexander Dale.

"Hawthorne," he snarls, eyes darting between me and Christopher with anger. "What are you doing here?"

I'm just about to launch myself into the room and across his wooden desk—which I notice has been replaced since my little late night adventure with Avery in here—when Christopher shoves me behind him.

"We need to begin psych appointments immediately," he states urgently, trying to take control of the situation—of me. "Patients are upset about the events."

Alexander huffs with an air of sarcasm from his leather chair pressed against the wall. "Upset? Those delinquents started this whole mess."

"Is that the bullshit story you're going with?" I laugh darkly, bringing myself to Christopher's left-hand side. "What's wrong? Scared the authorities will find out the cold truth and realize you're the real criminals? No," I pause thoughtfully. "You're scared that the press outside may end up getting wind of the facts and tarnish your pretty little reputation."

"Grey, shut up," Christopher hisses quietly. "Let me handle this."

"Nah," I say lazily, patting his shoulder patronizingly. "I've got this, *Doctor*. Besides, I want to speak to Whittingham one-on-one."

My eyebrow lifts with a challenge, knowing full well Arthur won't accept it. He's nothing but a coward, hiding behind his web of lies. Arthur's jawline twitches at my test, eyes softening as he turns to the detectives and laughs calmly.

"Patients," he starts. "They keep us busy."

"Leighton Pierce is dead," I loudly announce to the room. "Killed by one of your guards. *I. Want. A. Name.*"

Hands creep toward concealed guns as detectives watch me carefully, sensing the danger reaching its peak in the room. But my issue isn't with them unless they make themselves a problem. I just want them here as witnesses.

Arthur stands from his desk, the color of the shiny new mahogany oak very similar to the blood I spilled over the old one. Maybe I'm an influencer now.

"The guards are currently receiving professional help for their traumatic ordeal. I'll give you one chance to return to your room, otherwise, I'll have these nice detectives take you on a trip downtown."

Oh—so the old cunt wants to play that game?

Next to me, Christopher is as stiff as a board, probably in a *psychological* state of panic. But he's stuck in his silence, unable to speak or walk away from the train derailment taking place in front of him.

"Where is Leighton?" I ask casually. "Is he in the morgue downstairs next to your dead receptionist-slash-lover? I am intrigued to find out how she died. After all, she's been there a few days now I assume. Always makes me curious when healthy people just *drop dead*."

Arthur's jaw clenches, eyes narrowing on me. To my left, Alexander doesn't appear shocked by this revelation. And why would he? I have no doubt he's involved somehow. But unlike Arthur, he's watching the exchange with disinterest, completely unfazed and not at all caring that I'm spilling their secrets. After all, who would believe me? It's just a shame the press can't hear us. I'd love to see the headlines since they rarely care about truth and justice.

"My beloved Dorothea suffered a cardiac event while at work. The coroner has already been called and she has been kept safe until such time as they are available. She'll be taken from the premises and reunited with her family later today," Arthur manages to spit out calmly.

Of course he'd use today's events to cover up his own dirty work. It's almost as if he anticipated some type of *event* to occur today. Slimy bastard.

The look on his face says it all. They knew that shit would go down. I now realize that this was all planned—exactly as they had hoped. Another ploy to set us up, to make us look like criminals to cover their own dirty tracks and strike us down. The only thing they didn't see coming was the marriage certificate. But if Alexander's calm demeanor is anything to go by, he already has a plan.

As my attention turns to him, he clears his throat, standing and buttoning up his business jacket. Facing me, he steps forward, a cunning stare on his smug face.

"I need to go check on my son in the hospital—make sure he's alive," he pauses, lip curling slightly with the idea of Damon's death. "From what I've been told..." He lingers off, switching his gaze to Christopher. "Other patients are also at the hospital, including my *daughter-in-law*. I'll be sure to check on her too."

My body moves in an instant, lunging forward as tight arms reach around my upper torso to try to contain me. The room erupts into chaos as Christopher struggles to hold me back, while detectives swarm toward us, drawing their guns on me.

"I'll escort him to his room after an immediate emergency psych session," Christopher yells desperately, digging his fingers into me. "It's fine. I'll sort it out."

Without breaking my stare with Alexander, I hiss at Christopher through clenched teeth, "Let me go or so help me God I'll throw you through the fucking window, Christopher."

Alexander laughs quietly, a dark undertone lacing the sound as he steps past me. Lowering his voice so only we can hear, he sneers at me. "I'll be sure to give Avery your best, Grey. I have use for her—*for now*. But as for Damon... I hope you said your goodbyes already."

An animalistic sound tears from me and I fling Christopher into the nearby wall, not giving a shit if he's hurt or not. Spinning around, I find Alexander stepping into the foyer, not bothering to glance back at the mess he's left in his path.

I manage to take two steps toward the door, ready to rip his intestines out through his stomach with my bare hands when electricity suddenly jolts through my body. Spasming, my body stiffens involuntarily, legs buckling out as I smash into the floor, a taser probe lodged into my lower back.

Those damn motherfuckers tasered me. Again.

The pain doesn't bother me, although the voltage makes everything burn like I'm on fucking fire. But it's the inability to stop twitching and lack of bodily functions that angers and frustrates me. I can't speak, and I'm helpless as I watch Alexander disappear from sight. All I can think of is Avery.

And how there's a monster heading her way and nothing I can do to stop it.

Chapter 4

Avery

"I'm sorry?" I splutter. I'm completely taken aback by Alyssa's words. How *do* I take them? My first instinct is to recoil, the basic breakdown of the words seeming like a threat. But there's nothing in her tone that suggests I should be chasing the officers and begging them to take me back to Lilydale.

As if sensing my internal panic, she smiles softly.

"July thirteenth and February first. Do those dates ring a bell?"

My brows furrow as I sink back into the pillow. Should they ring a bell? Most of the time I can't even remember what I did last week, let alone months or a year ago.

But somehow, my subconscious knows. Our minds hold onto trauma and knowledge without us realizing. It embeds itself into our existence.

My hand circles to my back, touching the scar in the middle of my spine.

Alyssa nods. "I was one of the nurses that assisted during your surgery to remove glass shards from your back. I was also working in the ER when you presented with a broken nose one evening."

Our eyes lock, mine wide with uneasiness. She's given me no reason to be on edge, but the reminder of my old life before Lilydale hits me hard like an avalanche.

"How do you remember?" I murmur quietly. "You would surely see hundreds, if not, thousands of patients."

"You're quite remarkable, Avery. Besides, most people don't present to the hospital for injuries such as yours—let alone *multiple times*."

I offer a dry, awkward smile. "I'm locked up now."

It's a weird addition to the conversation, my attempt at the world's unfunniest joke. But her words and presence make me feel like I'm worthy of attention, like she wants to hear my story and what became of me.

After all, we're just victims. Nothing more, nothing less. Despite people like Arthur Whittingham trying to condition us to believe otherwise, the truth is we were failed. Let down and given up on.

Don't get me wrong; I still did bad, unspeakable things. But if the past few months have taught me anything, it's that I need to stop blaming myself. And I have.

While there's still a tiny voice that lives in my brain, revisiting the guilt and *what-ifs*, I know better now.

Alyssa is one of the first people I've come across who actually sees me as a human being. It's because of that, that I feel the need to tell her what my outcome was.

"Lilydale," she confirms, glancing down at what I now deduce is my file. "I'm glad you didn't go to prison. You didn't deserve it."

"You don't know the things I did," I point out half-heartedly. "To be fair, I nearly ended up there."

Alyssa visibly grimaces. "I wasn't on duty that night," she tells me softly. "But the next morning, my colleagues filled me in on the girl who was brought in from a house fire. When one of them mentioned your first name during a debriefing, it didn't take much to put the pieces together. I knew right then and there that there was more to the story."

My heart beats strangely in my chest. For the first time, someone on the outside of Lilydale is looking at the old me... *without judgment.* Truly seeing me as the walking cry for help I was.

Too bad that girl is dead now. But I have no regrets. Lilydale saved me. Not in the way the welcome brochure promised, but the people inside, the ones who speak to the darkest parts of me—they did. They saw me as *everything.* Not the victim, not the familial killer, not the girl with mental illness... they saw what was inside and dug out the potential—the real me that had never had an opportunity to flourish.

"There *was* more to the story. But no one realized until it was too late," I say firmly. "That's okay though. Maybe everything happens for a reason. I think I'm exactly where I needed to be."

I state it with such weight and force, that it makes her pause for a moment, letting the words sink in.

Finally, she closes the file, placing it on one of those overbed tables that wheel around the bed. "I always knew you were strong," she remarks. "And if it helps, even in the tiniest bit, I did actually raise your case with my charge nurse and suggest they contact the appropriate authorities to investigate. We suspected abuse but the system is just so overwhelmed..."

Trailing off, guilt appears in her eyes. An invisible hand clutches around my heart at her own blame—because there's no way in the world she'd ever be able to stop or protect me from the monster I lived with. No one could.

"Alyssa," I say gently. "We both did the best we could. And that's okay. *I'm okay.*"

She nods, letting out a sigh. "I suppose we should get back to the matter at hand. Are you injured from what occurred today?"

Suddenly, I don't feel the need to lie or make up some bullshit injury. Instead, I just shake my head. "No. But my husband is. He's here somewhere."

Surprise crosses her face at that, and to be fair, I think my expression matches hers too. Saying the words out loud still feels *weird*—a good weird though.

I think.

"Your husband?" she repeats. "What's his name?"

I swallow, reality hitting me in the face at full force again at our conversation. "Damon." Pausing, I internally sneer as his surname hangs on the tip of my tongue, an unpleasant reminder of Alexander and the fact he's the fucking reason that Damon is hurt. "It's Damon Emerson Alexander Dale. His late mother is actually the reason Lilydale exists."

Not entirely sure if I should be revealing such personal information, but at this rate, my desire to protect Alexander is as low as humanly possible. Fuck him with a cactus and one of Grey's shivs. He's the reason Lily is dead, and he is the reason Damon is in this hospital right now, fighting for his life.

Alyssa pokes her head out through the curtains. "I'll go check for you," she says quietly. "No one should bother you. I'll just be a minute."

I watch as she disappears behind the pale, patterned curtain. Around me, the old familiar sound of hospital noises ground me. Machines beeping, feet shuffling on floors, doctors and nurses talking. It doesn't hurt or frighten me as much as I thought it would. I used to be terrified to come here, the fear that Dad would punish me for it. I guess his death brought me a freedom I didn't expect.

The hospital used to be such a triggering place for me. Always here for the wrong reasons, ignored and having to be treated like a number in an overwhelmed, under-supported system. Just needing to get the patients in and out as quickly as possible, the staff fighting to survive—just like us.

Maybe others like Alyssa did want to save me...

They just couldn't.

As I wait, my mind drifts back to Damon. It helps knowing that he's nearby, somewhere in this building. I feel strangely at peace knowing both of us are away from Lilydale temporarily. They can't hurt us here.

Damon... I need him to be okay. I can't lose him when I've only just gotten my chance with him.

Marriage was never something on the cards for me but I'm happy to take it. But being a widow? I'm not willing to accept that.

Damon deserves happiness.

I deserve happiness.

We all do.

After a few minutes, Alyssa reappears, acting very much like a spy on a mission. Her body is hunched, eyes darting around, and suddenly it feels like we're in a B-grade James Bond movie.

"Okay, I found him. He's in surgery at the moment."

"Is he okay?" I ask urgently, shooting up from the pillow. "Is he alive?"

Slipping into the room, she sits next to me, and I notice she's now holding an iPad. "The main concern was hypovolemic shock." Pausing, she clarifies, "Severe blood loss."

"I figured..." I whisper in horror.

She skims over the screen, flicking the page down with her index finger. "The surgeons are working on him but it appears there was no damage to vital organs. They are trans-fusing him with saline and blood products while repairing the wound."

"Will he be okay?" I ask warily, holding my breath for her answer.

Alyssa looks up, giving me a tight smile. "I'm not a doctor so take everything I say with a grain of salt. They haven't put any operative notes in yet since he's still in surgery, but initial imaging suggests no major organs were hit. As long as they can stop the bleeding, he should be fine, sweetheart."

It's not the definite *yes* I was hoping for, but it's something at least. It gives me hope to cling on to.

"And what about me?" I ask quietly. "Will you need to send me back straight away since I'm not hurt?"

She frowns, pulling my paper file back to her lap. I guess they have updated their systems since my last visit.

"What do you mean, Avery? My notes right here say that you are being treated for shock and bruising. You'll be here until tomorrow for observation."

Standing up, she gives me a wink, taking the folder and iPad with her. Holding the curtain, she smiles at me again.

"And since you are married, it means you'll be able to see your husband when he's out from surgery. I'm going to go find you some food, then we'll take a look in case there's any other injuries we need to tend to. I'm sure you'd love a shower too."

According to the doctor who comes to see me a few hours later, Damon is okay. Lucky—but okay.

It feels like I was holding my breath the entire time, not relaxing at all until I heard those words.

They mentioned I can see him soon once he's out of recovery, but for now, Alyssa has taken it upon herself to bring me all the food the hospital has to offer.

Previously, I was strictly against hospital food. But, Cirque des Morts food aside, this is a damn sight better than the raw garbage they serve us at Lilydale on a day to day basis. No offense to Tony and the kitchen staff...

It's as if my appetite has returned full force once I got the news that Damon was alive and safe. I've managed to inhale everything Alyssa has brought to my little room—Jello cups, sandwiches, roast beef and vegetables. Hell, even the questionable looking stew went down like a lead balloon.

Even better was Alyssa casually telling me that because we're still patients of Lilydale, it means they have to cover our hospital bills. Suck on that Alexander and Whitface.

My temporary newfound freedom is strange. I've been given permission to wander a little in the ward. There's not much to do other than go to the restrooms, watch the grainy

TV or visit the nurses' station—which I do a few times to chat to Alyssa while I wait—but walking around like a normal person is something I'm enjoying. It's amazing the things we take for granted... like freedom and autonomy.

I decide to take a second shower for the hell of it. Before I stuffed myself full of food, I took a quick one to get rid of the blood and dirt from my skin, and changed into fresh clothes courtesy of Alyssa. But at the time, the need for Damon's survival weighed heavily on my mind and I was on autopilot, not able to enjoy the unusual luxury. Breathing easier now, I take full advantage of it, washing my long hair thoroughly and lathering myself with lemon scented soap without timers and lurking guards.

When I emerge into the hallway, hair damp and freshly braided, I stop dead in my tracks at the figure by the nurses' station. Unfortunately, he spots me at the same time, a smug smirk crossing his face.

"Avery," Alexander greets, turning away from a tight-lipped Alyssa. "How *lovely* to see you."

My first instinct is to run—far away—but instead, I walk over with my head high, determined to look this asshole in the face. He doesn't deserve my fear, and he sure as hell isn't going to get my tears.

"What are you doing here?" I ask, annoyed. "And don't tell me it's to make sure Damon's okay because we both know that's bullshit since you're the one who pulled the fucking trigger."

Out of the corner of my eye, Alyssa watches our exchange with suspicion. But judging by her expression, she already knows who he is and has made her own calculated assumption.

Protect Damon, Alyssa... Please. Don't let Alexander near him.

"As the Chairman, it's my duty to ensure all members are looked after—including my new daughter-in-law."

His words leave a sickening taste in my mouth, like charcoal ash coating my tongue. Being married to Damon is one thing, but legally tied to this evil asshole? That's a whole issue in itself. But I love Damon, just like my guys love me despite having had a useless, pathetic father too.

"I assure you *our* relationship," I gesture between us. "Is on paper only. I want nothing to do with you."

Alexander cocks an eyebrow, dropping the charade. "The feeling is very much mutual. But we'll be spending plenty of time together, dear Avery. After all, being a shareholder means you have responsibilities *to me*. And if Damon is *incapacitated*, you'll have to step up in his place as his... *wife*," he says, spitting out the word in disgust.

"The only responsibilities I have," I scoff. "Are to Damon—which I *thoroughly* enjoy. But rest assured, Damon and I will take great care of *our* business. I doubt you'll be involved much longer."

He takes a step toward me, and immediately, Alyssa jumps up from her seat, coming around from the side of the desk to place herself in front of me.

"Mr. Dale, as I have already mentioned, you are not an approved visitor—regardless of your threats. You need to leave now before I contact security and have you escorted from the building."

Narrowing his eyes on her, I grab her arm and pull her back, taking her place in his line of fire.

"You heard her," I say darkly, interjecting before he can speak. "Fuck off and don't come back. You're not welcome here or anywhere else where it concerns Damon."

Alexander straightens up, adjusting his tie with a tilted forced smile. "I *will* be seeing you soon, Avery. Damon, as well."

We watch as he turns and heads toward the exit without a backward glance. Once out of sight, Alyssa puts her hand on my back.

"Well... isn't he a bundle of sunshine? Come on, sweetheart. I just got word that your husband is out of recovery and has been placed in a room. I'll take you to see him."

Chapter 5

Damon

Opening my eyes, the first thing I discover is the annoying abundance of physical pain. Accompanying that, sound logic indicates that perhaps my father finally finished off the job and I'm firmly in Hell for the rest of eternity.

But the second thought I have is if I'm in Hell, why is there a goddamn ethereal woman with her face buried into my bed?

Glancing down, I lift an eyebrow at the ebony locks sprawled out over the white blanket. The top of her head is resting against my leg and when I move the rigid muscles, she suddenly bursts upright with alarmed, wide eyes. As quickly as she moved, pink lips part with relief, eyes softening as she takes in my semi-amused expression.

"Damon..." Avery breathes out, jumping to her feet.

And just like that, I forget that it feels like I've been dragged miles over broken glass by a speeding truck.

"Aren't you a sight for sore eyes?" I say in a cracked tone.

"Are you in pain?" She asks, ignoring my comment. As if needing to feel helpful, her hands start running over my legs like she's assessing me for the answer. I'm not sure that's the proper way to determine pain levels in a patient but I resist bursting her little doctor bubble. Maybe she just wants to make sure I'm actually alive and not a figment of her imagination.

Only a short time ago, she probably would have wished I was dead. After all, she did aptly name me *Demon Boy* for a reason. How the times have changed.

"I'm fine."

Leaning over me, I catch sight of her reaching for something—a button. At first, I think she must be buzzing for a nurse. But as my eyes follow the length of the cord, I spot a PCA machine attached to it beside me.

"Don't bother," I say, voice still hoarse. "I said I'm fine."

"Shut up," Avery shoots back coolly, hitting the button. The machine beeps in response, and a cold sensation enters my wrist.

Fucking machines and IVs. The only thing that should be attached to my body is her—permanently, if I had my way.

Avery pretends to ignore me despite her flustered cheeks giving her away. It's almost *cute* that she thinks she's in control and is attempting to take charge.

"*Wife*," I say sharply, noticing her still immediately. Her cheeks turn an even darker shade of red, uncontainable emotions clearly visible on her face as my words cause a visceral reaction. But to her credit, she quickly shoves them away, stubbornly turning her attention back to providing medical care. "Drugging me now, are you? And on our honeymoon."

"Please," Avery scoffs, acting unaffected. "If someone wanted to take advantage of you, they would have done so while you were unconscious. Not while you're high and probably seeing dancing unicorns or neon-flashing knives."

"That sounds oddly like Grey's delirious state of mind—not mine."

She leans against the bed, hip jutting into the crocheted white blanket as she crosses her arms. "And what would yours be, *dear husband*?"

Smirking at her, I don't let on how *her words* are affecting *me*. There's something about Avery acknowledging our newly *not exactly spoken* vows which makes me want to be possessive of her.

"You," I answer back as I attempt to sit up. "Maybe that's why I'm seeing you here. You're just an apparition."

Avery snorts, giving my chest a gentle shove and forcing me back down. "Perhaps I used my powers to get in here to murder you. Turns out it was easy. The hospital staff love me."

"Murder me?" I say, amused. "Join the queue after my father. As for the hospital staff, they will need to get in line as well."

"Are you saying you find me lovable?"

Our eyes lock, and behind her playful expression, I see her curiosity.

"Do *you* love me, Avery?" I challenge back.

Her lips twitch into a smile before she glances over at something on the wall. "There's two minutes left of your birthday and our wedding day. If either one of us is planning to make a declaration of love, now is the time."

We both fall silent, waiting to see who breaks first.

"You're insufferable and a bit of an asshole," Avery mutters when I don't speak. "Also, just because you got shot, don't think you're not in trouble for the stunt you pulled."

The morphine starts working its way into my system, my body relaxing as I laugh. "And now you're married to me."

"Bastard."

"But you love me."

She narrows her eyes but her smile contradicts it. "I might love you—a little bit."

The seconds continue to tick by, annoyance creeping onto her face when I remain quiet. I can see her internal rising panic, and when the final ten seconds start counting down to midnight, I grab her hand, forcing her to uncross her arms.

"I love you as well."

Avery's body relaxes in relief—and frustration. "You asshole."

If I wasn't injured, she looks as though she might actually hit me again.

Climbing onto the edge of the bed, she carefully leans on one knee, grabbing my face. I notice that she's trying to be careful not to put any pressure on my body, so I reach for her hips, pulling her against me. She falls on top of me and her eyes widen, mouth falling open to no doubt curse me out. I don't give her the opportunity, leaning forward to shut her up with my mouth.

Our first kiss as husband and wife, even if it's now technically a day late. But I never was one for tradition—that much is obvious.

Pulling back just enough to speak, I rest my forehead against hers. "You were, by far, the best birthday present I could have received," I tell her, running my hand up her spine. "I always thought the ultimate gift would be my father's death, but I was wrong."

"Maybe that can be your Christmas present," she murmurs. "A little murder goes well with mistletoe."

I chuckle, capturing her bottom lip in between my teeth. She moans softly, searching for my mouth again but I've already pulled back.

"That's too far away. But I like your way of thinking and generosity. Make sure you extend that to Grey and Theo as well."

Avery shuffles her weight, straddling my body so she can lean back. I might be numb from the damn drugs she forced into my system, but my dick certainly isn't. It twitches to life underneath her, and I know she feels it too because her hips squirm into it.

I'm about ready to rip the IV from my wrist and fuck her through the bed when her gaze stops me in my tracks.

"I have to go back to Lilydale tomorrow. Well, today," she sighs. "You'll be here for a few days until you're stable enough to be transferred into the care of Dr. Markel."

Irritated, I raise an eyebrow at the idea—because that's what it is—not a decision. There's no chance in hell I'll be letting that old quack treat me. "Absolutely not."

"Damon," Avery says sternly, before softening her tone. "We need you fully recovered. We need you strong again. *He* was here before."

She doesn't even need to say his name for me to know who she is referring to. My eyes flash dangerously, darkening as I glance at the doorway for a split second as if daring him to appear. "And what did the bastard have to say for himself?"

Probably coming to check if he finished the job...

Avery's face contorts with disgust and my suspicions are right. "He wanted to see you."

"And I'm assuming he didn't since I'm still breathing."

"No. Alyssa and I wouldn't let him."

"Who the hell is Alyssa?"

There's a small clearing of someone's throat by the door and my eyes drift back over to find a nurse in teal scrubs standing where I expected my father to be. "I'm Alyssa, sweetheart. How are you feeling?"

Avery's face softens at the sight of our newcomer, and for a brief moment, it kind of makes me want to kill the health-care worker. But then I remember she said this woman also stopped my father from coming into the room and stabbing my unconscious body. So, she can live—for now.

"I'm fine," I grumble, and another beep makes me growl at Avery as she takes advantage of the distraction and hits the medication button again. She seems completely unfazed at the fact she's been caught kneeling over me, leaning back on her heels as cold liquid shoots into my veins. "Give me the button, Avery."

"No."

Climbing off me, she keeps the pain controller firmly in her hand, taking a seat in the visitor's chair next to me. The nurse wanders over, pressing buttons on another machine and I feel a cuff inflate on my bicep.

Despite my wishes, the morphine is oddly relaxing me—well, my body anyway. My mind is very much focused, albeit annoyed that I'm physically weakened at this moment.

"Your father is an *interesting* man," the healthcare worker mumbles, and I'm not surprised to hear he's made a lasting impression on her. This woman would be terrible at poker, her face showing all her disdain.

"He's good at charming people," I say, but she just scoffs in reply.

Removing the blood pressure cuff from my arm, she attaches a pulse oximeter to my finger. "Charming is not what I would use to describe him."

Avery laughs softly, still holding the button out of my reach. "He threatened her. And me."

"What?" I snap, turning to look at her. "Tell me what he said so I can remind him when I'm putting the asshole six-feet under."

"He doesn't approve of our marriage," she replies simply with a shrug. "I told him to fuck off and that I very much enjoy fucking his son, and we look forward to having him removed from the business in the near future."

My eyebrows shoot up in surprise. Avery is evolving, growing into her true self more and more each day—and I have to say I'm loving it.

When I first met Avery, all I could see was an out of control, spiraling woman, unable to control her emotions. Grey insisted she was a dark horse, capable of more than she let on, and he was right.

After what they did to her at Lilydale, no one would blame her for breaking. It would be expected even. The few that returned from the sociopathic doctors downstairs never recovered—most killing themselves within the first few weeks despite us trying to save them.

But Avery? She fought back. Sure, she was a little broken when I first rescued her. Her mind was reliving their torture and making her question her self-worth and our ability to care about her. But she still kept fighting, even putting a bullet into a guard to protect me. And when I finally let her in and she saw my most vulnerable parts, she didn't run away, choosing to fight for me and pulling me back from the edge instead. She could have turned a blind eye—many others would. But she never did, never once abandoning me like I had done to her before.

I was incorrect to ever think she was weak. She's perhaps more dangerous than most in the asylum. No wonder Avery has such a hold on Grey—he sees that darkness in her. Theo as well. Her light doesn't just call to their darkness and compliment it. Her own darkness found companionship, and slowly over time, she's growing into it. Instead of just letting the emotions control her or avoiding them until they implode, *she's* starting to control *them*. Well, most of the time...

The nurse laughs at Avery's response, seemingly amused as well. I wait for her to complete whatever checks she needs to do, mentioning something briefly about a doctor coming in soon to speak to me. When she leaves, I turn to Avery, stony faced as she pulls the button further out of reach.

Holding my gaze, her eyes flash with determination before she presses it again, earning herself another annoyed growl.

"Chill," she scolds. "There's no point being in pain."

Speaking of pain, I say the next words even though neither of us want to hear them.

"You need to go back to Lilydale today."

Despite the fact she already confirmed that she's being forced to go back, her face still twists sadly—as if she can't bear the thought of leaving me. But that's exactly why she has to.

Here, I can't protect her. And if my father is able to get to her so easily in the hospital, there's no guessing when he will try again. At least back at Lilydale, she'll have Grey and Theo to protect her. It's also important that we start planning our next move immediately and get defensive measures in place.

No doubt Arthur is on his high-horse, spinning a tale of affliction. It's a PR rep's worst nightmare, but that just means his anger will be redirected toward the patients. This whole mess started with him bribing and coercing patients into voluntary experimentation. I have no idea if that will continue—but if I was a betting man, I'd say yes.

Cirque des Morts needs to act—now. And if I can't be there myself, I need Grey and Avery to take over. It's her marital duty and right now—her legacy to create. Trust is a tough concept but I trust Grey and Avery with my life. I know they will protect the Lilydale patients.

"I know," Avery whispers back, shifting closer to me. Finally surrendering, she places the PCA button on the mattress next to me, giving me unspoken control back. We've been married less than twenty-four hours and she already knows me better than most. The thought of me being in pain is hurting her, but she understands what I'm asking of her—the *control* I'm giving her. And now, she's giving me control back too.

"You and Grey need to take over in my absence," I tell her firmly. "Check on everyone. I have no idea who is injured. We need to make sure Arthur doesn't try anything while I'm stuck in here. Byrone will help too. Tell Grey to bring on Louis and Mark. He knows who they are and what to do."

Avery nods, even though it probably makes little sense to her. Silence passes between us, saying everything neither of us can speak out loud.

The idea of being away from her is far more painful than being shot. But I trust Grey, and Theo by extension. We didn't come this far to give up now and let those bastards win.

Shifting over, I tap the mattress beside me with my hand, gesturing for her to lay with me. I half expect some lecture again, but it doesn't come. Avery just stands, carefully climbing back up onto the bed, and tucking herself into my side. There, we stay wrapped up in each other's arms, until the time we both dread comes, and Avery is taken away from me back to Lilydale.

Chapter 6

Avery

When I arrive back at Lilydale, in handcuffs of course, it's breakfast time. Except unlike the usual buzzing of patients in the hall, it's relevantly *dead*.

Staff I don't recognize in black coats walk past me, carrying trays of food toward the dorms. Apparently, by the looks of it, we're in a classic Whittingham timeout—though I don't think it's one of the *punishments* we all detest. This is nothing more than a show of control, to calm the chaos and keep us silent.

A few detectives wander the halls, chatting among themselves, and barely even glance at me. They do, however, acknowledge their colleagues on either side of my frame, and when we pass Whitface's office, I dare a peek while they are distracted. To my surprise, it's empty with not a single soul in sight. Well, Whittingham doesn't have one but he's not there either.

Nausea rises into my throat when we stop at the door that leads to the patient side of the facility. It means I need to pass *that* hallway again. Captain Asshole bangs on the door twice, and a few seconds later, there's a beep on the other side before it swings open.

Relief floods through me at the familiar sight of Dr. Smith, who takes a couple of seconds to scan over and check my physical condition before gesturing for me to follow him.

"I've got her from here. Thank you."

The asshole in blue undoes my cuffs, unnecessarily shoving me toward Dr. Smith before leaving as if the building is on fire and he needs to evacuate. Perhaps he's terrified he'll catch the *craziness* if he lingers too long. If there was a fire in the building, I know without a doubt that he'd leave me inside.

"How are you feeling, Avery?" Dr. Smith asks as we start to walk to his office, but I can't answer him. My eyes immediately look down the corridor, inspecting it for the evidence from yesterday.

Even though I know Damon is alright and very much alive, it still terrifies me to spot the warzone where everything went to shit. Thankfully, it's been somewhat cleaned but I can still see remnants on the floor and walls. Much like other sections of Lilydale, blood is a bitch to get out of everything.

I do my best to avoid looking directly at the place where Damon had laid, letting Dr. Smith guide me into his office.

He closes the door behind me and I drop into the chair across from his desk with a shaky breath. It's been a whirlwind twenty-four hours, and without Damon's presence to steal my focus, my mind is suddenly buzzing with flash-backs, questions, and a whole lot of anxiety.

"Here," Dr. Smith says, handing me a mug. "It should still be hot. I made it when I got word that you were on route back to Lilydale."

The smell of fresh coffee fills my nostrils, and I don't hesitate to take the mug from him. "Thank you."

Sitting across from me, he waits until I've taken a few sips before re-asking his question. This time, I finally have the ability to reply, knowing he's probably just as nervous to know what's happening outside these four walls.

"Damon is okay," I tell him. "Awake and recovering. I'm fine too."

Dr. Smith nods, relieved. "Good. Did Alexander turn up at the hospital?"

My eyes widen slightly at the question. "How did you know?"

"He made a point of *announcing* his intention to do so."

Well, that checks out. Though, I have no idea why he would tell Dr. Smith that. Wasn't he fired?

As if sensing my own question, he smiles softly. As I study his features, I realize he has dark bags under his eyes, meaning he's had as little sleep as I've had. "My termination was temporarily rescinded pending the authorities' investigation into yesterday's events. However, I have been locked out of certain staff privileges."

"I see. Where are Grey and Theo?" I quickly shoot back, not overly interested in going into excessive detail about his employment now that I have an answer. "Are they okay?"

His eyebrows furrowing together set off alarm bells. It looks like he's gone stiff in his chair, concerned etched across his face.

"Grey is currently in solitary confinement," he answers slowly. "Only until later today. We had a bit of a... *situation*."

Situation...

In Grey terms—blood was probably spilled. The thought of him downstairs alone almost tips me over the edge right away, but I focus on the fact that he's safe and I'll see him soon.

"And Theo?"

"In his room along with all the other patients."

I nod, unsure where to go from here. "I need to see them."

Dr. Smith offers a wary, tight smile. "I'll do my best, but with my restrictions, it may be difficult. Arthur has only just restored power to the facility—though, it's minimal. From my understanding, electricity is on but he's still got everything else switched off to minimize *disruptions*."

Both of us turn our head to the camera in the corner of the room, perched high on the ceiling. There's no flashing red light, and it only confirms that Dr. Smith is correct. No security means no access—in or out of the rooms unless they allow it. And something tells me they have no desire to open any doors.

"They can't get out," I try to ask, but it comes across as a solid statement. "Everyone is locked in their rooms."

Confirming, he nods once. "My staff card will only work for the general corridors at this time. They also changed the pin code again."

"Again?"

"This is the third change since your arrival. I was provided with the details from another colleague and while I'm sure Damon's people will figure it out quickly, most access paths are blocked."

"What is the code?"

I'm surprised by my tone—strong, a little demanding. Not at all like my usual self. Dr. Smith appears taken aback too, pausing for a second as he processes my request. I don't break eye contact with him, letting the seconds tick by while he psychoanalyzes me from his desk. Will he decide that I'm having some type of psychotic break? Or maybe he'll recognize it for what it really is. Either way, I refuse to let Damon down—or anyone. This is the time for action, to step up and prove that I'm better than my demons.

This is what I survived for. What I'm meant to do.

"The code?" he mutters. "It's Aunt Lily's wedding anniversary—0314."

A dry laugh escapes my lips. "Of course it is. Alexander sure has an odd sense of humor. A dishonorable homage to my own wedding date, no doubt. For a rich man he sure gives Temu style gifts."

I cock an eyebrow, holding my gaze steady as I finish. My silent question doesn't slip past the psychiatrist, awkwardly squirming in his chair.

"Yes, I married you. You signed the marriage license in here the other day."

"I suppose this is why they always tell you to read a document before you sign," I murmur sarcastically.

He hums thoughtfully. "Would it have made a difference if you knew beforehand?"

Would it? I haven't had time to consider what I would have done if he had told me what I was signing. It was a shock when that little bombshell was dropped, but I didn't hate it. I'm fully onboard Team Destroy Alexander and Arthur. The only thing I feel is guilt—knowing that Theo and Grey aren't able to marry me too and wondering how they feel about it.

Shit. That's assuming they would even want to marry me one day. I'd say I'm jumping the gun but I'm already wed at this point so it's all moot. Were they okay with the decision? Either way, I need to have strong words with all of them about making decisions like this without my knowledge. Goddamn possessive psychos.

"No," I answer confidently. "It wouldn't have made a difference. I would have still signed the paperwork."

I scan his face for a reaction, wondering if he'll hide it from me. To my astonishment, Dr. Smith begins laughing. "You continue to surprise me, Avery. In good ways. You've come so very far from your first day here. And if I'm being honest, Damon too."

"Don't let him hear you say that," I joke. "There's no doubt in my mind that he'll still be able to inflict pain even with his current physical condition."

Dr. Smith smiles. "Agreed. Anyway, I'll need to escort you to your room soon. They left the door unlocked so I'd be able to get you inside. There are minimal guards on duty at the moment. Though, this situation still needs to be dealt with."

"We have it under control—or, we will at least. I need you to get me access to Grey and Theo as soon as possible. Also, can you reach out to my social worker?"

"Your social worker?" he repeats, standing and waltzing over to the filing cabinet. I'm a little annoyed to find it unlocked after what happened with my file, but let's be fair... at this stage nothing is private or sacred in Lilydale. It's bizarre to consider the reality that my files being leaked has not been my worst experience during my time here. It felt like it when it happened—like the worst possible thing that could happen to me was my secrets being revealed. But being turned into a human pincushion and tortured takes a top spot easily. And watching my husband take a bullet for me. Besides, I'm not the same person who walked through those doors anymore. The past is in the past.

Sitting back down, he flicks open the file, reading it. "Margaret?"

"Yes," I confirm. "I want to speak to her. I also want you to get new cell phones for us since our other ones were confiscated. Communication is essential. I assume Whitface destroyed them after having a good snoop."

"Whitface," he chuckles, not seeming like the self-proclaimed professional I've come to know over the past few months. "I'll see what I can do."

I nod, pleased with... *myself*. If I had more time and patience, I'd psychoanalyze *him*. It's becoming clear that even the most put-together individuals wear a mask and pretend to be fully functioning adults. I have a strange feeling that Dr. Smith hasn't been completely honest with us, or me, but that's not important right now.

We need to be on our guard, ready for their next move. I know revenge and war is coming.

And we'll be ready for them.

My room is just how I left it. Except something is amiss.

There's no fingers in roses or belongings missing, but I can just sense that someone has been in here. Maybe it's the lingering scent of old spice or a crease on the blanket, but regardless, I can sense in my gut that someone combed through my personal space.

It makes me angry, beyond pissed off that they continue to violate us in every way possible. If they were searching for clues or contraband, I doubt anything was useful. We're smarter than that. Everything we need is locked inside Damon's mind—which is a weapon in itself I've come to realize.

With nothing else to do, I decide to attempt to take a nap, convinced that I'm stuck in here until at least tomorrow. I'm completely spent, even though my mind circles back and forth in agonizing loops. I'm impatient for updates, ready to go positively feral to find Theo and Grey. At least if I'm asleep, time will move faster, instead of this paralyzing loop with no exit that I seem to be stuck in.

When the door swings open, startling me awake, I jolt upright instantly. My heart bashes violently in my chest while adrenaline rushes through me as if I'm under attack. It takes me a few seconds to gauge what I'm actually seeing, almost convinced that I'm dreaming.

Gray eyes soften as they focus on me, and I launch myself out of the bed, feet barely touching the floor as I leap into Grey's awaiting, wide arms.

"Little killer," he murmurs into my neck, unfazed that I'm near straggling his neck in a tight hug.

"You're okay," I say relieved, catching sight of Dr. Smith over his shoulder. He gives me a small smile and nod before continuing on down the hall, leaving us alone.

Grey places his hands on my waist, keeping hold of me as he steps back slightly to scan my face with wary eyes. "Are you alright? How's Damon?"

The question is full of softly spoken urgency and it makes my chest ache. Cupping his face, I give him a reassuring smile. "He's good. Still stubborn as hell but definitely alive, kicking, and ready to slaughter Alexander."

Relief floods his expression for only a split second before he smashes his lips to mine. It feels so good to be home in his arms, my chest melting into his as I kiss him back with just as much need.

I nearly lost them. I nearly lost being able to do *this*.

Our intensities match perfectly, affirming his desperation was just as destroying as mine was. Time has finally brought us back together, all our emotions releasing at once in each other's arms.

Swinging me around effortlessly, I barely feel my back colliding with the wall, our mouths not breaking apart for a single millisecond. I feel his fingers leave bruises on my hips from his tight grip and I relish the safety his protective, strong hold provides. I love when he marks me, especially as his tongue reminds me of all the things it can do.

Finally coming up for air reluctantly, Grey rests his forehead on mine. We stay still, savoring the moment for a little longer until slowly, he retreats.

"Come on, pretty girl. There's still one more stop I need to make."

Chapter 7

Grey

Seeing Avery in person is even better than the rush I get after slitting a neck wide open. Warmth that fills you so thoroughly that you want to bathe in it and let every primal, unhinged instinct take over.

It's a mystery as to why Arthur decided to turn all the systems back online. I can only assume the authorities have left so there's no more need for a big song and dance. He also knows and fears that the longer we're left caged and prodded, the harder it will be to subdue us.

Although things are back to normal—somewhat, anyway—we can't become complacent. Arthur is well aware that this means we can move freely from the rooms. Once the security systems came back online, it only took Byrone and Jillian mere seconds to override access. I bet Arthur vacated the premises well before that, likely hiding somewhere away from here until things settle.

Changing the code was a nice touch though. Christopher has been oddly helpful, providing me with the new code as soon as I was released from solitary confinement. Alexander and Lily's wedding anniversary? Nothing says murder and mayhem like a personal touch.

My patience is wearing thin at their antics. I've imagined ripping out their spines with my bare hands more times than Hallman could count.

I'm curious who picked the new code—whether it was gutless Arthur or Alexander the Great Cunt. I can just imagine the two of them having a good laugh at our expense—another dose of dead mother reminders for Damon.

Given our latest news about nuptials, I can guarantee it's a tribute to Damon and Avery. Alexander loves sending messages, and while he has always refused to admit directly that he murdered Lily, it's implied in his methods. To the docile, naïve faceless specimens of the world, Lily Emerson-Dale died of an overdose. However if even one person was worth their paycheck, they'd be able to see that the toxicology report was inconclusive, vastly different from the initial findings to reflect a large quantity of narcotics and sleeping pills in her system. An error, they called it.

Money can buy you anything in this world—even murder.

That's the difference between them and us though. While they buy their power, we don't need to. That's true authority and strength.

They are sorely mistaken if they think taunting Damon will do anything other than motivate him. They are so far lost to their schemes that to them, this marriage is nothing more than a weapon. While that might be the case on a surface level, and we bent a few teeny-tiny laws to get there, the relationship between Damon and Avery holds more meaning than anything Alexander has ever experienced in his entire life—or what he's capable of feeling.

As I lead us through the corridor, Avery keeps a tight grip on my hand. Patients are just starting to emerge from their rooms eagerly, in time for lunch. And of course, to save face, we're allowed *free time*. Nothing is free if there's a price attached to it. Arthur considers it a reward, I call it bribery.

Judging by the expressions on passing faces, they are in agreement with me. It's not some prisoners' special, designed to make us feel warm and fuzzy.

Word is spreading quickly about the massacre that went down. Trauma holds a lot of space, and even without knowing the full story, people are shaken up. Stories are spreading like wildfire—some of them nothing more than fabricated fiction. I don't mind though, especially the ones where I allegedly slaughtered guards. I need to keep my reputation intact. Maybe I'll start my own rumor and tell everyone that I shoved a taser up Arthur's ass and he shot his load all over Alexander's face.

But seriously—fuck that cunt who stunned me. Once I get my hand on a taser, I'm returning the favor.

An influx of guards signal that things are *back to normal*. Many of them I don't recognize, just as they don't appear to recognize me. That can only mean one thing—new recruits. Arthur works fast. These poor fuckers must have a death wish, but I suspect Arthur distracted them from reality by shoving money in their greedy faces. It's all he can probably do to stop them from realizing their untimely demise is within reach.

We wordlessly walk into the Westwood Wing, and I can't stop the grin as Avery's eyes light up. She knows exactly where we are heading, her shorter legs suddenly gaining speed and traction as if Theo's tether is pulling her forward.

I openly play with the staff card in my hand, flicking it between fingers as I stroll past some new guards who gawk at me with sheer confusion. I can tell they are struggling to figure out what my deal is, easily noticing my carefree attitude to their presence.

Watch and learn quickly if you know what's best for you.

The group of guards are making their way room to room to escort patients out, and when we reach Theo's door, I'm pleased to find we've beaten them—they can thank me later for making their workloads lighter.

Swiping the card, Avery bounces in excitement next to me, waiting for me to punch in the code. The moment the door cracks open an inch, she's on the move, pulling it open and launching into the room.

I manage to catch sight of Theo, lounging on his bed, for only a brief second, before Avery crash tackles him into the mattress. Like with me, she's hellbent on choking the poor bastard with her limbs, but Theo doesn't appear to mind in the slightest.

"Theo," I greet warmly, leaning against the wall as I give them a moment to enjoy their reunion.

Dark eyes peer over Avery's shoulder at me. "Good to see you in one piece, Grey."

"Shame no one else is in pieces though," I murmur playfully, frowning at my chipped nail polish. Those fuckers ruined my hard work.

Theo hums in agreement, the sound immediately muffled as Avery kisses him, nails leaving fresh marks along his jawline as she holds him firmly. It's interesting to watch—we all know he's not going anywhere, but on some subconscious level, it's as if Avery is determined to keep a tight grip on us in case we suddenly vanish or float into the ceiling. Oddly enough, I share the same sentiments and would happily hand stitch her body to mine if I could.

As I wait, I sense someone approaching. A guard appears in the doorway, one of them finally game enough to investigate our appearance. He gives me a stern look of annoyance and disapproval, and when his attention switches to Avery and Theo on the bed, I start to see red.

"Keep fucking moving if you plan on waking up tomorrow."

I may as well have bitch slapped him across the face, his stunned reaction reminding me of a gaping goldfish out of water. He hesitates for a moment, probably trying to decide if I'm all bark and no bite, before a familiar face creeps up behind him.

"Connor! Fancy seeing you back here." I grin.

My reaction is genuine. After all, Arthur fired him as soon as Connor disobeyed him in favor of us. Whoever handled the dirty work for Arthur and did the new hires clearly missed the memo, desperate for all the help they could get. This will work great for us, and I make a mental note to reward Connor later.

"Grey," he answers with a sharp nod.

"It would be wise to instruct your new friends on the appropriate expectations," I tell him, locking eyes with the goldfish wannabe. Avery and Theo are watching our exchange, my dearest boyfriend-in-law looking ready to unalive both of them if they don't leave in the next five seconds.

Connor nods again, muttering something to the other guard before they both disappear from sight.

Turning back to the two of them, I decide to lighten the tension. "In the arms of another man already? And so soon after the wedding. You bad girl."

Avery picks up Theo's pillow, flinging it at me. "You assholes could have at least told me the plan."

"We could have," I agree. "But I also just really wanted to see your face when we told you the surprise."

She raises an eyebrow. "A surprise is a gift, Grey. Like a box of chocolates. Not a whole ass damn marriage."

Theo snorts quietly behind her. "Grey does like to do things to the extreme."

"Hey, asshole. I'm right here," I tease. "I could have left you in your room and fucked Avery in the library."

"No, you couldn't."

Avery chuckles quietly at our friendly banter, climbing off Theo to sit on the bed. He slides in next to her, and when she pats the free spot on her other side, I toss myself onto the bed with an enthusiastic bounce. Draping my arm around her shoulders, I tilt my head back against the wall. "How do you feel about the little surprise though?"

"I would have said yes," she replies heatedly before relaxing her tone. "Especially if it means fucking Alexander over. But the real question is why did *you* agree to it? Either of you? I assume you both knew beforehand."

"Because it doesn't matter which one of our names is on a piece of paper. You're still mine," Theo answers first, giving me the side-eye.

His arm is stroking her lower back, and playfully, I shove it off. "Actually, she was mine first. Just saying."

Theo huffs a laugh, unfazed at my stunt—still completely unbothered when I pull Avery into my lap.

"Because saying yes meant protecting you, little killer. Saying yes means we have a chance at setting you free from this place. I'll stop at nothing, do anything, kill everybody to keep you safe."

Avery leans down, gently pressing her lips against mine. "I'm still yours," she breathes out. "And Theo's. Nothing will ever change that. All three of you have my heart."

Hearing her words against my lips, my control starts to slide. I'm vividly aware of the small movements her hips are making in my lap. The way she claims me—us—like we do her makes me want to kill them all now so that I can fuck her in their blood while knowing that she's safe and ours forever.

My hand slides up her leg, enjoying the plush material of the teal sweatpants she's wearing. "I love you in anything but seeing you in sweatpants, I have to say it's getting me hard," I comment, grinning as she pulls back to glance down at her attire.

"Alyssa gave them to me," she says simply. I have no idea who Alyssa is but she gets the Grey stamp of approval. "The top as well."

Our girl clearly has a type. No wonder she was torn between the two of us, because it's glaringly obvious now that Theo and I are two peas in a fucking mental pod. He mimics my thoughts, reaching over to slide the thin strap of her top down her shoulder.

"They don't exactly have a closet full of bras and underwear in the hospital," Avery retorts, understanding where our minds are at. "That's why I'm not wearing any."

Swallowing a groan, I slip my hand under the waistband of the sweatpants to check. And fucking hell—she's not lying. My hand immediately finds her wet cunt, and I waste no time sliding my finger up her slit and dipping in to stroke her clit.

"I'm starting to think you enjoy your men possessive," I murmur. "You're so fucking wet for us already."

Avery rocks her hips into my hand, biting the inside of her bottom lip. "Enjoy the outfit while you can. It won't be long before I'm forced back into dull, monochrome colors that do no favors for my complexion."

"I'll rip every single uniform off you and leave a trail from your cunt to Arthur's office," I growl, pushing my finger inside her. She inhales sharply, her tight cunt instantly squeezing around me. She's already lost in our little bubble, not noticing Theo shifting off the bed until he's standing behind her back. We look at each other for a quick second, exchanging a silent conversation as she relaxes and melts into him.

His name leaves her lips in a whisper, tilting her head back for him. Theo leans over, starting his attention on her neck as he pushes the straps further down her arms until her tits are in my face.

My mouth encloses around the hardened, sweet tip, making her hips jerk. My fingers are still buried inside her and I trace circles around her clit with my thumb. None of us care that the door is still wide open, at risk that another guard could appear at any second. I'd have to kill them then and there if they do, because no one except the three of us are allowed to see her naked body.

I feel her getting close, Theo's hand wrapped around her throat and choking her as they kiss. He's silencing her moans, but we both know she's on the edge, speedily approaching breaking point.

"Don't stop," I hear her beg. "Please."

"They would have to pry my cold, dead body away from you to get me to stop," I respond lowly. "If I don't kill them first."

Theo's fingers tighten around her throat, cutting her breathing off. "Break for us, Aves. Give it to us."

Her lips part silently as her cunt undulates sweetly around my fingers as she comes. The hand around her throat disappears, her voice cracking as she cries out for a brief second before Theo swallows the sounds with his mouth.

I don't stop fucking her with my hand until the last of her orgasm drifts away in waves, slowly removing my fingers when she slumps against Theo.

Avery's eyes are hazy and almost unfocused, but she watches me as I taste her on my fingers. Holding up my hand to Theo, he snatches my wrist, almost crushing my bones in his grasp.

I grin as he maneuvers my hand to Avery's lips, guiding my arousal covered finger into her mouth. She moans in surprise but sucks hard, my eyes darkening with violent greed.

Removing my hand, Theo bunches up her hair in his fist, jerking her head backwards. He leans over the top of her, shoving his tongue into her mouth in a brutally passionate kiss, tasting her off her tongue.

If we didn't have important business to attend to, I'd take away her ability to walk for the next three to five business days. But instead, I will myself to calm down, knowing that it will be that much sweeter when I take her later and fuck her cunt into oblivion.

When Theo and Avery finally separate, I swoop in and capture her mouth in a quick kiss, biting her bottom lip.

"Come on, little killer. Time to go fuck shit up."

Chapter 8

Theo

To none of our surprise, we're the last to arrive at the hall for lunch.

Grey mutters something about joining us shortly, and I give a quick *whatever* nod before leading Avery over to our usual table, fingers still firmly entwined.

She watches Grey closely as he approaches another table in the middle of the room, full of people from their little club. I suppose *our club* now. I wasn't given much choice in the membership, but I'll follow Avery wherever she goes.

Circus society—whatever they call it. It's all the same to me.

There's an unsightly amount of knockoff SWAT guards lined up against the wall, covering every entrance and exit to the hall. Their beady eyes scan the hall like metronomes, hands hovering over their weapons.

I'm not sure what bullshit story Whittingham has fed them, but I wouldn't be surprised if they got trigger happy and started shooting up the place at the first misplaced sign of commotion.

Tension is thick. People aren't stupid though. Even the most ignorant patients here would be able to sense trouble—if the blood splatter in the corridor didn't give it away.

People keep their heads down, chattering among themselves as they pick at the poor excuse for food that's barely fit for human consumption. Avery can sense it too—not bothering to join the tiny queue to grab some lunch.

She keeps flickering her gaze to Grey, spare hand clenched tightly in a ball as she waits for him to re-join us. I can tell she's worried that the guards may accidentally—or deliberately—shoot him, but if Damon can survive a gunshot wound, I'm sure Grey would be fine too.

"Are you going to eat?" I ask her.

"No," she answers with a small shake of her head. "You should though."

When I don't respond, just raising an eyebrow at her clear self-abandonment, she turns her attention to me. A smile suddenly breaks out on her face, as if she's forgotten about the babysitters watching us.

I admire that after everything she's been through, she's still able to beam as happily as she does. It uses less muscles to frown, and frankly, giving minimal effort to people is more rewarding.

But not to Avery.

I suppose after her brief trip away from this madhouse, she's probably feeling somewhat refreshed. Even five minutes away from the soul sucking void would be a breath of fresh air. I'm glad she was able to be away for one night—just a fucking shame there was a price we all had to pay to achieve that.

Damon is fine though. I've been briefed on his situation and from what I understand, Avery and Grey are stepping into his place as locum. They are organizing a meeting straight away since there's no telling what the Lilydale cunts will do next.

I thought my family was messed up. Apparently, Damon's is on a whole other level. My parents abandoned me—a surprisingly better alternative than firing a bullet into my abdomen.

"You should eat," I tell her firmly. Despite my tone, she just smiles brighter, immune to my deadly demeanor.

"I ate my weight in hospital food," she says proudly. "It was better than the shit they are serving here on a daily basis."

"As long as it wasn't—"

"Don't say pineapple on pizza," she interjects. "You're wrong. Just admit it."

I snort, giving her a rare smile. "Make me, Avery."

Rolling her eyes and dismissing the challenge, her cheeks still turn pink. "Why don't you make me?"

I'm ready to pick up what she's throwing down, or rather, throw her down onto the table, but Grey climbing onto the real metal version grabs everyone's attention.

"Listen up," he says loudly to the room. It falls quiet immediately, and when the guards tense up and focus on him, Avery sucks in a nervous breath. I squeeze her hand for support, silently reassuring her that they are nothing more than gutless spectators, probably terrified of their own dicks. "A situation has gone down. Stay vigilant and keep together. Do not allow staff to *trick you* into false promises. If you see anything worth reporting, see me immediately."

It's short and sweet, the sound of his heavy landing echoing around the quiet room as he jumps off the table and makes a beeline for us.

Sliding in next to Avery, he throws her a grin. "Hey, baby girl. You okay?"

"You're going to get shot, you adorable moron," she grumbles, tilting her head toward the guards.

"By those assholes? Unlikely," he shrugs off, kissing her cheek.

Avery huffs under her breath, but the sudden, sharp gasp she makes has both our attention immediately. Grey and I glance at her in unison, her eyes narrowed on the main entrance.

Twisting my neck, I spot what has caused her reaction. The head cunt himself stands in the doorway, muttering low to a guard.

As if sensing our heated glares, Whittingham pauses, looking in our direction. His eyes mainly settle on Avery, and if I knew I'd get away with it, I'd walk over and snap his neck into multiple pieces just for looking at her.

Hostility and anger radiates from him, directed at the three of us. Grey slowly lifts his hand, rotating it until his middle finger is solidly pointed up in his direction.

Whittingham's cheeks puff out, his stocky frame vanishing out of sight as he storms off, the guard close behind him.

"Asshole," I hear Avery mutter angrily. "I've never wanted to kill someone more and I killed my father. Well, maybe Alexander. I wish he'd vanish off the face of the planet too."

I can't stop the smirk that I flash in her direction. There's something about hearing her desire for acts of violence that speaks to the monster inside of me. Grey apparently agrees, his eyes darkening as though he's ready to fuck her in front of the entire room.

Eyes darting between us, Avery blushes, suddenly turning shy. She clears her throat, looking at Grey. "Did you speak to everyone?"

Grey takes a moment to respond, probably still mentally undressing her. "Sure did. Want to handle the food again?"

Avery nods eagerly. "Have Byrone and Jillian managed to access the systems yet?"

Shaking my head, I leave them to their conversation, almost lost and not overly interested in being *that* involved in Damon's business.

I start scanning the room, taking note of everyone. People are easy to read if you know what to look for. Now that Grey has made his little speech, I'm curious if anyone begins acting suspiciously.

From what I've been told, Whittingham has a nasty habit of trying to blackmail patients to get them to do his dirty work. Whether that's demanding them to be spies or attempting to harm one of us if they have a death wish, we need to ensure that there's no other threats lurking nearby.

Everyone has happily returned to their food, a few sneaking glances in our direction as if trying to find out what the situation is that Grey speaks of. They don't come across as disingenuous though—merely curious like normal human beings.

Patients in Lilydale all have one thing in common. Trauma. And with that comes forced personality traits.

Untrusting, anxious, fearful.

It's the main reason why the psychiatrists struggle to engage with anyone here. Even professionals come across as a potential danger—and in Lilydale, they have good reason to be wary of them.

"Teamwork makes the dream work," Avery snorts with amusement.

Grey cackles. "I'm sure Deadman is absolutely thrilled being stuck in a hospital bed."

"Oh, please. If he was here, there would be no teamwork—just follow the leader."

"That's your husband you are talking about."

Avery points her index finger into his chest. "Are we going to continue this vicious cycle? Because I'll go another round if you want to bring up the marriage thing again."

I lift my eyebrow at her. "My condolences," I cut in. "For having to work with *him*." Tilting my head in Grey's direction, Avery fights back a laugh.

Grey threads his fingers with Avery's other hand, mustering the most serious expression he can manage. "Just think of all the late night one on one time I'll have to spend with her. I bet your pillow gives good hugs though."

My eyes glance over our hands, Avery holding onto both of us. We're almost like that stupid fucking Spiderman meme where the three of them point to each other. Except there's no chance in hell I'm holding Grey's hand to complete the triangle. Though, it would be rather bemusing for the patients. They are used to blood, violence and promises of death from Grey and I. But linking palms? Their remaining sanity would cease to exist and the whole facility would erupt into chaos.

"Would your face like to find out?" I shoot back.

"Play nice," Avery teases, though she knows we're just exchanging friendly banter. Death threats are the epitome of friendship for us now.

"I'm always nice," Grey exclaims happily. "Do I need to remind you just how *nice* I am? After all, I do prefer to complete things in sets of three. So, I should be extra nice and give you two more *nice* orgasms with my tongue."

She shifts slightly, thighs obviously clenching together. "Anyway," she murmurs, deflecting. "I'll organize the food if you can ensure the library gets set up. Hopefully we don't experience any access issues tonight."

"Whittingham won't be back tonight," I say confidently. "He hightailed it out of here awfully quick like the gutless fucker he is."

"I agree," Grey nods. "We're in the clear for now."

Avery's face flashes, as if a light bulb has gone off above it. "Damon said something about Mark and Louis—whoever they are."

Using his middle finger, Grey points out two men sitting at a table down the other end of the hall. They are large men—built like linebackers. Judging by their antisocial behavior and annoyed expressions, they keep to themselves.

Intelligent, unlike others here.

"Right," Grey answers in surprise. "That's good thinking. I'll catch them after lunch."

They continue talking, dropping more names I can't be bothered to learn. As I continue my initial observation of patients, someone grabs my attention.

That new patient keeps glancing over at us. I didn't take much notice at first—everyone was doing the same. But as the hype has worn off with people going back to their conversations, he's continuing to sneak glimpses.

I lower my head so as to not make it obvious that I'm watching him, and when he lifts his head again for another peek, I check to see who he's looking at.

Well, it appears Rian Thatcher has a kink for pain. Because I'm going to cave his face in and rip out his eyes since he's so fixated on my girlfriend.

Aves has temporarily forgotten about her leadership role, engrossed entirely in a sandwich that's as big as her head. To my surprise, there are no pizzas at all tonight, let alone a single piece of pineapple. Instead, Avery has opted to arrange sandwiches and finger foods for the circus gathering.

I linger close by to her, sending Damon's minions in the other direction if they attempt to approach while she's eating. They can wait. Avery didn't eat lunch and I wouldn't put it past Whittingham to resort back to old tactics of starvation if he can find his balls.

Without warning, said sandwich is thrust into my face, Avery grinning at me. "Try it. It's good."

I shake my head, amused. Her eyebrows pull together in frustration, stepping closer until she's got me caged in against the wall.

"Eat, Theo Ashwood," she demands.

Snorting, I hold her locked gaze, leaning down to take a bite. She looks satisfied, ready to step away when I grab her waist and pull her against me.

In my peripheral vision, I spot Grey watching our exchange, grinning while chatting to the one who's permanently attached to a laptop—Byrone, I believe—and as I focus, I catch little snippets of their discussion.

From what I can make out, someone died during the hallway ordeal. He's briefing the guy quickly and quietly, probably while Avery is distracted with her desire to shove the sandwich down my throat like we're on a cute couple's picnic during a random Tuesday afternoon.

That's good though. Avery doesn't handle death on her conscience well. Grey probably wants to sort out a plan before he updates her so that she doesn't have to do anything in regards to it.

When she starts to glance around, likely searching him out, I grip her chin and face her toward me.

"How are you feeling?" I ask.

I know she's handling things exceptionally well. I'm proud of her for that. But the exhaustion and stress is still present in her eyes as well as a lingering longing and sadness. It's clear who it belongs to—the one person who should be here, dealing with this.

I never thought I'd see the day where I cared, let alone, acknowledged, Damon's welfare. But he's grown on me as well. It's evident he loves Avery and will protect her with his life, and despite my desire to remain away from people, I believe in morals.

Damon is a loyal man, and he treats people well—most of the time. He's looked out for me despite our differences, and I respect that. This dynamic was never going to be easy for everyone, but we've all made it work, and by bringing me into his circle, I've given my loyalty to Damon. As long as he treats Aves well and doesn't hurt her, it will stay like that.

I appreciate the fact he took a bullet for her. We'd have all done the same, but we're here with her—he's not. He's paying a price that we'd all struggle with, while still ensuring that she's protected and loved.

Madison deserved that. And she paid the ultimate price for people's selfishness.

While I never saw eye to eye with Damon and Grey, we can all agree on one thing: Avery is the priority.

She has brought us together. What was it that Grey called us? Brothers-in-law? I guess that rings true now that Avery is a married woman.

It did cross my mind to warn Avery of the plan. The three of us discussed it in great detail. Ultimately, we all agreed that we needed things to be as authentic as possible with as few people involved. A dick move for sure from Avery's point of view, but we couldn't risk someone hurting her. We needed to move fast, and Avery likes to weigh up all the pros and cons.

I believed her when she said she would have agreed. There was never any doubt in my mind. But she would have dwelled on the details and guilt, sending her mind into a spiral, and time was of the essence.

When she asked how we felt about it, I was completely honest with my answer. A piece of paper means nothing to me. I'd already given thought about polyamorous marital situations with Madison—long landing on the point that love doesn't always need to go by the societal book and *normal* standards.

Avery is mine, in every way, shape and form that's important. Her being legally wed to someone else doesn't take away from what we have. What we have is unique, consensual, and customized to suit our individual relationships with her. She wears my ink and marks on her skin, I wear her on my dick. And she has my little black bleeding heart in her hands. That's all that matters.

I keep my arm tucked around her waist as she ponders my question.

"I'm okay," she answers honestly. "Just worried about everything."

"And about Damon," I point out.

She nods. "I know Alexander won't stop. He made that clear when he cornered me at the hospital."

After she filled us in, detailing all the events from her departure from Lilydale to her return, I can't say I'm surprised. Alexander Dale is a sly bastard, completely self-absorbed and obsessed. He's dangerous, and I won't hesitate to subject him to the same fate that led me here if he comes near Avery again.

"We won't let him," I promise her, meaning every fucking word. "Or that pathetic excuse for a shit stain that sticks to him."

"Whitface will already be planning something. He's spiraling. Did you see his face at lunch?"

I nod, watching as Grey finishes his conversation and heads in our direction. He comes up behind her, Avery shooting him a smile as she kisses his cheek.

"I think I know a way for us to find out," Grey says, clearly having heard the last part of our exchange.

"Oh?" Avery perks up. "How?"

Grey gestures toward Byrone and the tech girl. "Jillian still has access to the cameras we placed around, including the one in his office. As long as the servers and connection stay online, we can monitor his conversations."

"I asked Dr. Smith to purchase some new cells for us as well," Avery responds. "That way we can communicate with each other. Whittingham hopefully won't take notice since he confiscated the other ones and likely won't be expecting us to have new ones so soon."

He grins at her proudly, planting a kiss on her forehead before taking a huge bite out of the sandwich still in her hand. Whether he knows my mouth was on it before or not, he doesn't seem to care.

Fucking brothers-in-law.

Madison would have liked him. She would have *lectured me* to like him. The two of them would have fed off each other's energy. He's almost the male version of her—if Madison was a homicidal maniac with a weird kink for blood.

Swallowing the food, I notice his change in demeanor immediately. He gives me a tight smile, before spinning Avery around to face him.

"Alright, little killer. I have some news."

Avery stiffens, nodding for him to continue as she braces herself for whatever's coming.

Grey cups her cheek, stroking it with his thumb. "Leighton was killed in the fight. One of the guards injured him."

She doesn't react, the only telling sign she's affected by the news are her eyes which become a little glassy. Still, she holds herself together, lowering her head.

"Shit," she mutters. "But that's not all, is it?"

Grey shakes his head slowly, grimacing. "We've completed a headcount on all the patients, checking to make sure no one else was injured."

"And?" I ask when Avery stays silent, her face suddenly full of dread.

His eyes dart over to me, gaze reflecting the severity of his next words.

"Four patients are missing. They weren't involved in the hallway incident. But they did sign Elsher's bullshit consent form for voluntary *treatment.*"

Chapter 9

Avery

The days that follow are strangely... *routine*. It's as if the birthday massacre—aptly named by Grey—never happened.

Except it did.

We're forced back into the usual formation, attending classes under watchful eyes, and shoved into the rooms of the questionable psychiatrists. Thankfully, I'm still with Dr. Smith, though he seems just as uncertain as the rest of us regarding his so-called employment. He doesn't voice it completely, but little comments and the change in his demeanor just confirm the shift in energy that's radiating through Lilydale. That doesn't appear to slow him down though. He makes a point of being overly engaging in our sessions, almost to the point of being obnoxious. We've gone back several months and it takes all my strength not to be annoyed at his persistent questions about my feelings.

I understand where he's coming from. I know he's taking his role very seriously now after everything that happened. But at the end of the day, I'm not okay. Maybe on the surface I am, but people are still dead. Not to mention Damon is still in hospital, patients are missing again, and at any moment, Alexander is going to pop up to make good on his threats. No one is okay—even though we have to pretend that we are.

Despite all the new guards on patrol, I've yet to see Whitface since the day he poked his ugly mug into the hall. And when we finally get our hands on the new cell phones, it's apparent why.

"There's a whole bunch of news articles," I murmur, swinging my legs from atop the desk.

Grey looks up from the library table, nodding in agreement. "A few reek of Arthur, but there's a couple of local newspapers that have clearly gone rogue. Read the one from the Herald."

I click on the link in the list of articles. My eyes immediately get fixated on the title, eyebrows raising at the blunt directness.

PATIENTS SHOT. MANY DEAD IN REHAB CENTER BLOODBATH

Last Friday, 6th June, authorities were called to the Lilydale Foundation Center after reports of an altercation between staff and patients.

Upon arriving at the facility, initial reports suggested that several people were injured, with some suffering from gunshot wounds. In addition, staff and patients were also being treated for injuries relating to physical altercations.

The facility supervisor of Lilydale, Mr. Arthur Whittingham, gave a brief statement on the steps of the center, advising that several patients had started showing signs of aggression. When staff were called to deal with the situation, patients allegedly became violent, resulting in four people being pronounced dead at the scene as well as multiple counts of injury.

"Unfortunately, it is part of the job to deal with situations such as these. We are well equipped at the Lilydale Foundation Center to handle our patients, and empathize that they are on detailed, intimate programs to help them rehabilitate from their past crimes and upbringings. Sadly, we lost members of staff today, and while we would never give up on patients, it is clear that some are not safe to return to the community despite our expert guidance and treatment programs," Mr. Whittingham stated to the reporters on scene.

Lilydale Foundation Center was established over half a decade ago by a private organization. During its tenure, it has claimed to have successfully rehabilitated hundreds of patients. However, this reporter has been unable to find evidence to support these statistics.

When asked about the deaths, Mr. Whittingham was unwilling to provide details. However, according to a spokesperson for the local hospital, several staff and patients were being treated for injuries, including one with a gunshot wound.

We reached out to Mr. Whittingham for further comment regarding this, but at the time of press, have not received a response.

"Wow," I murmur, lowering the screen. "They know about Damon."

"I'm not surprised," Theo says from the corner of the room. He's leaning against the wall, one leg propped up with his arms folded. "Reporters will go to any lengths for a story. One even tried to sneak into Madison's funeral just to get inside details."

Frowning, I share a look with Grey, unsure just how much he knows about Theo's history. He nods in agreement about the reporters but doesn't prompt Theo for more information.

"And how did that work out?" I ask knowingly.

Theo shrugs. "I broke his camera... and his hand."

Yep. Called it.

Grey taps away on the keys of his cell, pausing before giving me a suspicious grin. "Check your phone in a minute, little killer."

I glance down at the same time it buzzes in my hand, a text message notification appearing. Clicking into it, I feel both sets of curious eyes on me, but it's momentarily forgotten as I read the message.

Damon: Hello wife.

"He's received the cell phone?" I ask excitedly, eyes blown wide.

Dr. Smith mentioned in our session earlier about taking a trip to the hospital to deliver the goods, but I didn't expect it to be this quick. Having a direct line to Damon suddenly feels like a weight has been lifted from my shoulders.

"Yep," Grey confirms, flashing me a Cheshire grin. "I'll no doubt be getting requests from him in the middle of the night. I'm fairly confident that Deadman doesn't actually sleep—or if he does it's with one eye open."

I don't respond, other than an amused snort, as I punch back a reply.

> You better be resting and taking those pain meds.

> Damon: Or what? Come and steal my buzzer again. I dare you.

"Arrogant shithead," I mutter, earning a laugh from Grey.

"You married him," Theo points out.

Swinging around to look at him, I cock an eyebrow. "Seriously. Again? You three are still in trouble for pulling that stunt without me knowing."

"Please," Grey laughs, tilting his chair back. "You sealed your fate the first day you slapped him."

Grumbling, I shake my head. "And here I thought the biggest issue was going to be Damon murdering me."

"It's still a life sentence. Just a different kind. It comes with benefits," Grey grins.

Before I can think of a witty comeback, the device buzzes again with a new message.

Damon: I trust the other two are looking after you. No doubt Grey is giving
you some kind of shit right now.

"He's on to you," I laugh, glancing over at Grey. "So, I'd behave."

He stands and rounds the table, plucking the cell from my hand. I assume he's just going to read the message, so all I can do is yelp when he moves behind me and lifts my shirt. Before I can react or unfreeze, his hand grabs my tit, an obvious camera shutter sound coming from the device.

"Motivation," Grey says lazily. "To get back here."

I snatch the cell back just in time to see the photo send, my chest on full display and being groped by Grey. "I'd ask if you're insane, but we already know the answer to that," I mutter, fixing my shirt back into place.

As soon as it was shower time after I arrived back from the hospital, the guards took my precious sweatpants and cotton tee, shoving me back into the dull Lilydale uniform. They have probably burned my gifted attire, a thought that pisses me off but at the same time is no surprise.

The library is quiet as usual, though there's still the lingering scent of food from last night. Grey and I both agreed that Leighton deserved a send-off in style, the whole Cirque des Morts family, sans Damon, honoring our fallen friend after Grey broke the news. We stayed later than usual, swapping stories and drinking in Leighton's memory. While it's all we can do at the moment, those assholes are going to pay for what they did to him—to all of us. They are going to burn for taking someone from us.

It was also a chance to feed everyone properly, the kitchen staff more willing than ever to prepare the menu I created. We're going to need all the energy we can get for what's coming. Something tells me the kitchen staff aren't too pleased with Whitface and his bullshit either.

"Uh, oh," I mutter as the cell buzzes with Damon's reply. This can either go one of two ways—either he's standoffish about it or...

> **Damon:** Grey, they deserve better attention than that. At least use your mouth.

"What did he say?" Grey asks, trying to sneak a peek.

I hide the cell, clutching it to my chest as I stroll over to Theo for protection. "Nice try," I tell him, leaning back against my dark, tattooed psycho.

Theo's arms wrap around me in a possessive grab, thoroughly shielding me from Grey. Stormy irises narrow at the challenge, and for a moment, I start to wonder who would win in a fight. They are both as strong and psychotic as each other. If I wasn't worried about them both getting hurt, I'd almost pay to witness that fight.

Before I can fall down that steamy mental rabbit hole, a hand trails down my collarbone, snatching the cell and catching me off guard. Theo recites the text message word for word, much to the amusement of Grey.

"You goddamn traitor," I grunt in jest to Theo, attempting to break loose from his hold but he pins me to his frame.

Grey stalks over slowly and I realize very quickly that any thoughts of the two of them squaring off are irrelevant when I'm the prey. I can't overpower one of them, let alone both.

"You heard Deadman," Grey grins, lifting my shirt again and ripping it off, taking the cell from Theo.

Muscular arms pin mine to my sides, making it impossible to squirm away. I feel Grey's warm breath on my nipple before his tongue flicks at the tip, engulfing it in his mouth while snapping more pics.

Well, this has well and truly backfired on me in the best way.

Grey's hand cups my breast, fingers digging in as he teases me with his hot, wet mouth. My back arches against Theo, the man himself still pinning me as I bite my lip to stay quiet.

"Well this won't do," Grey tsks. "Don't you dare hide from us. We want to hear *everything*."

He drops to his knees in front of me, hands reaching for my shorts. In one swift move they are at my feet along with my underwear, leaving me bare and exposed. A shiver runs through me but it's nothing to do with being cold. It's because both of their eyes and hands are on me, burning me faster than I can prepare for.

"Put your leg over his shoulder," Theo instructs, lifting my thigh without waiting for a response.

Between the two of them, they hoist my body into position, and I barely have time to brace myself before Grey's mouth is on me, dragging his tongue up the entire length of my cunt.

When his mouth finally stops on my clit, my hips jolt with a small moan. Theo holds me and suddenly I'm thankful for his hands because I'm not confident that I'd be able to stand when my grounded leg starts to shake.

"Theo," Grey murmurs against me, and I'm too distracted to spot their sneaky hand switch with my cell. The shutter sounds faintly register in my head but I'm too preoccupied with *Grey's head* to take much notice. His tongue swishes around my clit, moments before his hand snakes up my inner thigh. Fingers press against my entrance, timing perfectly with more clicking sounds from the cell as they invade my body.

"Are you going to come on his fingers?" Theo whispers in my ear, teeth nipping my earlobe.

All I can muster is a small nod, feeling the pleasure grow in my body. It crashes through me hard and fast, my knee buckling as strong hands circle my waist and keep me upright.

I'm still working my way through my climax when Grey brushes against my torso, the thick head of his cock lining up with my body. He pushes inside, the movement shoving me back into Theo as the two of them sandwich me between them.

Pleasure rushes through me again as I stretch to accommodate him, pulsating around his length as he begins fucking me into Theo.

Lips fall onto my neck, my head tilting sideways to give Theo more room. I'll never get over this feeling, how they make me feel as if I'm floating through different dimensions with their bodies.

There's another shift of hands as I'm passed off to Grey, his arms lifting me off the ground entirely. My ankles cross themselves behind him on autopilot as I wrap my arms around his neck, smashing my mouth into his.

It feels like mere seconds have passed before I'm lowered back against Theo again, but I'm instantly aware that it's a different sensation. I can feel his warm skin against mine and when I turn my head to confirm my lack of clothing suspicions, his lips crush into mine.

Sweet distractions serve their purpose, my mind fizzling with static. It's only when Grey stops moving, his cock buried deep in me, do I realize what's happening.

"Theo?" I mutter with hesitation.

"Sshh," Grey soothes, using his weight to hold me still and freeing a hand to grab my face. "Eyes on me."

A finger strokes the junction where Grey and I are joined, my body tensing when it pushes inside. Even just the sole digit makes me aware of the stretch, burning as Theo gently coaxes his finger inside. My eyes widen, a range of emotions flooding through me.

Shit. Theo has his finger inside my cunt while Grey is bottomed out in me. Another finger joins the mix, stretching me further until after a few gentle pumps the burning goes away and is replaced by ecstasy.

Grey groans, hand digging into my body as he rests his face against the crook of my neck. "Fuck, you're squeezing me so tight."

I can't form words, my frame sagging between them. And when I feel the unmistakable head of Theo's cock swapping with his fingers, I gasp.

"You're not going to fit," I argue quickly, swallowing hard.

"Relax," Theo murmurs, lips brushing the nape of my neck. "Grey..."

I have no idea how he manages, but somehow, we turn into a life-sized game of Twister, Grey's hand leaving my face to push between us. His fingers stroke my clit, relaxing me. When I've stopped tensing, Theo slowly pushes forward.

It's like nothing I've ever experienced. My breath staggers as I'm stretched beyond limits, Theo's hardened cock sliding in alongside Grey's.

I barely notice that I'm holding my breath until I start to see spots in my eyes, their soft groans bringing me back to reality. Taking a deep breath, I whine quietly, letting Theo kiss me like his life depends on it.

A hand wraps itself around my twisted neck, and Grey's calming voice infiltrates my ears. "You're taking us so fucking well, little killer."

There's something so fucking *hot* about the fact their dicks are both rubbing against each other in me. Shivers shake through my body, a small moan escaping into Theo's mouth, and the two of them take that as their cue to start moving. I stop breathing again for a few seconds, mouth falling open against Theo's lips. My eyes roll into the back of my head, and as suspected, my brain has left the building. But that's okay—because I'm more than fine when my body adjusts to the two of them, fingers still dancing around my clit.

They take turns thrusting into me, my legs still locked around Grey's back as I'm held upright by Theo. Breaking my mouth away from the man behind me, I change my focus to Grey, our tongues battling for dominance.

As if sensing my need to lose control, Grey slows his movements, tongue gently gliding over the tip of mine, drawing out every little sensation in my body.

Speed increases against my clit, my orgasm ripping through me faster than I can see coming. I scream into Grey's mouth, the two of them suddenly fucking me in unison with no holds barred.

My vision crashes into shades of white, body spasming around them as I fall over the cliff. No, not fall. I'm thrown head first, frantically clawing at the two of them wherever my hands can reach.

There's a wetness under my fingertips on Grey's back as I dig my nails in, earning me a low groan as he jerks hard into me, his release coming out of nowhere.

Behind me, my other hand fists Theo's hair, and in any other circumstance, I'd worry about hurting him with how rough I'm pulling the strands. He just growls deep in his chest, arms crushing me against his body as he joins us in the climatic bliss, stilling while he fills me like Grey.

And that's the last thing I remember. Grey takes me into his arms as Theo bends down, retrieving something from the floor. There's a quick clicking sound and a flash of light in my direction, and then I pass out.

Chapter 10

Avery

I had missed the boredom from classes, only just now relishing the monotone script Charmaine recites as she talks about biology.

Out of the corner of my eye, Grey twirls his pencil, focused on our teacher as she slowly paces the front row while holding open a textbook.

I have to give her credit. After everything that has gone down recently, Charmaine is holding it together. But there's still an air of tension emanating from her, bags under her eyes as she drones on.

Part of me wonders if she's tired and stressed because of the situation in general, or whether she holds concerns for her own life.

Death is normal in Lilydale—a concept I knew from day one. But lately, it seems as if that's all there is here. We're in some fucked-up version of reality, staff and patients constantly dropping dead by various means.

I don't think Charmaine has anything to worry about though. Most of the recently deceased had reason to be killed—be that their behavior or their actions. As long as she's not fucking Arthur now that Teddy is dead, she's safe.

Her back turns to face the front of the room, and a hand reaches out, squeezing my thigh. Smiling, I turn my head to spot Grey watching me, still lazily toying with his writing instrument.

He winks when he has my attention, giving me another grab further up my leg before sitting back in his seat.

Yesterday is still playing on repeat in my mind, and by the sultry glances he gives, I think I can assume the same about him.

After our library mischief, I spent last night texting Damon. I've never known someone to get shot and still act completely unfazed. He likes to be kept up to date, though there's little information to provide at the moment. According to him though, no drama means something is brewing. And I'm inclined to agree.

We currently have the society searching for answers on the new missing patients. So far, we've managed to narrow down the patient count to four. Given how many people were lined up for their bullshit excuse to bribe patients into being tortured, it only feels like a small positive. Four out of ninety-nine patients is such a tiny percentage, but after experiencing first-hand their inhumane methods, it may as well be everyone missing.

My stomach is in knots with worry. Lilydale's gen pop count is minimal, easy to tell when something is out of place since everyone knows everyone.

When I heard the names of missing patients, it took all of my willpower not to vomit everywhere. Two guys and two girls—unlikely to be a coincidence. Nothing is accidental in this place. Even worse, it's Siobhan and Eliana that are missing. I may not know the women in depth, but I've had enough interactions with them to make the judgment call that they wouldn't do something like this if they knew the truth.

Siobhan can be a little unstable at times, but she's not going to torture herself. Maybe after her brother's passing she was a little off the rails, but it's not characteristic of her to go and do something rash like this. Eliana has always been so sweet toward me, a friendly face who keeps to herself and befriends everyone. It wouldn't make sense. Plus, they speak to Vivian. I have no doubt that she would have relayed her experience to them as a warning.

So, where are they?

I feel eyes burning on me, an uncomfortable feeling niggling at my insides. That's how I know it's not Grey burning holes in the side of my face. His heated looks always cause an intense reaction, but not like this.

Twisting my head, I spot eyes watching me from the back of the room. Rian Thatcher doesn't slink away at all when I catch him. Nor does he show any reaction. He just continues to stare at me with blank, dead eyes.

Grey, sensing my movement, turns to me with a puzzled look of question, before following my line of vision. His pencil stops twirling in his grasp, stilling as Rian's gaze shifts from me to Grey. Finally, Rian loses interest, turning his attention back to Charmaine as she saunters down our aisle.

"Eyes up front, Grey," she scolds gently, whacking him in the head with the textbook. "You too, Avery."

Now I feel multiple sets of eyes on me, my cheeks reddening as I face the front. As she continues her path, Grey looks over at me, cocking his eyebrow. No words need to be spoken between us, his eyes asking the silent question. I just shrug in reply.

I have no idea why Rian is watching me. There's been something off about him since the day he arrived. I know Damon and Grey have kept a close eye on him, and despite assuming he had some sinister motives orchestrated by Whitface, he hasn't really been a threat to us.

Yet, at least.

We need to keep a closer eye on him. I know all too well what it's like to be threatened and bribed by Whitface, especially as the new kid on the block. But Grey was quick to remind him of proper etiquette.

Still, I can't fight the feeling that perhaps we have more enemies than we realize. People will do almost anything when they are desperate to survive. Damon may have most of the power, but he doesn't have the ability to offer any of these people what they really want.

I make a mental note to discuss it with Grey when class is over, and as usual, we're on the same wavelength.

We dip into the hall briefly while Byrone releases people by their numbers—my mind unhappy with the information that I'm still in group one. It's obvious though. I can't see my danger level decreasing any time soon. In fact, I'm probably enemy number one right now to Whitface and Alexander. I'm a damn shareholder in this place, legal heir to the Lilydale legacy after Damon.

It's a bit unnerving, I'm not going to lie. Knowing that they no longer want to just torture me, but kill me as well, that's unsettling. Even my father didn't really want me dead—he just wanted me to suffer and use me to release his frustrations. Now, I have people that wish and pray for my demise.

Fuck. The idea that people want me dead is next level. I suppose it's not much different to Whitface secretly giving me a razor blade and insinuating I should kill myself. But the motives are in a different league now. I was just a problem back then, collateral damage in their scheme to dissemble Cirque des Morts and hurt Damon. Now, I'm an obstacle, standing in the way of their plans and power. If Whitface can kill Teddy for lesser reasons, I really need to be careful and smart.

As group five is ordered to start free time, I gaze around, taking note of the *safe ones*. None of us are safe really, and when Theo stays still next to us, that's when it really hits me.

He slipped in so quietly with the rest of his class, but I felt him immediately. I'm drawn to all of them the moment we are in close proximity.

"Are you group one now?" I ask him, sensing Grey listening in.

The two of them share a look over my head as Theo nods. "We're in the same club now, Aves."

Confirmation still stings, but if anyone can handle themselves, it's Theo. I have to say I'm surprised though. After what he did to Dr. West, any smart person would stay far away from Theo. I guess the unwavering desire for science and research surpasses self-preservation when you are as sick and deranged as the doctors downstairs.

"Not really a club I wanted any of us to join," I murmur quietly so listening ears don't overhear.

Theo gives me a tilted smile, placing his hand on my lower back. "Anywhere you are, I'm there too."

"Come on," Grey says to us when Byrone gives the signal.

The three of us return to the library, checking the aisles to make sure we're alone. Besides the cameras, it's just us, and I have to wonder if our constant sexcapades in here are watched.

Okay—that's a thought I don't want to ponder. I can just imagine Whitface's disgusting face staring at the footage, and just like that, the library is tainted.

"What's the deal with Rian Thatcher?" I ask Grey, leaning against the table. "Do we need to worry about him?"

Grey sits on the table near me, practically leaping up with unnecessary force. "We'll keep a close watch on him, but I think it's fine."

"The new kid?" Theo interjects. "He keeps watching Avery. But the scrawny thing near pisses himself whenever he walks past."

A hearty laugh bubbles out from Grey. "Well... don't I have a funny story about that."

My nose wrinkles in repulsion. I was filled in about his bathroom visit with Rian, and frankly, if someone rubbed my face in urine, I'd be running in the opposite direction and steering clear of all bathrooms in my future.

Of course, Grey can't resist retelling the story, Theo enjoying it unlike the disgust I feel. But hey—we all have our different types of humor. I like jokes. Grey and Theo love violence. Opposites attract, right?

"Let's keep him on our list for now," I tell them, legs dangling off the table. "In the meantime, I want to chat to Vivian. I'm really worried about the missing patients."

The guys nod, giving me the green light.

"Theo, I need you to rough up some of the new guards. Find out what they know and if Arthur has bribed them with anything in particular. I'm willing to bet he's put a target on us. We need to be on alert in case they have plans to drag us downstairs."

I can't suppress the shiver that rolls through me at the memories. It makes me sick thinking about the missing patients. "We need to locate them asap," I say quietly. "I can't stand the thought of them being hurt downstairs while we sit idly by."

"Byrone is looking into it," Grey confirms. "We can't get down there though. The staff cards aren't working for those particular doors and they have tightened security for the camera zones."

"Oh," I mutter, disheartened. "That doesn't help ease my concerns at all."

"If anything, it just affirms that they are likely being held in the rooms," Theo says darkly. "Perhaps they allocated the access permission to the solitary confinement card."

"Which, we all know, is in Arthur's possession," I finish.

Grey hums to himself. "We need to get that card. But there's no doubt in my mind that he's either hidden it, locked it away, or it's on his person at all times."

"Can't we just smash the access pads?" I ask, glancing between the two of them.

Theo shakes his head. "They upgraded them. Those doors now have a new pad in place. I already tried."

"Fuck," I hiss quietly. "It's really happening, isn't it? Did the four missing patients sign the consent forms?"

"I don't know," Grey admits. "Perhaps Christopher knows."

I jump off the table, flattening my shorts back into place. "Then we need to find out. Who wants to pay a visit to Dr. Smith?"

At the end of free time, I'm paired up with a short, wide guard who looks no more than twenty-one. Even though he's clearly new, he doesn't harbor any nerves about his position, staying quiet as he leads me toward the Eastwood wing.

But as we near my room door, he grabs my arm, yanking me further down the corridor.

"My room is there," I point out, pulling my elbow to loosen his tight grip.

"You have a meeting," comes a gruff reply.

There's nothing I can do but be practically dragged further down, zigzagging until we reach the end door—and I know who this meeting is with.

Whitface is standing waiting for us, his office door open as we cross the foyer. Nerves fly through me as the cell phone suddenly feels heavy in my pocket. I can't let him take it away. It's our lifeline to Damon and each other.

If I had known what was coming, I would have called or texted Grey and Theo, but I'm stuck now, only able to hope that Jillian will see me entering his office on the live camera feed.

"Ms. White," Whittingham greets coldly. "Marriage becomes you."

Shit. Fuck. Shit.

"What is this about?" I force out, keeping my cool despite my insides turning to liquid.

He sits down casually, tilting his chair back while affixing his gaze on me. The guard stays close by, lingering too close for comfort as I wait for answers.

Finally, a sly smile breaks across Whittingham's face. "We've just been notified that your husband will be returning to Lilydale tomorrow under the order and care of Dr. Markel."

I try to contain my relief and excitement, face expressionless as I stay silent. There's more coming... there always is. He's building up to something and whatever it is, it can't be good.

"Take a seat," he gestures to the spare chair in front of him. I don't get a choice in the matter, the guard hastily gripping my arm and dragging me to the spot. I'm thrown into the chair, hands reaching out to the desk to steady myself as the legs tip and threaten to spill over.

"What do you want?" I ask more firmly. "Just hurry up and come out with it."

His murky eyes narrow on me, unamused by my attitude, but alas, he continues. "The Lilydale board is prepared to offer you a deal."

"You mean Alexander," I scoff.

"Your freedom," Whittingham states, ignoring my comment. "In exchange for an annulment."

Chapter 11

Grey

Christopher doesn't appear surprised to see me when I darken his proverbial doorstep. But he does shoot me an annoyed glance, eyes darting to the patient across from him.

"I'm happy to wait," I say casually, leaning against the doorframe. "Bit late in the day for professional appointments, isn't it?"

To be fair, it's not all that much of a shock. After the latest events, the staff will be run off their feet *consoling* patients. At least, that's what they will be telling themselves.

The meek woman in the guest chair jumps at the sight of me, her timid frame almost curling into itself. She has nothing to fear or worry about though. I know all about Charity Williams. Nothing more than the usual *charity* case that is sent to Lilydale, she's been here for nearly a year. Like Avery, Charity suffered a lot of abuse by parental figures until one day she snapped, blowing someone's head off in the middle of the street.

But unlike my little killer, this victim of society is just apprehensive in general. There's no spark or fire that harbors like it does within Avery. No anger or need to prove herself.

She's just, by medical standards, introverted and *broken* in their eyes for lack of a better word.

There's nothing wrong with being seen as broken. I love being underestimated, and if Dr. Smith is worth his pay-check, he'll be able to make her see that—learn her worth. As with most patients here, Charity is too lost to the system, eaten alive by guilt and stuck in a cycle that no one is trying to help pull her from. They don't believe anything anyone says about them being good, but she will believe that I'm the danger that everyone warns about.

"You know as well as I do why we're still hosting sessions this late in the afternoon," Christopher mutters firmly. "Wait outside. I'll be finished in ten minutes."

Turning my attention to Charity, I give her a friendly smile. She recoils still, eyes blown wide with fear. "No need to tremble, Charity. I won't bite."

"Grey!"

"Alright," I laugh, holding my hands up in defeat. "I'll be outside."

I deliberately leave the door open when I step into the hallway, leaning against the adjacent wall. Christopher stalks over and slams it closed to my face with a glowering look.

Amused, I do wait as promised. It gives me time to survey the hallway, noting the blood stains on the walls and floor. I wonder which poor sucker had to clean up our mess.

After the allotted ten minutes have passed, true to his word, Christopher walks Charity out. She gives me another shy glance before following Connor.

"You can't just be walking around like this," Christopher scolds, beckoning me into his office.

"Of course I can."

Taking the guest seat, I spread out, resting my arms along the top of the chair. Christopher sits at his desk, running his hand through his hair.

"Damon will be back tomorrow," he says suddenly. "Stanley briefed me."

"And how is dear Dr. Markel?" I ask. "Ready to take on Damon's care?"

An annoyed glance comes my way, the two of us well aware that Damon won't be letting Markel touch him, even with a ten foot pole. According to Avery, it's also unlikely that Damon will take any drugs offered by the old bat. Which means we're going to have a very cranky Deadman on our ass.

I don't blame him though. I wouldn't take the drugs either after what happened to Avery. Arthur would jump at the chance to drug any of us.

"Funny," comes the blunt reply. "Anyway, get to the point, Grey. What do you want?"

"Aww, trying to rush me? And here I thought you loved my company."

Christopher cocks an eyebrow. "You have three seconds."

"Fine," I sigh dramatically. "I take it you and Elsher confer at times?"

Even the mere mention of that cunt makes my blood boil. He's lucky he's still breathing. I can't help but notice that I never seem to be able to catch him alone. Always with a guard or storming off in the opposite direction when I approach. But that's okay—I love to hunt. He can only run for so long before I catch him.

"Not as much as we should be," Christopher informs me. "Even less now since my so-called termination."

"Well, that's about to change," I tell him. "I need you to find out whether or not the missing patients signed those forms. Avery tried to come ask you but you weren't here."

I leave my sentence there, letting him fill in the blanks. When his face scrunches up painfully, I get my answer. Christopher suspects they are experimenting on them too.

"They have been cornering patients," he says quietly. "One on one, seeking signatures still."

"What?" I snap. "Did you not think to perhaps relay this information?"

Christopher's eyes shoot up. "Watch your tone, Grey. I'm already on the outs because of you and frankly, not everything concerns you."

I nod my head toward the canister on his desk. "I'll jam that letter opener through your eye, Christopher. It works well. Ask the guard that caught Avery and I in Arthur's office. Oh, wait. You can't—he's dead."

Alarm crosses his face. "Stop killing people," he orders.

"I don't take demands from you, Christopher," I say delightfully. "You're not my father—who I also killed. And you might have the same blood, but you're not Damon either."

"Normal people don't go around murdering others."

"Thank fuck I'm not normal then."

The two of us enter into a stare off. I refuse to give in, just flashing my teeth as I grin at him.

Finally, he relents, rolling his eyes with a heavy sigh. "I'll see what I can find out. But be on guard. Now that Damon is en route to return..."

"Arthur and Alexander will be getting ready to strike," I finish confidently. "I'm aware of this, Christopher. Give me a little credit."

He nods. "Unfortunately, I'm not sure where the patients are."

"Yes, you do," I point out. "We all know where they are and with whom. But the assholes have upgraded the system to ensure we can't rescue them short of knocking walls down."

"This was never meant to happen," he mutters quietly, and it's almost like a statement to himself.

This time, I raise my eyebrow. "Really? Did you really think that Alexander had a personality change and would genuinely want to help people? Be smart about this, Christopher. Your whole career has been a sham. You were just a pawn in his game—someone to use for his benefit."

I half-expect him to argue, to disagree, but he doesn't. Disappointment shines back at me, and for a brief moment, I feel a little sorry for the bastard.

"You're right," he says, defeatedly. "That doesn't change what's happening."

"It doesn't. But you can't just sit back and let them pull this bullshit. Track down those forms and see what you can find out about Arthur's beloved extra-access card. We suspect that it's the key to getting downstairs. Teddy used to have a copy too."

Christopher nods slowly, voice gaining traction again. "Alright. Leave it with me."

"Put it in harder," I growl. "Thrust it in. Put your damn back into it."

"I'm fucking trying," Theo snaps. "Why don't you do something instead of standing there and attempting to look pretty? By the way, it's not working."

I grin. "That's because I'm already fucking gorgeous, brother-in-law. Even you aren't immune to my charms."

Theo stops, lifting the blade to my neck. "Want to make a bet? I can give you another little scar."

My eyes dance in amusement, the cold blade pushing against my throat. Anyone else in this situation would be terrified. But me? This shit is the stuff dreams are made of.

Theo doesn't look away, the two of us staring straight at each other with matching expressions. I raise my eyebrows, wiggling them. "Come on then. I'm waiting. Impale me on your knife."

"You sick fuck," he grumbles, pulling it away and jamming it into the side of the access pad again.

"Says the man who fucked Avery in a mortuary cabinet," I tease. "Didn't know necrophilia was your thing."

Theo continues messing with the metal access pad, attempting to find weakness in the structure. "I'd fuck Avery on your dead body."

"If she's naked, I'd die a happy man."

I start working on the other side, annoyed when it doesn't give. We're at the door near the stairwell, sussing out the new access pad in closer detail.

Both of us have discovered that punching it is fruitless, so we've resorted to the old faithful of trying to rip the cords out. Except, the metal is practically fused to the hard walls. There's an extra layer of steel securing the panel to the reinforced concrete walls to protect the box. The screws affixing it are tiny, making it near impossible to get the tips of our blades into.

"Maybe we just need to kick the door down," Theo suggests, gripping his handle tightly.

"Been there, tried it," I murmur, remembering how much it sucked trying to break through the door in my room.

"Blowtorch?"

"Hey," I drag out. "That's not a bad idea. Maybe Christopher can sneak us in a blowtorch."

Theo cocks an eyebrow. "I was joking. Somehow I doubt that it would work."

He's right. Cell phones are one thing but dear old Chris bringing in tools and machinery? Likely to be seen and confiscated by the old cunt known as Arthur since Christopher can barely keep a straight face and act inconspicuous.

I toss the knife, the blade reflecting and dazzling in the light as it spins before I catch it in the palm of my hand. "We'll just have to find a new Plan C if we can't get hold of an access card."

"We just gut Whittingham and steal his card?"

"I like the way you think," I grin at him.

The more I get to know Theo, the more I start to wonder why I ever really hated him. I mean, sure, there was the little issue of him stealing Avery from me, but I guess we can say with confidence that she has a type and perhaps she knew on some level we'd be good friends. Mentally deranged, psychotic, unhinged. Even Damon fits into the category. Although I still often consider killing Theo for the thrill of it, I don't think I can imagine life without him now. He's the violent brother I never had—slipping in easily with our little group of blood-loving lunatics.

Straightening up, Theo narrows his eyes at me. "What? You have that stupid look on your face."

"Just remembering all the sweet times I wanted to kill you," I say lovingly. "Still do."

"The feeling's mutual, asshole," he replies, but lacking the usual venom.

I open up my arms, palms as wide as the grin on my face. "Hug?"

"Fuck off."

"I love you too," I snort, tossing my arm toward him and jabbing him with the tip of my knife.

Theo looks down slowly at the blade resting into his shoulder, lips tugging into an amused smirk. See—*brother-mates*. Not quite soulmates, but something along those lines.

"Remove your damn hand before I give you a rectal massage with it."

"With the knife or my own hand?"

"Take your pick."

Flipping it back toward my chest, I catch the blade in my palm, enjoying the small sting it gives as it threatens to pierce my skin. I pocket it, motioning that our work is done for now.

"Come on, little psycho. Let's go find our girl and tell her the good news about Damon."

Chapter 12

Avery

It feels as though an ice bucket has been dumped over me, a shiver chilling me to the bones. "Excuse me?"

"We're prepared to release you from Lilydale and advise the Court that you have fulfilled your requirements of your stay. You'll be released back into the community and free to continue your life."

"But you want me to sign an annulment?" I question, the disgust visible in my tone.

Whittingham nods. "Reverse the damage you did and leave this all behind. Besides, it's for the best, isn't it? You don't need to be tied down to certain *people*."

Folding my arms, I hold his intense stare. He's trying to shake me down, dangling a carrot in my face. But he's made a grave mistake.

While he and Alexander have no qualms about hurting people to get where they want, I don't share the same view. And it's devastating to realize that he thinks this is all a game—that I solely and only entered into a marriage contract to fuck them over.

I mean sure, I didn't know I was entering into it... and they don't need to know that. But the thing he fails to recognize is my connection with Damon... with Grey and Theo, is more than revenge.

I'm nothing without them. They are my whole existence now—the three who saved me from my demons, my enemies, and freed me from the chains holding me back.

Whittingham takes my silence as a sign of contemplation, pushing a piece of paper toward me. Curiously, I lean forward, spotting the words 'ANNULMENT' along with a bunch of other text that holds no meaning.

"Just sign and walk out the door, Ms. White," he says coolly. "It's that simple."

My eyes fall onto the pen he's holding out, beady little eyes watching me eagerly. Shifting forward on my chair, I take the pen from his grasp, his eyes lighting up with greedy success.

Clicking the pen to eject the ballpoint, I lock eyes with him.

"You won't regret this," he encourages with a nod of his head. "You're better off without them."

A smile breaks across my face, his posture relaxing as if he's the cat that's got the cream. He's so sure that he has me won over, that he doesn't notice me moving until it's too late.

I lurch forward, gripping the pen tight in my fist. There's a sickening crunch and squelch of flesh as it embeds its way into his hand, sticking out.

Whitface lets out a loud yell, other hand immediately ripping out the pen as blood flows from the wound onto his desk, soaking the annulment paperwork. The guard, unprepared too, latches onto me, pinning my arms behind my back as I'm lifted off the chair and pulled away from the desk.

"You pathetic little—"

"What?" I cut Whittingham off. "What am I?"

There's no answer as he holds his hand against his expensive suit, staring daggers at me. Fury flashes back at me, his tone crisp and laced with pain. "Take her to solitary confinement," he directs the guard.

I don't cut my gaze from him as I'm dragged backwards, a snarky smile on my face. The idea of solitary confinement has always been terrifying, but I'm too pumped up on adrenaline to care.

I'm still learning things about myself every day. Even after all I've been through at Lilydale, if you asked me last week how I felt about harming another person, I'd probably say I hated the idea. I'm so used to being the one hurt that I could never picture myself inflicting pain on another. But something about the smug look on his face, the way they are trying to strongarm me into turning my back on my loved ones, just unleashed... *darkness*.

There's no regrets. Only... relief.

The office starts to vanish from view as my shoes whine against the flooring, my body being dragged heavily toward the patient side of the facility. But I keep my gaze fixed on

Whittingham until he slams the door closed, cursing and groaning.

It's then I realize I'm laughing out loud, the sound bouncing around the walls. The guard tenses behind me, a little panicked as he tries to keep a firm grasp on me while punching in the code and swiping the card I saw him grab from Whittingham.

I don't bother to assist him by walking normally. Consider this your cardio workout for the day, champ.

The high-pitched nail-on-chalkboard sound from the heels of my feet draws attention, both Dr. Markel and Dr. Smith poking their heads out of their offices as we pass. Equally horrified gazes find my face, and all I can do is throw Dr. Smith a wink.

"She has blood on her face!" the old, sing-songy doctor exclaims, near stuttering in some medical fashion of panic.

Huh—must have flung on there from Whittingham ripping the pen out. The thought doesn't freak me out as much as I expect. In fact, when the bane of my existence, Dr. Elsher steps out of his room to also see what all the commotion is about, I take advantage of it.

Catching his eye, I cock an eyebrow, smirking at him.

Psychoanalyze me now, fuckface.

Unlike his colleagues, he's not horrified or surprised. If anything, he sneers in response at my presence, and I flip him the bird happily.

Grey might be onto something here about the whole blood situation. Did that asshole's DNA accidentally soak into my pores, infecting me with all those traits that they love and use to hurt us? Or maybe—just, maybe—I'm fed up with being used.

What gives them the right to fuck with me? To dangle freedom in front of my face in exchange for stabbing someone in the back? They are nothing but cowards in expensive attire, hiding behind a wall of muscle.

"Ow!"

It slips out before I realize, my heels hitting the concrete steps heavily as I'm dragged into the darkness. The guard just grunts in reply, panting and probably contemplating his life choices after hauling me from one side of the facility to the other. Well, surely he knew it wouldn't be an easy job.

He repositions himself, curling an arm around my neck, forcing me into a chokehold while trying to open the cell door single handedly.

Fuck him too.

I dig my nails into his arm, doing my best to create semi-crescent markings through the black sleeves that poke out of the tactical gear. He squeezes harder, huffing in frustration before finally getting the door open.

Without giving my existence a second thought, he flings me into the darkness, my knees hitting the hard ground. I'm a little embarrassed by the yelp and groan of pain that emerges from my mouth, but he's already gone, the door slamming shut behind him.

Shit—Theo wasn't kidding when he said it was dark in here. I can't see anything, not even my own hands. The so-called flickering light doesn't appear to be on and as quickly as it appeared, the adrenaline leaves. I shiver, softly at first before it starts growing more aggressively.

Using my hands, I feel my way around, expecting a bed. There's a thin mattress on the floor but no bed frame, and I maneuver myself until I'm perched on top of it with my back pressed against the wall.

Checking to make sure there's no blinking red lights, I extract my cell. I need to alert Grey and Theo to the situation, but, of course, there's no signal down here. The light provides a little relief and I turn on the torch function, inspecting my surroundings.

Solitary confinement is smaller than my room, the walls painted black—at least, that's what it looks like even with the torch light. Large metal pipes crisscross on the roof, leading to God knows where.

The hard wall is scratched to pieces from my betters before me, scuff marks and stains of blood smeared on the wall. There's even a questionable larger stain about face level, and I shiver thinking about the idea that someone headbutted themselves into a mess in here.

But I can understand why.

I was warned about this cell.

Fuck. I stabbed Whittingham. Everything hits me at once as I circle back to his office, my mind replaying the events.

Asshole had it coming—there's no doubt about it. I don't regret it at all, surprisingly. The adrenaline has faded but I still feel justified in my reaction.

I have no idea how people like him can live and breathe with so much hatred. They get off on the idea of hurting others, determined to do whatever it takes to get their way.

For someone that claimed I could be saved when I first arrived at Lilydale, all I can do is shake my head. He lied from day one. There was never any intention of saving me. I was just a chosen project in their eyes. After feeling unworthy for most of my life, it was a shock to realize that I was worthy to people society deemed important—my story, at least.

I was personally selected to come to Lilydale. That hotshot attorney fought for it, not realizing he was putting me on a silver platter. They ate up my sob story, my tragic background, seeing nothing but dollar signs. From the day they accepted my application, I was worth a price.

No, that's a lie. I was the price.

I paid the price.

Still. Whittingham lied to me and Margaret, promising me great things about Lilydale. Yet, he watched Damon bleed out on the floor. He instigated my kidnapping, knowing what I was about to be subjected to.

He's a fucking monster.

Minutes turn into hours, and hours into years... Well, it feels like it. The only saving grace for my sanity is my cell phone. No reception is a killer, but at least I can view the time. Except it feels like it's lying to me too. Four hours pass but it feels like days.

I pass the time by scrolling through my gallery, not even embarrassed by the sex photos stored in there. I'm clinging to the thought of my guys.

It's distressing knowing that I'm stuck here until Whittingham decides it's enough. They couldn't even get Theo out when he was thrown in here.

How long will it take? Days? Weeks?

And then I realize I'm exactly where I don't want to be—at the mercy of Whitface. Only he can access me, separating us when I'm the biggest target in Lilydale. It wouldn't take much for Alexander to come down here, corner me all alone and end my life.

He'd use a gun, no doubt. Alexander and Whitface are all about the theatrics. It's why they use Lily's—my mother-in-law's—important dates as codes. Sending a statement is meaningful to them. The assholes love flaunting their power, and I've potentially walked right into their trap.

Well... what alternative did I have? I wasn't about to sign the annulment and just hand over everything to Alexander.

No, I decide, this was the better option. Even if they kill me, I will have saved innocent people from their clutches. Just as long as Damon survives me. My shares will revert to him, keeping him the majority shareholder.

The thought is troubling. I can't help but run through the other scenario. Where would my legacy go? Legally, it falls down the family lineage. But I don't have any family. Maybe a few distant cousins who probably barely remember me, but other than that... no one.

All my family is here in Lilydale.

I check the time again, not surprised that only a short period has passed. Left alone with my thoughts, I'm stuck envisioning the worse case scenarios. But once again, I tell myself it's okay.

Because I'm the badass who stabbed that motherfucker with a pen.

Chapter 13

Theo

My fist slams into the guard's nose, enjoying the sickening crunch that vibrates under my knuckles.

Doubling over, the miserable sad sack of existence makes a choking sound, blood guzzling into his mouth as he fights for air.

"What the fuck do you mean she's in solitary confinement?" Grey mutters darkly.

He's calm. Well, as *calm* as he can be. And by that, I mean the type of eerily quiet calm that radiates danger. The guard knows this, whimpering as he holds his hands up and waves the proverbial white flag.

"I don't know! Jonathon didn't say much. Just that she attacked Mr. Whittingham in his office and he was told to take her down to the holding cell."

The words are a jumbled mess. I'm surprised he isn't stuttering, though I suppose he's had time to get his story straight. After all, it was that guard—Connor, or whatever his name is—that warned Grey of the situation.

That soon to be dead cunt Whittingham went on a power trip while under our noses. All we know so far is that Avery was escorted to his office after free time and when we noticed her absence at dinner, Grey made it his personal mission to track her down before I could say anything.

My idea was to just decapitate everyone until we found her. His was to go to the guard they have in their pocket to ask for intel. Both effective methods if you ask me, but mine is a little more fun.

Connor was already on his way to us when we located him. Word gets around fast. It sounds like the new hires can't keep their mouths shut. Since I'm unable to slice anyone's head off, I've decided the next best thing is to put them all in jaw wires to make sure they don't speak.

After all, we need to set an example. These pathetic pieces of shit think it's a bragging right—to claim victory over their treatment of the patients.

I'm well aware that this particular guard was not the one to take Aves to solitary confinement. But he seemed a little *too happy* at first, reciting the events when we cornered him.

"And where is Jonathon now?" Grey asks, his voice as dangerous and threatening as mine right now.

"I'd hurry up and answer while you can still speak," I warn.

He cowers again, physically trembling before us. If he pisses himself, I'm going to rub his damn face in it. I'm losing my patience very quickly, and it's apparent Grey isn't far behind.

"His shift finished at mealtime," he offers weakly, hands shaking as he points to the exit door for good measure. "Back tomorrow."

Grey and I share a quick look, silently seething at the discovery we can't go straight to the source.

This is a waste of time. We're not going to get any more information from this motherfucker, so I put him out of his misery, delivering my promise.

I hit his jaw with precision, another crack and crunch ringing out, followed by a throaty, pained groan. He spills to the floor clutching his jaw, eyes rolling back in agony while I step over his discarded figure.

"Christopher," Grey murmurs, unfazed by the guard. He steps over him too, but a sudden high-pitched squeal indicates that Grey gave no fucks and squashed his hand as he passed.

The two of us head directly to Smith's office. Everyone is locked away in their rooms, the last of the shower groups just returning from the bathrooms.

I don't bother to voice the question to Grey as to whether or not Smith is still on the premises, the answer presenting to me when we reach his door.

It's open, revealing the man inside. He's hunched over his desk, reading something, and when our footsteps announce our presence, he looks up with a devastated face.

"You heard," is all he says, eyes darting between us.

"What the fuck happened?" Grey asks sternly, kicking over the trash can by the desk.

Smith looks at me, slouching back before focusing on my hallway companion. "I'm not entirely sure. Arthur ordered Avery to be taken to solitary confinement, and promptly left Lilydale. I assume there was an altercation of sorts. She had blood on her face."

"Wait, you saw her?" I snap. "And you didn't do anything?"

Grey nods furiously at my words. "I swear Christopher, I'm *this* close to losing my shit with you."

Unlike the guard that turned into a fumbling mess, Smith just shrugs with a frown. "I couldn't," he starts, attempting to sound apologetic. "It happened very quickly and by the time I investigated, she was already locked up and Arthur was gone."

"Fix it," Grey orders, emphasizing each word. "Before I send you on a first class express ticket to the morgue."

"And what would you have me do?" Smith argues back. "Break down the damn door myself? Arthur has both key cards and he's not here."

I walk over to the desk, slamming both hands down as I force the psychiatrist to look at me. "Figure out a solution," I advise him. "Don't be fucking stupid. There would have to be another way to get in. You expect us to believe that only two particular cards are able to unlock it?"

Smith's eyes widen slightly before peering over my shoulder to Grey. "I can't," he answers, not directly addressing me. And it pisses me off.

Swiftly moving around the desk, I grab him by the collar, yanking him from the chair. His feet dangle off the ground slightly as I hold him by the scruff of his suit. "You can and you will."

Grey mutters a curse, dragging my attention away from the man in my fist.

"What?" I snap at him.

His cell is out, resting in his palm. "It's not ringing."

"Lack of service," I reply, remembering I experienced the same thing last time I was in there. "If she moves around, she might be able to find a small bit of reception."

Grey nods. "Take us down there," he orders Smith sternly.

Dropping the man, he lands on his feet, huffing quietly as he adjusts his lapels. "Fine," he concedes, snatching his staff card from the desk. "But don't touch me again, Theo."

"I'll break your fingers one by one," I promise, the two of us following as he takes off into the hallway.

Both Grey and I know the path well, only pausing to let Smith open the doors to the dark stairwell. When we finish descending, Grey shoves Smith out of the way, tapping softly on the door.

"Little killer?"

"... Grey?"

I position myself next to him, listening as I hear Avery shuffle around inside. Her muffled voice becomes clearer when she's by the door, a hint of relief in her tone.

"Grey?" she says again. "Is that really you?"

"It's me," he confirms. "And Theo."

Even through the metal door, I hear her sharp intake of breath at the news. A rare smile, only reserved for her, falls onto my face. "Are you okay, Aves?"

"Yes," she murmurs, but there's an air of uncertainty.

I don't voice my concern. Solitary confinement is a fucked-up place to be—we already know that. From the start, I knew she'd never be able to deal with it as well as I can—or Grey. But sending her into a panic and being flustered is not going to help any of us.

Grey's façade cracks a little, his guard finally lowering. His eyebrows furrow together, his hand resting on the door as if he can feel her through the metal. "We're not going anywhere," he says confidently. "One of us will stay here the entire night."

"You don't have to do that," she murmurs sadly. "You'll get caught."

"She's right—" Smith cuts in but I hastily snap my head toward him.

"Shut. The. Fuck. Up."

Avery clears her throat, surprised. "Is that Dr. Smith?"

"Unfortunately," I confirm to her, still locking eyes with the psychiatrist. "*He* won't be staying though."

Grey squats down, running his finger along the gap at the bottom of the door. "What happened, little killer?"

I wait for some kind of recall, but when Aves starts cackling on the other side, Grey and I share a look. It's a chilling laugh, one full of sarcasm and disbelief. Still, I can't stop the smirk that appears on my face and neither can Grey.

"Whitface tried to bribe me," she finally reveals. "My freedom from Lilydale in exchange for an annulment."

"What?" Grey growls, turning to face Smith. "Did you know about this?"

"Of course I didn't," he huffs.

Avery, obviously listening, hums thoughtfully. "It's Whitface and Alexander coded. Be nice to Dr. Smith."

I sneer at the psychiatrist, wanting nothing more than to cave his skull in. "No."

Grey sits on the ground, making himself comfortable. Pressing his back against the metal door, he rests his hands on his curled-up knees. "You didn't sign it," he answers matter-of-factly.

"Of course not," Aves replies, clearly holding in a laugh again. "But I did stab him through the hand with the pen."

All of our eyebrows forget gravity exists. A small chuckle breaks free from me, while Grey stares ahead, impressed.

"Well, that explains the blood," Smith murmurs to himself.

"Why are you still here?" I snap at him. "Beat it."

Smith takes a step toward the door, and for a moment, I can't help but get excited that perhaps we're about to square-off. But instead, he raises his voice so Avery can hear.

"Are you okay, Avery? You'll be in there overnight. You weren't harmed, were you?"

Fine. He can live—for now, reluctantly. But I narrow my eyes at him, a warning not to tempt me.

There's no doubt about it that he cares about our girl, but he's far from innocent and kind. It was his delusions that caused Avery to be arrested in the first place. The ripple effect trickled down until she was fully on Damon's father's radar. Then, the more he's involved himself with the situation, the more harm he's brought her.

He should have left the protection detail to us. We can handle it. While he may have his own reasons for wanting to protect her—call it good doctorhood or whatever—he has no idea how to deal with this. And I'm getting a little fed up with him being in our faces.

Grey seems to share the same sentiments. He stays quiet though, waiting for Avery to answer the question.

"No," she says, and we all breathe a sigh of relief. "Other than being a little banged up from the guard dragging me here."

"We'll deal with him," I comment, Grey giving a firm nod of agreement.

Standing, Grey steps toward Smith, cracking his neck as he moves. "We're staying down here. Go see if you can figure out a way to get this door open."

Much to my annoyance, Smith nods, listening to Grey.

Asshole.

After he leaves, the two of us adjust our positions, backs pressed against the door as we stand guard for the night. Avery fills us in on a little more detail, specifically Whittingham's words and how she's using the torch on her cell to see around the dark room.

To my astonishment, we're not interrupted the entire night. I suspect Smith has redirected the guards in Whittingham's absence, ensuring we're not disturbed.

There's no fooling anyone though. We can all agree that it's for the guards' benefits—not ours. This cold floor will be their last resting place if they dare step foot down here.

Avery manages to catch some sleep, but Grey and I stay awake the whole night, listening to the faint, soft sounds of her deep breathing. And when morning comes, we've mapped out a plan, promising Avery that she'll be out of that cold box really soon.

If that means slaughtering every person in this place, then so be it.

Chapter 14

Avery

I send Theo and Grey away at the first sign of morning light. Of course, I'm using the term loosely since it's still pitch black in here.

Thankfully, my cell manages to stay on, the battery holding out since the only function I used all night was the torch light.

I don't know why, but there's something about daytime that feels safe. Like the monsters can't harm you when the sun is out. Maybe it's because fear stems from darkness and the unknown.

Knowing it's a new day, I feel a little more in control. My appreciation for the guys continues to grow, especially after they sat on the cold floor the whole night, making me feel protected.

Being able to speak to them, even through the door, erased that weird sense of time paralysis that I first experienced when I was locked in here.

I remember Theo mentioning that food only comes once a day, and my stomach rumbles at the thought. The gap under the door isn't big enough for the guys to sneak snacks, but

I'm remaining optimistic that perhaps they will be able to convince someone to let me out of here.

The hours continue to pass though, and I keep checking the time, trying to keep a sense of reality. By early afternoon, I find myself nodding off into a light sleep, my entire body out of whack by the constant darkness in the room. Outside noises echo downstairs and in my sleepy state, I don't hear the door open.

Footsteps start to bring me out of my slumber, but when I blink rapidly, attempting to wake, all I can make out is a blurred shadow in the corner.

What the fuck.

Maybe I'm imagining it. Hallucinations are probably a side effect of this room, and even though my heart starts pounding against my chest, I convince myself that I'm just seeing things.

"Hello wife."

My eyes snap open, flinging myself upright so quickly that my tailbone rubs uncomfortably against the thin mattress.

There's no mistaking it, not a single doubt that I'm imagining the voice that came from the shadows.

"Damon?" I ask warily, pushing to my feet.

Well, this is going to be awkward if the shadow evaporates when I reach the corner. But as I approach, a more solid outline comes into view.

My hands brush against a tall frame, body jerking slightly from my touch. But I feel it—soft padding like a bandage on his torso.

It's him.

Damon lets out a grunt as I throw my arms around him, squeezing his body in a tight hug. Hands snake around my back and I bury my face into his chest.

"You're back," I mutter into his shirt.

"You seem surprised," he teases. "You were told, weren't you?"

Laughing quietly in relief, I shake my head. "Yeah. I'm just so glad to see you."

The faint smell of lemons hits me and I recognize it as the cheap hospital soap. It doesn't feel like he's in the usual Lilydale attire, probably gifted with new clothing like I was. My fingers trace the outline of a zipper—a hoodie I suspect—and when they reach the bottom of the material, grazing against his lower abdomen, he grabs my hand gently.

"I can't leave you alone for five minutes apparently," he says, indicating my current predicament.

"I was overdue for a trip to solitary confinement," I joke dryly. "Blame Whitface."

Damon hums in agreement. "Yes, I've been informed of the situation. You stabbed him."

Amusement coats his tone, and I almost recoil at the perplexing feeling of pride I feel. That can't be a normal reaction—what type of sick person has a praise kink over stabbing someone?

Well, obviously Grey would. That man and his strange stabbing kink. Part of me jokingly wonders if he was jealous that I didn't stab *him* instead. He's been literally begging for it since day one.

"He deserved it," I answer. "Wanted me to sign an annulment."

"I thought you would have run from me at the first possible opportunity."

I link our hands. "You said you'd just chase me if I did."

"That I did," he agrees fondly. "But I suspect you'd *want* me to catch you."

"Always," I breathe out, pushing up on my tippy-toes to find his lips.

When our mouths touch, suddenly solitary confinement is the least of my thoughts. He tastes exquisite, my body bursting with excitement and energy that Damon is right in front of me.

Alive.

In perfect Damon fashion, he takes control, gripping me tight around my waist, pulling me flush against him. His tongue demands entrance, and I give it without hesitation.

I'm on the verge of climbing him like a tree when I remember his wound, pulling back. "Does it still hurt?"

He lets out a disgruntled sound at the sudden breakage, hands yanking me forward again until I'm pressed against him. "Stop worrying about it for a minute and just kiss me."

I don't need to be told twice, though I am planning to circle back to the pain discussion at a later time. Whether or not Damon admits it, he went through a lot. And even him, with his Superman powers, isn't immune to bullet wounds. But he has Grey to protect him, even if Damon insists he's fine.

I wouldn't put it past Alexander to try to take advantage of his weakened physical state. But we have a whole goddamn circus of survivors to defend our territory.

My tongue presses against his as my body pushes up as I try to hold my balance. I hate that we're in the dark, and I have a million more questions for him, but right now... this is perfect.

His hands slide down my waist, holding my hips. Damon, taking control of the situation as usual, surprises me by slipping his hand under the waistband of my shorts. My breath catches, feet slamming flat on the ground as I blink rapidly in the dark, trying to summon night vision.

Before I can discover any newfound abilities, his finger pulls the crotch of my underwear aside, dipping into my heat. Then, without dragging things out, slides straight into me.

"Damon," I breathe out. "What are you doing?"

I'm no stranger to random sex locations within Lilydale, but this I didn't see coming.

"Consummating our marriage," he replies, holding me still with his arm. His finger thrusts in and out of my cunt, and despite my best argument laying forgotten on my tongue, my eyes roll back in ecstasy.

"What if someone catches us?" I ask with a small moan.

"Let them."

"But you're hurt."

His thumb draws lazy circles around my clit, my breathing intensifying and coming out to ragged pants as another finger slowly penetrates me.

I no longer trust myself to stay quiet, my hands cupping his face and lips seeking out his. It doesn't take long until I'm falling apart on his hand, Damon swallowing my cries as my legs begin to shake.

Just when I think we're finished, he switches us, my back hitting the wall. Dropping to his knees, he slings my leg over his shoulder, his tongue lashing out against my clit, immediately bringing me toward the edge again.

Not once do his fingers leave my body, not that I'd let him. I'm clenching so hard that for a second, I worry I might break his bones, if that's even possible. Before I can contemplate it and let my mind run wild with panic that I could be hurting him, especially being on the floor, his tongue and fingers hurl me over the cliff.

"There," he murmurs, getting to his feet. "That's all the pain medication I need." I let out a squeal as he lifts me off the ground, pushing my back against the wall.

"Oh," I try to joke, barely able to breathe. "So, I'm essentially doing you a medical favor? That's the story you're running with?"

"Avery," he says sternly. "If I don't bury my cock into your cunt right now, I might actually succumb to my injuries. It's all I've been able to think about while stuck in that awful hospital bed."

I let out a sharp gasp as he impales me in one swift motion, my body stretching around his length. "Your injuries though..." I argue.

"Respectfully, shut up. Your husband is fucking you right now."

He emphasizes each word with a brutal thrust, hitting that spot deep inside me. My head falls back against the wall, moans increasing in volume as he continues to fuck me relentlessly.

"Touch yourself," he demands. "I need to feel you come on me."

I reach down between us, cringing as my arm brushes against the bandage on his abdomen, but he doesn't flinch or waver at all. Stroking my clit, I roll my hips as his cock dives in and out, until I'm screaming his name. It echoes around solitary confinement, sending him over the edge.

"Fuck, Avery," he growls, thrusting into me once more and shooting his release.

Pressing my lips to his in the dark, I stay wrapped up in his arms until he lowers me to my feet a few minutes later.

"Are you okay?" I ask breathlessly. "Did I hurt you?"

His reply is cut off with the sound of footsteps coming down the stairs outside, my frame tensing up.

Shit—the guards.

"Are you lovebirds ready? Did you consummate yet?" Grey's voice calls out. "Free time is kicking off and I'm worried Avery will get even more pale if she remains in there. She needs more Vitamin D."

"Let me guess—you have a shot for her?" Theo answers, deliberately ruining the bit.

"Why you gotta out me like that?" Grey groans, his shadow entering the room. "Wow—smells like sweet little killer in here."

Kicking off from the wall, I muffle a protest, thankful that no one can see my face. "Get me out of here. Please," I beg, desperate to get away from this room.

Grey reaches out through the darkness, gripping my hand as he starts to lead me toward the door. "Deadman?"

"Coming."

"I bet you did," Theo quickly interjects, earning a gasp from Grey.

"You asshole. That was my line!"

Turns out that the moment Damon arrived back at Lilydale, he all but kicked in Whittingham's door. The asshole still wasn't present, probably nursing a bruised ego and busted hand, but his office was unguarded due to his lack of presence.

I don't know why it didn't cross my mind before, but I found out there's a safe in his office, hidden behind the desk. No one knows the code of course, but Grey had filled Damon in prior to his return about my situation. No idea how he managed it, but he made a pitstop on the way back to Lilydale with Connor, grabbing a few supplies.

Mainly a crowbar and blowtorch.

And wouldn't you know it... the spare key card was in the safe. Mocking us.

Somehow in my sleep deprived state, I also missed Damon using his new toys to open the door to solitary confinement. I'm assured that it didn't take long, the white noise of the blowtorch probably lulling me into a deeper state of unconsciousness since I'm only hyperaware when it comes to the sound of footsteps for some bizarre reason. Even though they had the key, they decided to destroy the door so that the room can't be used against us anytime soon.

Grey and Theo had stood guard upstairs, ensuring my *prison break* wouldn't be disturbed. With Whittingham away from the premises, the guards are walking around in confusion, just manning the halls with no direction or instruction.

I have to hand it to the guys though—they really do think everything through. The blowtorch is going to make an excellent addition to Cirque des Morts' tool stash, lined up next to open the damn doors at the end of the hallway by the stairwell.

They run me through their plan, and I'm told it's similar to what they had to do when rescuing me from the hands of the mad scientists. We're going to start working on a plan tonight, Byrone and Jillian already working on breaking through the security systems. They are getting close to finally cracking it without detection, so I'm a nervous ball of energy waiting.

It might take a few days before we can fully get downstairs. In the meantime, Theo and Damon are checking the new door panels to determine how quickly we can pry them open with a blowtorch while Grey is working on *hand toys*.

If I thought he was proud of his shiv, it's nothing on the new one he nearly flings at my face during a trip to the library.

"What do you think?" he asks quickly, excitement lacing his words.

Gripping the metal handle, I run my fingers over the cool texture, carefully looking at the angular blade poking out. "It's great," I say amused. "Reminds me of a Stanley knife."

He nods, like all his Christmases have come at once. "That was the general inspiration. Do you recognize the blade?"

I glance at it, not noticing anything special at first until I spot some gaps in the middle of the silver. "Is this a razor blade?"

"The very one you smuggled from the showers."

My mouth falls open in awe. "The one I had to clench between my ass cheeks?"

Grey grins, clearly solely focusing on the mention of my ass. "This fine peach deserves protection. I made this for you."

"Wait," I pause. "This is for me? Like... a present?"

The small dip of his head is my confirmation, and I jut my bottom lip out, taken aback by emotion. No one has ever really gifted me a present before—except Paige of course and my father made sure to destroy it.

I don't know why but I've always valued sentimental, homemade gifts over expensive belongings. It feels personal—made just for me. And knowing Grey's attachment to his weapons, this is the most thoughtful present I've ever received alongside Theo's tattooing skills to hide my burn scars.

"Ooft," he groans as I fling myself into his chest, knocking him into the bookshelf. "If I knew you'd love it *that* much, I would have started giving you knives sooner."

"It's perfect," I mumble into his chest, the handle resting against his shoulder. "I fucking love it."

Grey snakes his arms around me, squeezing our bodies together so tightly that I struggle to breathe—and love every damn second of it.

"Are you done yet?" Damon calls out from the tables. "We need to make a start on these plans. No banging Avery in the aisles. The floors are still relatively clean."

Throwing a sly grin my way, I can't stop the squeal that falls out of my mouth as I'm suddenly hoisted off my feet and slammed into the bookcase.

Grey decides to take Damon's words as his own personal challenge because before I can even respond, my shorts are ripped aside and I'm filled to the brim with Grey's cock.

"Fuck," I moan, announcing loudly that we've detoured and gotten distracted.

"You feel so fucking perfect," Grey groans, smashing his hips into mine.

Feeling inspired, I grip the knife firmly, pressing it against Grey's neck. His eyes sparkle maniacally, somehow managing to fuck me even harder against the bookshelf as I cry out from the sheer force.

I dig my nails into his shoulder to balance myself, and to ensure I don't actually end up slicing his throat. The pain from my grip spurs him on further, his hands grabbing my thighs hard enough to leave finger marks.

"I love the knife so much," I breathe out, holding it steady against his skin.

Grey leans forward, startling me for a moment as I quickly move to readjust my hold. He nearly impales himself on the blade, completely unfazed as he captures my lips in his.

My climax crashes through me quickly when his tongue molds into mine, hand shaking and accidentally nicking his skin. Before I can panic over drawing blood from him, he growls heatedly, the cut sending him over the edge as he hastily slams into me a few more times before shooting his release into me.

A droplet of blood drips down his neck, staining his shirt as we keep kissing passionately, still wrapped up in each other.

Pulling back for a moment, Grey calls out, "We're going to need a few more minutes, Deadman. I'm not done with Avery yet." Then, making good on his promise, Grey and I, plus the blade, go round two.

Chapter 15

Avery

If I thought the atmosphere in Lilydale was intense before, it had nothing on Damon's return. It's almost as if people thought he wouldn't be coming back, and seeing him was a stark, cold reminder of the entire situation.

Patients were still talking, the stories continuing to grow more outlandish by the day. On the plus side, I did hear one tiny rumor that I killed a guard which is why I stabbed Whitface when he allegedly tried to kick me out of Lilydale.

Needless to say, I haven't bothered to correct anyone. Damon was right—having people fear you was something else. People no longer saw me as invisible and barged into me in the hallways. For the first time in my life, I wasn't the girl in the glass box, watching life go by like a forgotten afterthought. I also wasn't the father killer who received pitying stares or disapproving looks.

I felt like the guys' equal.

Walking down the hallway with Damon, Grey, and Theo, people move out of our way, nodding to us. They can sense the power shift, and I think Whittingham made a big mistake at overlooking the patients. He's treated everyone as if they are nothing but an inconvenience, a charity case he can use to his advantage. But they are smart—hyper aware and vigilant because of their trauma. And with patients missing, people are starting to connect the dots.

We're not the real villains.

Speaking of which, as the days continue to pass by, I'm getting more agitated at our lack of access to downstairs. We still haven't been able to access the stairwell or figure out the code, even with the extra-access staff card. Damon has tried every combination he can think of in relation to his mother, but so far, we've come up empty handed.

At least we have the blowtorch but that's going to take some planning. With the guards wandering around, looking for trouble, we've only got a short window to act. One chance to save our friends. If it goes wrong, then they could end up like Leah...

Knowing what I went through downstairs, and how volatile things are, my imagination runs wild with possibilities and scenarios, just picturing what they could be going through. Two more patients have been counted as missing, and vomit threatens to rise every time I wonder if it's because our fellow peers aren't with us anymore.

Are they replacing test subjects? Or just expanding operations? Both are indescribable options.

When we enter the hall, I do a quick scan of the room, patients lining up for lunch. My eyes fall onto the meek blonde sitting alone, and I turn to Damon, grabbing his hand.

"I'll be back. I need to go speak to her," I say quietly, though I have Grey and Theo's attention as well.

Damon follows the trajectory, narrowing his eyes suspiciously. He knows we have no reason to suspect her now, but this is more than just general Cirque des Morts business.

"Fine," he agrees.

Before I can step away, he catches me off guard, swooping me around until I'm dipped backwards. His lips fall onto mine, and there's a clatter of metal as food utensils are dropped in shock and awe.

I'd probably find it amusing if I wasn't so entranced by his kiss, my mind floating away into space.

It's not like Damon and I have hidden anything—holding hands in the corridor and him pinning me against walls in plain sight—but he's never publicly *claimed* me before.

Slowly, he breaks the kiss, standing me upright. My head is still woozy and I've barely started to recover when Grey flies in, swinging me around to heatedly kiss me as well.

Frigging Neanderthal.

Next to us, Damon makes a scoffing sound in his throat, clearly catching onto Grey's tactic too. He grins against my lips, pulling back only enough to whisper to me, "Can't let him have all the glory."

I snort, giving him a quick peck before straightening up and looking at Theo. "Get over here."

He doesn't need to be told twice, but unlike the other two, he doesn't lunge at me. It's slow, mesmerizing, and taunting.

Steady footsteps, his warm hand cupping my cheek as he leans down and lightly kisses my lips.

It's dead silent in the hall now, my skin burning with the eyes of ninety-odd patients. And just like them, I'm also hypnotized and breathless. For our onlookers, it's confusing—not only seeing Damon and Grey make me theirs, but Theo's stark contrast to his usual behavior.

They don't know what I know though. Only I get his softer side.

As for me, I'm struggling to handle all the different approaches, and for a second, I forget what the conversation was before all this happened.

"Oh, right," I mutter to myself, stroking my thumb over Theo's cheek. "I'll be back."

He gingerly nods, heading off to the food line and leaving the other two in his wake. Damon and Grey wait for me to head over to Vivian, her green eyes plastered on my approaching frame.

"What the fuck?" she asks quietly when I reach her table, but it's more puzzled than anything.

Sitting down across from her, I take in her pale cheeks, and slender frame. Vivian has always been a petite woman, but there's something nearly sickening about her current physique.

Her plate in front of her barely has any food on it, only a few vegetables. The fork is still on the table next to it, completely untouched.

"You're not eating," I point out, temporarily bypassing the main reason for my impromptu visit.

She shrugs. "I'm not hungry."

Offering her a grim smile, I glance away for a second, understanding all too well what she's feeling. "We're going to find them," I promise her.

Vivian lets out a sad sigh, resting her chin on her palm. "Will you though? They are probably already dead, Avery."

I know she's close to Siobhan, and probably Eliana too. I remember when Whitface told everyone that Vivian was dead, Siobhan lost her shit.

"They have to be okay," I tell her. "There's no other option."

As we lock eyes, I see tears swell. She's on the verge of breaking down, and I hurt for her.

"Do you think...," she pauses, swallowing hard. "Do you think they are going through the same as what we did?"

Fucking hell. I never thought I'd see the day I trauma bonded with Vivian. Neither of us deserved what happened. I don't know Vivian's back story and what led her to Lilydale but it's clear that she's deeply disturbed by the recent events.

I don't blame her. The thought that other patients are currently being locked in ice cold water or electrocuted is sickening.

"I hope not," I mumble. "But I can tell you one thing—Dr. West is dead."

"Good," she replies carelessly.

Theo ending his miserable existence was the relief I needed. He'll never harm someone again in the name of science, but that doesn't mean there aren't more doctors in his place. Dr. Cromwell—fucking Melanie—is still on the loose. She was so eager to learn and please, acting empathetic and pitying me.

I don't need their pity. I needed to be protected.

We all do.

"Please look after yourself," I say, lowering my voice. "They don't deserve your tears—or your pain. Live... *for you*. Be their worst nightmare."

Vivian doesn't respond but her eyes sharpen at my words, as if I've hit something buried deep.

Standing up, I give her a quick nod and tight smile before joining the guys at the other end of the hall.

"Not going to lie, it feels a little crowded," I joke, taking a seat on the edge of my bed.

It's been nice being back in my room after solitary confinement—even if it did get a little *heated* in there. When all three guys insisted on walking me here after free time, I said yes immediately.

Having all of them here though, just reminds me how much of a shoebox we're forced into. Or maybe it's their overwhelming physical sizes. Either way, I'm not complaining.

Damon stands in the middle of Grey and Theo, taking his usual leader role. I'm not even sure if he realizes he's doing it. It's all second nature to him.

He reaches into his pocket, pulling something out. At first, I'm fixated on the lily—smiling as I recognize it from the Cirque des Morts calling card from my first ever meeting. But then he pulls something else out, my eyes widening on the black box.

"What is that?" I blurt out, amused and confused.

My eyes dart behind him to Grey and Theo, eyebrows shooting high as they watch me carefully.

Why is my heart racing like this? Goosebumps are forming on my skin, tingles running up my arms.

Grey grabs my attention, his grin wild like a kid on Christmas morning. Even Theo doesn't appear overly out of place, his head held high, locked stare unwavering.

"Avery," Damon says, and I swing back to look at him. "The three of us have been speaking, and we decided that perhaps we were a little too *rash* with our decision to exclude you from this moment. Therefore, we only felt it was appropriate to rectify this."

The velvety, square shape is telling, but I still can't bring myself to connect the dots. I'm completely paralyzed—not with fear, but with... something else.

Hope.

Want.

Need.

Damon opens the box and I suck in a breath, staring at the singular piece inside. Shit—is that what I think it is?

Inside the box is a ring, the black band woven in a distorted circle. The center piece is a red gemstone—a ruby, perhaps—with white tiny diamonds edging the band.

"Little killer," Grey murmurs, reaching forward to clutch my hand. "You've had my little black heart from the first day I laid eyes on you."

He comically moves my hand in front of Damon toward Theo, who takes it without hesitation.

"You're my favorite tattoo, Aves."

A man of simple words, he passes my hand to Damon, who's already removed the ring from the box.

"Avery," he pauses, sliding the ring onto my finger—*yes, that finger*. "You're already my wife legally, but will you do all three of us the honor of officially being ours?"

They become blurry, and it takes me a few seconds of stunned silence to realize it's because tears have welled in my eyes. The three men I love with all my broken heart are asking me to be theirs, promising to love all of me. Flaws, trauma, background, file that says I'm mentally insane.

Me.

No one speaks as they wait for me to pull myself together, and I can't hold back any longer. "I've been yours—all of yours—since the beginning. You consumed me from the moment I stepped foot in Lilydale. And my life doesn't make sense without you in it. I'm yours."

"Good," Damon answers coolly. "This was going on your finger no matter what." He adjusts the ring so it's centered on my finger, and I'm stunned to find it fits perfectly. It's then I realize that Damon also has a ring on his finger—a matching black band with a thick red center insert, chunky black markings decorating it.

Instantly, my eyes scan the other two. Grey dips his hand into his pocket, extracting a matching ring and makes a show of holding up his hand and slipping it on. Snapping my attention to Theo, he lifts his hand casually showing me his band.

We have matching bands.

Oh, my god. Am I engaged? Wait, no—I'm already married to Damon. Whatever it is... I love it.

I love them.

"À nous pour toujours jusqu'à ce que la mort nous sépare," Damon murmurs, gently clutching my hand and kissing it. "And all the lifetimes after."

Chapter 16

Damon

Markel scurries away without pushing the point like a smart man. He tried, just once, to finally corner me, to see if he can fulfil his duties as my appointed primary care physician. I didn't need to speak—my glance alone told him everything he needed to know.

Fuck off.

I don't need some bullshit doctor force feeding me narcotics. Even if I wanted to take painkillers, after what happened to Avery, there's no chance in hell I'm allowing them to drug me.

The pain is still there but it's nothing a glass of whiskey won't fix. Besides, it's easing each day.

It's a damn pain in the ass being shot, but I'd do it a thousand times over. I know my father aimed specifically for me or Avery. He might be a lousy shot, but even a moron could hit their target at close range. I'm just lucky that with all the commotion and movement, he managed to hit somewhere unimportant.

Most of all, I'm glad Avery is safe.

When they organized the Lilydale escort from the hospital, I wasn't surprised to find Connor waiting for me. I knew it was only a matter of time before they had to hire more guards, and with his loyalty, he volunteered since most weren't keen to be my glorified babysitter.

Call it fear or laziness, but Arthur is slipping with his desperation. He's well aware of Connor's ties to us, but when no amount of money will persuade your staff to accompany a certain patient, you have little choice but to give in.

I insisted we make a pitstop on the way back. I could have sent Christopher for the blowtorch, but what kind of *husband* would I be if I didn't buy my wife a proper ring?

Of course, I needed to make sure I included Grey and Theo. After all, Avery isn't just mine.

They were fully on board with the idea, and after some searching at the jewelry store, I finally found a ring that complimented all of us. It's perfect really, symbolic of our individual relationships with Avery.

Diamonds to represent my strength and commitment to keeping Avery safe.

Red for Grey's fascination and love of blood, and the stone being centerpiece since he was Avery's first love.

And black banding to signify Theo's ink that he insisted on marking Avery with. But I told Grey it was because of our black hearts. He enjoyed that notion.

One quick call to my financial advisor using Connor's cell and we were in business. He detests my father as much as I do—the two of them having a run-in many years ago when he refused to bend to my father's will. Before I was locked up in Lilydale, I suspected my father would pull some bullshit stunt. I set up a separate account, and before I lost access to the trust fund, I transferred a generous sum over. Since I didn't have a bank card to use, he provided the card details over the phone and I had the clerk manually put the details into the machine.

My father has no idea about the other account. Of course, he meticulously checked the transaction history and knew funds had been moved, but he had no power to stop it at the time. I knew he'd move fast to try to take me down, so I moved faster.

Avery is going to wear my ring proudly. Pissing Arthur and my father off is an added bonus.

As I round the doorway, glaring at Christopher, he looks up, sensing me.

"You look like shit," I point out, unable to resist the urge.

He sighs, throwing his pen down. "I feel like shit. But at least I wasn't shot."

I crack a smile. "If you had, you'd still be in a hospital bed, whining and flirting with nurses."

"Good to see nearly being killed hasn't affected your sense of humor," he mutters dryly.

"The missing patients," I say, ignoring him. "Is everyone accounted for today?"

So far, we're up to six. I'm doing everything we can to tighten surveillance but without knowing how or when they are being taken, it's difficult.

People are becoming antsy, noticing their missing peers as well as Arthur's lack of presence. Even though the whole facility breathes easier when he's not lurking around, it's still causing turmoil—as if things are slipping out of control.

There's very little that patients control here, and what they do is slowly being taken. I imagine Christopher has his work cut out for him, probably another reason his termination was temporarily rescinded. William Elsher is unlikely capable of managing the patients and their growing hostilities. Plus, knowing Arthur and my father, they want to keep Christopher where they can see and control him. That way, if they notice his insubordination, they can step in.

Attempt to, anyway.

"Yes," Christopher confirms, sounding relieved. "Have you had any luck with the security systems?"

"Not yet. But we are aiming to strike soon. It's a fine line. If we act too quickly and aren't prepared, it's likely the missing patients will become collateral damage."

"But leaving them is causing irreparable harm."

I lift an eyebrow. "I don't see you attempting to rescue them, Christopher. Feel free to try if you feel as strongly about it as we do."

"You know I can't," he growls in frustration. "Besides, I've been locked out of certain systems and no longer receive the staff updates."

"Then shut your mouth and let me sort it out."

The two of us fall silent, entering into a stare-off. I continue to hold it until Christopher relents, rubbing a hand over his face.

"I don't know what to do, Damon."

"Who are the missing patients assigned to?" I ask firmly.

He frowns. "Psychiatrist wise? Let me check."

Tapping his laptop, I wait patiently as he cross-checks the notes. When his mouth purses into a violent line, I have my answer before he's voiced it.

"Elsher's patients," I say confidently. "No surprise there."

Christopher nods once. "They all signed consent forms too. So, technically, what they are doing is perfectly legal."

"Bullshit," I laugh sarcastically. "That form was nothing more than a cover-up with minimal details."

"It gave the doctors free reign in terms of scope."

"You can't contract out of human rights," I point out. "I need a list. Give me all the names of patients assigned to Elsher and who have signed the form. I'll have my people do a risk check."

Christopher rolls his eyes. "Oh, yes. The infamous numbering system," he mutters. I'm not surprised he knows about it. Most people within Lilydale, patients or staff, don't understand it. They just do as they're told. But Christopher knew the ins and outs of what was brewing beneath Lilydale, and it doesn't take a genius to piece it together.

"My methods are effective."

He gazes over at me with a hardened stare. "If you say so. I'll put the information together. In the meantime, you should probably know that Avery asked me to contact her social worker. Arthur needs to sign off on it first, but I think his hands are tied. He'll have to since it's her legal right."

"Arthur doesn't care about legal rights," I reply. "But I agree. He'll sign off on it so it doesn't come back to bite him. Did she say why?"

Christopher cocks an eyebrow at me. "Maybe ask your *wife* that."

I laugh quietly. Clearly, Christopher still gets a kick out of the whole situation. No doubt he'll hold it over my head for the remainder of time but frankly, I don't give a fuck. He knows as well as I do that it was our only loophole to temporarily stopping my father. Not that I have a problem with it. Being married to Avery isn't a chore or business transaction.

My mother would have loved her.

"I fully plan on questioning my wife," I respond to Christopher, turning to leave. "But remember—she has a husband with a nasty streak. So, I'd do as she says."

Grey enters my room, holding a fresh stash of snacks from the kitchen. He whistles to himself, giving me a small nod as he heads over to the desk, restocking my drawer.

"I spoke to Christopher," I tell him. "I've asked for a list of patients under Elsher's care. I think he's the culprit."

I notice he stiffens, likely recalling the Avery situation too. One day soon, we'll get our hands on him and make him suffer for his part in her kidnapping.

"Good idea," Grey answers. "Speaking of which, I've organized a meeting for this evening. Tony is even going to make your favorite."

"How do you even know my favorite food?" I ask, amused.

He knows I'm being satirical. It became known when he organized his first *Cirque des Morts* meeting. Practically hounded me for the information until I relented, deciding that him knowing wouldn't be the worst thing. Grey was eager to please from the beginning, showing his loyalty from day one and ensuring he always had my back.

"I know everything about you, Deadman," he laughs, pausing as he lifts something. "How long have these cigarettes been here? They are stale as fuck."

I shrug. "Beats me. I haven't smoked in months. You can have them if you want."

Grey pockets them. "The only drug I need is Avery. But I'm sure they will come in useful as rewards. People are stressed. We'll be gods amongst men giving them out in exchange for information."

"You do love a little bit of bribery in the mornings."

He hops up on the desk with a grin. "You know me so well."

I offer him a tilted smile, his damn infectious mood getting the better of me. "Where is dear Avery anyway? I thought she'd be with you."

"Our little killer is with Theo in the library. She's helping set up for tonight."

"She's certainly taking her new responsibilities seriously," I mutter, admiring her newfound leadership skills.

Grey grins. "Dark horse," he winks, reciting one of our earlier conversations.

I guess he was correct. He saw her potential before anyone else. Even though I trusted his judgment—most of the time—I was still surprised at her progression. If I had to narrow it down, I'd say that's what ultimately won me over.

She's much stronger than she appears. And with the right people supporting her, we're finally seeing Avery's true colors.

Just like a true Emerson-Dale.

At the conclusion of free time, Grey and I head to the library to double check things are ready. Tonight has to run smoothly—it's imperative.

Everyone has been escorted back to their rooms, Theo confirming with us that Avery is safe and sound.

We decide to be a little adventurous, planning to head to her room when we are finished. I want to brief her on tonight's agenda, as well as inform her that she'll be heading up part of the next operation.

She's ready. I'm confident in her ability. It's time that the society sees that as well. While I know they respect my decisions and will listen to whatever I say, it's vital that they see Avery in full swing. For her benefit, not mine.

Avery has spent her life tiptoeing around people, submissive and timid. She needs to believe in herself that she has the strength to lead, and by doing this, it will provide the opportunity for her to do so.

After we confirm the library is ready for nightfall, the two of us start making our way down the corridor toward the female dorms. There's a loud bang that echoes in the distance, the sound of a door slamming but I pay it no mind.

The two of us continue to exchange idle chit chat as we approach her room, when suddenly there's a bone chilling scream that stops me and Grey in our tracks.

Avery.

Chapter 17

Avery

The scream rips out of me before I can stop it, my stomach heaving as I quickly cover my mouth. Despite my best effort, I have to run to the tiny en suite in my room, stomach emptying into the toilet in violent waves.

When the door to my shoebox opened, I was expecting one of the guys to be on the other side. No one pushed open the door, so I got up from the bed to investigate.

Outside my door was a tiny white caddy, unmarked but clearly discarded. For a moment, I thought it was a gift from one of the guys, a surprise since they have been so generous lately.

How wrong I was...

I jump a foot in the air as my door crashes open into the adjacent wall, wild footsteps rushing into the room before a body appears in the doorway.

"Little killer?" Grey breathes out, relief flooding his face at my seemingly okay figure.

I'm far from okay. I fear I never will be okay again after what I just witnessed.

Damon peeks over Grey's shoulder, wide eyed with semi-composed Damon level panic. "What the hell was the screaming about, Avery?"

I can't muster words, a fresh rush of vomit coming when I try. All I can manage to do is point my finger in the direction of the door.

Grey shares a look with Damon before stepping into the bathroom to hold my hair. Out of the corner of my eye, Damon vanishes, en route to investigate.

"Well, fuck," his voice mumbles, completely different from his usual unfazed tone.

It's obvious that part of Grey wants to see what's caught our attention, but he stays put, stroking my scalp as he gently holds back tendrils from falling into the path of my partially digested meal.

"What is it, Deadman?"

"You better come see this, Grey."

I motion with my hand that I'll be fine for a moment, gesturing for him to go look. I'm fairly confident that I've gotten it all—at least, I hope.

There's nothing but silence from the pair of them. I don't dare leave the bathroom, leaning against the wall as I resist the urge to lose my shit or cry.

Monsters.

Grey heads back into the bathroom a minute later, arms outstretched. "Come here."

Moving with speed that would almost be impressive considering what just came out of me, I launch myself into his chest. "It's bad..." I manage to mumble.

I feel him nod above me. "Are you okay?"

Pulling my head back, I gawk at him wide-eyed. "Absolutely not. There's a fucking severed head at my door."

Teddy's head to be exact...

Fucking hell. I thought her body had been escorted from the property. I was told that Whitface had organized for her to be released to her family. More lies.

It never ends.

Damon hovers in the doorway, and I do a double take at his face.

"What?" I ask, dreading the answer.

It looks as though he's fighting the idea of whether or not to tell me, but with a sigh, he does. "There was a note inside."

I definitely didn't see any note but to be fair, the half a second glance I had inside sent me sprinting. "What does it say?"

Grey's arms tighten around me. "Deadman," he warns.

"She needs to know," Damon replies sharply. "No more secrets, remember?"

"I'll take a secret marriage over this any day," I mumble, dry-retching before quickly recovering with a hand over my mouth.

Damon offers me a tight smile. "See—the idea of being tied to me isn't so bad now."

"You're deflecting," I grumble, waving my hand. "Tell me."

He suddenly looks standoffish, almost worried about delivering this news. But I already can sense it's something messed up. In fact, I have a pretty good idea of what it says.

Bringing his hand up from his side, I spot the blood-covered paper in his grip. It's scrunched up, crinkling sounds way too loud as I wait nervously.

Damon flips the paper around so I can see the words, and it's exactly what I suspected.

YOU'RE NEXT.

I'm not sure what's more disturbing; the fact that I'm doing this... or that it was my idea.

In theory, the reaction of the guys should probably be up on that measurement too, but when you're dating psychopaths, it's easy for moral compasses to get a little lost.

"Cameras are offline," Damon confirms, giving me a sharp nod.

The three of them are staring at me with different expressions. Damon looks determined, like this is just another everyday mission. If gravity wasn't a thing, Grey would be bouncing off the ceiling with excitement. And Theo... if we weren't in the open corridor, he'd probably throw me against the wall and make me forget what I'm holding.

"Let's do this," I answer, face tight.

Damon takes a single step forward, lifting his hand to gesture for me to go first. I know it must be difficult for them—their instincts wanting to kick in and walk ahead of me like protective guard dogs. But this is about me.

Glancing at each of them a final time, I start walking down the corridor, the sounds of their footsteps following immediately. We pass the staff rooms and I'm unable to resist peering inside. I'm disappointed to find Elsher's door closed, probably in session with an innocent patient. For a moment, I'm tempted to kick his door down and put on a show for him. But I know this will get back to him regardless. We can save him for another time.

Dr. Smith has his door wide open, alone in his office. His neck nearly snaps with a loud crack as he does a triple take, mouth falling open in horror as we stroll by. Grey cackles behind me, obviously amused by the chaos we're causing.

Fuck—I'm going to be grilled in my next therapy session. Alexander should really pay Dr. Smith more because my mental health alone is disastrous enough for the man to handle.

Damon hums quietly to himself, and if I had to guess, I'd say his mind is somewhere along the same lines as mine—more likely amused at his cousin's distress than anything.

Of course, Theo says nothing. Swiveling my head, I check that he's still following, his eyes immediately finding mine as I do. He gives me a small smile, silently reassuring me that he has my back and I'm safe.

Safe.

I can't ponder the alternate reality that if I'd never crossed paths with these three that my existence in Lilydale would be anything but safe. I'd already be dead, or even more broken than I was when I entered.

Pausing as we reach the final door, I wait for one of them to unlock it. To my surprise, a staff card is handed to me over my shoulder.

"Damon?"

He holds the card out. "Yours, Avery."

I guess we're actually doing this and not cutting corners.

Nodding, I take the card with my free hand, swiping it on the keypad before punching in the code that Damon had me recite before we left the rooms. The light on the access pad flashes green and I waste no time pulling open the door. There's no hesitation, no fear. We're fucking doing this.

Stepping into the Lilydale foyer, the sound of our four sets of footsteps echo around the marble. Whittingham's door is wide open, his head down as he pours himself over paperwork. I actually wonder if he does much work or if he just spends all his time planning malevolent ideas.

His head jerks up, and despite my best efforts to keep my face expressionless, I can't help but smirk in amusement at his sudden panic. He stands before we even reach his doorway, and I spot his eyes darting between our distance and the door, probably wondering if he has time to lock us out.

He doesn't, of course.

Behind me, Grey growls low in his chest, his own amusement left back in the corridor now that we're face to face with the man who stars in all of our nightmares.

"Whitface," I greet, strolling straight over to his desk. "A displeasure as always."

Normally, there'd be some snarky reply or threat, but Arthur Whittingham is completely speechless. And I don't blame him.

Lifting my arm, I drop his present in front of him, a sickening bang drawing his attention.

"You lost this," I say calmly—my tone surprising even me.

Whittingham's eyes widen, glaring at me before dropping down to the severed head of his lover on his paperwork.

Damon steps up beside me to my right, placing his left hand on my shoulder. Whittingham looks at it, eyebrow twitching as he takes in Damon's wedding band.

"Threaten my wife again and next time it will be your head," Damon promises coldly.

I'm not sure if they practised it but as if on cue, Theo and Grey split, closing in on Whittingham on either side of the desk. The older man stumbles back at their advance, unable to hide the sheer horror and fear at realizing the four of us have him blocked in.

"I have no idea what you're talking about," he spits out, moving behind his cushy chair and using it as a barrier.

Grey grins at him, reaching down to grab the beloved letter opener from the stationery canister. "I used this to pluck your guard's eye out. If you even look at our girl the wrong way, I'll shove it so far up your dick hole that you'll be pissing out of your belly button."

"Good luck with that," Whittingham snaps heatedly, although his expression fails him. "You'll be out of here by the end of the day."

Damon smiles saccharinely. "Because of the cameras, you mean? The cameras that are currently switched off?"

I fail to hide my grin as his eyes check the corners of the room, omitting the usual red light.

Theo stalks forward, grabbing Whittingham's arm and violently pulling him forward before slamming him back down into the chair. "When Grey's finished with you, I'm going to drag your bleeding useless carcass downstairs and fry your mind so much that you forget your own name."

"Don't touch me!" Whittingham yells, slapping his hand away. "I'll have you all arrested, you delinquents."

"Big word for a little man," Grey laughs. "Did you learn that from your friend, Alexander?"

At the mention of his father, Damon stiffens next to me. I reach out and grasp his hand, threading our fingers. The act doesn't go unnoticed by Whittingham, a look of disgust crossing his face as he spots my ring.

"We'll prove that this marriage is illegal. This is only tem-porary."

I lean forward, patting the top of Teddy's head as I hold eye contact with him. "I'm not next, Arthur. You are. And don't even think about coming after my guys." Pausing, I reach down and collect the paperwork from under her gray neck, tossing it in his face. "And when you're in here, taking your last breath, we're going to kill your good buddy Alexander and send you both to Hell where you belong."

Chapter 18

Avery

"Just do it," I mumble, peering at Theo with one eye closed.

His lips twitch into a smirk, hand paused like he's waiting for me to change my mind.

I won't though. I'm determined to prove him wrong.

"Last chance," he warns. "Are you sure you can handle it?"

"Give me some credit."

Theo shakes his head, clearly amused as he lowers the needle to the sensitive skin. We're doing the other side of my ribcage today, but sadly, there's no Grey to distract me from the incoming pain.

I remind myself that this is our therapy and that I'm doing this because it's *romantic*. Sure, it's probably not as romantic as severed fingers in flowers or homemade shivs, but at least I'm being original and not stealing their ideas.

After we nearly lost Damon, it dawned on me that I'm alive because of him. Even when I hated him—or thought I did—I was always safe because of his protective scheming.

The night I spent with him at the hospital, I barely slept. I became fixated on watching him sleep, counting his breaths. It was terrifying wondering if his heart would just suddenly stop or his poor excuse for a father would stroll in and stab us both in our sleep.

The monitor next to the bed had been my safe haven, showing me visual proof that he was alive. As long as his heart kept beating, that was all that was important in that moment.

Alyssa had periodically snuck into the room to check vitals and when I asked her for a favor, part of me expected her to laugh. But she didn't even flinch at the idea.

Let's just hope Theo has a steady hand.

"How much are we doing?" he asks, glancing down at the piece of paper in his lap.

"Two or three inches," I answer, letting out a deep, controlled exhale.

"So, just the tip?"

I start laughing, making him pause with an annoyed scowl. The needle is dangerously close to my skin but it's not my fault that the great quiet Theo is ripping out dick jokes while tattooing me.

"Oh, stop giving me that look," I scold playfully. "You started it."

He places his hand firmly on my torso, pinning me down. We're in the library again, using the table as a makeshift bed. Damon and Grey are off doing Cirque duties, and I figured there was no time like the present to organize a... present.

"This will resemble a flatline or a heart attack if you don't stay still," he grumbles, strumming his fingers along my skin.

"Well don't threaten me with *just the tip*."

Theo's lips twitch, fighting against a smile. He doesn't respond, waiting until I'm completely still before pressing the ink covered needle into my skin.

Okay. It fucking hurts.

I already knew this of course. But nothing quite prepares you for tattooing bony spots.

I'm doing this for Damon though. If he can take a bullet for me, I can get a tiny tattoo for him.

My head flops to the side to catch sight of the paper in Theo's lap—a tiny print out of Damon's ECG results. The rhythm of his heart in black and white, proving that it was still beating. Now, it's being memorialized on my skin since my heart beats for him too.

A short while later, Theo announces that he's done, handing the paper back to me. I shove it down my bra, sneaking a quick look at the ink before fixing up my shirt.

"Can I do you now?" I ask, sitting up and stretching my arms with a small crack.

Theo nods. Except when he reaches for the other needle, I stop him. My fingers circle round his wrist, and in a somewhat awkward maneuver, I crawl along the table and sit back on my heels.

"I didn't mean tattooing," I say.

Grabbing his face in my hands, my mouth crashes into his without warning. He's ready for me though, instantly kissing me back as he loops an arm around my back.

I let out a small squeak of surprise as he pulls me off the table and into his lap, but we don't break apart. My legs dangle on either side of him, lips heatedly tracing his jawline down to his neck.

My freshly painted black nails—courtesy of Grey—match his hair, and when I dig them into his skin, there's a crash as the chair flies backwards and my back is slammed onto the table.

Strong hands remove my shorts before my brain can catch up and process the moment, and while I'm still in a static state of malfunction, Theo slaps his length against my clit.

"Fuck," I breathe out, grabbing his forearms. "Hurry up and get inside me."

I should have seen it coming. If the previous conversation wasn't an omen, the smug smirk is. Theo fists his cock, holding it steady as he slowly enters my body—then pauses.

Just the fucking tip.

"Theo," I groan, trying to seemingly scold him but it comes out desperate and breathy. "Please."

"Please, what?"

"Fuck me."

He chuckles, reaching down to draw lazy circles around my clit with his thumb. "You can beg better than that."

Part of me agrees, almost chomping at the bit to beg, cry, plead, scream... while another part, the winning bratty part, falls silent.

Two can play that game.

"No," I say sharply, rocking my hips in an attempt to sink him in deeper. "Make me."

Theo raises an eyebrow, pausing his administrations. "You want me to make you beg?"

Shrugging nonchalantly, I hold his gaze. "If you think you can."

A silence falls between us at my challenging words. Despite the calming ink depicting Damon's steady heartbeat on my torso, my own is pounding inside my chest cavity.

A groan of disappointment escapes my lips when Theo steps back, leaving me empty. That's nearly enough to make me start using my nice words, but hands grab my thighs, flipping me onto my stomach.

Theo snatches a handful of my hair, yanking my head back. My back arches with the movement, his dick pressing into my ass from behind.

"Tell me you want my cock in you, Aves. That you need it and crave it like I crave you."

My body clenches at his words, a moan slipping from my lips against my will. My resolve is crumbling, brutally being replaced by an unwavering, dying need to have him in me.

"I need you," I breathe out. I don't even have the strength to be mad at myself for caving so easily—not when this man obviously wants me as much as I do him. Together, we're a force. Without him, I don't make sense. The three of them fit my broken, jagged parts in a way that only make sense to the broken.

Inch by inch Theo pushes into me, a slow, agonizing speed that has me sounding more animal than human. His grip doesn't loosen on my hair, and when he bottoms out, I roll my hips against him, every nerve ending in my body firing to life at the sound of approving ecstasy that comes out of his mouth.

"You belong to us," he murmurs, starting to move inside me. "Only us."

I nod my head, not trusting my voice. He silences me in a way that I can only describe as heavenly—ironic since we're in hell. But sometimes it feels like I forget, because he's shielded me from the beginning.

"You," I manage to choke out, hoping he understands the broader words that fail to accompany my statement.

My head is ripped back further, a delicious wave of sharp pain traveling down my neck. It causes my cunt to spasm around him, eyes rolling back. Now I know why they say there's a thin line between pleasure and pain... and I want all of it.

The sound of our skin slapping together echoes around the library. My hands grip the table for dear life, not able to find easy leverage. I start to leave scratches along the wood from my nails but I'm too far gone to care.

Every thrust brings me closer to the edge and it feels like I'm having an out of body experience. I'm floating while falling at the same time, willingly descending into the obsidian abyss where we belong together.

I let out a little mewl of disappointment when Theo re-leases the hold on my hair, but his hand immediately takes place on my throat, gripping the sensitive skin in a choke-hold. With each new thrust into my body, the pressure tight-ens, slowly taking away air. I don't need it though—who would? All I need to survive in this moment is him.

Eventually, I realize that I'm holding my own breath, not that it would do much good. Theo's hold is so tight that I'd be lucky to breathe in small fragments of air. Black spots start to appear in my vision and as if sensing my breaking point, Theo's free hand snakes around to the front of my body, easily finding my clit.

His fingers move effortlessly against me, circling at first until he presses against it. A slap follows, making me jolt, and I find myself at the precipice.

"Beg for me, Aves," I hear him say with a tight, low tone.

My throat bobs against his hand as I try to speak words, but nothing comes out. It's enough for him though, the vi-brations a silent plea for release.

He lifts his hand again, sending another slap onto my clit, and I explode. The pressure from my neck vanishes, a rush of oxygen entering my lungs, heightening my climax. Still, nothing comes out except pants and whimpers as I shudder, falling against the table.

Theo continues to fuck me, his hands finding home on my hips as he leaves finger marks. His movements become erratic, off-beat, until he stills with a small growl, shooting his release into me.

Leaning down, he gently brushes my hair aside, kissing the nape of my neck without pulling out. My skin tingles at the contact, and slowly, I turn my head as much as possible so my lips can meet his in a slow, thorough kiss.

We stay like this for a few minutes, his cock softening in me as our tongues massage each other's and my heartbeat slows.

Despite everything happening in Lilydale, it's moments like this that keep me grounded. I find little fragments of peace, strength to fight and hold on to.

Theo helps me get cleaned up, checking the fresh tattoo once more before we finally leave the library just before the end of free time.

I can't fight the grin as we locate Damon and Grey, the two of them walking and chattering quietly along the hallway in our direction. When they realize we're waiting for them, the two of them pause their conversation, eyes lighting up when they look at me.

"Are you going to show him now?" Theo leans down to whisper in my ear.

I shake my head, gaze still locked on the approaching men. "I have an idea, but not here."

He nods in acknowledgment just as Damon and Grey stop in front of us.

"You have that sneaky, suspicious look about you, little killer," Grey grins.

"Do I?" I ask innocently, lifting an eyebrow.

Damon narrows his eyes on me. "What are you hiding?" he asks coyly.

I shrug. "You're not the only one who knows how to keep a secret," I reply with clear amusement. "You'll just have to wait and see."

Damon scowls, clearly annoyed that there's information to know but that he's not allowed to be privy to. Ah, well—payback's a bitch.

Stepping forward, I kiss him, his icy demeanor melting instantly as he roughly kisses me back.

Dominating little shit.

Regardless, I let him take charge, giving him this moment of control as I groan into his mouth. His soft lips ravage mine mercilessly, and by the time he pulls back, I'm breathless and nearly ready to throw him against the wall and put on a show for the other two.

"I'll drag it out of you later," he threatens quietly, an almost edge of danger to his promise.

Grey laughs beside us, reaching over to grab my arm and pulls me against his chest. "I think you've finally met your match, Deadman," he murmurs in amusement before brushing his mouth against mine. "But you're certainly rubbing off on our pretty girl."

Chapter 19

Avery

Is it wrong that I'm having murderous thoughts about permanently deleting Dr. Christopher Smith? And no, I'm not reflecting back on the time he accidentally framed me for murder... or the fact he secretly and illegally married me to his cousin.

I'm referring to the fact that he's *apparently* off sick today.

He better hope to God he's shitting out a storm or vomiting like the girl from *The Exorcist* because I may set Grey or Theo loose on him when he returns.

"Ms. White. Are you planning on wasting my time?"

I scowl at Elsher from across the room, my arms tightly crossed against my chest. "You do that well enough on your own."

That's right. Thanks to Dr. Smith's explosive diarrhea I've been forced to attend a session with Elsher. Okay, I don't know if it's diarrhea, but I'm telling myself that it is. Painful, gut breaking, Hell on Earth norovirus because even then, being in this room with this man is more agonizing.

If I had some prior warning, I would have feigned illness myself and spent some quality time with Dr. Markel. Unfortunately, I only found out five minutes ago when I was shoved into his room by the guard.

Elsher sighs heavily, tossing my file onto the desk. He leans back in his chair with a bored expression and starts... *ignoring me?*

The clock on the wall ticks obnoxiously loud and I swear I can feel my eye start twitching.

It's only an hour, Avery. You can do this.

My leg bounces as the minutes pass in complete silence. It feels like some kind of test, the two of us seeing who will crack first.

Sadly, I have too many thoughts. In the time that we play this game of chicken, I have a full internal conversation with myself, swearing and cursing this pathetic excuse of a psychiatrist. Eventually, the verbal vomit starts to filter out.

"So, kidnapped anyone else lately? Are the missing patients being cooperative downstairs? Or have you just killed them already?"

A little extreme, I'll admit. But it gets the desired reaction.

Elsher snaps his angry gaze to me, knuckles white as his fists ball up. "You're out of line, Ms. White."

"Ooh... tragedy," I say sarcastically. "At least you'll have some gossip to report back to Whittingham later when you braid each other's pubes."

He straightens his chair, leaning forward as his calculated gaze lingers on my face. "It's a shame that you're beyond help. You could benefit from some of their treatment methods."

"Oh, you mean like being forced into ice cold water. Or, being electrocuted? I have to admit that one was rough. But the icing on the cake for me was nearly overdosing on drugs and being forced to watch pornography. I bet you sick fucks had a good laugh at that one. In fact, I wouldn't be surprised if you all sit around Whittingham's office and jerk off to videos of patients fucking. Have I provided enough content?"

My words are sharp and laced with venom, but there's still a sickening squeeze in my stomach at the thought. I know there's cameras everywhere and no doubt they have captured their fair share of sexual encounters. I mean, the library sees more action than a hotel and that's where they originally got their footage of Grey and Leah.

Elsher laughs dryly. "Your words mean nothing, Ms. White. There isn't anything you can say that can hurt me. My training—"

"You mean that bullshit excuse of a degree?" I cut in. "I assume you have no morals or ethical dignity left since you choose to use your training to be the most deplorable, vile human known to man."

"Interesting sentiment coming from someone who murdered someone."

I shrug. He's used this same tactic multiple times now that it's useless. Besides, I already mentally beat myself up enough about my father's death that people can't hurt me as much as I can hurt myself. But those days are slowly moving behind me. I refuse to let this man—no—this monster, make me feel any less of a person because he favors victim blaming and manipulation.

"Karma."

He cocks an eyebrow at the singular word, surprised. "You honestly believe that you can justify your actions by calling it *karma.*"

"Sure," I agree light-heartedly. "Same way as you justify your torture as so-called *treatments.*"

You can hear the pipes in the walls rattle. The room falls so quiet that for a brief second, I start making contingency plans in case he launches himself across the desk and strangles me. My eyes dart around, looking for makeshift weapons. If Grey has taught me anything, it's that anything can be a weapon if you use it hard enough.

I mentally note the pair of scissors atop his desk, pausing for a second as it hits me that I've never seen a pair of scissors in Lilydale. For good reason obviously...

Patients might be likely to grab them, either planning to harm themselves or others. But of course, there's no shock at the thought. Elsher is probably secretly hoping for that.

"Theo Ashwood," Elsher murmurs, ripping my attention back to him. "Interesting patient."

My blood boils. How dare he utter his name? He's not worthy of even breathing the same air as Theo and I'll kill him if he even thinks about touching him.

"Theo's baby toe is more interesting than your entire existence," I shoot back. "Jealous?"

When a smug smile appears on his face, I brace. I can already sense what's coming—know his next move.

Still, it lands exactly as he hopes.

"I'd love to experiment on him one day."

I act purely on instinct, launching to my feet and rushing toward the desk. My fist curls around the scissors and to my delight, Elsher's eyes widen in disbelief and... *fear?*

Holding the sharp end in his face, it takes all my control not to shove the pointy tip into the bridge of his nose. "I promise you," I start. "If you even look at him the wrong way, I'll send you to Hell myself."

He quickly recovers, masking his expression. But there's still a flare of anger, as if he's annoyed at my audacity to lash out at his words.

It makes me feel a little warm and fuzzy, the thought that he never expected me to react like this. He probably assumed I'd yell or cry, or merely threaten with my words. But as I've told him, over and over, he doesn't know me. He doesn't know anything. I wasn't the monster before Lilydale that he thinks I was... but I sure as shit am now.

Having something to lose makes you dangerous.

I won't let anyone come between us again. No one will touch my guys. I don't care if I have to pay a price for their safety. They would do the same for me.

"Put the scissors down, Ms. White," he growls, maintaining eye contact.

There's a warning to his tone, a final chance for me to back down and comply. But we're past that. No matter what happens now, I've set my fate. I may as well see my promise through.

Leaning forward a fraction more, he lets out a mangled choke as the tip of the scissors pushes against his skin—right between his eyes. It's not enough to hurt him by any means, and let's face it... I'm not about to kill him right this second. Not unless he gives me a reason to.

But he doesn't know that.

I only kill when necessary. A fucked-up version of Batman, I guess. Vigilante villain. Maybe I'm the love child of Batman and the Joker. That would be cool.

"Listen here." I drop my voice low, allowing the smirk to creep onto my face. "I'm everything you think I am, but nothing at the same time. If you think I won't kill again, you're mistaken. I would feel absolutely nothing at ending your life—no remorse, no guilt. Only relief knowing that you'd never hurt anyone else again."

I drag the tip down his pointed nose, lips twitching as his throat bobs with unease. Trailing the tip along his lips, I suddenly understand the desire to carve a smile into his cheeks. I'm probably being way too dramatic and theatrical, but it's working. Elsher is completely paralyzed with fear... because of little old me.

"I'll slit your throat," I promise, grazing a line across his stubble, mimicking Grey's scar. "And fuck all of my boyfriends in your blood."

His eyes flash but I'm not done.

"Then," I pause, smiling. "I'll pay Whittingham a visit and deliver your pathetic excuse for a penis to him to use as a coffee stirrer."

Pulling back, I raise my arm, letting the scissors go with a crash. They bounce off the top of the desk, making him fly backwards in his chair.

"Put the fucking scissors away," I scold him. "Before someone uses them."

Turning, I head to the door, pulling it open. To my surprise, the guard isn't waiting in the hallway. I close the door behind me while I quickly figure out my next steps. The guys are probably in their rooms and I don't have the staff card on me to enter the dorm. It also means I can't get back to my room either.

I'm not safe out here. Elsher is probably already on the phone, calling for guards and backup. I need to get out of here before I find myself in solitary confinement—or prison since the door is out of action.

The library is too obvious. That's probably the first place the guards will search.

I could hide in Dr. Smith's office but that would look suss. Markel is an option but if the guards come for me, I doubt he'd fight to keep me there.

There's really only one option. One safe place where they probably won't think to look. Plus... it has certain benefits for me.

My feet start moving quickly, eyes checking for approaching bodies until I slip through the doors. The sound of my footsteps resemble a racing heart, erratically moving as I slip through another closed door.

"For fuck sake! Who hasn't put the water on?"

It takes them a few seconds in the chaos before someone finally spots me lingering by the door. Like a domino effect, they stop—one by one, glancing at me with uncertainty and confusion. I give them a small smile before I round the countertop and approach the loud voice.

"Hello, Tony."

He glances up, a large knife in his hand as he frantically chops greens—well, brownish looking greens.

"What can I do for you?" he growls, unfazed by my presence. "It's not the best time. We're getting ready for the lunch rush."

I nod, completely understanding. "I'm not here to place an order," I tell him, walking over to one of his nearby colleagues. The younger cook is dishing out bowls of spaghetti bolognese for the kitchen staff, her eyes wide with apprehension as she watches me approach. "Can I have a bowl?" I ask, tilting my head toward one.

"S-sure," she mutters quietly, looking over my head at Tony for double reassurance. He must shrug or wave her off because no one says anything as I reach for one, also pinching a clean fork from a pile.

"I'm not here," I tell them all, heading toward the large walk-in freezer. "You never saw me."

I don't wait for their reply, grabbing a can of pop from the fridge before slipping inside the cold box and taking a seat on an empty vegetable container.

And just like that, I enjoy a well-deserved delicious meal in silence until Grey finds me a little while later.

Being cold was a small price to pay for freedom. It tasted just as good as the fresh pasta I devoured. But nothing compares to the euphoric feeling of replaying the look of fear in Elsher's eyes when he realized I was becoming his worst nightmare. Maybe Damon was onto something—having people fear you is a rush I never knew I'd love.

Chapter 20

Grey

*** Three Years Ago ***

He's in one of his *joyous* moods again.

I'd just managed to fall asleep when his excessive stomping and huffing around the house woke me. Normally, that wouldn't be troublesome for most people. But when it's accompanied by heated whispers and self motivating pep talks, it's cause for alarm.

I toss back the blanket with a sigh, rubbing a hand over my face. I'll need to go deal with him before he ends up naked outside and traumatizes Mrs. Miller next door. The poor woman is newly widowed and I'm not sure seeing my father's dick in the middle of the night is on her bucket list. Garden tools? Yes. Wrinkly midnight dick? No.

It's frustrating because the past few weeks, I've already had trouble sleeping. It's that time of year when flashbacks re-emerge as if my mind is a fucking Google calendar.

Oh, hey. Remember the time Mom took you to the alpaca farm and you tried to ride one like a horse? Mom's birthday is coming up—maybe send a card and remind her that you exist.

I stopped caring after she walked out and left me to deal with my father alone. I don't blame her for wanting to break free—he's more than a handful. His schizophrenic episodes have been getting more frequent over the past few years. I caught him laying a hand on her during one of them. She wasn't strong enough to fight him off and I had to do it for her. He didn't take too kindly to me putting him through the glass coffee table, but I digress. If a method is effective, then that's all that matters.

But still, she didn't have to just *leave* like that.

When people want to exit relationships, you see a lawyer. Not your dentist. Though, I suppose they are renowned for their oral skills.

I'm not sure what she thought would happen when she blurted out the infidelity to him. Even someone without a medical degree could guess it would take a negative turn.

To be fair, I think she tried to stick around for as long as possible before riding off into the sunset with Dr. Pussy Eater. I just don't understand why she didn't take me with her. I guess a stepchild would dampen the thrill of an affair or she assumed I'd be fine to handle Dad. Or perhaps she felt so guilty about cheating with their dentist that she left me as a consolation prize.

Either way, tonight I was finally able to fall asleep peacefully after work. I've only been at Angus' Butchery for three months and we were run off our feet today with an upcoming barbecue festival. So many knives to play with, so little time.

Creeping out of my bedroom, I listen for the rambling, tracking his location. It sounds like he's in the kitchen.

The fridge door slamming closed all but confirms my suspicions and I head in his direction. It doesn't take long to find him in there, his tense body pacing with wide eyes as he mutters to himself.

"You can't go. Don't go. He did what?! I know you said that. The boy is an imposter. They are watching. Are you watching? Grey is dead. He killed him."

I slump against the doorframe, eyes following his path. He hasn't noticed me yet, in full conversation with himself.

"Dad," I say firmly. "Go to bed."

He stops abruptly, spinning to face me. My eyebrow lifts at the knife in his hand. No surprise where I developed my kink from. I guess it's true that you inherit kinks from your parents.

"What are you doing here?" he snaps in a low, husky voice. "Our son is upstairs."

"I'm your son," I remind him, recognizing he's in an episode. "It's me—Grey."

Dad laughs maniacally, waving the knife around carelessly. "I see how it is." His pewter eyes look at me unfocused. "You think you can fool me."

Fuck me. I just want to go back to bed. I have to be up at dawn for another shift.

"Dad—go to bed," I repeat. "You need sleep."

The doctors warned us that his drinking and lack of sleep could make his symptoms difficult to manage. For a while there, he was doing well. But gradually after Mom left, he stopped caring too. I guess I get my poor sleeping habits from him as well.

When his body stiffens like a statue, I straighten up. It's the same cycle as usual. We argue, he gets defensive and physical, then retreats. I can read him like a book.

"You can't have her, Brent. Anne is *my* wife!"

"You're right," I agree, holding my hands up in an act of resignation. "I'll leave and never come back. She's all yours."

This is the equivalent to a movie I've watched a hundred times. Same lines, same scenes. I've got my act down to a fine art.

Panting, Dad relaxes slightly, seemingly satisfied. I take a few steps forward as his head dips, pain on his face.

"Come on, big man. Let's get you up to your bed to Anne."

I place a hand on his bare shoulder, pleased that at least he's got shorts on today. He's calming down, and my bed is singing my name in sweet, melodic tunes like a siren.

As I swivel sideways to make room for him to pass, I feel him tense under my hand.

Oh, no. That's not the usual reaction.

Before I can turn back, I spot the knife swinging around toward me. I just manage to lunge out of the way into the sink, Dad stumbling off balance.

"Oh, come on," I groan. "Bed—now."

He catches his footing, spinning to face me. His eyes are wild again, and I'm pretty sure life is having a laugh at my expense. You want to go to bed? Ha. Too bad.

"You can't have her!" He yells in full battle cry mode, moving at an alarming speed.

"Fucking hell," I grumble, dodging again. "Just go for a run then. You have shorts on."

Apparently, my words fall on deaf ears. He continues to launch himself at me with a stream of jumbled words and threats. I'm going to have to subdue him before one of the neighbors calls the cops for noise disturbance. It wouldn't be the first time they have paid us a visit. And part of me feels a tiny bit guilty at the thought—having the house to myself to get sleep sounds pretty fucking awesome.

But I'm responsible for this man, even if he is swinging a knife at my face.

"That's enough," I grunt, grabbing his wrist and halting the blade in mid-air. "I'm getting annoyed now."

I expect more fast spoken sentences but instead he lets out a blood-curdling yell. My ears ring as I squeeze my eyes shut. Who knew he had a set of lungs on him?

"Oof."

The wind is knocked out of me when a fist connects with my stomach. I guess that's what I get for closing my eyes.

I still have his wrist in my hold but he's using his other hand to strike me, shoving his weight into my body as my back hits the countertop behind me.

"Let go," I growl, bending his wrist backwards. It has to hurt, nearly snapping the bone but he seems indifferent to it. When his fist clocks me in the eye, I push him back to gather myself, well and truly pissed off now.

Except he's on the move again.

Fast.

All I see is the reflection of the ceiling light on stainless steel as it rushes toward me. Pain erupts through my head, and that's when I lose control.

I briefly register the first hit I lay into him. And the second.

Then suddenly, I'm staring at white walls, chained to a hospital bed with a bandage on my neck and a fuzzy recollection of his dead body beneath me.

*** Present Day ***

There's something satisfying about new toys. It's like that feeling at Christmas, when your whole body is filled with excitement after ripping open a brand new toy that you'll inevitably break within a week.

Holding the blowtorch in my hand, I feel the same way. That's the best part about being an adult—more expensive toys to play with.

"This is amazing," I murmur, grinning at Deadman. "Compact too."

He nods, completely unfazed by my overly enthusiastic reaction. "Portable handheld torch. We just need to be mindful of the butane canister. Don't go wasting it."

"You're no fun," I pout, whirling it around like a lightsaber. "Pew pew."

I quickly hide it behind my back when there's a small knock on Damon's door. I leave him to do the honors, wondering if there's someone on the other side that I'll get to use my new toy on straight away.

"Connor," Damon acknowledges, and I feel a pang of disappointment.

Damn.

"I have some information for you," Connor grunts out, giving me a small nod as he notices me.

"Go on," Damon says, only partially interested.

"It's about Avery."

Well, that grabs both of our undivided attention. I slip the blowtorch out from behind my back, Connor glancing at it for a brief second as if it's nothing more than a shoe. I suppose he did help Deadman purchase it so there's no element of surprise.

"Dr. Smith is absent today. Some of his sessions have been rescheduled with Dr. Elsher."

"Avery better not be with him," I cut in, clearly echoing Damon's thoughts as he nods sharply.

A pained, constipated expression appears on Connor's face, confirming the worst. That motherfucker. I'm going to melt his face off and sizzle his balls.

"She was," Connor quickly answers, noticing the change in my demeanor. "She left though. The guards have been instructed to look for her."

Damon steps toward him. "What do you mean *she left*?" he asks dangerously.

"Walked out of session. We've been warned that she could be hostile."

A laugh bursts out of my mouth, startling our friendly little guard. He jumps, pursing his lips as he glances at me cautiously.

"Avery, hostile?" I repeat, amused. "Come on. That's just being overly dramatic."

Connor nods. "I don't disagree. But according to Dr. Elsher, she threatened him so the guards have been instructed to take her to Whittingham once she's located. They've deemed her a flight risk."

My little killer threatened him? I need to find her now before one of the guards do, but given the fact my dick is hardening at the news she threatened Elsher, we might need to make a pitstop on the way back.

"A flight risk?" Damon spits out with disgust. "She's not a risk at all. Do not let anyone touch her. Grey—"

"I'm on it," I answer, begrudgingly handing the blowtorch back to him. While the idea of setting things alight sounds delightful, I don't have the patience to be stopped by one of Arthur's minions for carrying a weapon.

I push past Connor and head straight for the library. It's empty to my disappointment, and a quick trip past Elsher's office confirms she's definitely not there either. Christopher's office is also vacant and for a moment, I'm actually stumped.

Normally, I'd consider the morgue but given we can't access the stairwell, there's no way Avery would be able to get past the doors.

The classrooms are also empty which only leaves one other option.

If I'm correct, which I believe I am, it means our girl is smart and quick thinking. It's the one place no one would check—practically in plain sight with witnesses.

Kitchen staff are wandering around the hall, setting up food for lunch. A few glance in my direction, and when one smiles uncharacteristically at me, I realize it's a sign I'm on the right path.

The doors swing open as I stroll in shamelessly, grinning at our good old grumpy friend. Tony pauses, letting out a sigh at my presence but not seeming surprised, before nodding his head to the other side of the room.

"In there."

"Well, thank you."

As soon as I rip open the freezer door, Avery glances up at me, her face softening. "Fancy meeting you here," she says with a smile.

I close the door behind me, tilting my head as I smirk at her. "Ever fucked in a freezer before, little killer?"

Chapter 21

Avery

I'm having the nicest dream about freshly baked cookies when I'm ripped back to consciousness. Pain shoots through me, jolting me awake, and through the dimly lit room, I spot two guards grabbing me. It feels like I'm reliving a nightmare from my past and I instinctively enter into fight-or-flight mode.

"What the hell are you doing?" I manage to croak out, a yelp following as my shin clips the metal frame of the bed.

Neither of them respond. I'm dragged from the room, mind quickly becoming more alert as I take in my surroundings while attempting to deescalate my racing heart. From the hallway, I can see the sun starting to rise outside Lilydale, the first light of the day already tainted and ruined by flashbacks and SWAT wannabes.

And of course, history repeats itself as I'm pulled painfully through the quiet corridors toward Whittingham's office. Besides the three of us, there's no other living beings in sight—not even Dr. Smith or Dr. Markel.

One of the guards releases his hold on me, pushing open the office door to reveal Arthur Whittingham and Alexander

Dale, dressed in their usual tailored suits. They both look at me casually, unbothered by my disheveled physique.

"Good morning, Avery," Alexander greets coldly. "I take it you slept well?"

The tone of his voice indicates he couldn't give a shit whether I slept at all. Before I can think of a snarky reply, I'm forced into a nearby chair by the desk, rough hands pinning me down by the shoulders.

I take a moment to survey the room, lips twitching with slight amusement at the bandage still on Whitface's hand from where I stabbed him with the pen. He scowls at me, flashing me a murderous look of rage.

"How's the hand?" I ask with a snort, any functions of a filter non-existent this early in the morning.

"Enough," Alexander cuts me off, leaning against the desk. "I'm not above having the doctors silence you, Avery."

"Given you shot your own son on his birthday, I think there's very little you wouldn't do, Alexander."

He chuckles quietly to himself as he reflects back on the memory like the sick fuck he is. "Is the transport ready?"

I know he's not directing the question to me, but I can't resist chiming in, blood running cold. "What transport?"

"Yes," Whitface answers dryly. "These two guards will accompany you and Ms. White."

"What is going on?" I snap.

Where the fuck are they taking me?

Despite the attitude I was happy to give, I'm suddenly drowning with panic. The absence of my cell phone feels heavy and my fingers twitch, desperate to run to my room to call for help. But I know I'd never make it there. The chances of me even making it to the foyer are slim, let alone the issue of no access card.

I'm in trouble.

I can't let them take me out of Lilydale, especially not with this maniac. Fuck—were they planning on taking me to a paddock to shoot me? I wouldn't put it past them.

Finally, Alexander acknowledges my question, a clearly beguiled expression on his face that reminds me of Damon. I think of all of the times in the past I thought Damon was ice-cold and heartless. But nothing compares or comes close to the monster standing before me.

"We're taking a little trip," he says casually. "But first—a change of attire."

He nods his head toward the guards. One steps away while the other tightens their hold on my shoulders, pressing down painfully. A bag is chucked into my lap, my eyes spotting bunched up fabric inside.

"Where are we going?" I ask firmly.

"Get changed," Alexander answers, giving me a dismissive wave. "Or if you're incapable of doing so, the guards will do it for you."

I'm given no time to respond, hands suddenly lifting me off the chair and ripping my clothes off. And when I say ripping, it's not an exaggeration. They shred the gray Lilydale pyjamas from my body, a cold chill shooting through me in more ways than one.

Four sets of masculine eyes scan my body from various directions. Tears threaten to spill as I do my best to cover myself with my hands, absolutely hating that I'm vulnerable right now. Even more flashbacks appear, threatening to paralyze me with fear.

I make the mistake of looking at Alexander. His cold, dead green eyes slowly hover over my body. It makes me want to tear my skin off and bathe in acid.

"Don't flatter yourself, Avery," he says when he meets my eyes finally. "I certainly can't see the appeal that my son does."

"You're repugnant," I spit out, quickly pulling the clothes out of the bag. Turning to face the guards—since it's the lesser of two evils—I swallow down bile as they stare at my chest. Hastily pulling on the clothing, I realize it's business attire—a black skirt that falls just above my knees and a lilac blouse that thankfully hides the fact I'm braless. A pair of ballet flats tumble onto the ground and I shove my feet in, ignoring the squeezing pressure from the too-small of a size.

I nearly choke out a sob when a hand strokes my hair, flattening some rogue strands. Slapping it away, I send Alexander an angry, teary-eyed glare. "Don't fucking touch me."

Smack.

A gasp slips past my lips as I clutch my cheek in disbelief. My skin burns with disgust and pain, his stare still unfazed.

"You won't speak to me like that again," he warns. "Next time, I won't be gentle."

He hit me. He actually hit me. And has the nerve to call it *gentle.* I'd be willing to bet there's a scum-sized handprint on my cheek, forcing some color back into my face.

This time, I have no witty reply or deadly glare to give back. He's slowly undoing months of healing and I can feel my body sinking back into that all too familiar survival mode—placid, submissive... timid. Exactly how I used to act around my father when I was walking on eggshells, scared of the next blow.

"Take her to the car," he orders the guards without breaking eye contact. "If she gives you any trouble, feel free to use whatever force necessary to ensure her compliance."

My body trembles with the threat, my mind shattering as I imagine just what the guards would like to do to make me fall into line. Their hands reach for me, dragging me by my elbows as I'm pulled toward the door. And for a brief second, I do something I'm not proud of—I look at Whitface with desperate, pleading eyes, hoping that perhaps he has a fraction of humanity after knowing and seeing the devastation that live within these walls.

Of course, there's nothing in his vacant stare. He subconsciously clutches his bandaged hand, silently telling me to go fuck myself with a pleased tilt of his lips. My head drops in resignation and when we step outside Lilydale, I spot a black town car waiting.

One guard opens the door while the other keeps a hold on me, the two of them sandwiching me in the middle of their large frames.

I hate that they are touching me. It feels like I'm suffocating. I curl inwards in an attempt to make myself small, holding back tears as I threaten to spiral. They make small talk with each other while laughing, and when the door opens a few minutes later, I glance up with hope.

Hope doesn't exist in Lilydale. I'm stupid to think that Damon could casually stroll out of the building to pull me out of the car.

Alexander slides in across from us, sitting opposite me. He cocks an eyebrow at my discomfort, and when I glance away, I realize there's a driver climbing into the front of the car.

"Ready, Sir?"

"Yes," Alexander answers, checking his cell. "They will be arriving shortly."

As the car pulls away from the main building toward the large gates, it takes all of my willpower not to vomit. The further we get, the more I realize the growing danger.

Months ago I'd have given anything to be away from Lilydale, to see the outside world again. Even the hospital was a nice change. Now, it feels like a death sentence.

I may not come back.

We join early morning traffic as commuters head into the city, skyscrapers coming into view. No one speaks in the car, and when we pull up outside a tall building full of glass windows, Alexander motions for the guards to exit.

"Avery," he sneers. "We're here to conduct business. I expect you to be on your best behavior."

I don't respond, sending a deadly glare in his direction.

Clearing his throat, he unbuttons his jacket, opening one side. My breath catches in my throat as I spot a gun tucked inside his pocket.

"Good," he says, taking note of my reaction. "We have an understanding. Now, you'll be required to sign paperwork. If you even think of putting a pen through *my* hand, be rest assured I'll put a bullet in yours. The board is aware of your position and are just as displeased about the situation as I am."

The board? As in... the Lilydale Board?

Alexander tilts his head toward the door. "Out."

I slide along the seat, shivering as cold air hits me in the face. The two guards are waiting on the sidewalk for us, immediately stationing themselves on either side of me.

Alexander walks ahead without glancing at us, and when I hesitate for a moment, I'm grabbed by the elbows.

"I can walk," I hiss at them, quickly moving and freeing myself from their grasps.

People bustle around the entrance, the monochrome and beige interior blending into the suits and briefcases. I must

look the part, or some acceptable level, because no one both-
ers to glance at us. Even having guards on either side of me,
there's no curious stares.

Alexander signals for the elevators and just my luck, we
manage to get the entire metal box to ourselves. Terrible
music plays through the speakers as we rise. My eyes stay
glued to the floor numbers, heart skipping a beat when we
stop at forty-two.

The doors open into a wide reception, the smell of clean-
ing chemicals leaving a sour taste on my tongue. A young
receptionist sits at a desk in front of the elevators, her eyes
widening in acknowledgment as she spots Alexander.

"Mr. Dale. They are ready for you in Conference Room
Three."

"Thank you, Evelyn."

I try to catch her eye—maybe to send an SOS. But she
doesn't pay me any attention, returning to her computer as
the phone rings.

Fuck.

I'm really in a world of trouble.

Conference Room Three is pretty easy to find. Large printed font on glass doors acts as a countdown, and when we
reach the third room overlooking the busy city below, a
dozen eyes fall on us.

The long table is filled all but for two seats, with Alexander
at the head. He doesn't sit down straight away, gesturing for
me to take a seat on his left.

"Ms. White," he murmurs sternly, reverting back to formalities.

A hand shoves me in my back, my feet stumbling as I move while every set of eyes watch me carefully. I sit down next to a middle aged man with short dark blond hair, his pale blue irises and thin lips sneering as if he's being punished by being sat next to me.

"Good Morning gentlemen," Alexander greets loudly when I'm seated. "Thank you for meeting me. We have some urgent business to attend to. But first, I'd like to take a moment to introduce you to someone *special*."

My stomach clenches painfully and for a split second, I consider running full speed at the glass windows to launch myself into the streets below. Anything to get away from this.

Alexander steps behind me, his cold hand gracing my shoulder in an almost intimate touch.

"This is Avery White. The newest shareholder of our corporation. And my soon to be former daughter-in-law."

Chapter 22

Theo

It's amazing how some people defy the laws of survival. Confidence and ill-thought wisdom tend to occupy the space in people's brains where they ought to have common sense.

Especially in a place like Lilydale.

How anyone could become complacent here is beyond me. Even without the knowledge of what lies below, we're constantly surrounded by other patients who could slip into their trauma at any given moment, and so-called professionals who get off on playing God.

I've been following this asshole for twenty minutes and he's still none the wiser. Grey would have realized within seconds if I was tailing him. Probably Damon as well.

But Rian Thatcher? Walking around as if he's taking a casual browse through a shop, completely oblivious to his surroundings.

I have half a mind to just take him out now. I'm almost at the point where it seems pointless to follow him. Clearly, he's not up to any good.

Most patients are either in their cells or attending professional sessions. So, the fact that he's just strolling freely

through the halls, peeking into rooms and wandering aimlessly is suspicious enough.

Especially since Avery is nowhere to be seen.

Grey, Damon and I waited at the table the entire time,
head-counting every patient that was escorted into the hall
for mealtime. She never showed.

It wouldn't be the first time that Avery has been kept from
the patient eating schedule, but something about the timing
feels off. My gut tells me this isn't a simple case of assigned
duties or punishment.

None of us waste our time with the bullshit therapy sessions. After we returned to the male dorms following breakfast, we quickly formulated a plan.

The other two are currently sourcing information while
I volunteered to check the facility for signs of her. I'm just
hoping she's not downstairs. Part of me wants to smash the
stairwell door in and check, but given they have patients
down there already, we put everyone at risk if we burst in
suddenly. It was the first place that came to mind, but all of
us quickly agreed that it's unlikely Whittingham would pull
the same move twice. I could sense the panic and uncertainty
in Grey and Damon's tones when we had that discussion—it
matched mine. One wrong move and it's all over. One incorrect agreement about her whereabouts and we run the risk
of getting to her too late.

But we have to think clearly and act rationally. They let her
get away once. If she was down there, they wouldn't allow

that again. She'd be killed and there's too many witnesses with the other patients. I'm *attempting* to be empathetic, but despite our warnings, those patients signed the fucking form. For all I care, they are a low priority right now. I know the others don't agree and Aves would give me a mouthful too if I relayed those thoughts, but she is the only one I care about. She is the one I'm going to save first.

I'm volatile and on edge with the idea that someone has their hands on her or could be hurting her again. If that's the case, they can consider this their last day on Earth.

After searching and being unable to find her anywhere, I was just about ready to head back when I saw this asshole lurking about.

He came out of the dorms without a guard which only means one thing—he has access in and out. And knowing that the luxury of Cirque des Morts hasn't been provided to him, I can only assume someone else has. And the only reasonable suggestion points directly to Whittingham.

I knew from his arrival that he was up to no good. Something is off with his body language, the way he conducts himself—as if pretending to be intimidated while saving face and acting brave. While I definitely believe he spiraled during his run-in with Grey, I'm willing to bet he's got a lot of motivation coming from somewhere. It's a good act—I'll give him that. But I see through his charade.

The way he was staring at Avery. The way he's kept himself small and seemingly out of view. It doesn't exactly scream mental patient.

At this point, either he's searching for something, knows I'm tailing him, or he's genuinely shit with directions because we've visited everywhere *and nowhere* in Lilydale.

The free time rooms, the hallway near the staff offices, the meal hall. I can't help but notice he glanced at the library door as he passed but didn't attempt to enter—exactly like he's trying not to be cornered.

If someone was actually trying to hide or have personal space, that would be one of the safest places.

No—this fucker is up to something.

Rian never checks behind him, not that he'd spot me.

Finally, he starts making an intentional beeline toward the psychiatry rooms, vanishing into Elsher's office when the previous patient exits to an awaiting guard.

Shame.

I was really hoping to have a one-to-one chat somewhere private.

I could wait for him, but I suspect he's going to be in there for a while and I need to see if there's been any updates about Avery.

Heading back to the dorm, I find Grey and Damon in the latter's room.

"Well—anything?" I ask straight away, inviting myself in without a care.

The two glance up, faces tight with matching expressions. It's Damon who speaks first though.

"They found our camera in Arthur's office. We've lost signal so Byrone assumes it's been destroyed."

"Avery was there," I state confidently, reading between the lines.

Grey nods, rested fist clenching atop his knee. "Connor said there's two scheduled guards missing as well."

That familiar burning rage flares up again as I narrow my eyes in his direction. "Missing or stationed elsewhere?"

"They clocked in for their shift," Grey replies and it sounds like he's on the cusp of escorting me on a murderous rampage. "The main camera feed captured them heading in the direction of Arthur's office, chatting about a *day trip*."

"What?" I snap. "She's not in the building at all? They've taken her outside Lilydale?"

Initially, I kept myself in control by deciding anything was better than her being downstairs in the hands of the fucked-up doctors. It never even occurred to me that there was a possibility they would take her outside of Lilydale.

We can't get to her if that's the case. They'd kill us before we'd even make it to the front gates. She's out of our reach.

I'm going to make them hurt so badly that every last moment of their existence is nothing but pain and suffering beyond comprehensible measure.

When neither of them answer, I break, turning to leave. I'll knock down every single door until I find Whittingham and make him talk.

"Theo," Damon calls out, demand clear in his tone.

Out of respect for Avery's love of him, I do actually pause. He has five seconds to voice whatever it is he wants to say before I go—with or without them.

"That's your wife, Damon. My girlfriend. *Your* girlfriend," I direct to Grey. "I'm not waiting around to see if they return her in one piece to us."

Damon stands, crossing the room until he reaches me by the door. "I am in complete agreement with you. But if we do anything right now, we don't know if they will hurt her. We need someone on the outside to try to track her down."

I raise my eyebrow. "And who would we ask?" I question sarcastically.

"Christopher," he answers simply. "He's still out sick. They likely won't anticipate him searching. We need to go dig further to see where she could have possibly been taken so we can narrow the location down. Byrone and Jillian are looking into it. Once we have an idea, we will send Christopher."

Begrudgingly, I nod. It's probably the best plan we have. I don't like feeling helpless, but he's correct. Last time we confronted them, it ended with Damon being shot and people dying. No one needs a repeat of that—especially when the sole target is Avery.

To my unpleasant surprise, Damon reaches up and gives my shoulder a reassuring squeeze. I bat his hand away with a scowl, but the asshole just dryly laughs, turning back to Grey.

"I'll contact Christopher to let him know the situation and to be on standby. In the meantime, lunch is about to start so we should go. Keep our eyes and ears tuned for any information or her return."

Grey appears as though he wants to disagree as well, but he nods once, standing up. "And classes after lunch?"

"Same deal," Damon replies. "We go and we blend in. We don't know if any of the teachers have intel, so we need to be on guard. That way, we're also in the public spaces if she does return."

"Do either of you have Thatcher in your class?" I ask, the two of them giving me a puzzling look.

"Mine," Damon answers. "Why?"

"Because I just followed that asshole aimlessly around the building before he disappeared into Elsher's office. He can get in and out of the rooms by himself."

I end the information there, letting them fill in the blanks. Grey suddenly pushes past us with a low throaty growl.

"If Avery isn't back soon, I'm going to make Elsher piss himself and then I'm going to drown that cunt Thatcher in it."

*** Two Years Ago ***

I hear it.

The moment I step into the house, soft sobs travel to my ears, unsettling me.

Madison.

Heading to the living room, I find her curled up on the couch, face red and puffy.

"What happened?" I demand angrily.

She jumps slightly, dissociating too much to register my presence until now. "Hey, little brother," she murmurs, quickly wiping her eyes. "I didn't hear you come in."

Deflecting again. It's becoming an annoying habit. She can spare me the protection privilege. I don't need to be shielded from her pain. I'm her brother, after all. Her being older is irrelevant. It's my job to protect her.

"Madi, tell me what happened?" I ask again.

"It's nothing," she mumbles, waving her hand dismissively. "I was watching *The Notebook*."

I raise an eyebrow, slowly turning my head to deliberately look at the unplugged television. "Want to try that again? Come on—give me another bullshit excuse. I've got plenty of time." I fold my arms, ready to stand here for as long as it takes.

The thing that Madi doesn't realize is I already know. I overheard her talking to our mother while the parents were packing for their bi-annual vacation. They leave next week, and apparently, we're old enough now to stay behind. Decoded—kid free vacation even though we're adults.

I just need to know which asshole it is this time. Joseph had her in tears three days ago and Richard the week before. These crying episodes are becoming so frequent lately that I can't remember the last time I saw her genuinely smile. Madi is miserable all the time, and typical Mom in all her wise glory merely said, "That's just how men are, sweetheart."

No. We are not.

It isn't a chromosomal trait to make women cry. Nor is it something to be proud of.

After all, those two assholes started this mess. From my physical inquiries I was able to deduce that Madi was a competition—two old friends vying for her attention. What they failed to realize is that her heart is big enough for more than one, and instead of accepting that, or doing the sensible thing and walking away, they decided to fight over her. Except they turned their sights onto Madi, insisting she picks. My people pleasing sister whose greatest fear in life is to upset others.

Of course she can't choose. She apparently loves both of them.

If they loved her like they claim, they wouldn't be making her cry every chance they get. Even our parents have turned a blind eye, uncertain how to feel about the whole situation. I know they judge her silently. They can't seem to grasp their heads around the fact that Madi has feelings for more than one person.

Who the fuck cares? It's her life.

Except she's not living.

It's a ticking time bomb. Which is why when the parents are away next week, I'm going to try to sort this mess out before Madi suffers more irreparable harm.

She deserves better. And I'll be damned if anyone hurts my sister.

Chapter 23

Avery

Soon to be former daughter-in-law.

A chill runs down my spine but I keep my face composed. I'm bleeding in a sea of sharks, and there's no way in hell I'm going to let them see me panic.

One could surmise that he's referring to an annulment, particularly after Whitface already tried to coerce and bribe me into signing one. But there was something in the way he said it—a threat—that has me envisioning other scenarios.

It hits me that every single man in this room not only despises me, but they are carbon copies of Alexander Dale and Arthur Whittingham. Rich, egotistical pricks who will destroy the world to climb the ashes. Alexander could whip out that gun and shoot me in cold blood, and none of them would flinch. They'd probably celebrate the destruction of another obstacle and feign innocence.

After all, isn't that what they have always done? Damon said that Alexander killed his mother. Yet, he never suffered the deserved consequences.

Whittingham too. How can you lie in bed with someone, accept gifts of love from them, just to end their life without a care in the world? That sick fuck actually decapitated her, disrespected her corpse. Well, let's be honest. He wouldn't have done it himself. People like that keep their hands clean and hide behind others, ready to throw them under the bus if a whiff of suspicion comes their way.

My body physically recoils and revolts as fingers dance along my shoulder blade. It doesn't go unnoticed by Alexander as he gives a small chuckle under his breath.

"We're here today to discuss the next fiscal quarter. As you are all aware, we suffered some... *setbacks* in recent times. However, I've been assured that those issues have been resolved and our financial contract is still in place."

Someone across the table clears their throat, leaning forward with interest. "And what of our newest shareholder? I believe your son's marriage restricted the Board's access to financial resources."

The man looks at me with a blank expression, dead green eyes curious. He looks almost familiar, but then again, all these men appear the same unless you gaze closely.

"Yes, you are correct, Henry," Alexander says, giving my shoulder a squeeze. "However, Arthur was able to proceed with the purchase of the replacement equipment and date it prior to the restriction taking place since it was already a contractual obligation. As such, we negotiated a continuance for the time being while our legal team reviews the trust deed."

It feels like spiders are crawling over my skin as everyone glances at me. I'm an inconvenience to them and it reads in their expressions.

I let out a breath when Alexander releases me, walking over to his spot. Picking up some paperwork, he scans it briefly before turning his attention to me.

"Now, down to business," he says with an almost sincere, calming voice. "Avery, Board regulations state that any documentation must be signed by the majority shareholder. Previously when it was just Damon and myself, we were *usually* unable to proceed with required business without a Court order since Damon wasn't... *compliant.* When I took over as the majority shareholder, it made things easier as I only needed to sign. However, your incoming position changed the order of proceedings. Fortunately, our legal counsel has advised that given there are three of us now it actually works in our favor," he smiles coldly. "Together, you and I equal a majority. And by Dr. Smith's admission that you were lucid enough to enter into a marital contract, you are able to now sign on behalf of the Board."

What?

He drops the paperwork in front of me. I drop my head, reading only the first sentence before I spin to glare at him.

"You want me to sign an agreement that allows you access to the trust fund?"

Alexander nods, as if he's asking for something simple and not the ability to access means to torture human beings.

"Damon was correct in that as majority shareholder his vote holds the most weight. But he failed to account for the fact that you and I can form a majority if in agreement."

"I won't sign it," I snap, pushing the paperwork away. "That's not your money. I'll never agree with you on anything."

"Let's circle back to that," he says, unfazed. Reaching down, he lifts the paperwork, revealing a second one underneath. "How about this one?"

Words printed in black and white stare back at me, my heart stopping completely as a shiver rolls through my body. I don't even react. I'm paralyzed by the document, tears threatening to spill as I register the double meaning of *this* document.

A pen appears in my peripheral vision as Alexander holds out a black ballpoint for me knowingly.

"Avery," he drawls when I don't move. "Sign it." There's a hiss and warning with his demand, and I do circle back—to the start.

I scan the room, checking for allies. Surely at least one of them disagree with this. Right?

Wrong.

The men all watch expectedly, some more annoyed than others at my hesitation. I realize I'm stupid to have hope, a fool to consider that any of these monsters would care about human decency.

I find myself looking through the large windows that separate the conference room from the hallway, pitifully searching for help. It's eerily empty for a busy corporate building—almost as if it was planned that way.

"I won't ask you again," Alexander warns. "I'm not a patient man, Avery. If you refuse, we'll just go with Plan B. Sign it."

I know I'm not the smartest person. And hell, everyone knows I've made some questionable decisions. I hurt Grey in the past. I abandoned Theo when he only wanted to be there for me. I painted Damon as a villain when all he ever did was try to protect us all. But I know what Alexander is referring to. I know what he's promising.

If I die, Damon would be my legal beneficiary by law. I don't own much—nothing except these goddamn shares. But they would go to him.

Unless...

This time, I can't stop the tear that slips free, rolling down my cheek. I don't bother to swipe it away. I want them to see what they have done.

Slowly, I accept the pen from Alexander, disgusted with the little huff of approval he makes.

My name is already printed at the bottom under a line where I need to sign. I never understood the expression *signing your life away*.

But I do now.

After all, it's here—clearly written....

THE LAST WILL AND TESTAMENT OF AVERY ELIZA-BETH WHITE

1. I revoke all prior Wills and Codicils.

2. I am married to Damon Emerson Alexander Dale.

3. I do not have any living children.

4. I appoint Alexander Dale as my personal representative and executor.

5. In the event of my death, I bequeath the whole of my estate to Alexander Dale.

6. I, the testator, being of sound mind and legal age, hereby exclude my husband Damon Emerson Alexander Dale from being a beneficiary or receiving any portion of my estate.

7. This last Will expresses my wishes without undue influence or duress.

The pen makes a scratching sound as I quickly sign, shoving the paperwork toward Alexander. He gleefully motions for two men to come over, the pair of them signing as witnesses next to my name.

"Excellent. Now since that small matter has been taken care of, Avery, the other document."

I close my eyes for a few seconds, unsuccessfully composing myself. I wish I could be as cool and calm as the guys, but I'm not. Alexander is literally holding a gun to my head—well, Damon's now. If I don't sign the Will, he'll kill Damon then me. And if I don't sign the majority shareholder agreement, he'll kill us both anyway. One way or another, he's ensuring he gets his cut. It's just up to me as to who gets the first bullet.

And I choose me.

Damon will find a way to stop him. But I can't. Damon is the key to freedom for everyone at Lilydale. I'm just the girl he fell in love with.

I can't choose my life and our marriage over the patients in good conscience. This isn't just my story. We're all victims. Maybe this is what I'm meant to do. No one was able to save me, but if I go down saving everyone else... That's a life well lived.

The guys have each other. They will stick together. And maybe, just maybe, I can chase the clock and figure out a way to fix this mess before Alexander gets to me.

Right now though... he needs me. We need to use that to our advantage.

If it was easy enough, he'd just shoot me right now in this conference room and use the Will. But he's asking me to sign the majority agreement—which means we have leverage. Somewhere. We just need to find it.

I quickly scribble my signature on the majority shareholder agreement, slumping back in the leather chair. Alexander nods happily at his little victory, looking way too delighted at my distress.

I hope he dies a slow and painful death at the hands of Damon.

"Our counsel will file the paperwork and we'll begin necessary preparations. Now, gentlemen—if you turn to the next items in your agenda, Henry will take us through the fiscal quarter projections."

The ride back to Lilydale was as silent as the first trip.

By the time we return, it's well after lunch but the thought of food makes me physically sick.

The hallways are vacant, the patients in their classes. I fully expect the guards to take me to my cell or to solitary confinement, to keep me away from the guys. But when they shove me through Charmaine's door without a care in the world, I realize that was Alexander's plan.

He wants me to tell them.

He's going to gloat through me.

I spot Grey immediately, his whole body straightening at my arrival as his eyes scan me over for inspection before shooting a murderous look at the guards.

"Avery, welcome," Charmaine says warmly. "Take a seat. We're just doing some reading. The material is on your desk."

All I can muster is a quick nod to acknowledge I heard her, my feet dragging as I head to my desk.

My ass has barely touched the seat when Grey leans over, unbothered that Charmaine will probably notice and catch him.

"What the hell happened, little killer? Where were you?"

Exhaustion seeps through my bones. I had every intention of coming back strong and determined, channeling that rage that has reared its head lately. But there's nothing but fatigue and sadness—and it's written all over my face.

There's no point sugar coating anything. Nor any reason to lie. I'm in a huge mess and it affects everyone, so I just come straight out with it. "Alexander happened, Grey."

He scans me over again, taking in the business attire I'm wearing. No doubt another bold move from Alexander in an effort to make a statement. I stand out like a sore thumb on the best of days, let alone in clothes that aren't the usual Lilydale gray uniform.

"Fuck this," he murmurs angrily, standing up and grabbing my hand. I'm pulled from my seat and dragged behind him. Charmaine looks baffled by our movement as we head toward the door, but to my surprise, she doesn't try to stop us.

As soon as we're out in the corridor, Grey stops and rounds on me, cupping my face in his hands. "Are you okay?"

I shake my head. "Not even in the slightest."

He lets out a low exhale, resting his forehead against mine for a few seconds, allowing us both time to pull our shit together.

"Come on. We need to find Deadman."

Chapter 24

Damon

I should have known he'd pull something like this. And I'm punishing myself for not being two steps ahead because he could have easily hurt Avery. There's no doubt in my mind that he wanted to, but by proving he could take her from me at any time, he's sending a message.

War has begun.

I'm exceptional at finding loopholes, but he didn't get to where he is by playing clean and by the rules.

When Grey pulled me out of that bullshit class, it only took one glance in Avery's direction to realize what had gone down. Theo was with them, but the expression on his face indicated he was just as uninformed as I was at first. None of us are ignorant fools though. We can piece together events by observing and reading between the lines.

There's only one person who would send Avery back into the devil's lair in formal business attire. Only one person who would willingly keep her alive for now when he needs and wants her dead.

The fact that I allowed myself to believe she was somewhat protected is beyond forgiving. Even with all our measures in place—cell phones, guards in our pockets, access to the facility cameras, our own streams—he still bypassed them easily.

We clocked that she was missing by breakfast, and immediately sprung into action. Our first initial fear was that they had taken her downstairs again—but that theory was quickly dispelled with the assistance of Connor and applying logic.

To no one's surprise, the majority of Arthur's guards are pathetic gossip seekers. A few inquiries from Connor and we were able to confirm that she wasn't even in the building at all. But other than that revelation, no one knew where she was. That part they had intentionally kept under wraps. Nothing is accidental when it comes to my father. Every decision, every choice is part of his master plan. He had *wanted* us to figure out that she was gone. He knows we'd catch on quickly, leaving just enough breadcrumbs in a trail until it goes dead.

I had already spoken to Christopher and set up a plan for him to search for her, but she was back before we could implement it. Typical Alexander Dale strategy—he had this organized down to the millisecond. While he may or may not have deduced that we would enlist Christopher's assistance, he focuses on timing and procedure.

It was no surprise that they dragged her out of bed before everyone else, to allow time for them to enact their plan before we even knew she was gone. And he'd know exactly how long it would take us to follow the clues and ensure that she was back at that specific moment.

The four of us are squared away in my room for this conversation. I no longer trust that the library is secure, even if Byrone and Jillian are able to send the cameras offline during our meetings. We need a plan, and we must start moving. Things are already in motion, and now that he's pulled off this stunt, it's going to send him on a power trip which is dangerous. He'll be adamant he's untouchable, and while I disagree, it means he will stop at nothing to bring us down.

We're still waiting for the specifics. My patience is already paper thin, but these two assholes ganged up on me, demanding I wait before interrogating Avery. It's frustrating watching Grey coddle her. Not because I want answers, which I do, but because Avery doesn't need it.

While it's clear that this morning rattled her and she's troubled by whatever went down, she's not on the verge of a nervous breakdown. If anything, I'm probably more inclined to suspect she's going to rage blackout judging by her tense posture and irritated expression.

"Can we move this along?" I finally snap, directing my question at Grey.

He coolly glances over his shoulder in my direction. "Chill, Deadman. Give her a few minutes to process things."

"Avery," I say sternly, shifting my attention to her. "Do you *need* processing time?"

Her light irises lift to meet my face, expression softening. I'll never admit this out loud, but that simple gesture alights something in me. To know I have an effect on her mood and demeanor, to have her look at me so fondly despite whatever turmoil is happening, it's addictive in a way I never anticipated.

I suppose that's a good thing since she's now stuck with me in unholy matrimony. It would be rather awkward if we returned to me threatening to wipe her from existence, and Avery slapping me whenever she got riled up by said threats.

"No," she answers after pondering the question for a few seconds, much to my amusement.

Grey laughs quietly, almost pouting like the competitive bastard just suddenly realized I'm on his level now and he'll have to try a lot harder to persuade Avery to take his side. He stands, holding up his hands in defeat. "Fine," he mumbles cheerily. "We'll do it the classic Damon way. Information first, therapy later."

He at least earns himself a laugh from Avery, who reaches forward to squeeze his hand.

"You can help fix me later," she teases.

I close my eyes, agitated that we're heading backwards on the fucking merry-go-round with these two again. They both get distracted by shiny things, which is counterproductive when they are both like black diamonds on a sunny, cloudless day—a never ending cycle.

My sanity must truly be slipping through the cracks because a second later, I find myself glancing in Theo's direction, silently requesting some assistance.

Theo stares back at me with a blank expression, but luckily, someone in this room still has some focus. He steps forward, slapping Grey up the side of the head. "Snap out of it, asshole. We've got work to do."

"Ow."

"Thank you," I muse before facing Avery. "Now, what did my father do?"

All playfulness vanishes from her face in an instant and it makes my blood boil. It's clear that whatever happened has unnerved her, but still, she persists, filling us in. As she details the ordeal, from the guards dragging her out of bed, to being forced to change in a room full of vile creatures, I secretly hope that it doesn't get much worse because I'm already on the edge of hunting my father down and being done with rationality.

But alas... that is never the case with him.

"... he made me sign some majority agreement so that we outvote you, as well as taking the liberty of organizing my *affairs*," she spits out in disgust.

"Affairs?" Theo asks.

Avery locks eyes with me. "A Will—leaving everything I own to him and excluding you."

"Deadman, we need to kill him—now," Grey mutters angrily. "No more delaying. Even if it means changing the plan."

"Fuck the plan," Theo interjects. "I don't give a shit about anyone else. He's planning on coming for Aves. We do something—now. I'm done fucking around and waiting."

On the outside, I'm managing to keep my composure while digesting this news. But inside, I'm in complete agreement with them for once. I'm probably seconds away from detonating and losing control, but I have to remain focused. That's what he's counting on. My father will be laying in wait, hoping I take the bait and charge in with guns blazing.

When you act on impulse, things become murky. There's no sense of judgment. No ability to see danger or control over your actions.

I still haven't spoken when Avery walks over to me, straddling my lap.

"Hey," she murmurs quietly, grabbing my face in between her hands. "You've got this."

I find myself searching her eyes, quickly registering her words.

Control. You've still got control.

Placing my hands on her waist, I don't bother to speak because truthfully, she can already hear me—read me like a fucking book. There's a silent conversation passing between us—Avery knowing my true reaction buried deep, and helping me stay grounded, and me, promising that no one will dare lay a finger on her and I'll protect her with my life.

Grey and Theo stay back and watch our exchange quietly, but incredulously there's nothing awkward about it. Nor do I feel threatened by them witnessing my mental recalibration. There used to be a time that I'd probably ensure their silence for viewing what could only be considered a vulnerable moment.

But despite my best instincts and everything that drives and embodies *me*, these three broke through those walls. We're family now—connected and founded by death. Just like *Cirque des Morts*.

Except where Cirque des Morts is my greatest creation, the weapon that will bring down Alexander Dale once and for all, this right here, this is my biggest achievement.

This is *my* family.

"We'll kill anyone that touches you, mon petit feu."

Avery's eyes sparkle. "You better not have just called me a little docile sheep or anything like that or we're going to have a problem, Demon Boy."

I chuckle quietly, lifting her shirt up. "The only problem I have right now is that I'm not buried inside you, Avery."

She shivers as I drag my fingers up her sides, but when something that wasn't there before catches my attention, I pause. "You have a new tattoo," I remark in surprise, tracing the black ink on her ribcage.

Grey moves closer, curious to see, but Theo stands in place, clearly her partner in crime.

"I do," Avery breathes out, still quivering slightly. "Do you want to know what it means?"

I nod, though it's fairly obvious what it is on a simple level. The significance on the other hand is still a mystery.

Avery places her hand over mine, flattening my palm against her skin. "It's your heartbeat, Damon," she says softly. "Taken the day we got married while you were fighting to come back to me."

To me...

Not *to us* or *Lilydale*. Not even the society. But to her—my wife.

Clearing my throat to attempt to dislodge whatever feels trapped in it, I wrap my arm around her back, lifting us both off the bed. "Theo, lie down. I need to ruin Avery's pretty little cunt while you fuck her throat."

"Aw, excluding little old me?" Grey asks playfully, but jumps up on the desk like it's an observation deck and he's taking a front row seat.

"Theo deserves this reward too," I tell him simply as the dark-haired man glides past us, shooting Grey a smug look as he does. It doesn't go unnoticed, Grey's eyes darkening with a threatening promise that will no doubt rear its head later.

Avery, willingly oblivious to it all, drags her hands through my hair before linking them together behind my neck. She leans forward and finds my lips, and I waste no time kissing her back while subconsciously registering the bed moving with Theo's weight.

The idea that she's permanently marked herself with part of me is sending me feral, the need to claim her too great to ignore. I catch sight of her ring on her finger, the gemstones flashing under the dull lights overhead and at this point, I snap.

I wrap my hand around her throat, guiding her backwards off me. I feel the tiny vibration under my palm as she whimpers. As I start to spin her around, another set of hands joins to assist, grabbing Avery as the two of us position her on her stomach.

She peers up at Theo with a look of wild hunger and a smile is shared between them as I hastily shove her skirt up over her ass. Her cunt is already glistening, shining brighter than our ring she wears proudly, and when I move behind her, I spread her open with my hands.

This makes her still, dropping her head into Theo's lap. I slowly run my finger up her wet cunt, smirking as she shivers under my touch. Slapping her ass, I relish the sound of her moan, sliding two fingers into her entrance.

"Wrap your mouth around his cock, wife," I order, burying my fingers deep and curling them to hit her sweet spot.

Avery tenses and rocks her hips back, but slowly, composes herself enough to reach into Theo's pants and retract his hardened length.

We all watch as she fists it, running her hand up and down in precise motions. Leaning over her, I grab her throat tightly. "Open those lips," I demand, my thumb reaching up to drag her bottom lip down.

Her warm breath tickles my skin as her lips part, and to my surprise, her tongue shoots out, the tip flicking my thumb.

It's cute that she thinks she's in control, that she can distract me with such tactics. She is, but she'll have to try a lot harder than that to take charge.

Prying her jaw open with my finger, I remove my hand from her body, grabbing a fistful of hair and pulling her head back. I lock eyes with her, giving her a coy smile.

"Adorable," I tease. "But you'll look a lot better with your mouth stuffed."

Without waiting for a response, I shove her head forward, pushing her onto Theo's dick. Avery moans—either in pleasure or protest—but makes no effort to move away, using her hands to brace herself on his thighs. Still gripping her hair, I control the pace, lifting and lowering her head as she takes Theo in her mouth.

I motion for him to take over, and when his hand rests atop her head next to mine, I shift back, giving him the reins. Lining up with her entrance, I hold the base of my dick, watching with fascination as it slowly vanishes into her pretty little cunt. My control snaps when I bottom out, Avery squeezing me while making muffled breathy sounds, and I pull back and slam into her. The force sends her jolting forward, choking on Theo's dick but she quickly recovers in time before I thrust hard into her again.

"Much better," I muse deeply, grasping her hips tightly. "Such a *good. Fucking. Girl.*" I emphasize each word with the slap of our hips.

Theo keeps his hand on her head, guiding her as his head tips back and he makes his own sounds of pleasure. Avery quickly becomes a whimpering mess between us, and I reach around her, spreading two fingers around her clit as I gently rub.

"Fucking look at me," Theo says, and I'm glad he's talking to her and not me. Avery must obey, because he gives her a little nod of appreciation, the two of them deep in each other's gazes.

Not one to be shown up, I focus on her clit, drawing figure eights around it.

Theo growls, grabbing her hair. "Keep those eyes open, Aves."

Avery makes a sound of protest as I rock my hips while circling her clit. A smirk tugs on my lips—I know I'm making it unbelievably hard for her to comply, but it will be good for her to learn some control. Learn to fight against your body and will your mind to be stronger.

"Keep them open," I voice, stroking her faster as I slide deeper into her pulsating cunt. "Or we won't let you come."

Grey chuckles from the other side of the room, and I can just imagine her giving him the side-eye. From what I can make out without directly looking away from her perfect ass, Grey's enjoying the torture as much as we are. He's leaning forward, watching her closely, while encouraging her to break.

"Come on, little killer," he grins. "Look at Theo while his cock is deep in your throat. You take them so fucking well, don't you?"

She moans loudly, shuddering as her hips push back into mine. She's close—chasing her orgasm while overwhelmed by all the sensations and voices. It's perfection, and I'm enthralled gazing at her fighting back, captivated by her sheer willpower as she resists and obeys simultaneously.

While one hand continues the attention on her clit, I bring the other to her ass, running my hand over the curves. I know what's coming before she does—her. My thumb grazes her little asshole, stroking the sensitive skin as Avery suddenly jerks at the new sensation. I don't relent, fucking her hard while pressing all her buttons, and before she realizes it's happening, her muffled cries are filling the room as she crashes into bliss between us.

"Fuck," I hiss as her body clenches around me firmly, ripping my own climax out of me. I quickly grab her hips for support, digging my fingers in as I thrust deeply into her body before spilling inside of her.

Somewhere in the mental haze, I hear Theo cursing, his hands gripping her head tight as his head tips back.

The two of us slouch forward, my body covering Avery's as I place a gentle kiss on the nape of her neck. Her breathing is ragged, her head drooped forward, and I move her hair aside as I lean to whisper in her ear.

"And it will keep beating for you, for as long as I'm your husband," I tell her, referring to the gift.

Avery twists her head to look at me, eyes focused and looked thoroughly fucked in all the best ways. "Forever?" She asks.

"Even when it stops, I'll still be yours," I promise. "Because you're ours now and no one is taking that from us—not even death itself."

Chapter 25

Avery

When the guards come to collect me for my mandatory psych session, I'm instantly in a bad mood at the thought of dealing with Elsher again. At least this time, the guys will know where I am if I suddenly disappear and find myself on the Lilydale most wanted list.

Except to my relief, we bypass Elsher's doorway and stop in front of Dr. Smith's. The feeling is short-lived though as I'm ready to give him a piece of my mind.

The guard opens the door for me and I don't wait for him to announce me or get the all clear, just barreling in.

"Did you have a nice little break?" I grumble, annoyed. Dr. Smith blinks at me in confusion, but I've already prepared for this conversation and have a full on speech prepared. "Seriously, Dr. Smith. Of all the times to be sick, you continue to have terrible timing. Why is it that I'm always affected by this special skill of yours?"

Okay. So, it comes out a little less angry than I practiced, but I'm still frustrated. Especially when he crosses his arms with an amused smile and leans back in his chair.

"Avery, you're fully charged today."

"I'm not a frigging cell phone," I shoot back. "Speaking of—some warning next time would be nice. That goddamn asshole—"

The words trail off in embarrassment as I spot movement out of the corner of my eye and realize we're not alone in the room. It turns to shock quickly, a gasp escaping my mouth.

"Margie!"

There, sitting in my usual seat, dressed in a pencil skirt and blouse is the old familiar face of my social worker. She blinks at me a few times, processing my appearance before her expression softens.

"Hi, Avery," she says, turning her attention to Dr. Smith with a small light-hearted laugh. "You're right, Chris. She's made incredible progress."

"I—" My brain struggles to compute the situation, planning to circle back to her comment. "What's going on?"

Dr. Smith gestures for me to take a seat next to her. "You asked me to try to get Meg here for you. That's why I've been absent."

Meg?

"So you didn't have explosive diarrhea?" It slips out unfiltered, and for a second, it's hilarious to see him become flustered. It's bewildering and concerning, watching as he scrambles to recover, attempting to form words. *What the fuck?*

His cheeks redden slightly and when he avoids glancing back at Margie again, it dawns on me why.

Oh, my fucking God. He likes her!

Holy shit. I absolutely called it during my first session when I likened them to each other, how they'd have cute little babies with perfect hair and wear tuxedoes instead of onesies. I just didn't think it would ever actually happen since they wouldn't have contact with each other... except for now.

Except for me.

Fuck. I'm a matchmaker. A fucked-up version of Cupid if he had three psychos as weapons instead of arrows.

Margie laughs softly at the obvious fumbling mess the psychiatrist has become and I decide to go easy on him, giving him a few seconds to compose himself as I sit beside her.

She smiles at me warmly. "You're looking well, Avery. How are you?"

"I can't believe you're actually here," I tell her. "How?" I direct the last part to Dr. Smith, deciding he's had long enough to pull his shit together. I need answers.

"It took some coordination," Dr. Smith grunts, messing around with some paperwork on his desk. It's obvious he's not actually looking for anything in particular though, just attempting to appear important. "I knew Arthur would try to avoid signing it if I presented it to him straight up. So, I buried the form in a pile of other requests and waited until he was too busy to actually check what he was approving. I've spent the past two days with Meg getting ready so that we could bring her in straight away before he realizes."

I nod sharply. "And no one has noticed yet?"

"Arthur is away at a meeting this morning," Dr. Smith confirms. "I cornered him late yesterday to sign off on everything. He was in such a hurry to leave that he didn't read anything. Then, we scheduled this appointment for this morning when we knew he'd be absent from Lilydale. But he will be returning at lunch, so let's make this productive."

I have no idea how to process any of this, and now with the urgency lingering over my head, I'm suddenly a flustered mess. At least I'm not as much as a hot messy expressy as the psychiatrist though. He stills looks a little green at the diarrhea comment.

"How much do you know?" I ask Margie, turning back to her. "They are horrible here—really horrible."

Her face saddens. "Chris filled me in about the procedures in place. I'm so sorry, Avery. I truly had no idea."

It's clear she's racked with guilt. It's in her tone and expression, as if she's placing some of the blame on herself for talking this place up. But she wasn't to know—no one did. They made sure of it.

"It's not your fault," I tell her confidently. "You did the best you could to advocate for me and you stayed with me until the very end. Well, to the start of my journey here. The concept was too good to be true. But people like Alexander Dale, they deliberately enticed the community to believe this facility was a place of refuge. No one would ever expect that it was actually a living nightmare."

Okay—I'm probably being a touch dramatic. But I'm not going to downplay my experience here. If we're going to try to get outside help, they need to know the truth. Everything. Because nothing about this is going to be simple. I have no doubt that Alexander and Arthur have covered all their bases. Everything about that fucking contract is legal somehow. They twisted reality to fit their agenda, so we need to think like Damon—find a loophole and exploit it.

"You were hurt," Margie states gently, laying her hand atop of mine. "And from what I understand, others are being harmed as well."

I glance over at Dr. Smith, for once relieved that he's broken doctor-patient confidentiality. Sure, I'll give him shit later for his lack of ethical behavior, but this time, he's done a good job. "It's true," I confirm. "Which is why we need to get this facility closed down once and for all. We'll all die in here if we don't. And if we survive, there will be nothing left to save. I didn't survive all that before just to have everything taken away from me now."

Both of them stay quiet at my words. I didn't expect such a reaction from them. Staring at them in turn, I'm surprised to find tears in Margie's eyes and... *pride* in Dr. Smith's. It makes me feel oddly pleased and uncomfortable at the same time. Fuck—why can't I just take a compliment? All I ever wanted was to be told someone was proud of me, and the moment someone is, I want the ground to open up and swallow me whole.

Stop looking at me.

Fuck.

"Avery," Dr. Smith says when I face away from both of them, clearly having a minor mental spiral. "It's okay to acknowledge—"

"Here's the plan," I interject, cutting him off. "We need to figure out a way to bring this to the attention of people who care. I don't know—authorities or something?" I trail off. "Isn't there an organization that deals with investigating human rights?"

He gives me a glance of annoyance, before shifting into concentration. "There are agencies that deal with ensuring facilities are compliant with regulations. But it may be difficult to prove that what they are doing is non-compliant, especially when the contract in place is held by the government."

He voices my own thoughts, but I'm already two steps ahead. "What about those consent forms?" I ask. "While they may have been able to involuntarily take me before, surely those bullshit consent forms that Elsher had everyone sign is a starting place? They can't claim that we have the ability to consent otherwise we'd be able to leave here. Or something."

"Your sentences are tied into your Lilydale admission," Dr. Smith starts, deep in thought. "But perhaps you're correct. If we can prove that they are having people sign when they are deemed unable to make decisions, it could trigger some kind of investigation. It still wouldn't be enough though—"

"Unless we prove that it's leading to inhumane experi-mentation," I finish sharply. "There has to be a limit on what that contract allows them to do to us. Some of their methods are banned and illegal. If they are breaching their obligations by conducting treatments that are not legal, it would force the agency to have to review the whole process. It's a starting point."

Margie nods. "I think she's right, Chris. If we can make the allegation that the forms are in breach of a patient's freewill, especially since they were apparently coerced with reduced sentences, it could put them under investigation."

I gaze at her in awe. "You heard about that?"

"We were reviewing the form," she admits. "To see what we were working with. It's pretty standard in black and white, but verbally, they have coerced patients into this which is morally and ethically a breach. Not to mention the heinous methods you endured."

"How can we prove it though?" I ask weakly. "Damon said they cleared everything out the first time. If they destroyed the evidence of what they did to me and the others, how do we prove that they are doing something illegal?"

Dr. Smith straightens up. "We catch them in the act."

I shake my head. "No—we can't leave them down there any longer. It's going to do more harm than good. If our re-port triggers an investigation, they will erase their tracks. We know they have killed patients before. We're getting them out."

Margie glances at the two of us in confusion, and I realize that he hasn't been completely transparent with her. It's obvious that she's not privy to the knowledge of Cirque des Morts, or even possibly Damon and his relationship to Dr. Smith. But the doctor recognizes what I'm saying, hearing my unspoken words.

Sighing, he nods defeatedly. "Then get them out," he answers quietly. "Do what you have to do. We'll lodge a report today and do everything we can to stress the urgency of the matter."

Before I can answer, a knock on the door interrupts us. My eyes instinctively move to the clock on the wall, and I know it's a guard coming to collect me—probably to ensure I don't get actual help. My appointments with Dr. Smith have been getting shorter each session, like they are attempting to disrupt him from doing his job. Standing, I smile at Margie as she rises with me.

"Please don't blame yourself," I tell her again. "I know what it's like to feel guilt that's misplaced. Neither of us are at fault. And for what it's worth if Dr. Smith hasn't filled you in, in a weird, twisted turn of events, coming here has saved me."

Puzzled, she tilts her head, urging me to continue. The door opens behind me, and when I check who's stationed there, I relax when I spot Connor.

"I found myself," I tell her peacefully. "And I found a real family where I truly belong. No matter what happens, I'm happy—well, as happy as I can be. But I came to Lilydale lost and broken, and regardless of how I leave, whether that's alive or dead, I'm leaving in one piece, put back together by people who love me and make me realize I'm worth more than I ever thought before I came here."

Connor motions for me to follow and I take a few steps, pausing in the doorway once final time as I smile at Margie.

"I'm everything I was meant to be but was too scared to become. And this asshole," I nod, laughing quietly playfully toward Dr. Smith. "Is now my cousin-in-law, and he was a big part in helping me open my eyes."

Chapter 26

Avery

We're all on edge waiting for nightfall, but no one more than the three guys. When they collect me from my room when lights go out, it's eerily quiet among the group, and it's nothing to do with the fact that we're trying to remain out of sight.

Even in the dark, I can see their tense muscles and stiff backs as we make our way to the library. The others are waiting for us, and I give a quick nod to Byrone and a wave to Jillian before standing next to Damon at the head of the table.

It's then I realize that everyone here is a ball of nervous energy, and it dawns on me why...

They already did this once...

"Alright," Damon starts, voice strong. "Let's go over the plan one more time. We'll move similar to last time, with Byrone and Jillian cutting the feeds. Arthur has left for the night and Connor is keeping track of the guards. He won't be able to stop all of them if they get the word to follow and attack. But we've provided him with a cell phone so he can communicate with us. That's our advantage this time people. Use the cells provided. We'll set up a conference call so that we're all in touch."

Grey shifts closer to my left, boxing me in between him and Damon instead of being on our leader's other side as usual. To my surprise, Theo is on Damon's other side, the four of us facing the awaiting group.

"And just confirming you four plus Louis, Mark and Andy will be heading downstairs?" Byrone asks.

Damon nods. "Given the number of patients we're dealing with, we need the extra set of hands."

I meet Jillian's eyes as they glance up from her laptop, the two of us sharing a tight smile. When we debriefed early about my meeting with Dr. Smith and Margie, it was a unanimous vote that we move tonight. Straight away, I strongly told the guys I was coming with them. Even though I could sense their hesitation, to my astonishment, no one objected. I'm not sure if it's because I have knowledge that we can use, or that they want to keep me in their line of sight, but either way, they weren't going without me.

This whole experimentation mess started with me and it's going to end with me. No one else gets hurt.

Reaching down, I slip my hand through Grey's. He's chilled and composed, but underneath those complex layers, there's something brewing. I know what this means to him as well. The fact that this is the third time they have had to do this is fucked up. Despite everything I went through, at least

I came out of it alive. Leah didn't. And I know that hangs on his conscience tonight.

It hangs on mine too.

These patients down there, they aren't just peers of ours—they are friends of mine in a way. It hurts me to think that they are suffering like I did, and I feel rage burning inside.

Dr. Smith managed to pull together a list of the missing patients and track down copies of their signed forms. None of us recognize their signatures for obvious reasons, but I have a hard time believing Eliana and Siobhan would sign. We're all desperate to get out of here, but there has to be more than meets the eye with this corruption.

Grey squeezes my hand back as he steps forward to address the room. "Since we know the location this time, the seven of us will stay together. Everyone else will remain here, assigned to their sections. If Connor gives the signals that guards are on the move, you'll distract them. No violence—just direct them to another task by having them escort you back to your rooms. But remain in your assigned pairs. They are less likely to be physical if they don't feel like they have the upper hand."

"When you receive our signal Byrone and Jillian, put the feed back on and make sure to record everything. We want evidence of their return so that if the patients happen to go missing again, we can place their whereabouts back up here," Damon says.

"What if the doctors attempt to overpower us?" Jemison asks, but there's no concern in his voice, just curiosity.

"Kill them," Theo interjects. "Don't give them the opportunity to grab you. They may try to sedate us."

I swallow, well aware of what went down between Theo and Dr. West when he confronted him. The idea that Theo might have been captured by that psychopath is unnerving, even if it didn't actually eventuate. Though, when you compare the two of them, Dr. West stood no chance.

My lips twitch into a smile, a few members of Cirque des Morts noticing and turning to look at me. Wow, good job, Avery. Way to look unhinged and deranged at the most inappropriate time.

I glance over at Theo, relaxing when he smiles at me. It's clear he knows where my head is at, and he steps past Damon to stand in front of me. "They won't touch any of us, Aves," he says threateningly. "We'll make sure of it."

Nodding, I lean on my tippy-toes to plant a quick kiss on his lips. "Good. Because I'll kill them if they touch any of you."

Grey chuckles under his breath. "Stop saying sweet things like that, little killer. You'll distract me."

"Grey," Damon says firmly, interrupting our little love triangle. "Grab the gear and head into the aisles. Help Avery suit up."

"Suit up?" I repeat excitedly. "I get my own mask?"

Damon's lips twitch in amusement but he says nothing as Theo drags me toward the library aisles, Grey in tow with a bundle of black material. The other members of our entourage wisely choose another aisle to get changed, and I feel a moment of giddiness as I start pulling on the black sweats and hoodie. It's messed up that I feel such elation any time I get the chance to ditch the crappy Lilydale attire, but if I'm being honest, that's not the only part that's sending me into the mindset of a sociopath.

My eyes lock onto the red plastic in Grey's hands as he steps toward me, smirking. "Let me do the honors," he murmurs, sliding the devil mask into place over my head.

It takes me a moment to adjust to my semi-restricted vision, blinking a few times to see past the black mesh holes. But then everything becomes clear when my mind trains itself to ignore it, beaming at Grey through the mask. Not that he can see it—though it's probably obvious by the way I straighten up.

"One more small touch," he says to himself, reaching into his pocket. I watch as he extracts my blade, the present he made me, and passes it over. As I take it, he groans quietly, taking a step back. He and Theo scan over me, still free of their own masks so I can see all their reactions.

And by reactions I mean if we don't remain focused they are going to take me to Paris in this aisle.

"Hurry up," I tease, nodding toward their own masks. "We don't have all night, you know?"

Grey's eyes narrow at me and he moves forward, leaning down so we're only an inch apart. "I'm going to fuck the living shit out of you in that mask later. Don't lose it."

"Oh, really?" I laugh. "Maybe I'll make you watch again. You're a good little observer."

"You're playing a dangerous game, Aves," Theo warns. "Because I'll pin you down for him if you keep giving us that attitude."

Movement behind me has me doing a one-eighty, but before I can check who has dared step foot in the aisle with us, their relaxed postures and the firm hands on my waist give me an answer.

"Stop getting Grey fired up," Damon says, tightening his hold on me. "I need him focused on rescuing, not being balls deep in that little perfect cunt of yours."

"You're no fun," I tease, leaning back into him. "Just trying to break the tension a little."

Sadly, I wish that were true. We could all use a little stress relief, but nothing is going to bring that feeling until we get out of tonight in one piece together. What would Dr. Smith say about my attempt to mask fear with sexual humor? I'm sure there's a medical term for it. Elsher would definitely contribute it to my *horrible* mental state.

I hate the sickening feeling that twists inside my stomach. Perhaps the real reason I'm being so blasé about the situation is because a part of me worries that everything might burn to ash. It wouldn't be the first time that we were suddenly in the middle of a warzone. Damon nearly died right before my eyes, and as much as I want to believe we'll be okay—because we *have* to be—I hate that there's a possibility someone could get hurt.

These doctors don't care about our wellbeing. They just want to protect their warped legacies and ideations of playing God.

And me. What will they do when they see me? Better yet—what will Grey do? Or Theo? Or Damon? We're all ticking time bombs, reliving trauma and pain from only a short time ago.

"Alright, it's time," Damon announces, tightening his grip around my waist as if he can sense my inner demons. "Let's make this quick. Stick to the plan. That means, *Avery*, staying close to one of us at all times."

I nod, glancing at the three masked covered men. "I will," I promise. "Same to you."

The arm around me squeezes—not in confirmation, but reaction to my desire to lecture the great Damon. I don't care though. He's my husband. That means I'm equally responsible for his wellbeing, just as I am for my two boyfriends. We're all in this together. We go together and we leave together. No plan B.

"Grey," Damon starts, leaning round me to hand something over. "You can do the honors."

I eye the item being passed between them. Through the mask I can sense Grey's excitement, and it's that moment of tension relief I was craving. "Why am I not surprised you're also a pyromaniac?"

"No need to slap words in front of maniac, little killer," Grey muses. "That one word sums me up pretty well. But if you want to get into the argument of fire..."

Scowling at him, I step out of Damon's arms and move closer to him. "Fire is significant, Grey. It can mean rebirth."

"Like a phoenix rising from the ashes?" he states playfully. "I feel like we're more akin to a bunch of crows."

"A murder?" I snort.

Grey taps the temple of his mask. "Exactly."

"Alright," Damon cuts in. "Time to move. Grey—you and Theo will remove the door as quickly as possible. Then, we go. Once we're done there, we split up into pairs and start gathering the patients. If my suspicions are correct, the doctors will hightail it out of there. They won't want to try to confront all of us. Just be sure to confirm through the phone line which patient you have so Jillian can mark them off the list. We need to ensure we find everyone."

We all nod, exiting the aisle to meet the other dressed members. It's a touch eerie seeing all the devil masks in a circle, but somehow, it also feels... *powerful*. This is what Damon fought for, what we all have prepared for. I'm not going to let him down.

Tonight, we prove to Whitface and Alexander that no matter what they do, we'll continue to stop them.

They can torture us all they want. Shoot us and try to end our lives. Tell us we are insignificant and a danger to society. But we know the truth. We see through their lies.

That's why we are the society—born out of pain and trauma. Sticking together and fighting for the voices who can't speak.

We'll be the monsters they claim us to be. Hell, we'll be the villains too.

But what we won't be... is their victims any longer.

They don't get to use our pain and pasts to fund and fuel their sick and twisted needs. We're stronger than what they make us out to be. And it's time we take them down once and for all.

Cirque des Morts isn't just a group of unhinged psychos.

We're a fucking legacy.

Chapter 27

Avery

As soon as we connect the conference call on the cell phones, Byrone goes ahead and disconnects the cameras. It's time to move. We know from experience that the notification will already be on its way to Whitface, which means he'll soon send word to the lab downstairs.

Grey and Theo have obviously planned their part perfectly, the two of them working in unison to remove the door by the stairwell. Sparks fly from the metal as Grey melts the outline of the door while Theo uses a crowbar to jam it into the lock. Then, they destroy the access pad with the blowtorch, sizzling the plate until it crashes to the floor with a clunk.

Between the weakened doorframe, warped hinges, and ripped wires from the access pad, the two of them pull the door off within minutes, lifting it and placing it against the wall.

At first, I'm a bit confused as to why—why wouldn't they just focus on the access pad like we've done previously? Then it hits me... they are making sure we can get back out. We can't have anything slowing us down, and we have no idea what condition the patients are in. If we need to carry them, stopping to disarm doors and rip out cords is going to eat into valuable seconds. This way, there's an open entrance to get through.

Sure, the guards will be able to get to us a hell of a lot quicker, but that's the risk we're taking. I know they are confident in handling the guards, so weighing that against the patients' conditions and the need to get them to safety wins out.

No one says a word as we fly down the staircase, weaving into the cold darkness. Even with the hoodie and sweats, I can immediately feel the change in temperature when we move underground.

The next door is subjected to the same treatment, much faster than the first, and suddenly, we're on foot toward those large double doors.

My heart beats ridiculously fast in my throat, stomach clenching as they come into view. I can just picture the mass panic on the other side, doctors scrambling to flee through hidden exits while either abandoning patients or ensuring they can never speak again.

A hand grabs mine, squeezing it tight as our group pauses. I don't dare glance up at Damon as he silently reassures me through our gripped palms, not trusting myself to snap. But I clench his hand back while focusing on Grey and Theo as they work on the doors at lightning speed.

I can't help but notice the access pads down here have been updated too—like they expected us to do this. I hate that thought. It means that they still think of themselves as better and stronger than us, not deterred by our efforts. Assholes.

It takes longer than the other two singular doors, and every second that passes, I feel myself creeping closer to the ledge. I need to get inside—a thought I'd never imagine myself saying.

The overwhelming necessity to make sure these patients are okay is sending rushes of adrenaline through my body. But to my surprise, instead of fear, I feel nothing but anger and the urge to avenge them.

I can sense Damon on edge next to me too, his hand in a vise-like grasp with mine, completely still and tense. It's the only sign that he's battling that control inside of himself, and together, we watch the other two work as a perfect team, ripping off the doors at the same time.

There's no care with them like the others, the doors smashing into the concrete ground with a deafening bang. But that's okay—we don't need to be subtle.

White light blinds us for a moment as the lab is exposed, a startled scream making my lips twitch as a flood of people rush in various directions while staring panic-stricken at us.

We must really look an interesting sight—the seven of us standing in the dark corridor, dressed in black with bright red devilish masks. It's obvious they have had a minor bit of warning, but our presence is shocking enough to disturb that.

Moving as one, we all storm inside. Damon lets go of my hand, but it's immediately captured by Grey as he pulls me left at the desk. I don't dare glance back at the room behind me where I suffered at the hands of their doctors.

Cowards. That's all they are.

A few doctors disappear into a doorway which I always thought was just another patient room, but I manage to catch a glimpse through the swinging door.

"It's an exit," I breathe out to Grey, nodding toward the obvious.

He nods. "Let them go for now. We'll deal with them later," he says, stopping as we reach the end of the corridor.

The door at the end of the corridor to our right is wide open, and my whole body jolts violently as I spot the electroshock machine. Except it's slightly different—more shiny. Even the straps on the bed aren't faded. It's been replaced.

I try not to dwell on the fact of what this means, turning to face the patient room door just as Grey kicks it in.

Wood shatters as splinters fly in multiple directions. As I spot a curled up figure in the corner, I completely forget about the room of nightmares, rushing inside.

"Siobhan!" I exclaim, kneeling in front of her. "It's Avery. Are you okay?"

Wide dark blue eyes peer up at me. "Who?"

I recoil, taken aback by her confusion. "Avery... It's me. Remember?"

Siobhan blinks a few times, and it's when I notice her eyes are unfocused.

"She's disorientated," Grey comments. "Move out of the way, little killer."

I step aside to let him in, but as he leans down to reach for her, Siobhan lets out an angry shout, suddenly bursting with energy. I yell for him to watch out, but Grey catches her fist and dodges her foot with ease. "Calm down," he tells her. "We're getting you out of here."

"Don't fucking touch me!"

"Grey." I put my hand on his shoulder. "We need to help calm her."

"We don't have time for that—"

"We make time," I shoot back. "Go to the next room and let me handle this."

Grey snaps his head toward me. "We're not splitting up, little killer. That's the only rule for this."

"We're not splitting up," I argue back. "Just keep checking the rooms next door while I try to calm her down. If we try to force her out, it's going to slow us down. We need everyone to be able to move on their own."

"No—"

"Do it!" I snap, shutting him up. "We're wasting time. She's vulnerable and her mind is in a bad place. Just give me two minutes—that's all I'm asking for."

Grey falls silent for a few seconds, contemplating my demand. Finally, he stands, grabbing my waist and yanking me into him. "You have *two* rooms," he offers. "Then I'm coming back and throwing her over my shoulder."

I nod with a sigh of relief. "Okay. Go."

He hesitates for a split second, glancing between the two of us before hastily heading out of the room. I hear him say something into the cell, likely updating Damon and the others on our—sorry, my—whereabouts.

Quickly, I kneel down again, lifting the mask off my face. If Siobhan's mind is in protective survival mode, seeing the masks is only going to escalate those heightened feelings.

"See," I try again. "It's me, Avery. Your friend. We're here to rescue you."

Siobhan blinks a few times at me, but doesn't speak. I take this as a good sign, holding up my hands in a calming gesture.

"I know what you're feeling right now. They hurt me too," I admit softly. "Which is why we need to get you all back upstairs to safety. I need you to help me. Can you do that?"

"I just..." she pauses. "I want to see my brother."

Remembering back to my first day here, I nod sympathetically. "I know. Your brother would want you to fight, Siobhan. He'd want you to be strong. Do it for him."

Something clicks behind her eyes, the dark blue irises widening. "Avery?"

"Yeah," I breathe out. "Let's get you out of her," I say, offering her my hand.

Slowly, Siobhan reaches for it, letting me pull her up. It appears we're just in time as a shadow darkens the doorway and Grey's voice floats in.

"Time to move, little killer."

"We're coming," I tell him, keeping a hold on Siobhan's hand as I guide her out into the corridor.

It's absolute chaos when I take in my surroundings. Spotting a few patients bundled together near the desk with Louis, Mark, and Andy, I watch as Damon stalks out of a doorway, holding a doctor by the scruff of their white coat. I only have a few seconds to study them, not recognizing them at all, before Damon flings the younger man into the adjacent wall head first.

I jump slightly as his head makes a cracking sound, the doctor falling to the ground in a limp heap. Yep, shit—I think he's dead. Either that or he's going to have one hell of a migraine tomorrow.

The three of us reach the group as I step over the unconscious, maybe dead, doctor. Is it wrong that I have zero fucks to give?

Scanning the group, I let out an exhale of relief at the sight of Eliana in the middle. She seems a little worse for wear, but finding me, I'm offered a tiny, broken smile.

I nudge Siobhan to the group, doing a mental head count. "Is that everyone?" I ask, searching for answers.

"One more," Damon replies, just as Theo emerges from my old room. Except it's not the male patient scampering out ahead that catches my attention, it's the doctor being dragged harshly by Theo.

"Please let me go," she winces painfully, trying to remove Theo's steel-like grip from her forearm.

My body stills as I watch, nerves going completely numb as she stumbles blindly. I glance down at the doctor on the floor before quickly finding the terrified face of the woman trapped by Theo.

"Wait," I say urgently, not sure what Theo's plan is. I don't *think* he'd yeet her into the wall, but then again, I'm not willing to bet on it.

At the sound of my voice, the doctor searches for me, cerulean eyes locking with mine. "A-avery?" she stutters, and I realize I've still got my mask up.

Dr. Melanie Cromwell stares at me as if she's seen a ghost—a nightmare from her past. And suddenly, I'm teleported back to my own nightmares—ice cold baths while begging for help, drugged induced hazes while heels click on the ground around my limp body, visions of Grey with Leah in the library while they study me like some lab rat. She was present for each single horrifying moment I spent down here, constantly boasting about my inhumane treatment being for the greater good.

I was nothing to her but a test subject. There was no sympathy like she's silently begging me for. No mercy. No help.

"You know her?" Theo asks angrily. "Was she one of the doctors who tortured you?"

I can feel Damon and Grey staring at me through their masks waiting for my answer. All I can do is nod slowly, while stepping toward her.

"Dr. Cromwell," I mutter, and I'm not sure if I'm telling them or greeting her.

It's strange being on the other side—in a position of power while she's restrained, scared shitless. Her legs slip on the flooring, heels sliding as she flails to keep balance while Theo holds onto her tightly.

"Avery, please," she begs, only looking at me.

"Why should I help you?" I say emotionlessly. "You didn't help me. You didn't show me any grace or compassion while you were torturing me. So, tell me, Melanie... why should I help you?"

Chapter 28

Theo

I'm well aware I'm bursting capillaries and cutting off the circulation of the fumbling doctor. She's still attempting to dislodge my grip unsuccessfully while speaking to Avery.

It's pissing me off. What gives her the audacity to even breathe in Avery's presence?

I already ended the life of that other miserable, pathetic man who dared lay hands on Aves. Regardless of the situation, I'll happily welcome her death too.

Grey is watching the exchange with growing, silent anger. It's practically filling the air, putting the patients on edge.

A few of them hunch together, the last patient being reunited with the group, moving away from the two of us, and for once, I don't think it's because of me. The way they are watching the doctor with trepidation and fear, it's clear she's made her mark on them as well.

But I control myself, allowing Avery to take charge of the situation. Damon seems to be in the same mindset, folding his arms as he digests their conversation.

That doctor on the ground is clearly dead. From here, I can see blood dripping from his ear canal, and his calvaria is misshaped from hitting the wall. Oh, well—play stupid games, win stupid prizes.

If I'm being honest, the only reason besides Avery that I haven't hurled this idiot into her colleague is because she's a woman. Not that she doesn't deserve it, because she does. I recognize her name from Avery's recall about her time down here. This was one of her main doctors who was assigned to her, responsible for all the vile torture methods our girl endured.

Avery is staring at her with a blank expression, but it's clear from the way her shoulders are tense that this is an unforgettable interaction for her. She's reliving the memories she's pushed down, forced to come face to face with her tormenter.

We knew this was a possibility with bringing her with us, but she was adamant we weren't leaving her behind.

"Avery," Damon says. "We need to start moving. What do you want to do?"

Glancing in his direction, she finally has some emotion break through—confusion. "We need to get the patients out of here," she answers monotonously.

He nods, stepping around the group to place himself in the middle of us. Temporarily blocking Avery's view of the doctor, he puts his hands on her waist.

"What do *you* want to do with *her*?"

"I—I don't know," she mutters with uncertainty.

Damon nods to my surprise, uncharacteristically patient with her. "Grey, take the others and head back upstairs with the patients. I'll be right behind you. Theo, can you handle this with Avery?"

"Of course," I answer without hesitation.

Grey moves in front of Avery when Damon steps aside, whispering something to her before lifting his mask to kiss her forehead.

The doctor starts flailing harder as the patients head toward the doors with Grey and the other men, leaving just the four of us behind.

"Please!" she begs louder. "I was just doing my job."

Damon strolls casually over to us, snapping up the doctor's jaw in his hand to still her. "You had a choice. You have no one to blame for the fact you chose wrong. This is called the consequences of your actions," he growls low, shoving her head back as he releases her. "Avery, I'll be outside waiting. You have five minutes. After that, Theo and I will decide for you because you're not spending a second more down here."

Softening her gaze, she nods at Damon. "Alright."

He heads in the direction of the group, disappearing in the dark corridor. When it's just us, Avery slowly turns to look at the doctor, who's starting pathetically crying and slipping in place.

"I'm sorry," she splutters. "Avery, I'm so very sorry."

"Are you?" Avery asks in disbelief. "Or are you just frightened and saying whatever it is you think I want to hear?"

The doctor shakes her head. "I was wrong. I just wanted to make a difference in the medical field. We wanted to save people—"

"Bullshit," Avery cuts her off. "You knew how much you were hurting me but you still ignored it, quoting it was for *the greater good*. You have no right trying to play God, Melanie. We're not your play toys—we're goddamn human beings. Did you do the same experiments on them?"

To both our astonishment, she answers quickly and shamefully, "Yes."

Avery looks away with disgust, deep in thought. For a moment, I see the hurt appear behind her eyes, but it's extinguished a second later. She gazes over at me, lowering her voice. "Let her go, Theo."

"What?" I snap. "You can't be serious."

"I am. Because I genuinely believe she's learned her lesson. Dr. West was too far gone and corrupt, but Melanie... I think she'll think twice as hard now about her chosen career path."

The doctor wails, and in a moment of frustration, I release her, launching her frame toward the floor. She trips and stumbles, landing in a heap at Avery's feet.

"T-thank you," she stutters, climbing to her feet as fast as her heels will allow her.

Avery straightens up, anger appearing on her face. I start to wonder if she's changed her mind, but then I realize she's allowing the doctor to see her pain, the direct effect of her actions. "Remember I showed you mercy, Dr. Cromwell. Remember that I, someone you deemed unworthy of being treated like a human, showed you compassion when you didn't do the same for me. That's the difference between us. I'm a good person. You are not. But it's my hope that you'll use your degree for good and change lives like you claim you want to do."

"Y-yes," Dr. Cromwell murmurs between sobs. "Yes."

That's all she's able to muster, taking off down the corridor to a door and disappearing from sight.

"You should have let me kill her," I say gruffly. "I would have done it quick and painlessly if you asked."

Avery smiles sadly, silently pulling me into a hug as she wraps her arms around my frame. "We're not like them," she mutters into my chest. "We're better than them."

"I'm not," I answer. "I have no qualms torturing them with their own devices."

She shakes her head amused, stilling when she starts groping the hardness pressing into her. "Is that something in your pocket or are you just happy to see me?"

Laughing, I reach into the hoodie pocket, lifting out the blowtorch. "Both."

Avery stares at the blowtorch for a moment. "What are the chances of the entire building burning down if we set the lab on fire?"

"Judging by the sprinklers along the ceiling, probably minimal if we do it properly."

"Good thing I'm well versed in fire," she murmurs, grabbing the blowtorch from my hand, turning on her heel and heading down the corridor.

Amused, I lift the cell phone from my other pocket to my ear. "Did you hear that, Damon?"

A sigh filters through the receiver. "Loud and clear unfortunately. Make it quick—we need to get her back upstairs. Connor has just given word that some guards are on their way. I'll distract them."

Following Avery, she heads into the room with the electroshock equipment—the same room I killed the other doctor in. Poetic, if you ask me.

She starts going through the cupboards, searching through chemicals until she pulls a bottle down. "I don't know what this is but it has a flammable symbol on it. That's a good sign, I think."

Dousing the chair and machine in liquid, I stand back as she fumbles with the blowtorch, pressing buttons until she finds the right combination and the flame shoots out. Doing one last check at the roof to confirm there's a sprinkler above, she lights the liquid on fire, quickly stepping back.

It engulfs in flames rapidly, the room lighting up as heat starts to warm up our skin. Avery laughs under her breath, the sound music to my ears as she gives me a smile over her shoulder.

"We should grab the files on the way out—just anything to prove what was happening here."

I nod. "Come on, pyro. The last thing I need is to be hauling your unconscious body out of here from smoke inhalation."

As we exit the room, Avery pouring a trail of liquid along the floor, I spot something out of my peripheral vision. Spinning around, I lift an eyebrow at the person standing in the walkway, watching us with interest.

"What the fuck are you doing here?" I snap, making Avery turn.

"Rian..." she gasps, squeezing the chemical bottle.

Crossing his arms, I narrow my eyes as Rian Thatcher stares at us unbothered. "Always causing trouble, aren't you?"

I knew this motherfucker was up to no good. Pivoting closer to Avery, I step in front of her, painfully aware of the building flames behind us. I'm going to kill this asshole because judging by his stance and seemingly different persona, he's not a patient escaping—he's down here willingly to confront us.

"What the hell are you doing here?" Avery asks, moving closer to me to get a better look at him. "Get the fuck out of here, Rian."

He smiles knowingly at her. "I plan on doing so, but you won't be leaving. Though, I was hoping to just find you, Avery. But two for the price of one? I'm not complaining."

"You won't touch a single hair on her head," I warn. "You've made a grave mistake following us."

Thatcher laughs. "Did you even realize I was following until now? You've lost your touch. I was warned all about the *great Theo* but to be honest, you've been quite the letdown. Did you think I didn't notice you following me the other night?"

Avery glances over at me with confusion. "What is he talking about?"

"Never mind," I tell her. "He's just a dead man walking."

"Cute," Thatcher replies. "But the only one who will be laid to rest is you pair. After all, that's what I've been paid to do."

I fucking knew it.

We suspected he wasn't an actual patient and this confirms it. Avery tenses next to me, angrily blurting out, "Alexander."

"Smart girl," he replies. "I was just meant to keep a close watch on you all, but then you had to go and get married. Well, now that the Will is sorted, there's nothing stopping me from executing our plan."

"How the hell do you know about that?" Avery snaps. "Who are you?"

"That's not important," he replies coolly. "All you need to know is that Alexander sends his condolences and goodbyes. Don't worry. I won't rip your head off like I did with the other one. I hope you enjoyed the little gift I left you."

"You did that to Teddy?" Avery gasps. "What the fuck is wrong with you?"

Thatcher shrugs. "She knew too much. Started putting her nose where it didn't belong. Just like you."

I'm rather aware of the heat creeping up behind us, sweat starting to form on my skin. Grabbing Avery's arm, I pull her closer to me as I step away from the flames behind us, noticing that the sprinklers haven't turned on yet. "I hope your affairs are in order because I'm about to send you to meet the Devil," I shoot back, charging toward him.

Thatcher whips out a knife from his pocket, but it doesn't deter me. I continue at him, kicking him square in the gut. He stumbles backwards, expression turning angry before he lunges at me, swinging aggressively.

I can hear Avery shouting behind me as the two of us start grappling, my fingers wrapped painfully around his wrist as I try to get him to drop the knife. Finally, it clatters to the floor as he releases it, his other fist connecting with my jaw.

I have to hand it to him, he's much stronger than I gave him credit for. But I still manage to throw him into the wall. He's back on me a second later, hurling blows into my ribcage while I pull him into a chokehold.

"Theo!" Avery calls out, and I gaze at her out of the corner of my eye. She's looking at the flames with wide eyes, the heat and smoke getting closer and starting to pool along the ceiling.

We have to get out of here—now.

Ignoring the blows to my side, I lock hands, strangling the other man. He hits harder in an attempt to free himself, but a second later, he lets out a pained cry, arms dropping to clutch his side. Avery is suddenly in my line of vision, holding up a bloodied knife as she surveys Thatcher's side.

Shoving him into the wall, I follow her direction, spotting blood oozing out of his side as he clutches it and stumbles.

"Aves, let's *go*," I growl, reaching for her.

"Not yet," she says back, stunning me as irritation builds. I need to get her the fuck out of here.

But the irritation quickly vanishes, replaced with surprise as she picks up the discarded chemical bottle, spraying Thatcher with it.

He splutters and coughs. "What the fuck are you doing?!"

"Sending my own condolences," Avery replies without hesitation, suddenly kicking him in the upper thigh just below the hole in his side.

Thatcher lets out a pained yell, hitting the ground with a thud. My eyebrows shoot up as I realize what's about to happen, hastily gripping Avery's arm and pulling her toward the exit. She stops again, and as I'm about to snap at her, I watch as she grabs an armful of files from the desk, just as Thatcher's screams start filling the room.

Avery and I pause as the fire engulfed man runs violently into walls as he tries to put it out to no avail. When he starts staggering in our direction, I grab her forearm and pull her toward the door, water hitting our heads as the sprinklers finally trigger.

But it's too late for the man, his screams still echoing behind us as we rush toward the stairwell, just as Damon reappears at the doorway.

"What the fuck happened?" he snaps, lifting his mask, eyes darting between the pair of us.

"Your father happened," Avery replies fiercely. "Now let's see them rebuild after we've burned their fucking lab down."

Chapter 29

Avery

Thankfully Theo was correct. The sprinklers being activated stopped any real damage to the ground floor levels, though from what we estimate, the lab is pretty much destroyed.

Oh, no. What a shame.

Besides the equipment which I ensured was out of action for a second time, several patient rooms and the main hallway have suffered too much damage and will need proper repairs. From what Damon explained, the contract only pertains to the medical equipment, so even if Lilydale was able to replace it, they would also be solely responsible for the facility repairs.

It could be worse, but since the underground levels are basically just a pit of concrete, the structure held up well so we're safe up here.

The biggest risk we have is Alexander trying to force my hand. I've already been forced to sign his bullshit document giving him access to Damon's trust fund for the purpose of fueling Lilydale's costs, but hopefully, we've done enough damage that it will cause legal issues. Likewise, now that we've destroyed the equipment again, it may have jeopardized the contract.

If Alexander and Arthur want to continue their torture clinic, they will have to outlay a lot of money to get it fixed. And that shit takes time. But if there's anything rich people hate more than poor people, it's having to spend too much money.

I suppose if I'm being honest though, the lab is probably the least of my problems. Rian made it clear that he was ordered to kill me. There's no doubt in my mind that the order came from Alexander—he wants me out of the way to steal my shares and fuck Damon over. We're all on edge now. While the guys had their suspicions about Rian from the start, we have no idea if he was just a disguise. For all we know there could be more of Alexander's spies hiding in Lilydale, waiting to do his bidding.

"I can practically see your mind running a hundred miles an hour," Grey murmurs from behind me.

We're curled up on his bed, resting while everyone else enjoys free time. Damon and Theo are together somewhere, working on finding out information.

"I'm getting a little sick of being a constant target," I grumble quietly. "But even more so that Theo was nearly hurt because of it."

Arms tighten around my torso, pulling me further against him. "He can handle himself," Grey answers, burying his face into the side of my neck. "We're more worried about you."

I laugh softly. "I can handle myself too."

Grey hums in agreement. "Yes, you can my little pyromaniac."

"Not just a maniac?"

"You?" he laughs. "No. You're too sweet to be a fully fledged psycho."

"I beg to differ. I set someone on fire. Well, twice. It's becoming a bad habit."

"I'm inclined to disagree," he murmurs. "Because I think it makes you a good girl."

I roll my eyes even though he can't see it. "Of course *you'd* think that."

Grey leans forward, reaching his hand down my body to skim my skirt up with his fingers. I glance down at the words marked into my skin on my inner thigh.

"Mine," Grey whispers, reading it aloud.

"Yours."

Brushing my hair gently from my shoulders, he places a kiss along the junction of my neck. "You're marked by all of us now. My scar on your thigh, Theo's ink on your body, and Deadman's heartbeat on your ribcage."

"You've taken over inside too," I tell him. "You own every part of me."

"Good," he replies against my skin, trailing his lips along the top of my shoulder. "But it's still not enough." His fingers play with the hem of my skirt, slowly inching toward my inner thigh. Slowly, he pulls my underwear aside, dipping his finger in.

Arching against him, I turn my head to find his face. "Oh? What else did you have in mind?" I ask breathlessly as his finger slides inside, curling to stroke my pussy.

"Ride me, little killer," he orders softly.

Well, when he says it like that, how can I refuse?

Turning around, I place a hand on his chest, pushing him back into the bed as I straddle his hips. Grey pushes his pants down, just far enough for his cock to spring out while I line myself up. Pulling the cotton aside, I slowly sink down on his length, the two of us moaning as he fills me completely. When my hips are flush against his, he grabs my waist, locking eyes with me.

"You feel so fucking good."

I nod, biting my bottom lip as I roll my hips. "So do you."

"This body was made to take me," he growls deeply. "So fucking perfect."

I push up on my knees and drop back down, my pussy eagerly engulfing his hard cock. Grey lets me take control, deciding the pace as he helps guide me up and down. Fingers dance across my skin to find their way under my skirt. His thumb draws precise circles around my clit while I ride him into the bed, the familiar rush of building pressure gathering in my lower abdomen.

"I need more," I say with a quiet groan, and Grey responds instantly, thrusting his hips upwards into me. A tiny cry escapes my lips at the sudden deepness nestled in me, the sound of our skin slapping together as he takes over, spearing into me from below.

"I could stay in this perfect little cunt forever," he murmurs, still playing with my clit.

My hands rest on his toned chest, using him for balance as he fucks me hard. "Then stay," I say clenching around him.

Grey pulls me down, slamming his lips to mine. "Don't tempt me."

I kiss him back, rocking my hips slowly. Our tongues find each other, stroking in time with his thrusts as he starts moving again.

"I'm going to come," I moan into his mouth.

"Then fucking come for me," he says between kisses as he starts fucking me harder and deeper.

It sends me—no, throws me—over the edge a few seconds later, my whole body shaking as I cry out into his mouth. He doesn't slow down, dragging my orgasm out of me as our hips smash together. Just as I start to come down from my high, Grey makes a deep throaty groan, stilling as he shoots his release into me while bruising my waist.

"Stay," he murmurs when I make a move to crawl off him. "I want to stay like this for a bit longer."

I lay down on his chest, our bodies still joined. I can hear his heartbeat through his chest as his arms tighten around my back.

It's exactly what I need right now. Because for a brief moment, life feels perfect again. Which can only mean one thing.

It's about to come crashing down on top of us.

"Christopher lodged a complaint," Damon tells us as we sit at the table eating dinner. "I gave him the files that Avery grabbed."

Theo is on my right, one hand holding a fork while the other rests on my leg. Damon is on the other side, ignoring his plate of food while Grey sits across from us, listening closely.

"That's good," I answer. "Do you think they will do anything about it?"

"Let's hope so," Damon answers. "Because Arthur is going to lash out at any second. Speaking of which; the patients are doing well apparently. Dr. Markel is treating them alongside Christopher. No permanent injuries thankfully."

"Physically, at least," I mutter sadly. "Mentally they are probably fucked up."

Theo squeezes my leg. "They will be okay," he says, surprising me.

"That's the most caring thing you've ever said about the other patients," I point out, amused.

"Don't get used to it," he shoots back. "I'm just telling you what you need to hear."

Grey nods. "He's right though. They will be fine. It will probably take them some time to process everything, but at least they are in the hands of Christopher now. He's no Freud but he's a damn sight better than Elsher."

"You got that right," I mumble in agreement. "Where is he anyway?"

"Probably hiding and licking his wounds," Damon answers. "Or Arthur's. I have no doubt that they are planning their next move and trying to salvage things."

"Good luck to them," I reply, pushing my plate of plain pasta away. "It's a lot of money to fork out. Even with the trust fund and Alexander's ability to access it, they won't want to. They are too greedy."

"Agreed," Damon says. "But it means they will turn their sights to us. We need to stay on alert. It's likely there's other people here that are willing to do their dirty work for them."

And by dirty work, he means kill me. Or any of us, really. Damon and I are public enemy number one.

"We need to keep Avery with us at all times," Grey comments. "Even at night."

"Implement the *ASS schedule* again?" I joke.

Grey grins at me. "Fuck that. Literally and metaphorically. You'll be staying with one of us. We'll need a new roster.

Unless of course these two assholes are happy to just let you stay in my bed every night."

"Not a chance in hell," Theo replies. "Aves can stay with me and the pair of you can cuddle."

"Damon cuddle?" I snort. "Not sure he's capable of such a feat."

Damon cocks an eyebrow at me. "Do you want me to cuddle you?"

"Is that code for strangulation?" I tease. "Because yes either way."

His lips twitch, fighting back a smirk. "It can be arranged. I'll leave you to question which one."

"He's after my wealth," I tell Grey. "Cashing in on the life insurance policy. Oh, wait—I left it all to his dad."

The three of them simultaneously put down their forks, glaring at me.

"Oops, too soon?"

"Theo, control my wife," Damon says. "That smart mouth of hers is going to get her in trouble."

The hand on my leg shifts higher. "I don't think she knows how to stay out of trouble."

I throw Theo a side eye. "You're one to talk."

"Speaking of talking," Grey interjects. "Perhaps it's time we tell the other patients what's going on. We need everyone to stay on alert and the only way we can ensure their safety is to have them on board."

"Will they even believe us?" I ask warily. "I mean, when you think about it, it sounds outlandish."

Grey nods. "It does, but now that we have nearly a dozen patients who have been subjected to their bullshit, it's more believable."

I frown. "Maybe we should have Dr. Smith help with this."

Damon deadpans. "He's not going to tell patients what is secretly happening behind closed doors."

"Maybe not," I agree. "But with some of their conditions, it could be upsetting. They need support. The last thing we need is for a bunch of struggling patients to lose their shit."

"She has a point," Grey says. "He doesn't have to confirm or deny it, but we can't risk the whole facility being triggered. People could get hurt."

"People are already hurt," Theo replies, unfazed. "Give them some credit. Most of them have never been given the opportunity to be in control of their own situations. If you tell them, while we run the risk that they might react badly, many may appreciate the gesture of being given information."

"You sound like Dr. Smith," I joke. "Who are you and what have you done with Theo?"

Theo narrows his eyes at me. "It's as if you like my angry side. Want me to practice on Grey?"

"Try your luck, asshole," comes the reply from across the table.

I hold up my hands in defeat. "Alright, wise one. Let's fill Dr. Smith in and start warning patients. Maybe it will be better if we do it one by one, rather than making a loud announcement where it will get back to Whitface."

Damon nods. "I agree. We'll arrange a meeting tonight and have the other Cirque des Morts members assist. That way we can get it done faster and all have the same story."

"Thank fuck," I breathe out, wrinkling my nose at my plate. "Tony's cooking has spoiled me. I definitely need the energy from better food if we're about to open the flood gates."

Chapter 30

Grey

There's never been a better time to be me.

During the meeting last night, we agreed to split the patients and created a list of which people we were responsible for explaining the clusterfuck that is Lilydale.

Little killer had voiced some concerns about patients' willingness to hear us out, but I wasn't worried about that. Especially since I've already completed my list.

When you tell people you need to speak to them, most will agree—either out of the incessant need to know information, or fear of repercussions if they refuse.

I kept it short and sweet, merely providing the bare minimum that we agreed was necessary. We were correct about the former missing patients though. People were much easier to convince now that missing patients were back and looking in bad shape. It made our story believable. Arthur hasn't helped his cause either. Turns out he's not well liked among the facility, even to most of the staff. No surprise, really. When you're a walking dickhead with a chip on your shoulder, you're bound to rub people the wrong way.

I'm using my free time to update our beloved *ASS Schedule*. It's fairly simple—an orderly rotation, but naturally, I'm first up.

Avery spent last night in Damon's room. Both are in good moods today despite everything, so no doubt they are also a little tired.

And speak of the Devil and he shall appear.

"Finished already?" Damon asks, strolling into the library.

I nod, grinning. "Piece of cake. And the few that looked as though they were about to enter into a panic attack, I provided stale cigarettes. See—told you they'd come in handy."

"Yes, but I believe it was for bribery."

"I bribed them not to lose their shit. It's a win-win if you ask me."

Damon sits down next to me, running a hand through his hair. "Avery is with Theo, I assume?"

"I think she was worried that he might frighten the patients, so they are tackling their lists together."

"A likely excuse."

I raise an eyebrow at him. "What's got you... smiling?"

By smiling, I mean he looks less murderous than usual. I could chalk it up to his bedtime extracurriculars, but this seems different. He actually seems a touch relaxed.

"Christopher came and spoke to me," he states. "The board is officially under investigation. Which means—"

"They can't touch the funds even if they wanted to," I finish, surprised. "Well, this is great news."

Damon nods slowly. "It is," he agrees. "Although, I'm expecting backlash. There's no telling how this investigation will go. If they are good at hiding their paper trial then nothing might come of it. But if they decide there has been wrongdoing..."

Leaning back in my chair, I process the unfinished sentence. We didn't quite plan for this. To be fair, anything is probably better than the current situation. But that leaves the question...

What will happen to Lilydale and us patients?

"I guess we just wait and see," I finally reply.

It's a little unnerving wondering about the possibilities. There's no precedent for the situation. What would happen to us all? It's not as if they can just release one hundred patients into the community. As for an alternate setting, facilities are at capacity. That's how Alexander was able to even instigate this whole scheme. He was 'doing a favor to the community'.

"At the moment, I've instructed the society members to keep a close watch on patients assigned to Elsher. While there's no immediate risk to them being subjected to experimentation, I don't trust him not to act out because of the situation. Christopher provided the list so we're just telling them all to be on guard during sessions."

The information makes me realize that somehow I ended up with a list entirely created with Christopher's patients. I can't help but feel it was deliberate—same with Theo's. The last thing we need is to scare the patients into blurting out information to Elsher. Deadman really does think of everything.

As I start to think back to the lists, it dawns on me that Avery *does* have some of Elsher's patients on hers. Smart move. The best way to gain allies is to share a common enemy. I actually think Avery may hate Elsher more than the rest of us. He seems hellbent on damaging her psyche, always telling her she's to blame for her behavior and personality.

She's perfect, just the way she is.

I can't wait to splatter his blood all over his office floor.

"Avery is with me tonight," I advise, tapping my fingers on the desk over my invisible schedule. "Theo tomorrow night. Then you'll have your turn again."

"No surprise there," he replies unbothered. "Try not to break her. We need to stay focused."

"You don't give me enough credit."

Damon laughs. "Don't I?"

Before I can respond, the library door opens and I glance over as Avery and Theo enter hand in hand. She gives me a warm smile, tucking a piece of paper into her pocket.

"My list is nearly done," she exclaims. "Theo's too."

"Good girl," I wink, beaming when she blushes.

Theo rounds the table behind me, using the opportunity to smack me up the back of the head.

"Ow, what was that for asswipe?"

"No reason. I just felt like it," he says calmly. "Damon," he greets.

"Theo. Always a displeasure."

Avery groans into her hands. "Stop beating each other up."

"I'm innocent," I gasp. "Control your boyfriend, Little Killer."

"Yeah, Aves. Control me," Theo responds.

She rubs her temple, turning her attention to Damon. "Want to take a trip to the morgue?"

"Well now, that's just mean," I grumble. "You know how I feel about morgue sex."

"You're only saying that because it's apparently Avery's favorite place to fuck," Damon says coolly.

"I didn't see you complaining," she shoots back playfully. "Besides I'm not the one who likes to chase through the dark hallways."

Damon smirks. "Fond memories."

Laughing, Avery relaxes, glancing between the three of us. "So, what now?"

"Now that you are both here, I do have an update," Damon tells us. "I did some digging into the board to see what we could find in the hopes that the investigation does the same."

"Oh?" I ask, interested. "Tell me you found something juicy."

Damon raises an eyebrow at me. "If by juicy you mean Rian Thatcher having connections to a board member, then yes."

"What?" Avery gasps. "Who?"

"Henry Thatcher. One of father's old friends. Rian's parental information was excluded from his transfer file. It didn't raise any red flags because it's not uncommon for patients to have missing details or have been through the foster system. But it's now apparent that he was planted here after Hallman's death to spy on us."

"We suspected this," Theo says. "I'm not surprised."

Damon nods. "Neither am I. Hopefully, the agency connects the dots and looks into why a board member's son was placed into Lilydale."

"Besides you," Avery points out. "Surely, two instances are grounds for review."

"My father has documentation to support my admission, even if they are forged bullshit," Damon comments. "But I'm willing to bet that Rian's documentation was also fabricated. I doubt he had the same volatile history with his father though."

Avery pauses. "What did you say his name was again?"

"Henry Thatcher."

I watch as her face pulls into a deep look of concentration before it's as if a light bulb goes off.

"I remember him," she answers quietly. "He was at the board meeting. I thought he looked familiar."

"What else can you recall?" I ask.

She thinks back. "He knew about the marriage. He mentioned it was restricting their access to financial resources. The asshole also witnessed my Will."

"Makes sense," Damon says annoyed. "He handles the board's financials."

Theo shakes his head. "What kind of parental figure would let their kid into a place like this?"

"Mine," Damon answers without missing a beat. "All the board members would do it."

Avery frowns. "Should we be checking their backgrounds? Make sure there's no other family members lurking around Lilydale?"

"It wouldn't hurt to check," I chime in. "Though, Rian was the only new patient in some time. It's likely if someone else had infiltrated the patients we would have already picked up on it."

"We'll look into it anyway," Damon states. "Just to err on the side of caution. My father knows no limits when it comes to these matters."

Strumming her fingers along the table, Avery turns to Damon. "Is Dr. Smith here today?"

"Yes," he confirms. "Why?"

"I have an idea," she murmurs, standing. "Grey, will you come with me?"

Grinning, I stand. "Of course. You're mine today, anyway."

She rolls her eyes with a laugh. "Yes, yes. The *ASS Schedule*. How convenient."

"Are you going to fill me in on this idea?" Damon asks, irritated.

"Nope," she replies coolly. "Better you don't know yet."

I can practically see steam billowing from his ears at the lack of information provided, so I quickly grab her hand, winking at Deadman. "Relax," I tell him. "Curiosity killed the cat. You'll find out soon no doubt."

Laughing, I let Avery drag me out of the library as Damon stares daggers at me. I give him a little wave and flip Theo the middle finger before we disappear into the corridor.

"Oh, you're playing with fire," I smirk.

Avery smiles, linking our fingers. "He'll survive. It will do him some good to be kept in the dark for a while. Learn some patience or something."

"Patience isn't his virtue."

"Don't I know it..."

When we arrive at Christopher's door, Avery knocks once before opening it. He glances up from his desk, smiling politely.

"And what do I owe for this visit?"

Pulling me inside, Avery closes the door behind us. I lead her over to the seats, motioning for her to sit on my lap. I half expect her to refuse in the presence of Christopher, but she takes a seat on me.

"I need you to help with a favor," she says casually. "I'm just not sure how to go about it."

Christopher closes his laptop screen, giving her his full attention. "Go on."

Avery clears her throat, concentrating. "Alexander made me sign a Will that he had drafted. He also made me sign the awful document advising I was in agreement with him so our shares can be combined to overrule Damon's majority percentage."

"Right," Christopher remarks, following along.

She glances at me over her shoulder. "We have two choices here. Either we have Dr. Smith sign off and say that I'm not lucid to make decisions, thus invalidating my signature on both of Alexander's documents."

"That could jeopardize the marriage certificate," I point out. "They will argue that if you aren't lucid now, then you weren't lucid enough to enter into a marital contract."

"Not to mention," Dr. Smith cuts in. "Considering I was the one to officially marry you, they will question my licenses."

Avery nods, turning back to Christopher. "Then our second option," she starts. "Is to prepare a new Will that overrides the one I signed for Alexander."

Interesting.

Christopher frowns at her. "If he gets wind of it..."

"He won't," Avery answers. "You will keep it somewhere secure. But it's a backup plan, just in case something happens to me. Lily was good at protecting Damon. I want to do the same."

"No one is going to touch you," I growl.

She twists her body, placing her arm behind my head and strokes the nape of my neck. "I know," she says softly. "But it's a safeguarding plan. At the moment, it's something we can do to override Alexander's motives. This is bigger than just me. We need to make sure we protect our legacy."

Our legacy... she really is one of us now.

I had no doubts. I knew she'd become this person. I saw the potential behind those sad eyes that first day in Charmaine's class. There was something about her that stood out, something different than the other patients that walked through those doors. I knew she'd be mine—knew she'd become one of the strongest people I'd ever met.

"I can type it up," Christopher offers. "I have some spare time."

"Good," Avery answers sharply without breaking eye contact with me. "Grey can be my second witness. Or Dr. Markel. I just have one condition."

"Yes?"

She smiles at me. "We find a way to incorporate Grey and Theo into it. All three of them are my life. It's only fair they are mine in death too."

Chapter 31

Avery

*** One Year Ago ***

Crash.

My choked up scream is drowned out by the shattering sound of the beer bottle smashing above my head. I only just managed to duck out of the way—this time at least. You'd think with all the practice I'd be getting quicker, but I'm just so exhausted I find it hard to do anything now. The only thing keeping me going is the natural urge to run. I don't even think about it, my body just springs into action, sheltering and doing everything possible to protect.

But I can't keep running. I'm tired. And he always catches me anyway so, what's the point?

I tried to convince myself that it was just easier to take it. On the good days, it usually blows over pretty quickly and then I'm rewarded with the eerie silence I've grown to love.

This is a bad day.

It feels wrong to try to categorize my father's moods into good and bad—there's nothing but anger and hatred. Some days it's just better than others. Some days, I come out of it almost intact.

Please walk away... please.

"Worthless... exactly like your mother."

I bite down on the back of my lip, staying quiet until he walks away. But when I don't respond or acknowledge his words, he storms toward me.

"Don't... please, don't," I beg desperately, pressing myself flat against the wall behind me. Dad lets out an ill-tempered shout before grabbing a fistful of my hair and slamming me face first into the ground.

A pained squeak forces its way past my vocal restraint as my hands and knees land heavily on the broken shards of glass.

Part of me wants to call for help. I stopped screaming for help a long time ago. No one ever came. And all it did was make him more upset.

"Shut up!" He roars, spit flying into my face as his fist connects with my jaw. "Shut the fuck up, Avery!"

How? How do I make it stop?

I curl into a ball as I try to shield myself from him, but that just rewards me with a kick into my stomach.

How?

There's no humanly way to stop the pained cry that slips out, no amount of strength I can muster. It still hurts so much from last week. The bruises on my lower abdomen and thighs are starting to turn that sickly shade of yellow instead of black, but everything still screams in agony.

The doctors at the hospital said it would take weeks before I fully healed. I know they were talking about the bruises and internal damage because I'll never emotionally heal from this—never recover from what he let his friend do to me.

I screamed so much that night that I lost my voice. I blame myself. If I hadn't been so loud, struggled so much, maybe it wouldn't have hurt like this.

All I remember is there were tiny little dots on the hospital ceiling. I counted them, one by one. The doctor treating me said something about reproductive scarring and inflammation but it sounded like a voice in a thick blanket of fog.

I'll likely never bear children now. Not that I'd ever condemn someone into my life, but still...

He stole it from me, and all Dad did was watch TV in the other room, completely unbothered. The volume kept increasing, the only sign that he could even hear my screams.

The doctors tried to make me feel better by telling me that at least I'll be able to have sex again—probably without pain. That alone made me feel sick because I'll never let anyone fucking touch me again. He stole my virginity, he stole my womanhood. No one will ever steal from me again. I'd rather be dead.

More pain erupts from my scalp as I'm dragged across the floor. But luck must finally find me because suddenly, he lets me go with a drop, trudging over to his cell phone to answer a call.

I block out the conversation, doing my best to stay completely still, hoping I'm now a forgotten afterthought. Footsteps move toward me and I whimper, the stench of beer hitting me in the face.

"I'm meeting Marty at the tavern. Do something useful and clean this fucking shit up. Or maybe I'll just bring him here again..."

My body trembles violently at the threat, not at all stopping even as the front door slams closed and I hear his car take off down the street. He's going to fucking kill someone—if not me, then someone on the road. He doesn't even have a driver's license anymore after multiple DUIs.

That's why Martin drove him back last week... That's how he got into my bedroom while I was asleep.

No. No, no. I can't do it. I can't do it again.

Forcing myself up from the floor, I scan the living room slowly, taking in all the mess. Once upon a time there were some better memories here, but I don't remember them anymore. Did they ever really exist? I can't be sure.

This house holds more tears than an airport, more pain than a hospital. Trauma is etched into the walls, my screams embedded in plaster. There's still permanent marks from where Mom killed herself to escape and I found her lifeless, blue body.

I never understood. Why am I not enough for *him*? Why wasn't I enough to make her stay?

Why am I just *not enough*? I just don't deserve to be loved—by anyone, let alone by more than one person.

A wave of calmness washes over me, my entire body suddenly feeling numb.

It ends now—all of it.

I'm not cut out for this life. I miss my mom. I miss Paige. No one here will miss me, so why even fight?

He's broken me, just like he broke Mom. But I won't let him break anyone else ever again in his house.

I'm going to burn it to the fucking ground. And maybe, just maybe, I'll find my happy ending in the ashes.

*** Present Day ***

I jump as another random scream fills the room. There's the sound of clattering food utensils as people hastily glance around to locate the source of the noise, before the chorus of echoing screams start.

One after the other. Again.

It's been this way all day. I'm starting to think we underestimated the situation. Perhaps we weren't prepared at all.

Slowly, it seems, the more the news sinks in about the truth behind Lilydale, the more people are processing it. Except... by processing it, I mean badly.

Someone stands up at their table, pointing toward a guard and hurling jumbled up words.

"Fuck," I hiss, sending Damon a panicky look. "It's happening again. What do we do?"

He drops his head and starts fiddling with something under the table. "I'll let Christopher know."

"The guards are moving in," Grey remarks.

"Should we do something?" I ask urgently, gripping the table.

It's too late. The guards grab the girl, sending her even further into a state of panic.

Fuck—this is all our fault. We've caused mass fear and it's a domino effect. People are spiraling at concerning rates, making it obvious that the patients know something. Now that the boulder has started rolling down the hill, we can't stop it.

"Christopher will intervene," Damon says, but there's an edge of concern to his tone that has me worried.

Dr. Smith surely can't handle all of this. Patients are dropping and losing control more and more quickly, inundating the staff as they try to calm them. Everyone is nervous, and when two other unrelated people across the room suddenly start physically fighting, I recoil in my seat.

I clap my hands over my ears, trying to drown out the sounds of flesh being hit and accompanying screams. It's still too raw, too triggering.

And we did this.

"Hey," Theo murmurs, lightly gripping my wrist to pull it away from my ear. "Breathe."

"I hate this," I respond quietly.

He nods. "Look at me."

I do, his dark eyes capturing my attention and instantly starting to ease the sickening pull in my stomach.

"Do you want to get out of here?" Grey asks, leaning into me. "We can skip class after lunch if you need some quiet space."

Shaking my head, I offer a small smile. "I'm fine," I lie, dropping my shaky hands into my lap. "It's better we are there in case anything happens."

Grey looks like he wants to argue with me but just kisses my cheek while Theo rubs comforting circles on my wrist.

"Arthur is probably going to step in soon," Damon comments. "He'll want to gain the upper hand on the situation, particularly with the looming investigation."

"This is when they need to show up," I mumble. "To see the damage."

Damon sighs. "It could be weeks before they fully investigate. And likely, they'll start with the board and all the legal side. This," he motions to some more patients being dragged out of the hall. "Isn't concrete enough evidence to back our story."

"We can't just let this continue," I argue. "People are getting hurt."

Grey rubs my arm. "I know, but this is still a damn sight better than having them downstairs. It's sad, but most people here are probably used to this on some level. They can survive it—they were unfortunately trained to do so."

"That's fucked up," I murmur dazed. Because it's the truth, isn't it? All the times my father laid hands on me. I learned to deal with the physical pain. In a twisting act of surprise, it was almost an escape from the mental anguish I dealt with. Scars fade and bruises heal, but mentally? You can't escape that pain. It lingers long after the physical touches are gone.

"There's the bell," Damon snaps with frustration. "Are you three going to be alright?"

It's nice that he's asking all of us when we all know he's aimed it at me. I nod, forcing a smile as I glance over at him. "We'll be fine. Let's go, Grey."

Famous last words.

We were not fine. Not in the slightest.

Charmaine does her best to placate the class, but realistically, all she can do is dodge the flying desks and fists as patients tackle each other like wild animals.

Guards rush in to assist, prying people off each other and dragging them away, but things continue to escalate.

There's not a big enough ratio of guards to patients, so I'm not surprised when we're quickly screamed at that free time has been cancelled. Everyone is ordered back to their rooms straight away, the more volatile patients forced by guards while the rest of us follow by dorm.

I throw a quick wide-eyed glance at Grey as I'm herded with a group of girls to escort back to our section of the facility, mouthing that I'll use my cell to contact him.

He angrily scans the guards surrounding us, completely oblivious to the chaos as people shout and kick around him. I silently beg him not to do anything, not to draw attention or lash out despite his obvious overwhelming need to get to me and keep me safe.

Thankfully, he remains calm, our eyes staying locked until we're pulled out of sight in different directions.

I need something else to focus on, so I take in the group I'm with, sucking in a breath when I spot Eliana. I shuffle toward her until we're walking side by side.

"Are you okay?" I ask, noticing her usual smiley face is absent.

She turns her head to face me, steps never faltering. "I don't know," she says honestly.

All I can do is nod in acknowledgment. Because like I said: we're not fine. No one is.

We've sealed the fate of every patient in here. And we have no idea what that means.

Chapter 32

Avery

"Did anyone notice all the fucking roses?" Grey grumbles, sitting down on the end of Damon's bed. "There's fresh roses everywhere. The damn classrooms, the bathrooms, the hall. They even put some in the fucking library."

"Arthur is trying to send a message," Damon answers while stroking my leg. We sprawled out with our backs against the wall. "He's fucking with us, a warning because of the patients starting to riot."

The guys managed to break me out of my room yesterday once the sun went down. We stayed in constant communication until then, and even though everyone is still confined to their rooms, Grey makes a valid point.

There's suddenly roses everywhere. Appearing out of the blue since yesterday, I can't help but agree with Damon. Whittingham knows we'd never stay separated, intentionally placing them around the facility for us to see. It's a message all right—we're still walking free but he's got something planned.

But still... what's the deal with the fucking roses?

Grey folds his arms. "He's about to fuck around and find out when my fist caves in his face. Hell, maybe I'll do a Uno reverse and slice off his head like he had that asshole do to Teddy. I could wear it as a hat."

"And hide that hair you think is so precious? Unlikely," Theo speaks up from the corner, one leg pulled to his chest.

The comment sends me into a fit of maniacal laughter. If I don't find humor in things right now, I may just slip into some abyss from all the mind fucks and games.

Grey shoots an offended scowl at Damon, who too, is smirking at the comment.

"Don't be mad at me," Damon shrugs, squeezing my knee. "She's the one cackling like a hyena."

I straighten up, pushing his hand off me playfully. "I beg your pardon. How is this suddenly my fault?"

Damon cocks his head to the side with a smirk. "You know I love it when you *beg*."

"Of course that's all you choose to focus on," I mumble. "But at least I'm not a *docile sheep* now."

Shaking his head, he turns back to Grey. "Did you find Christopher?"

"Yeah," he confirms. "Deep in a session with a patient who was screeching at a level that only bats can hear. Something about conspiracy and this place being a gimmick."

I shake my head. "I hope Alexander gives him a raise for having to deal with all this bullshit."

"He doesn't need a raise," Damon says. "A new personality maybe."

"What's the time anyway? I have a session with him this morning," I ask.

Grey pulls out his cell. "You've got about twenty minutes. I told Connor where you are so he can be the one to come collect you. We'll walk with you though."

"You're not staying for my session though," I point out. "How else am I meant to dissect the clusterfuck that is my life if you're too busy taunting the psychiatrist."

"Consider it training," Grey grins. "It's improving his skills."

I glance over at Theo. "Are you still going to speak to Dr. Markel today?"

We decided it was best to suss out the old man again. In conjunction with Dr. Smith's extra workload to help calm down the patients, Markel has been required to provide medicinal support. Though, I'm not entirely sure there's enough sedatives in the world to help regulate our nervous systems at this point.

Theo nods toward Damon. "We'll do it while you're in session. That way we're close by."

Twenty minutes later, the four of us plus Connor head to Dr. Smith's office. Christopher? I'm not entirely sure what to refer to him at this point. We're technically family but he's still my doctor. Wait, aren't doctors supposed to *not* treat family members?

It doesn't matter. We're well and truly past the point of ethical practices.

I bid the guys farewell, closing the door as their footsteps head down the corridor toward Dr. Markel's room. Sitting down across from Dr. Smith, the bags under his eyes stand out, business shirt unbuttoned at the top like he's been tugging at the collar.

"You look like shit," I tell him politely.

"I feel like shit," he replies without missing a beat. "I slept in my office last night."

"You could have used my room," I shrug. "It was empty."

Dr. Smith smiles. "I figured as much. But I'm not going to invade your privacy. Also, I don't have the time to deal with Grey when he inevitably comes for my throat."

I tap the side of my neck. "I see what you did there."

He relaxes with a laugh. "How are *you* doing though?"

"I feel like I'm walking on eggshells, every second of every day," I answer honestly. "It's torture waiting for something to happen. Everything is outside of our control and people are spiraling."

"Does it make you uneasy?"

"Yeah."

It's full of confidence, no hesitation. There's no point sugar coating it—it's not a donut.

Clearing my throat, I elaborate. "It reminds me of home. Not the good home, but the life I lived before. I wish I could take their pain away."

"And what about your pain?" he questions sharply.

"I have three guys who love me for that. They make me feel so alive that I forget about the pain most of the time."

Dr. Smith's eyebrows furrow together in thought. "That's a really amazing observation to make. You sound like you've accepted the idea of love."

"Because it's not just an idea," I mutter. "They actually love me. How could I deny that?"

"But do you feel worthy of it?"

"Yes," I answer straight away. "I do."

He leans back in his chair, cupping his hands together. A smile crosses his face, confusing me.

"What?" I press.

"Think about it," he says, rolling his hand. "You feel worthy. That's huge, Avery."

"I—"

How do I respond to that? When did it happen? Somewhere along the line, I fell head over heels for these three guys, accepting it completely. I never believed it was conditional, attached with a price tag. I've never felt used or less than anything.

"They make me feel that way," I mumble, awkwardly shifting in my spot. "They forced me to believe it until one day I just did, I guess."

Dr. Smith beams at me. "I had a feeling it would happen."

"Because I was so desperate to be loved that I greedily accrued multiple partners to fill the mass void in my chest?" I snort sarcastically.

"I think they each bring out different parts of you."

Like each part fits together to make one piece. Maybe I was too broken, in many pieces that I needed more than one part to be put back together.

I think that's why I tried to fight it. To hide it.

I never thought that even one person could love me—all of me, broken shards and fragments—but they did. Yet, at every turn I expected them to walk away.

Every time I started to feel happy, there was a voice in my head that told me to push them away. Because people leave. Everyone leaves.

They leave me.

That mindset nearly cost me everything with Grey. I should have just spoken up about my fears, confided in him and given him the opportunity to reassure me. Instead, I broke his heart because I couldn't figure out how mine worked.

I'm just so thankful we found our way back and made this work. The four of us together, we fit. Four broken pieces with jagged edges, sharp enough to cut, but somehow, we piece together perfectly.

"They do bring out different parts of me. But I don't think any of us could have seen this coming," I muse.

Dr. Smith shrugs one shoulder. "I had a suspicion that you and Damon would become more to each other."

"Bullshit," I laugh. "We hated each other when I arrived months ago. He only tolerated me because of Grey. God, he threatened to kill me on more than one occasion."

"Murder threats is Damon's love language," Dr. Smith jokes. "But in all seriousness, Avery—you are so much like Aunt Lily. Always trying to please everyone while fighting silent demons. You see the good in people, often when it's well hidden."

"I think I just see the good as a way to convince myself that they won't hurt me," I admit.

He nods. "Definitely. It's a survival strategy, conceived by your mind. And also if you can make someone good, have them prove to be different than who they proclaim to be, then it will validate in your mind that not everyone is like your father."

Ouch.

I hate to agree with him but he's making way too much sense for a Thursday morning.

"So..." I start slowly. "I basically forced them all to fall in love with me for validation. And secretly they are walking red flags that I overlooked to prove a point?"

Dr. Smith cocks an eyebrow. "Interesting theory but I'm inclined to disagree. You're missing one key factor here."

"What's that?"

"You."

I jolt back, confused. "Me? Where do I fit into this equation?"

He smiles again. "You think *you* forced them to fall for you, to *put up* with this dynamic," he says, using air quotes. "But have you stopped to consider the possibility that you perhaps helped heal them?"

Blinking, I become speechless. Now he's talking trash for sure. I haven't healed anyone. If anything, I've probably activated a gene in their bodies to turn their hair prematurely gray and provide daily doses of anxiety.

"Maybe," he interjects when I don't reply. "You also wanted to save them like you feel they saved you, because you harbor some guilt about past things outside your control."

"My mom... Paige?" I answer weakly.

Dr. Smith's lips purse to fight against a frown. "Your father too. Because if you can save someone from their demons, that little inner child feels safe again."

Something jerks me out of my trance. I realize it's a tear sliding down my cheek. I quickly wipe it away. "This is a bit too personal right now," I laugh jokingly, attempting to deflect. "There are patients out there with real problems—like psychopaths leaving roses everywhere and dumping patients in ice water. The goddamn roses, am I right?"

"Avery." He leans forward, forcing me to look at him. "Everything you feel is valid, regardless of the situation. You should be so proud of how far you've come. Look at what you told Meg—you said you were happy and have a real family now. That you're not the person who walked through those doors. Give yourself some credit—you've come so far, and while doing that, you've become a strong woman who is trying to free everyone. Plus," he laughs. "You did the unthinkable—you made Damon fall in love."

"Yeah, well... being trapped in caskets will do that," I murmur quietly. "Forced proximity and all."

"What?"

"What?" I repeat, cursing myself as I play stupid.

The two of us stare at each other, Dr. Smith appearing increasingly concerned and confused. Quickly, I change the subject. "So, why do you call Margie, Meg?"

That appears to do the trick as he becomes flustered slightly, tugging at his collar. "Well, her name is Margaret. It's a nickname," he chokes out.

"You like her," I laugh. "Ooh, she makes you nervous."

"No, she doesn't," he argues back. "It's just warm in here."

"Sure," I tease, folding my arms. "Whatever you say, *Chris*."

His stunned face looks as though he's been slapped by a fish. Snorting, I nod toward the chessboard that's been sitting ignored since the beginning of our session. "Do you want to play?"

"Do you remember the rules?" He asks, glancing at the board.

"Yeah," I confirm softly. "Protect the King, right? That's what you were telling me along, isn't it? Protect Damon?"

Dr. Smith's eyebrows shoot up. "Like I said—I had a feeling you'd be special to him. Or at least hoped someone could knock him down a few pegs."

"I'm going to tell him you said that," I mock, sliding off my chair to the floor as he grabs the chessboard and places it on the ground. "No secrets between spouses."

"Except when it comes to Wills," he mutters knowingly.

I hum in agreement. "And marriage licences apparently. Or is that just our new cousin thing?"

Chapter 33

Avery

After our game of chess, I stand in the hallway awkwardly.

To my surprise, there's *no one*.

No guard, no sign of the guys.

And since everyone is still in their rooms, no patients.

It's dead.

Dr. Smith appears in the doorway behind me, frowning. "They aren't here yet?"

I shake my head. "Not unless they found a way to make themselves invisible. As tempting as ghost sex sounds, I'm going to guess they *aren't* here."

"I didn't need that imaginary, but thank you," he sighs, motioning for me to follow him. "We'll check the other rooms."

We reach Dr. Markel's rooms but that's empty as well, not a single lullaby to be heard.

"Maybe the male dorms?" I offer, suddenly hearing the sound of footsteps as soon as the words leave my mouth.

Turning around, I expect to find the guys heading our way, but instead, we're face to face with Whittingham.

"Christopher," he snarls. "Ms. White—you are required to head back to *your* room after session."

My eyes darken and narrow. "We're just fine without the directions, thank you."

Dr. Smith places his hand on my shoulder. "I'll escort her there now. We were just looking for her assigned guard."

Whitface cocks an eyebrow. "They are currently busy dealing with an urgent matter. I'll accompany you to the Eastwood Wing."

I don't like the sound of that, but what choice do we have?

Slowly, I pivot, walking ahead as I start to make my way to the girls' dorm. What the hell did he mean they were busy with an urgent matter? That must be why the guys aren't here.

Oh, my God. Are they hurt? Has someone done something to them?

I want to voice all my concerns out loud to Dr. Smith, to send him on the search, but with Whittingham bringing up the rear, we can't risk it. Dr. Smith is smart though—surely he'll do it anyway. Plus I'll try calling them when I'm back in the room. My cell is down my bra, concealed as best as possible. I wouldn't put it past anyone to check my pockets, so the boobs are the safest bet.

Stopping in front of my room, Whittingham opens the door when Dr. Smith makes no effort to do it for him. Holding it open, he motions for me to enter.

"Inside, Ms. White," he snaps irritably.

I chuck a quick glance at Dr. Smith over my shoulder, hoping to hell he can understand what I'm pleading with my eyes. He gives me a quick, subtle nod when Whitface isn't looking, and knowing we're on the same page, I step inside.

Facing the door, I meet the supervisor's eyes, the two of us sharing a mutual heated look of hatred. But then his lips twist into a dark smirk, unsettling my stomach.

The door slams closed in my face, and immediately I dive for the cell in my bra, ignoring the terrible boob sweat that coats the cell.

I try Damon first, pacing as I listen to the call go unanswered. When he doesn't pick up, I try Grey with the same result. Theo's cell doesn't even ring at all which scares the hell out of me.

Is he in solitary confinement? Did they fix the door that they blowtorched off?

Clutching my stomach, I think I might actually be sick. I try to gaslight myself that everything is fine—that there's a perfectly reasonable explanation for all this. But that smug bastard's smirk plays over and over in my head.

Something is happening, I just know it. There's no other possibility as to why the guys are nowhere to be seen and aren't able to answer their cells.

We promised we'd stick together in numbers. They wouldn't leave me alone.

Trying a different tactic, I breathe out a tiny sigh of relief when the feminine voice floats down the line.

"Avery?"

"Jillian," I choke out. "Do you know where Damon is? I just finished my session with Dr. Smith and I can't find anyone."

I hear shuffling noises in the background before the unmistakable sound of a laptop opening and whizzing to life.

"I'll check the cameras," she says. "I'm still stuck in my room."

"What?" I question. "Can't you just let yourself out?"

"I could," she confirms. "But Damon asked me not to. He doesn't want to alert anyone to our movements. Byrone and I have been keeping a watch on the feeds but nothing unusual has happened according to our observations."

Rubbing my forehead, I squeeze my eyes closed. "Something is happening. I just know it."

"They are in Markel's office," she announces. "The three of them, talking to him by the looks of it."

"N-no," I sputter. "That's not right. I just checked his office. It was empty..."

More gaslighting—except this time it's not self-inflicted. I definitely was just at his office and there was no sight of them. If they went there after we left, we most definitely would have crossed paths with them. Not to mention that my session time is over. They know what time it finished so they would be looking for me.

"Are you sure?" she asks, unconvinced. "I'm looking at the camera feed right now."

"I'm sure," I murmur warily. "Jillian, are you sure you're watching the correct feed?"

"What do you mean? It's a live feed."

"Is it though?" I question sharply. "They were heading in the direction of Markel's office at the start of my session. That was over an hour ago."

She falls silent, clicking a few keys before letting out a soft hiss. "Shit. You're right. The time stamp is off."

"Jillian, they are replaying the feed. They know you're watching so they are fucking with us. Something is *happening*," I reiterate urgently.

"Okay," she murmurs, her own panic laced in her voice. "Let me call Byrone and we'll come check. Just hang tight for a few minutes and I'll break you out."

I can't speak. My throat is closing up. All I can manage is a nod, and even though she can't see it, she hangs up anyway to dial Byrone.

Trying the guys' cells again, I keep ringing over and over like an obsessed psychopath.

A few minutes later, I hear the tap and ding outside my door, springing to my feet to greet Jillian. As I go to reach for the door to pull it open, I stop dead in my tracks at the unexpected figure. Or more so, the gun pointing at my face.

"Avery," Alexander greets coldly, standing in his usual freshly pressed expensive designer suit. "Come with me, please."

When I make no effort to move, completely frozen in place, he cocks the hammer in warning. "Don't test my patience today, child."

"Fine," I snap, launching into action. "I'm coming."

He looks pleased at my compliance, using the gun to direct me to walk in front of him.

The female corridor is empty, but as I pass Jillian's door, I notice it's cracked slightly. "Where are we going, Alexander?" I ask with a raised voice to alert her to the situation.

"You'll find out soon enough," he responds sharply.

Weaving through the Lilydale maze, I find myself in Whittingham's office, the man himself sitting behind the desk. I shoot him another glare full of disgust, my heart racing when I realize we're the only three people here.

Where are the guys?

"Now, Avery," Alexander begins, pressing the gun into my spine. "It's come to our attention that *someone* made a formal allegation against the board in regards to the conduct of the facility. You wouldn't happen to know anything about that, would you?"

I shake my head. "No idea."

Whittingham purses his lips, narrowing his eyes on me. "You're lying."

"Nope," I answer casually, voice surprisingly strong despite the panic that's flooding through me. "I assume you're here to fill me in on the details as a shareholder."

I wince as Alexander shoves the barrel harder into my back. "We're not here to play games, Avery. We are well aware that you know of the situation. It's thanks to your little stunt that all our records have been seized and we've been provided notice that they are coming to do a check of the facility."

"Not to mention the state of the lab downstairs," Arthur adds venomously. "We saw the footage. You set it on fire."

"I have no idea what you are talking about," I say through clenched teeth. I'm well aware that there's cameras down there, so chances are they most definitely watched me burn it. That also means they witnessed me killing Rian Thatcher. I can already sense where this is going. They are going to throw me under the bus, blame me for murder. Anything to distract the relevant authorities from the truth.

Footsteps behind me alert us to another presence. I don't dare move, but judging by Whittingham's look of acknowledgment, it's someone I don't want here.

"William. Finally," he says, and my eyes darken as the man appears in my peripheral vision.

Elsher watches me closely before turning his attention to Whittingham. "The guards have managed to subdue them downstairs."

My chest clenches painfully when I realize they are talking about my guys. What the hell were they doing down there?

Alexander spots me tensing up, dragging the barrel down my back. "You really should know better than to head to the morgue unsupervised," he taunts.

"What are you talking about?" I snap back angrily, earning myself another painful jab.

Whittingham laughs darkly, his amusement pissing me off. "We sent them down there to search for you. Damon's team are quite easy to fool. All we had to do was replay old footage of you and they walked straight into our trap. Ironic, given they passed you in Christopher's office and didn't stop to check. We should thank you, really."

"Why?" I croak out, feeling my strength start to fade into panic.

Alexander's cold hand brushes my hair off my neck. I resist the urge to vomit as his fingers caress the junction between my throat and shoulder. "You're the weakness we've been waiting for—the one thing that Damon loses focus over. Now, once we kill you, we'll be able to finish what we started. So, thank you, Avery."

I refuse to cry. I refuse to let these men see me beg for my life.

They are wrong. I'm not Damon's weakness—I'm his strength. And whatever happens to me, I've protected Damon. Alexander won't get his grubby hands on those shares.

Elsher growls, stomping over uncharacteristically toward me. I have no time to react, even without the gun pressed into my back, as he flings his arm forward and slaps me hard in the face. "Not to mention you killed my nephew. You are exactly who I thought you were, Ms. White."

I stumble into Whittingham's desk with a wince, clutching my cheek as my ears ring. Fuck—he hits even harder than Alexander. "I didn't kill anyone," I lie through clenched teeth, feeling blood dribble down my cheek.

Arthur leans forward, hitting a key on his laptop before spinning it around to face me. There, in black and white, is me and Theo in the downstairs lab. I'm very visibly dousing chemicals everywhere before Rian steps into the view of the camera.

My eyes widen in horror—not because they have me on footage committing murder, but because...

"Rian was your nephew?" I finally mumble at Elsher.

He doesn't reply, but the loathing in his eyes confirms my question.

Swallowing, I ignore the footage playing, willing myself to stay calm. "I thought Rian was related to a board member—Henry."

If I distract them, maybe it will buy me some time. I'm also hoping that somehow, the cameras in here will pick up our conversation and Byrone can access it. If investigators are coming, this is the evidence we need to bring them down. Our camera was destroyed, but maybe Jillian can access to Lilydale feed if they haven't been blocked out.

If I can talk about the investigation, maybe I can incriminate them.

But they know this too... and they are still willing to kill me for it. If they are going down, then what do they have to lose?

Alexander knows we've backed him into a corner. Knows we've fucked them. I'm the punishment, the collateral damage as they resort to extreme measures to bring down Damon before their world comes crashing down.

"My brother-in-law," Elsher spits out. "You little bitch. I knew you'd kill again. That's all you're capable of."

I bite my lip painfully when Alexander moves the gun to my head, pointing the barrel directly into my skull. "Any last words, Avery?"

"Yeah," I breathe out, shooting a quick glance at Elsher before sneering at Whittingham. "Go to fucking Hell."

Bang.

Chapter 34

Damon

*** Five Years Ago ***

"I'm so sorry for your loss, Damon."

I instantly recognize the softly spoken voice, and despite my deliberate efforts to ignore everyone here, I choose to turn and acknowledge *her*.

"It's nice to see you, Mrs. Whittingham."

She looks a lot better, unlike me to be honest. Divorce is a fresh start, an exit from toxicity. Death is just... final.

"Your mother was an amazing woman," Mrs. Whittingham murmurs, placing a hold on my arm. "I owe her my life."

And Mom paid with hers.

I don't blame this woman though. If anything, I'm happy she managed to escape the clutches of her abusive husband.

"She will be sorely missed," I confirm emotionlessly.

She offers a sad smile, but my attention is forced elsewhere. Someone is yelling, and Mrs. Whittingham sighs out loud at the exact moment I pinpoint the culprit.

Arthur fucking Whittingham.

That pathetic, useless excuse of a man is pointing at us, while my father nods sternly. Clicking his fingers at security, Father gestures to us.

Red, hot fury begins to pulse through my veins. He can't even give her *this*—the last time any of us will ever come together for Mom and he's trying to control it. Manipulation is what he loves best, and I'm not surprised in the slightest that he's attempting to ruin this moment.

A bulky security guard in black wanders over, puffing up his steroidal chest. But before he can utter the expected words to Mrs. Whittingham, I punch him square in the face.

The small crowd around us gasp and cry out at the commotion, and I take a moment to enjoy the stunned looks of disbelief on the faces of the older men. It just proves that my father doesn't know me at all. If he believes I'll let him pull his bullshit today, he's dead wrong.

"Everyone stays!" I say in a raised voice while glaring straight at him across the lawn. "Today is about Lily—my *mother*. We're here to honor her memory and *everyone* is welcome."

It does the job as people—strangers, colleagues, distant family members—all turn to gawk at my father like he got his audacity on sale or stole it like the tightass he is. He sputters angrily, storming off toward his awaiting private town car.

I knew he wouldn't stay long. This was nothing but a publicity appearance for him. Today, he's playing his most hated role—a husband. Being a father a close second.

"Thank you," Mrs. Whittingham whispers, giving my arm a squeeze. "You're just like her, you know that? Lily would be so proud of you, Damon."

I wish I could believe that. I was Mom's pride and joy, but let's not pretend I'm not a carbon copy of the asshole escaping the consequences of his actions.

Mom was beautiful, elegant, graceful. She was the sunshine, the moon, and the whole fucking galaxy. But my father and I are cut from the same cloth. We crave power, control, fear. Caring and emotions are weaknesses that should be hidden at all costs. And Mom's death is the exact reason why.

He knew I loved her, so he removed the perceived obstacle out of the way. This was nothing more than a strategy to hurt us both, and now, he's going to come after me, to exploit that love I had for my mother. He uses people against each other, pawns in a chess match where he believes he's untouchable. This is why we don't love, why we don't give someone any reason to find weaknesses.

It's my fault she's dead.

Alexander Dale is all about appearances. Having a doting wife in public helped him. But the more I stood up to him and protected her, the angrier he got. Because she chose me over him. Until finally, he took her from me.

She was collateral damage in our game of war.

And it didn't help that Mom helped Mrs. Whittingham escape the clutches of her asshole husband. Because in his eyes, if Mom was willing to do that for another woman, what was to stop her from walking away too?

"Look after yourself, Mrs. Whittingham," I say with finality, needing to get out of here before Christopher comes over and I am forced to bury him in a vacant shallow grave. He's had his eye on me for the past five minutes and I'm in no mood to deal with my cousin and his snide remarks right now.

"You too, Damon," she replies. "And for the record, I've reverted back to my maiden name. But please... call me Rose."

"Next one goes in your fucking head," I warn, gun pointing at my father. I can see the bruise forming on Avery's face, blood trickling down her cheek as she fights back pain.

They fucking touched her.

My. Fucking. Wife.

That bumbling idiot of a psychiatrist flattens himself against the wall while Arthur ducks down behind his desk. Of course, my father doesn't flinch at all, grabbing Avery's shoulder and spinning them around as he uses her as a human shield against me.

Wrong choice, asshole.

"I'm disappointed in you, Damon," he remarks, his own barrel pressing into Avery's temple. "Your ability to protect your wife is just as impressive as your skill in keeping your mother safe."

Avery's eyes are blown wide, trained on me as she stays still. I meet them for a brief moment, silently telling her that I've got her. If anything, she appears more terrified by my presence, eyes darting between me and the gun lined up with the side of her head. Like she's worried *I'll* get hurt.

I know this emotional manipulation tactic is merely an attempt to throw off my control. He brings up my mother whenever he can, in the hope that I'll overreact and provide him with a clear opportunity to overpower me. Clearly, it hasn't worked before. Which is why he's now using Avery as well.

When Byrone called me to inform us that Avery was spotted heading downstairs solo, I admit I did make the wrong decision. I should have known that she wouldn't be doing that, but in the moment, all I felt was the unwavering need to protect her and simultaneously scold her for being stupid. I panicked. We should have checked Christopher's office, but they led us to believe he was leaving the facility in a rush. I had no reason to doubt Byrone, nor did it occur to me that it was a trap. All I knew was I had to get to her before it was too late.

I stupidly thought that with an investigation underway, no one would dare step out of line. After all, appearances matter. But I overestimated Alexander Dale. For once, *he* overreacted. Instead of doing the smart thing and lying low until the authorities did their checks, he let his emotions get the better of him—knowing we've got him right where we want him. And in turn, I was foolish to expect him to be sensible.

And now... he wants to take away the only other person I've ever loved. Just like he did Mom.

Guards had immediately swarmed us downstairs, but we knew they were coming. Barely downstairs for longer than a few minutes and Connor had alerted us to what was really happening. Still, it took a bit of time to deal with them all. Grey and Theo handled most of it, giving me the opportunity to head straight here. I knew this is where I would find my father. And as soon as I realized what was going down, I anticipated this moment, stealing Connor's gun.

Even though I was prepared to find Avery in some kind of trouble, I'm still having difficulty keeping my control in check, watching as he threatens her life. It's taking all of my willpower to remain focused, to not let my emotions get the better of me. One wrong move and Avery is as good as dead.

"I'm disappointed in you as well, Father," I tell him casually. "It's unlike you to make stupid decisions. I guess we both feel deceived in that regard."

He scowls at me, anger washing over my entire body as his hand grasps Avery painfully, her face contorting as she soundlessly tries to hide the fact she's hurting.

"We're at a crossroads," Father points out. "What are you going to choose, Damon? Your wife or your so-called self-proclaimed legacy?"

"It's remarkable that you assume I only have one option," I say coolly. "But rest assured, I intend to fulfil my promise today. You've just sweetened the motivation that much more. Even if you did try to sneak in that board member's son."

Cocking his eyebrow, he laughs sinisterly. "That boy was nothing but a failure. But I think you have forgotten one key factor, Damon."

"Enlighten me."

"Once I end Avery's life, I become her sole beneficiary. If you attempt to harm me, you'll never leave this place. My estate documents ensure that you'll never receive anything, nor will you be able to gain any power with the board. Legally, you'll forfeit any position of power you have, and you'll be transferred to prison for the rest of your life. Everyone you care about in here will remain under Arthur's supervision, and I promise you—they will wish they were dead when we're through with them. This investigation will blow over and your efforts will have been for nothing."

Avery's lips twitch, capturing my attention. Her eyes relax, almost as if she's internally laughing. For a moment, I admit I'm perplexed—questioning her mental health in this moment. My father still has the tip of his gun pressed into her head, yet she doesn't seem fazed at all now.

On cue, he notices that my attention is elsewhere, and despite my best efforts to hide the suspicion from my face, he correctly deduces that Avery has done something. Her poker face isn't as perfected as ours, and I nearly snap and break when he grabs her chin, aggressively twisting her face toward him.

"What are you doing?" he growls at her.

I take a step forward, gun trained on him but Avery just laughs out loud. Every sensation in my physique is heightened as danger grows, my finger resting against the trigger, ready to pull it at any moment.

"You're wrong," she tells him amused. "How does it feel?"

"What are you talking about?" he demands loudly.

Her eyes dart over to me before returning to his. "You're not my beneficiary," she answers calmly—too settled for the tension in the room.

An eerie silence drifts over the room while everyone attempts to process her words. My father changes positions, shoving the barrel under her chin with quick precision.

"You signed the Will," he snarls.

"I did," she agrees, smoothly lifting an eyebrow. "But you failed to realize one simple thing..."

"Spit it out."

Avery smiles, eyes dancing with unhinged delight. "You failed to realize that I could just sign... *another one.*"

There's about a three second delay as her words sink in before utter chaos breaks out. My father's face flushes bright red with rage while my chest expands with pride.

She created another obstacle. Another barrier to block him. All by herself.

Her death would give me the power to bring him down, unless he was able to kill both of us before we retaliated.

Which we all know there's no chance of that. She sacrificed herself, destroyed part of his plan, making it worthless.

It's as if everything moves in slow motion; his body tensing, finger twitching against the trigger. That near perfect control breaks as his emotions overpower him—embarrassment, failure. Everything he hates.

I have only a fraction of a second to react, knowing what's coming if I don't move quickly.

Aiming, I don't hesitate to pull the trigger, the bang deafening the room. My bullet hits him in the shoulder, his arm dropping and the gun moving away from Avery as he clutches his bleeding wound while snarling and cursing.

William attempts to rush forward to grab Avery from behind, but I fire at him too, hitting him perfectly in the forehead. He drops to the ground like a sack of shit, dead before he can even stain the carpet. I wanted to prolong his torture, but in this moment, I'll settle for his death.

I spot Arthur duck behind the desk again like the coward he is, and I cross the threshold, ripping Avery behind me as I stand in front of my father as he hunches over, trying to stop the bleeding.

"Allez en enfer," I tell him in French, knowing just how much he hated Mom's fascination with Paris. It's why I learned the language, after all. Why I named the society *Cirque des Morts*.

His eyes widen as I bring the gun to the bridge of his nose, smiling fondly as I pull the trigger without another thought—twice for good measure.

Bang. Bang.

Alexander Dale drops to the floor as blood splatters over my face and chest, quickly pooling at our feet. I barely notice Arthur scampering out from behind the desk, rushing to the door to run away.

I'll get him later. Right now, I take a moment to enjoy the feeling of seeing my father's dead body on the ground.

It's over. He can't hurt anyone ever again.

My chest heaves with deep breaths as reality sinks in. I finally fulfilled my promise to Mom, and fuck it feels so damn good.

Arms curl around me from behind, Avery resting her forehead against my back.

I spin around, searching her face carefully—checking for signs that she's terrified of who I am and what I'm capable of. But there's nothing, just need as she grabs my face and smashes her lips to mine.

As I kiss her back, I hear running footsteps screeching to a halt, before Grey's voice float into the room.

"Ohh," he says amused. "Look at that. We missed all the action. Ding dong, the bitch is dead."

Chapter 35

Avery

"I'm going to miss this place," I sigh heavily.

"Should we be concerned?" Grey jokes. "I mean... it *is* the morgue, after all."

The four of us stand in the cold room, Grey on my left and Theo on my right. Damon is behind me, and I can feel his sarcastic stare on my back. No doubt there's some witty comment on the tip of his tongue.

But I don't care.

I don't have it in me right now to worry about what this says about my mental health. Most people's favorite locations that they share romantically with their partners are restaurants and breath-taking views of mountain ranges. Not morgues.

"Maybe I'm just broken," I murmur. "This will always be a stand out memory and that's not normal."

A hand slides along my waist, a chest pressing into my back. "You were beautiful when broken, Avery," Damon replies. "And you're still beautiful now. But not broken. You're much stronger than you give yourself credit for."

I lean back into my husband. "It's ironic. The place I felt most alive in Lilydale is the one place the dead come."

"You came too," Grey points out. "Thankfully, still alive."

"Sick fuck," Theo mumbles under his breath.

"I didn't mean it like that," Grey shoots back. "Who invited this guy?"

Theo twists his head to smile at me. "I was here first," he says, eyes darting over to the mortuary cabinet knowingly.

"Yes, you were," I laugh. "Still not sure how we managed to fit in that damn thing."

"Or the fact you made a sex tape," Damon murmurs in amusement. "Except if anyone dares to watch it outside of us, I'll be forced to kill them."

My shoulders slump forward, sadness creeping in. "What if we never see each other again?"

Grey cups my face with his hand. "Hey, don't think like that, little killer. This is only temporary."

After everything that went down with Alexander, the police arrived as expected—accompanied by the investigation team. Turns out he knew they were planning on making an appearance that day and had decided to take matters into his own hands. He just didn't anticipate that Damon would get to me so quickly. See, he might have known Damon, but he wasn't prepared for one thing—our family. No one could prepare when the three of them banded together as a team or the lengths I would go to protect Damon. Because Alexander was incapable of love. Our selfishness for one another was something he couldn't foresee because he didn't have the ability to do the same.

Still... having the authorities walk in on two dead bodies and patients losing their minds didn't exactly help our cause. Even with the evidence they had managed to collate from the board's dodgy documentation and motives, it's hard to explain cold blooded murder.

Damon told all of us to cooperate and immediately instructed Byrone and Jillian to hand over the footage before Whittingham could have the chance to wipe it, wherever he was. They had managed to override the loop that was being fed and saved a copy to exonerate us of any wrongdoing. Alexander had made it quite clear what his intentions were and that they had planted Rian here. That, along with other previous footage should be enough to prove that Lilydale was nothing but a coverup.

The only problem is the video evidence of me burning down the lab and killing Rian. Police took my statement but until the investigation is complete and they have their official ruling, I'm looking at charges. Given everyone's mental health and the allegations of what we've endured, we've been granted a pardon from being held in prison until everything gets dealt with.

But Lilydale can't stay open.

Which means they are sending us to another facility to be held until they can figure out what to do next. The only information we have is that they need to split up the patients due to spacing issues.

And it's tearing me apart.

I just know in my gut that I'm going to be separated from them. I've already been given my departure time and it's different from theirs. The chances of Lilydale being reopened are slim and with me facing potential murder charges... *I can't even say the words.*

"We will sort it out," Theo comforts, giving my hand a squeeze. "It will be alright."

Turning around, I throw myself at Theo, wrapping my arms around his neck. He hugs me back, resting his chin on the top of my head.

"I can't say goodbye," I whisper into his chest.

"It's not goodbye," Damon answers from behind me. "Like Grey said, it's only temporary. We will figure it out."

I peer at him over my shoulder. "I love how confidently you say that."

He smiles at me. "If you think for one second it's not tearing us apart to be away from you... you're wrong, Avery. But I still mean every word. We *will* find you. We will come for you."

"'Til death do us part?" I try to joke, voice cracking with unshed tears.

Damon steps in behind me, boxing me in between the pair of them. "And forever beyond that, wife."

"Come here," Grey coaxes, holding out his hand. "I know what you need." He's still wearing his black hoodie and I place my palm in his, letting him pull me toward the steel table in the center of the room.

Lifting me up by my waist, he plops me onto the cool metal, digging into his pocket.

I muffle a laugh as he pulls out his red Cirque des Morts mask and slides it onto my face.

My legs dangle off the side of the table as I stare at them through the darkened holes, thighs clenching together at the look of hunger that washes over their faces.

Grey drops to his knees in front of me, running his hands up my legs. "Lift," he orders when he reaches the waistband of my shorts.

I comply, holding myself up on the palms of my hands as he slides my shorts and underwear down my legs and lets them fall to the floor. Pushing my legs apart, he hums in approval as he takes in my exposed cunt, wasting no time as he lowers his head. His tongue darts out and drags a line up my slit, repeating it a few more times until I'm squirming on the examination table.

I try to hold myself up while leaning back, but I'm tense, worried about falling back too far and doing a backflip off the table. Damon rounds the table, standing behind me. His arms loop through mine, holding me securely against his chest as he leans me back allowing Grey better access.

"Fuck," I breathe out when the tip of his tongue finds my clit. He drags slow circles around it, and my breath hitches even more when Theo drops to his knees next to him and starts kissing up my thigh.

Spreading my legs as far as possible, my eyes roll back as the two of them eat my needy cunt in unison. A shadow crosses my face before the mask is tilted up, lips pressing into mine as I wrap one arm around Damon's head as he kisses me upside down.

Fingers tease my entrance, dipping in before vanishing, and circling. My hips buck as I desperately try to sink myself into them, but whoever is touching me pulls back. I'm completely distracted by Damon's mouth, his tongue massaging mine that between all the sensations overwhelming me, I crash straight into an orgasm without warning.

My cries are swallowed by Damon, body still working through my climax when I'm suddenly clenching someone's fingers. I break the kiss to glance down, lips swollen and tingling, and when I catch sight of Theo and Grey working me together, I immediately feel the start of another orgasm building.

Holy fuck.

Damon's hand comes down on my throat, holding me still as his mouth works me into a frenzy. Is it possible to come from kissing? Because the way his tongue moves effortlessly in my mouth, I'm not confident that I won't spontaneously combust. Of course, having my two other boyfriends between my legs certainly has some... benefits.

His hand squeezes my throat, cutting off my air supply, but I still feel like I'm breathing the most intoxicating scent. Fingers slowly leave my body much to my disappointment, but I moan into Damon's mouth when I feel something larger pressing against my entrance. One inch, two inch... my cunt stretches to accommodate the hardened length pushing into my body, my back arching as I push further into Damon's hand.

Just as I start to see spots and stars in my eyes, he eases the pressure at the same time I'm fully filled.

"Please," I beg against his lips, glancing down again when he pulls back slightly.

Grey is standing now, hands digging into my thighs as his cock is buried inside me. "Put the mask back on her, Deadman," he demands.

The devil mask snaps back into place, but I hyper-focus on Grey through the eye sockets, loving how his irises darken.

"Fuck, little killer," he growls, pulling back before slamming into my cunt. "You're so fucking wet for us."

I can't respond as he begins moving his hips quickly, smashing our hips together as he fucks me hard and fast. I don't dare look away though, determined to watch every expression that crosses his face. I want to remember them, and I'm fairly certain by how hard he's fucking me that he wants me to feel him long after I'm gone from Lilydale.

"More, Grey," I beg, needing him to ruin me.

He growls, digging his black coated nails into my thigh, breaking the skin slightly as he thrusts into me hard. My back rhythmically hits Damon's chest in time with Grey's movements, and I groan when warm hands lift my shirt and bra over my chest and cover my tits. Damon pinches the soft pink tips, squeezing and groping them as I career into another climax, screaming Grey's name.

His hand moves to my back, yanking me forward so fast that I fall off the table toward him. But he catches me, lowering me to the ground. I already know what's coming, shoving the mask off and opening my mouth as I peer up at Grey from my knees.

"So fucking perfect," he breathes out, taking a moment to observe me. "Our little killer."

I don't wait for him to move, shooting forward as I take his cock in my mouth, tasting my own arousal on his length. He grabs the sides of my head, holding it still as he fucks my face. "Fucking beautiful," he murmurs before groaning low and I feel his release hit the back of my throat.

I swallow everything, running my tongue up and down his cock eagerly, until finally he pulls me off with a sharp hiss.

I'm barely given time to compose myself before strong hands lift me from the floor, Theo's mouth slamming into mine. He rips my shirt and bra off completely, tongue exploring my mouth in a kiss so frenzied that it leaves me light-headed.

"Bend over the table," he orders, hands positioning me as my stomach lands on the metal. Kicking my legs apart, he's buried inside me a second later, hands gripping my hair as he pulls my head back slightly.

"Fuck, Theo," I groan, throwing my hips back to match his tempo. He's just as rough as Grey, fucking me deep as my body screams in both pain and pleasure. It's the best kind of pain, the promise that I'll definitely be feeling this for days to come. I wouldn't have it any other way.

Damon leans down in front of me, still on the other side of the table. Grabbing my face, he forces me to look at him, eyes dancing with lustful need.

"You're taking him so fucking well, Avery. You're going to take everything we offer," he demands. "And you're going to come on his dick. Understand?"

I nod, my hands gripping the side of the table. "Yeah."

"Touch yourself," he orders. "I want you to feel that dick fucking your tight, little cunt. You're going to write our names on your clit with your finger, and you're not allowed to come until you finish all of them."

Fuck.

Reaching down with a shaky hand, my fingers trail through my wetness, dipping lower until I find where Theo and I meet. My breath catches as I feel him thrusting into me, my pussy clenching around him. He growls, tugging on my hair as his rhythm falters slightly.

"Write it," Damon orders sharply. "Tell us who you are doing."

I find my clit, biting my lip as I have to fight back my release. My swollen clit aches under my fingertips, but I shakily start drawing.

"T... h...," I whimper. "e... o."

Theo groans behind me. "Fuck, Aves."

"Next," Damon instructs.

I repeat the motion, this time spelling out Grey. "Hm... Grey," I breathe out.

A hand trails down my spine, Grey's voice reaching my ears. "Good girl."

"Next," Damon says sharply.

My body is violently trembling, ready to crash over the edge. But I manage to write it out, desperate for release. "Damon..." I cry out through clenched teeth.

"Come for Theo," he responds, grabbing my throat, and forcing me to look at him.

I barely get a choice in the matter, instantly barreling into my climax, mangled moans getting choked out.

I'm still pulsating when Theo pulls out of me, his strong hands picking me up and throwing me onto the table. He steps to my head, pulling me by the arms until I'm dangling off the table upside down.

"Open those pretty lips," he says, stroking my cheek.

As soon as my mouth is open, he pushes forward, fucking my throat while I'm upside down. A hand flattens on my chest, holding me firmly as I'm left battling for air. But I take his thrusts, clinging to his muscular thighs until he's shooting his release into my mouth.

When he steps back, I'm left panting, the blood rushing to my head. Damon grabs my hands, pulling me upright.

"My turn," he smirks, looping an arm under my knees and another around my back. He picks me up bridal style off the table and carries me to the side door.

I shoot him a bewildered look, too delirious to actually speak words. Opening the door, I take in the room with the caskets. Damon moves straight to a particular one, and it dawns on me it's the very same casket that we hid in from the guards.

Lifting the lid, he takes a moment to remove his clothes, dropping them to the floor without a second thought.

Damon climbs into the casket, laying on his back. "We're going to finish what we started," he tells me, fisting his cock and running his hand up his length.

I smile, moving on shaky legs as I step into the box. Dropping my knees on the side of his hips, I place my hands on his chest.

"You going to kiss me again?" I tease, lining him up with my entrance before slowly sinking down and taking him inch by inch.

"You better believe I am," he says, hastily grabbing the back of my head and pulling me forward until our lips touch.

I rock my hips, lifting and dropping as I ride him. Our mouths never separate, tongues frantically pressing against each other's as we fuck in the casket—where we had our first kiss.

Grey and Theo step into the room, clothes back in place as they lean against an adjacent casket and watch us closely. But I'm completely mesmerized by Damon—by his touch, the feel of him, the full circle moment. It's everything.

He reaches between us, spreading his fingers on either side of my clit as he gently massages the sensitive spot. I throw myself down his length, engulfing him as if my life depends on it.

The two of us groan in unison, swallowing our pleasure as his expert fingers send me higher and higher until I'm spasming around him, crying out his name. Damon takes over, lifting his hips and fucking me from underneath, the sound of our skin slapping together filling the room.

"Come in me," I plead. "I need to feel you inside me."

"Beg for me," he demands.

"Please," I whimper.

"More."

"Please fucking come in me, Damon."

Damon growls and groans underneath me, spearing into me with frantic movements before stilling as he finds his release. I fall to his chest, spent as his cock continues to pulse, until finally, he softens and slips out.

Neither of us make any effort to move despite the fact I can feel him dripping down my thigh, some of it getting on the casket floor.

"I love you, Damon," I murmur weakly. "I love you all so much."

Damon kisses my cheek. "I love you too, wife."

Turning my head, I find Grey and Theo. "I love you, Grey. I love you, Theo. Please remember that."

"Love you, Aves."

"I love you as well, little killer. But hold onto that thought because you're going to tell us again when we see you soon."

Closing my eyes, I rest my head against Damon's chest. I need to remember this moment, savor it. Because in a few short hours, it's all over. And whatever happens next, I need to remember how they all feel, how they love me.

It's the only way I'm going to survive.

Chapter 36

Avery

The Ridgeview Valley Rehabilitation Home is worlds apart from Lilydale.

Our bus pulls up at the entrance, no one speaking a word as we stare out the window at our temporary new home. I hate being here already.

I remember I felt the same about Lilydale when I first arrived. The pristine white building had offered promises of healing, the roses a stark contrast in color as though we were meant to be mesmerized by its beauty. But inside was my own beginning of Hell. Except... it did save me. Just in a way no one saw coming.

Instantly, I feel the different vibes. The older beige building may not look as flashy, and the only floral additions appear to be neatly trimmed hedges along the front of the property, but the sickening feeling of dread comes from inside me.

A middle aged woman floats out the white front door, skipping down the steps in dark blue jeans and a white button-up blouse. When she reaches the doorway of the bus, the driver opens it, allowing her to step inside.

"Good morning, ladies," she says warmly with a bright smile. "I'm Dell, the manager of Ridgeview Valley Home. We're excited to have you here."

Despite her welcoming demeanor, which is a nice change from Whittingham, no one seems to share her sentiments. Why would we? Lilydale was the place we went to die—in every way possible. Now, we're left reeling, trying to adjust to new changes with no resolution in sight.

Who knows what will happen next? Maybe we'll be here forever, never to see our male friends and partners again. I refuse to live in a world without Theo, Damon, and Grey. All I can think about is where they are now. Maybe they are nearby, about to enter a new facility while our fates hang in limbo with someone else's decisions.

"Follow me, please," Dell says softly, jumping off the last step to the ground as people finally start descending from the bus.

I spare a quick glance toward Jillian, giving her a small sad smile as we join the line to exit.

The breeze is crisp and fresh once I step onto the gravel, finding myself in the center of the group as we huddle sub-consciously together.

When everyone is off the bus, Dell climbs the steps of the building so everyone can see her. "I understand it must be incredibly overwhelming being here," she starts. "Especially after what you have been through. But please be rest assured we are here to help. We're a family at Ridgeview and here to take you under our wing. I know many of you are hoping for answers," she pauses, scanning our group. "And as soon as we have information, we will update you. In the meantime, our rehabilitation team is eager to meet you and help you get settled in."

We head inside slowly when she gestures for us to follow, a few people whispering among themselves. I stick close to Jillian, hoping the familiarity will keep my sanity in check.

Everything hurts. My heart, my body... but nothing more than my soul. It's as if it's missing three parts, no longer whole. But I promised them I'd be strong, promised that I'd get through this and see them again.

For a brief moment as I take in the high ceilings and warm brown tones of the foyer, I can't help but worry that maybe they will forget about me. What if they get out and I don't? What if they meet someone new and I become a fading memory—a ghost that reminds them of their worst nightmares?

Unlike the day I arrived at Lilydale, there's a dozen staff members waiting inside. They are all dressed casually like Dell, ranging in age with the same carefree smiles. Not a single expensive suit among them.

Dell grins at them, quickly whispering to a young man at the end of the line and taking a blue folder from his hands. She turns to us, flicking it open.

"We're a co-gender facility as well and encourage mingling. You'll be paired up with a bunkmate. We understand that you likely have relationships with one another so we'll give you a few minutes to chat among yourselves and pair up if you'd like to be with anyone in particular. Once you have someone, come forward and we'll assign you a room. Each counselor here will take two pairs under their guidance and get you set up."

My eyes scan the line of staff, before catching Jillian's eye. She understands my silent question, giving a small nod.

"I can see you all have uniforms from Lilydale. Now, you are welcome to stay in them if you wish, however we believe in a more casual approach. If you would like a change of clothes, your assigned counselor will escort you to our Willowbrook Closet where you'll be able to pick out some new clothing which will be dropped to your room. We're very lucky to receive donations from the community and have quite a range. Hopefully everyone will find some pieces they enjoy."

I finger the bottom of my shorts, knowing immediately that I want to get these off my body. I don't even remember what my style was before I went to Lilydale, or if I even had one. But at this stage, I'd be happy wearing a trash bag if it meant getting rid of the gray, flimsy cotton. Judging by the expressions of the other patients, they agree.

Dell gives us a tight smile, sensing the tense atmosphere. "We have a camp-style buffet set up in our dining hall for you. Your counselor will let you know the times the dining hall is open and where you can obtain snacks from, but you're welcome to explore once you are settled in. We have recreational rooms, daily activities and optional hobby classes for you to enjoy. The only requirements are that you are to return to your rooms by 8 p.m. each night. The doors do lock after that to ensure the safety and wellbeing of all, but if you need anything, each room is fitted with a speaker and we have staff available around the clock. Now, take a moment to pair up then step forward."

A few people start to visibly relax, smiling with each other. But I quickly realize that they are the lucky ones. As I scan, I can't help but notice that the ones who lived the pain of Lilydale, like myself, Vivian, Eliana and Siobhan, we don't smile. We don't look excited.

Everything sounds like a dream. Even if you were to take Lilydale out of the equation, this is the type of place we should have been all along. Not prisoners, treated as less than because of our backgrounds. But even dreams can be disappointing.

As much as I hate to admit it, I'm still in Lilydale. Physically, I'm not. But every other single thing about me is. It's almost like a location version of Stockholm Syndrome.

I can't decide if I'm broken or just messed up.

Jillian and I step forward together, one of the counselors noticing and meeting us halfway. The woman looks to be in her late-twenties, all smiles like her colleagues in a tie-dye rainbow shirt and white cotton shorts.

"Hiya! I'm Marissa, but you can call me Ris. Are you guys bunking together?"

"Yeah," I answer at the same time as Jillian.

"Fab! Full jinxing mode—I like it. Follow me and I'll get you checked in," Ris announces, heading to the reception desk and being handed two swipe keys from the older gentlemen behind it. He beams at us, blue eyes twinkling and for a second, he reminds me a little of Dr. Markel.

Ris holds out the keys toward us. "One each because even though sharing is caring, everyone deserves their own."

Sharing is caring, indeed. But this isn't what I want.

We're taken down an open corridor at the other side of the room, my eyes finding portraits and photographs of laughing patients, families and painted artwork of seemingly important people. Well, at least I assume given they have gold engraved plaques beneath them.

"So, Ridgeview Home is *very* open plan like Dell mentioned," Ris says, acting as tour guide. "All the rooms are scattered through the facility rather than centralized in one area. You'll notice on your keys that there's a letter in the top right corner."

Glancing down, I see the uppercase C, nodding to confirm I'm following along with her spiel.

"A Block starts over to the left, and it goes in order," she pauses, glancing at my card. "You lucky ducks! C is the middle block which is where we are now. But these rooms," she points to the open doors as we pass, our eyes spotting people inside. "Are some of our rec rooms. That's arts and crafts, this one is music, and over there is sewing."

"You let people handle needles," I ask, confused.

Ris blinks at me from over her shoulder. "Well, of course!" she answers bubbly. "As long as they pass the counselor check and get a tick of approval and we know they will be safe, patients are free to do what they like. We're here to help heal, not hinder."

Jillian grumbles under her breath. "This is... weird."

I nod, watching Marissa's reaction but she just laughs coolly. "Totes understand why you feel that way. We heard that Lilydale was a little strict."

"Strict doesn't quite cover it..." I say. "So, we have mandatory checks and sessions?"

Opening an unlocked door for us, she points with her thumb to motion us through. "Sessions, yes. But they aren't completely mandatory. Some days, you just don't feel up to chatting and we understand that. But we find most patients are happy to take advantage of our mental health program."

"Are the patients here involuntarily?" Jillian asks.

We enter a large airy corridor, immediately blinded by sunlight. Squinting, I realize it's from the large windows overlooking a courtyard, people wandering around enjoying the warm weather.

"We get patients from time to time who are on a mandated holding period. But before they finish, we offer them a place to stay voluntarily. Most do."

"I can see why," I mutter, shaking my head in disbelief. A young woman in the courtyard who could be our age is licking an ice cream, laughing with two guys. It's hard to grasp that they are patients at first, dressed in summer clothing and sprawled out on a picnic blanket.

What the fuck even is this place?

On the other side of the courtyard, we trek down another corridor with closed doors, and as I take note of the numbers and compare it with the key card in my hand, I realize we've arrived at some of the bedrooms.

"So, what number was it again?" Ris asks.

"317," Jillian answers for us.

"Perfect! Here we are," Ris announces, stopping in front of the door. "Who wants to do the honors?"

"You can do it," I tell Jillian.

She nods, swiping the card. "No code?"

Ris laughs. "No code. Just a single swipe."

The light flashes green and Ris pushes it open while standing back, letting us explore first. My mouth nearly lands on the light blue floor when I focus on what I'm seeing.

Two beds are on either side of the room, a window in the middle. The lack of bars is astonishing, and from here, we can see mountains.

At the end of each bed, there's a set of drawers for clothing, and an adjoining bathroom.

"We have communal showers which are open from 6.00 a.m. until 7.30 p.m. each day, but there's a sink and toilet in all the rooms. Though if you need a shower outside of those hours, just buzz us," Ris murmurs, hovering behind Jillian and I as we look around the spacious room. It's at least twice the size of our Lilydale cells.

"And what time do the doors open?" Jillian questions, and I bite back a smile knowing that she'll be able to let us out somehow if we need.

"5.30 a.m. We have some early morning programs for those early birds. But you're welcome to stay in your room for however long. The dining hall times are posted on the wall under the window along with the speaker."

I spot the intercom, and I'm genuinely lost for words.

"You guys are probably hungry now after a big morning. So, follow me and I'll show you the dining hall! And if we hurry, there might be some fluffy pancakes left."

Chapter 37

Avery

Despite laying on the most comfortable bed I've experienced in years, I don't sleep a wink.

Jillian woke a little after first morning light, the two of us heading to the dining hall for a quick breakfast and gathering snacks for the room. Yes, snacks.

The camp-style buffet was correctly described, the food outshining Lilydale's regular menu by far. Last night they offered Sloppy Joes, salad, baked vegetables, and some vegetarian alternatives—something that had plant protein and tofu. As wonderful and inclusive as it sounded, no one was going to stop me from diving face first into a Sloppy Joe. In hindsight, I should probably feel a little grateful that the guys weren't here to witness the massacre. I'm certain toddlers eat more dignified and graceful than I did last night.

In the dining hall, there's a long table that fills much of a side wall. Snacks are scattered throughout, housing everything from chocolates to potato chips, miniature bags of popcorn, Twinkies, pretzels and fresh fruit. I grabbed a few packets of jelly beans and M&Ms to take back to the room while Jillian opted for Reese's and potato chips.

Neither of us had any desire to check out the recreational rooms yet, not even after finding out there was a computer lab. I asked Jillian why she doesn't try to contact Byrone, but all she said was that it wouldn't work at the moment.

I tried not to let my disappointment show. Truthfully, I was hoping that if she could reach him, it would also give me a direct line to the guys. But short of using some type of messaging app, the chances of us being able to have everyone online at once was slim—that's if they even have access to computers. The guys could be anywhere. When we left Lilydale, they still hadn't been provided with details of their upcoming transfer, and as far as I knew, they hadn't been told where we were going either.

Do people still email? Maybe Jillian could do that if Byrone had an email address.

Except I have no damn email addresses to contact the guys. I imagine it would be something like *littlekiller69* or *touch-me-and-die* but there was the possibility that the men didn't go somewhere as nice as Ridgeview Valley. Maybe they went to a prison or a stricter facility where they can't just roam freely and stuff themselves stupid with snacks.

The only way I could have potentially contacted them was the cells. But naturally, they were confiscated prior to our departure from Lilydale. So with each passing hour, I feel myself fading a little more.

What if I never see them again? What's going to happen to all of us?

From what we were told by Ris, this facility had to discharge some existing patients voluntarily to make room for us. They initially didn't have enough beds to accommodate all of us, but they managed to make room so that we wouldn't be split up among multiple facilities. And to lessen the burden on the social work team assigned to the Lilydale patients by the investigation agency, they decided it was just easier to separate us by men and women for now.

I understand the logic, I really do. But it still doesn't make it hurt any less.

By mid-afternoon, Jillian and I agree to go for a walk for the sake of our mental health. Even though she's not showing it, I know she's struggling just as much as I am. Everyone is.

We could take away all the fucked-up nonsense that happened and it would still be a challenge to adjust. We went from strict routines and being treated like a problem, to suddenly given the freedom to do what we want—well, almost.

Change is never easy at the best of times. This... this is torture.

Eventually, Jillian declares she's done peopling and heads back to our room. I choose to stay outside, distracting myself. It's all I have right now, especially when they have *asked* us to consider speaking to some of the in-house psychiatrists. I don't even know where to begin.

I explore some of the rec rooms and to my surprise, I run into Vivian, Siobhan and Eliana in a small reading room.

Ignoring the stabbing feeling of library reminders, I invite myself in with their blessing.

The room is about a quarter of the size of the Lilydale library, and aside from the books scattered on the floor, there's no shelves. I can only assume there's another room with all the books and this is merely the reading space. Beanbags are spaced out in various bright colors, with motivational posters on the wall. I blink at one of a golden retriever, grinning with a ball in its mouth and the caption *'Don't be afraid to make mistakes. Life's a ball!'*

"Fuck me," I mumble, taking a seat on a bright lemon colored bag next to Vivian and Eliana. "The toxic positivity is practically dripping through the walls here."

Eliana laughs quietly. "It's humbling, that's for sure."

The four of us are in some lame attempt at a circle, and I take a second to scan all of them. We all wear the same exhausted expression, run down with misery that no one can shake off. It's sickening when you think about it.

This place is everything we needed. Supportive, caring, freeing. Yet, it's nothing but a reminder of the hell we survived.

Survived physically, I mean. Because inside, I'm barely keeping it together.

Time will heal us, but the reality is we will always carry the scars. I hate that we've been bonded by trauma and have finally found something relatable to each other—torture.

"They want us to be happy," Vivian points out. "It's killing me."

Siobhan nods. "These assholes have no idea. None."

"They really don't," I agree. "But at least they care, I guess."

"Do they?" Siobhan snorts. "Or is it just another trick to confuse us?"

I frown. Are we that messed up that we can't even let people care about us without questioning if there's an ulterior motive? I get it. Dr. Cromwell kept telling me the experimentation was for the greater good—to help people. People like Arthur Whittingham promised to save me... just for us to find out it was a lie.

No wonder we don't have the ability to see good anymore. Every single time we thought we found it, it turned out to be a fake fantasy. Or disguised while people used and hurt us.

"I think..." Vivian starts quietly. "They genuinely do care. But we're too broken to be fixed."

Flashbacks of her mental health following Sam's death swirl in my mind. She stares at me, as if knowing where my mind is at.

"I'm fine," she tells me. "Just over everything."

"I get it," I reply. "I really do. But you know what? They don't get to have that. We went through hell and those assholes don't deserve to still have a hold on us."

Vivian lifts an eyebrow in disbelief. "Easy for you to say, Avery. At least you have something to look forward to. I have no one."

"You have me," I shoot back. "And look, while I won't pretend that Sam was a good person, I know you were grieving. I know you probably went through shit before Lilydale and then you had to deal with that. Not to mention what they did to us downstairs."

The three of us shift awkwardly, clearly recalling their own experiences.

"Avery is right," Eliana murmurs softly. "We didn't deserve that. And maybe now's our chance for a new beginning. A do-over."

"Why bother?" Siobhan huffs, folding her arms. "All I've got left is a dead brother and a mind that drives me insane."

"You have the chance to tell them motherfuckers to go fuck themselves," I point out. "Don't let them win. We're worth more than that."

Vivian sighs, sliding back into her key lime beanbag. "I just hate how chirpy they all are. It was easier dealing with cranky bastards all the time. At least the food is better. Well..." she trails off, glancing at me knowingly.

"Tony's food was the fucking shit," I mumble, not wanting to dwell on the subject. Vivian was ejected from Cirque des Morts, and I don't blame her for any ill feelings of missing out on the food we got to indulge in. "At least they have snacks. And we can wear jeans."

I nod toward my denim shorts and oversized tee. Ris took us to the closet and let us pick up a few pieces each before showing us where the laundry was. We have to do our own naturally, but at least it's free and there's a range of clothing variety. I can't help but notice that none of the Lilydale patients opted for anything gray shaded.

Eliana is in bright pink and blue, while Vivian and Siobhan are wearing black shorts and shirts.

"We aren't stuck in the rooms," Vivian adds quietly, and I'm happy to hear some improvement in her tone.

"Who did you end up bunking with?" I ask everyone.

Siobhan points to Vivian, while Eliana mentions another Lilydale patient.

"She snores," Siobhan scoffs, eyeing Vivian.

"And you talk in your sleep," she shoots back. "Tough shit."

They glare at each other for a few seconds before breaking out in faint smiles, obviously just as happy not to be alone as I am.

"You know," Eliana starts. "I heard a rumor from my counselor. Apparently, they might end up reopening our cases."

Vivian's eyebrows knit together. "What do you mean?"

"They are trying to figure out what to do with all of us. And given some of the initial findings from Lilydale, they might be allowing appeals so our sentences can be adjusted. Otherwise, it's putting pressure on the facilities to accommodate everyone. So, some of us might go free."

"Free?" I repeat. "But we all have mental health disorders. How would that work?"

Eliana shrugs. "I'm only speculating of course, but some may end up staying here. Voluntarily or involuntarily. I'm not sure. There's a lot of things to work out apparently. It's going to take some time."

My heart sinks. "How much time?"

"Probably months," Vivian sighs. "Nothing gets done quickly in the legal system. I waited six months before I even had my trial."

Six months...

I don't know if I can last six months.

Siobhan grumbles. "No one will let me go. Besides, where would I even go? I got no family, no money."

"Whatever is meant to happen, will happen. Life always works out," I say, earning a glare from the three of them.

"Argh," Vivian groans. "Stop being chirpy and optimistic, Avery. It's gross," she jokes.

"I'd be happy too if I was getting dicked down by three guys," Siobhan says.

Eliana's eyes light up. "Did it ever happen... you know... at the same time?"

"What?" I laugh awkwardly. "How did this turn into a discussion about my sex life?"

"Oh, it so did," Vivian snorts. "It's written all over your face."

"Shut up," I snap, but end up laughing with the rest of them.

Siobhan leans back, folding her hands behind her head. "I'd maybe... stay here for a bit if I got offered the choice," she admits.

"What?" Vivian gawks at her. "You would stay in a facility?"

"Maybe," she shrugs. "I dunno. I'd want to... *maybe* get better."

There's uncertainty and embarrassment in her tone, but I can't help but smile, nodding at her. "I want to get better too," I chime in. "We all deserve to heal."

"Yeah, we do," Eliana agrees. "It will take time, but we'll get there."

Vivian stays quiet, staring at the ceiling in thought. I lean over, placing my hand on her forearm.

"You're a good person, Vee. You get to call the shots for your life now."

She looks at me warily. "I really am sorry, Avery. For everything."

"Me too," I breathe out in relief at the mended gap between us, squeezing her arm.

"We're not hugging though," Vivian snorts, looking over at Siobhan, amused. "I draw the toxic positivity line at physical affection. This one sleepwalks and near spooned me to death last night."

Chapter 38

Avery

** *Six Weeks Later* **

"All rise for the Honorable Judge Shannon Sherwood."

My fingers strum my hips nervously as I watch the Judge enter the room from a side door, her black robe billowing behind her as she walks powerfully towards her seat.

The whole room is dead silent, the bailiff motioning for us to sit once her Honor is settled into her chair.

I've been counting down to this moment, desperate to know what's in store for me. When we got wind that the agency investigating Lilydale decided to reopen all our cases, I wasn't sure how to feel.

For the past few weeks, the Court has been summoning patients one by one, reviewing the previous charges that led us to Lilydale. Apparently, the facilities can't hold onto all of us long term, and with the only other viable option being prison, someone recommended that we should be re-trialed or attempt to appeal our sentences. Even sending us all to prison would be a burden on resources, and given the torture and experience we all had in Lilydale, it was deemed necessary to review everything thoroughly.

Everyone had been hopeful when we found out. Except me.

The idea of my past being scrutinized again made me feel sick. Even more so the fact that there's a possibility I could go to prison. Or what if I'm released and the guys are still found guilty? Too many factors lay in the hands of others, and my track record with allowing people to decide my fate isn't great.

Peering over my shoulder, I spot Dr. Smith and Margie in the courtroom gallery, the two of them giving me reassuring smiles.

From what I've been told, they have been to every court appearance to date, supporting patients. The guys apparently haven't been summoned yet and only a handful of women have returned to Ridgeview Valley Rehabilitation Home so information has been limited, to say the least.

When I got notice yesterday that it was my turn today, I didn't sleep a wink. Jillian had managed to use one of the computers in the facility to help find precedent to argue my case, but at the end of the day, it all comes down to the public defender next to me and the Judge.

Lilydale was... traumatic. And no doubt that will work in my favor. But I still killed. Not only my father, but I killed while in Lilydale.

Police had scoured Lilydale after everything went down, securing the footage to watch to help the agency with their investigation. There's literal evidence that I committed arson and murder, not to mention the guys. We can argue that it was self defence, but we were in Lilydale for a reason.

"In the matter of the people versus Avery Elizabeth White, the Court will now review the original charges and evidence presented during the trial," the Judge recites, glancing at me briefly before switching to the public defender. "Mr. Lovett, as you will."

The public defender reminds me a lot of my hotshot lawyer from the first time round—young, ambitious. Except he also looks tired. I don't blame him though. He suddenly had nearly one hundred cases thrown at him with little time to prepare. The system is ridiculously overwhelmed and he lifts my file in his hands, hazel eyes meeting the Judge's as he clears his throat.

"Thank you, Your Honor. The defendant was previously brought before the Court in relation to a homicide charge pertaining to her father. The Court will note that previous evidence provided by the Defence indicated that the defendant was the victim of domestic abuse. Due to the mitigating factors of the case, the charge was downgraded to involuntary manslaughter as the defendant claimed to not have intended to harm the deceased. Due to her mental state at the time, she was allegedly attempting to end her own life and was not aware her father had returned to the property prior to starting a fire."

I rub my scars nervously, focusing on the tattoos covering them. The whole courtroom is getting a first hand recount of my life, and it's only going to get worse from here.

"I see," the Judge answers casually, not giving anything away. "And her sentence?"

"Originally sentenced to prison time, however was offered a place at Lilydale Foundation Center after her legal representative applied on her behalf."

Glancing over my shoulder again, I meet Dr. Smith's eyes. He gives me a small nod of reassurance.

"Ms. White," the Judge addresses me, my head spinning back to face her. "Please proceed to the stand to be sworn in."

Part of me expects the Bible to sizzle and burn when I put my hand on the cool leather. Following the prompts by the public defender, I link my hands nervously, trying to will myself to calm the fuck down.

"Now, Ms. White," he starts, brown hair perfectly smoothed back. "You began your sentence at Lilydale around a year ago, is that correct?"

"Yes," I answer quietly.

"Can you please tell the court about your time at Lilydale Foundation Center—specifically your treatment program?"

I hesitate as I look over to the prosecution table. I've watched enough *Law and Order* to know that they are going to try to rip me apart. But as I wait for them to object, to accuse the defender of leading me, I'm surprised when they don't move at all.

It's as if they want to hear my story—want to hear what I have to say.

"Well," I start nervously, twisting my hands in my lap. "When I arrived I was told that the program was set up to help rehabilitate patients so that they could go back to society. We were strictly guarded and had a set treatment program of professional appointments, including mandatory psych sessions." Pausing, I smile tightly at Dr. Smith. "We also had access to a physician who helped manage my chronic pain from previous injuries."

The public defender jumps in, "Injuries that were a result of your father's abuse?"

"Yes," I confirm. "Prior to the fire, I had been to the hospital a number of times for his abuse. Broken bones, removing beer bottle glass from my back, and other things..." I trail off uncomfortably.

"Could you please elaborate on what you mean by *other things*?" he presses.

My heart beats violently in my chest. But I realize I have a choice here. I can retreat into my mental shell, or I can take this opportunity to speak up for the first time in my life. Everyone here wants to hear what I have to say. Even at the back of the courtroom, reporters are staring at me intensely with notepads, eager for a story. From what I've heard, the whole Lilydale ordeal has created a media frenzy lately.

What benefit is there to staying quiet? What about other victims that are too afraid to speak up? To talk about their pain. Abusers get away with too much. My father may be dead, but it's not my job to protect him. He never protected me. I had to fight to survive every step of the way.

Well, fuck him. And fuck Lilydale.

Clearing my throat, I do my best to keep my voice strong. "The week before I accidentally killed my father, he had arranged for his friend to rape me," I say loudly, voice cracking only slightly. "I was the prize in some stupid game or bet. The incident left me severely injured."

I can practically feel the tension in the room at my words, a few people not hiding their shock and repulsion. It spurs me on, the public defender nodding. "Tell us about these injuries."

"Scarring and inflammation to my reproductive organs. I was told I will never be able to conceive children. I also suffered severe bruising from attempting to fight back."

My face feels warm as dozens of eyes watch me but I stay focused on the public defender. He eagerly nods, indicating I'm doing well.

"And was your father present that day?"

"Yes," I frown. "He was in the living room. I know he could hear me screaming because the volume on the television kept increasing. He basically sold my virginity and didn't care."

A few murmurs sound around the room but I pay them no mind. Anger and pain rush through me, memories flashing into my mind. I didn't deserve that shit—any of it.

"And what happened to lead to the fire?" The public defender pushes.

"That night my father was in his usual bad mood," I recall. "He threw a bottle at my head and dragged me through the glass while kicking me. During it, he got a phone call and left to go meet that friend. He threatened to bring him back for round two."

It's so quiet you could hear a pin drop. But the faces of the observers and jury give me the power to continue, their horrified expressions clearly working in my favor.

"I'm so sorry," he sympathizes. "So, you felt the only option you had was to end your life."

"That's right," I admit, not bothering to brush away a tear that glides down my cheek. "Except I didn't know he had come back home. I wanted to burn the house down. My mother had killed herself in it too because of him. I just wanted to escape him—not harm him."

"And you ended up in Lilydale?"

"Yes."

"Tell us more about Lilydale. Were you supported by the professional staff there?"

I meet Dr. Smith's eyes again. "Some, yes. But unbeknownst to us, they were conducting experiments on patients. I was one of them."

As I enter into my recollection of Dr. West and Dr. Cromwell's torture, I notice people around the room covering their mouths in horror and disbelief.

Then it hits me.

I'm so close to freedom—if I can just prove I'm not mentally unfit and should be kept in a facility for the rest of my life.

"Despite everything," I start to tell the room. "I worked with my psychiatrist at Lilydale to help heal. And I feel like I've come far. I worked through the blame I held, and how much I hated myself. I actually fell in love there. And for the first time in my life, I believe I deserve a second chance. I deserve to live my life."

The public defender nods, smiling at me. "Thank you, Avery. No more questions, Your Honor."

It's a long morning, pushing into the afternoon when finally, after everyone has spoken, including Dr. Smith, we are excused while the jury deliberates. I stay outside the courtroom with Margie while Dr. Smith keeps his distance, apparently so as to not cause any tampering issues or something according to Margie. Since he spoke as a witness, it's best that we aren't seen talking until the verdict comes back, in case they try to say we're colluding, even though he's on my side.

Hours pass, and finally, we're called back in.

I might actually vomit. Like enough to drown in.

My legs threaten to shake and buckle as I stand next to the public defender, heart pounding painfully.

Shit. This is it...

Whatever they decide, that will seal my fate forever.

"Has the Jury reached a decision?" The Judge asks the lead juror.

"Yes, Your Honor."

"And in your relation to the original charge of involuntary manslaughter, how does the jury find?"

"Guilty, your Honor."

I suck in a breath, panic threatening to send me into madness. How? Why? Do they not care at all about what I had to say?

The public defender touches my back gently. "Just hold on," he whispers.

The Judge nods, face completely vacant. "And the new charges of murder and arson relating to the defendant's time and conduct in Lilydale Foundation Center?"

It feels like minutes pass, and I realize I'm not breathing. But the lead juror glances over at me quickly before looking back at the Judge. "Not guilty, Your Honor."

Not... guilty.

Holy fuck. That's... a start, right?

"Thank you. The Jury is now excused," the Judge says, waiting as the bailiff escorts them from the room.

"What happens now?" I whisper to the public defender.

He nods toward the Judge. "She'll review your original sentence."

I just nod, hugging my frame as I stay standing while the rest of the room sits. The Judge reviews the paperwork in front of her before peering down at me.

"Ms. White, I want to start off by making it clear that what you suffered is unacceptable and inhumane. However, we're guided by law and precedent, and regardless of the circumstances, you unfortunately still fulfilled the definition of involuntary manslaughter."

Tears prick in my eyes but I force myself to maintain eye contact. I give her a little respectful nod of acknowledgment.

"That being said," she continues. "I'm taking into consideration time already served. This, along with the mistreatment you received while under the care of the Lilydale Foundation Center."

Fuzz circles in my brain, static electricity humming in my ears. What is she saying?

"In a perfect world, Ms. White, you would not have been found guilty. Nor should you have endured such mistreatment while you should have been receiving professional help. Unfortunately, that isn't always the case in complicated matters such as these." Pausing, she clears her throat. "Taking into consideration the witness statement from your treating psychiatrist, the report submitted by the Ridgeview Valley Rehabilitation Home in relation to your current stay and cooperation, the investigation report pertaining to Lilydale and the evidence submitted today, I have reached my decision."

I wait, holding my breath as she watches me closely.

"I'm ordering that your sentence be deemed satisfied and final. And with our deepest apologies for what you have endured, I wish you the very best in the next stages of your life. You are free to go."

Chapter 39

Avery

"Holy shit," I breathe out, turning to face Dr. Smith and Margie. "Is it over?"

The courtroom has cleared out for the day but I've been unable to bring myself to leave, still frozen in place. The public defender had given me a quick pat on the shoulder, before grabbing the next file and fleeing to review the information before the next case. I barely noticed though, just replaying the Judge's words in my head over and over.

You are free to go...

It doesn't seem real. Any moment now I'm going to wake up in my room, desolate and bereft as I cling to memories and wishes.

"It's over, Avery," Dr. Smith confirms, giving me a wide smile. "You made it."

I shake my head in disbelief, glancing at Margie. "Thank you so much."

"Of course," she says softly. "You were so brave on the stand, Avery."

"I..." Trailing off, I look around. "I don't even know what to do now. What happens now? Where do I go?"

Dr. Smith clears his throat. "I may have been a little dishonest with you," he starts. My brows frown in confusion.

"What do you mean?"

"I know of three people who probably have a good idea of what you're going to do next..."

Heart beating rapidly, I stare at him wide eyed. "Don't play with me, Christopher..."

He nods his head toward something behind me, smiling.

I spin around, gasping. Standing in the doorway of the courtroom is Damon, Theo, and Grey, dressed casually with matching grins.

My feet move on their own accord, nearly barging Dr. Smith and Margie out of the way as I sprint down the aisle. I launch myself at them, unable to decide who to go to first. Limbs become entangled as I try to reach for all of them, Grey letting out a pained groan as his head collides with Theo's.

"Whoa, little killer. Careful of the award winning face."

"Shut up," I breathe out, grabbing his cheeks and kissing him into silence.

He's only just started kissing me back when I release him, sucking the life out of Theo before moving onto Damon. It's only when someone awkwardly clears their throat behind me that I remember we have an audience, and that I have a million questions, so I pull back.

"You're here," I croak out, voice breaking. "But I don't understand."

Theo reaches for my hand, rubbing my wrist with his thumb. "Grey and I were released last week. Damon was let go a few weeks ago."

I stare at Damon. "Weeks ago?"

He nods. "They decided to set my trial first, given the situation and my involvement. Once I was able to provide all the evidence relating to my father's scheme, the board's corruption, and the treatment suffered in Lilydale, it was basically a domino effect for the rest of the patients. Especially with the investigation findings."

"Except Theo," Grey adds. "He nearly didn't get let off."

"What?" I mutter in horror.

Theo shrugs. "I was brutally honest that I had no issue with killing the people I had."

"But then the public defender jumped in and explained *why*," Grey tacks on. "Idiot here left out some key details."

"I have nothing to hide," Theo explains. "But they basically ruled any conduct at Lilydale as self-defense and reluctantly moved to a ruling that I'd served time. With a warning, apparently."

"Apparently?" I press.

"I don't consider it a warning. Just a suggestion."

Shaking my head, I wipe away tears. "Fuck. This is really happening? We're free? But some people didn't come back to the facility I was in. I thought they had been taken away..."

Damon nods. "A few patients, particularly those struggling still, were admitted into treatment programs. Some voluntarily, others mandated for a fixed period of time to be reviewed. Others were released. Everyone has been happy with their results."

"I can't believe it," I murmur, starting to become over-whelmed with emotion. "Shit—it's over. This is real?"

"It's real, little killer," Grey grins, spinning me around.

I squeal, throwing my arms around his neck. When I'm back on two feet, I ask the question that's bothering me. "Why weren't you guys in the courtroom then?"

"That was something you needed to do on your own," Theo answers. "To fall back on your own strength without having us there to distract you."

"And she did it perfectly," Dr. Smith adds, walking over. "You'd be proud."

"I'm always proud," Grey says, winking at me.

Taking a breath, I wipe away more tears, on the verge of a full sobbing session. "I still can't believe it."

Damon puts his hands in his trouser pockets. "To answer your previous question about what happens next—I've got that sorted."

"Oh?" I ask, eyebrows shooting up.

He nods. "The trust has been immediately released back to me, along with my mother's possessions. If you're up to it, I have a house ready. It needs a bit of work since it's been vacant since her death, but it's big enough for all of us."

"All of us," I repeat, chest tightening in wishful thinking as I glance at Theo and Grey. "The four of us?"

Grey laughs, throwing his hands up. "I know. I gotta live with that asshole," he nods toward Theo. "But I think we'll manage."

"Until I suffocate you in your sleep," Theo bites back.

Ignoring them, I walk into Damon's arms, pulling him into a hug. "I go where you go," I tell him. "I'll follow you three to the depths of hell and back. Oh, that's right. I did..."

Walking into the large white house, my jaw practically scrapes along the ground.

It's beautiful. Perfect.

On the outskirts of town, the house is surrounded by green pastures, large trees and gorgeous gardens. The back of the house overlooks paddocks, and further back there's a small pond, little ripples floating along the surface in the wind.

I'm captivated by the chandelier in the open plan kitchen, fingers grazing the pastel blue walls as I'm given a tour of my new home.

Apparently, Damon has spent the past few weeks getting it ready for us, hiring tradesmen and gardeners. It's been sitting abandoned since he was forced into Lilydale, Alexander opting for a more modern, luxurious penthouse in the city on Lily's dime. Which... now belongs to Damon too. Turns out Alexander's precious Will was deemed invalid due to his actions, the court awarding everything to Damon as his only living child.

There's a strange feeling swirling in my stomach that knowing the real Lily Emerson-Dale lived here. Like my old house, this home is full of memories too. When Damon gives me a tour, I notice an empty room upstairs, the walls ripped apart with holes in them, the carpet partially ripped up and no furniture in sight.

Indents in the remaining carpet resemble the legs of a desk and it doesn't take me long to put two and two together—Alexander's office.

I guess Damon is more like me than we thought. Except instead of burning down the house, he's completely smashed this room to smithereens and is rebuilding it. Probably a better option in hindsight...

"We each have our own rooms," Damon tells me, opening the door to a large bedroom, completely full of new furniture. The smell of fresh paint reaches my senses, the lavender color doing nothing to stop the excitement rushing through me. So much for a calming color.

I head over to a set of large double doors, gasping when I discover they open onto a balcony. I must be above the kitchen, because I have the same perfect view of the grassy fields, my hair billowing in the gentle breeze.

"This is mine?" I ask, leaning back into him as he curls his arms around me.

He nods against me. "The other three rooms are next door and across the hallway. Grey is already working on a new *ASS schedule* as to who gets you every night."

Laughing, I turn to face him. "Do I even get a say?" I joke.

"No," he answers without missing a beat. "Though I'd suggest locking your door. I wouldn't put it past them to sneak in and make an Avery sandwich in the middle of the night."

"I'm not opposed to sandwiches," I say casually. "As long as you sneak in as well."

Damon narrows his eyes with a smirk. "I might just keep a spare key under my pillow."

Grinning, I grab his hand, leading him back downstairs to the living room. It's at the front of the house, with big bay windows and a fireplace to keep us warm. Grey and Theo look up from their spots on the couch as we enter, giving me warm smiles as I curl up on the new fluffy sofa. I could just sleep *here* and be happy. It feels like a damn cloud.

"What do you think?" Grey asks. "I picked the color for your room."

"It's perfect," I breathe out. "I just can't believe this is our new home."

Theo glances at Damon. "Have you told her the other news yet?"

"What news?" I quickly question, snapping my head around.

Damon leans back against the couch, resting his arms behind his head. "Arthur got arrested," he tells me coolly. "We may have provided footage of him and Teddy. Turns out we were correct. Her body was never released to the coroner—obviously since we had her head. He's been charged with her murder. They finally caught up with him three days ago. Locked up in prison awaiting trial. His ex-wife Rose is also planning to testify about his abusive behavior."

"Please tell me you're not kidding," I bounce up, shuffling to my knees. "My heart can't take it."

Grey laughs. "Well, that's one charge anyway. Alexander is dead so someone else has to take the fall for the board's corruption and involvement. Arthur and the board members have been charged for their contribution to the Lilydale scheme."

Best. Fucking. News. Ever.

"That's not all," Theo presses on, shooting me a knowing look. "I may have made a call to the medical board when I was released. That woman doctor has also been charged and has her license suspended pending investigation into malpractice. The other *surviving* doctors as well."

"Dr. Cromwell?" I splutter out. "Shit. No Christmas or birthday presents will ever compare to this."

"I still intend to give it my best shot," Grey replies.

I turn to Damon, unable to fight the smile off my face. "You really did it, Damon. I'm so proud of you."

He lifts an eyebrow. "Team effort, wife. You three also played a pivotal part in this. Along with the others, of course."

Byrone and Jillian were released a few days ago. From what I've been told, the pair of them immediately headed North, back to Byrone's home town to be near his family. They still keep in touch though and have promised to come back for Thanksgiving.

"So, what happens to Lilydale?" I ask. "After the investigation is finished, I mean."

Damon shrugs. "Technically I own the building. I'll probably demolish it and sell the land."

I slope back into the couch, pulling my knees to my chest. "Or..."

"Or what?"

"Okay," I murmur. "Hear me out. What if we—you—turn Lilydale into a proper facility? Like the one I was in over in Ridgeview Valley. They are obviously desperate for more space to accommodate patients. We could turn Lilydale into everything it was meant to be. A proper home to help victims."

The three of them watch me carefully, my cheeks reddening. Was it really that terrible of a suggestion?

"I actually like that idea," Grey finally chimes in.

"It would take a lot of work," Damon responds thoughtfully. "We'd practically need to tear down the whole internal structure and start fresh."

I nod. "No one would want to step foot inside any old format of Lilydale. But we could transform it into a real place of support. It would be the perfect fuck you to Alexander."

"Alright, I'm sold," Grey laughs. "Any fuck you to Alexander has my tick of approval."

Damon's eyes stay trained on me, a smile appearing on his lips. "Mom would have liked that."

"So, it's settled," Theo says. "Lilydale gets a makeover while I spend the rest of my days buried inside Avery."

"Sharing is caring," I laugh. "That's what the *ASS Schedule* is for."

"I'm going to order takeout," Grey announces, standing up from the couch. "Something tells me Avery is going to need all her strength tonight."

Resting my head against the couch, I smile at all of them, feeling completely at peace and loved for the first time in my entire life.

I guess Whittingham was right about one thing—Lilydale did save me. It was just in the form of three unhinged psychos.

And I have no complaints about it whatsoever.

Epilogue
Grey

Sometimes we take for granted just how nice the fresh night breeze can smell in summer.

The wind dances around in soft whispers, and when the wet belch interrupts the night sky, I nearly enact my plan early. This fucker is killing my vibe when I should just be killing him.

He wasn't hard to hunt down. People rarely change. When Avery gave me the minimal details she knew, such as the name of the bar her father frequented and his friend's first name that violated her, I found him within hours.

And that's being generous.

I was much quicker—I just took my time to make sure I was one-hundred percent certain.

After waiting for him to arrive at the bar like clockwork, I got to work, pulling up the fake Tinder profile I'd created with Theo.

Of course a good-for-nothing sleaze like him couldn't resist swiping right on a young, beautiful girl. Once a predator, always a predator.

Just how stupid must you be to believe everything you read online. In a world full of social media and catfishing, the older generation still hasn't quite grasped the fact that they are the easiest to scam. So much for their generation telling us not to talk to strangers and if something is too good to be true, it probably is.

It was easy to lure him into the open. Martin Goldsberg thinks he's meeting eighteen year old Jessi tonight. He wandered out of the bar, stumbling over his own feet at the exact time I told him too. Judging by his poor coordination, he didn't understand the instructions as to our meeting location, but given he's a pathetic excuse for a man and lack of ability to grasp consent, I'm not surprised.

Two single letters, one small word.

No.

I'm nothing if not a teacher. By the end of tonight, he'll have a firm understanding of the word. I'm already taking bets on how many times he'll mutter those words himself, desperate for them to have meaning.

The alleyway is dark, bricks wet from the earlier rain. He's stomping so heavily that he can't hear me behind him, following in the shadows.

When he finally reaches a dead end, confused and lost, I step out into the light, shiv in my hand.

"Who's the fuck are you?" he slurs, tripping over sideways as his eyes narrow on me.

"I'm your worst nightmare, pumpkin. Consider me the grim reaper, coming to collect."

Martin's flabbers are gasted, eyes widening and squinting rhythmically like he's having some kind of electrical shortage. He still has no idea I've just led him into a trap. To him, I'm a cockblock, standing in his way of meeting his next conquest.

"Move aside, son," he says, and although I know the words are nothing more than a seniority thing, it cuts deep, spilling open my own wounds.

"I wouldn't try that," I tell him, nodding my head toward his staggering frame as he attempts to move around me.

One step, two step, three step... floor. Well, ground. Martin finally loses his footing, colliding with the brick wall as he clings to it and fights to stay upright.

It's pathetic really. Part of me hoped for a decent fight rather than a mercy killing. Because even though I plan to mutilate him, it *is* a merciful killing. If I had it my way, I'd escort him back to Damon's house—our house—locking him downstairs in the basement. Every day I'd visit, inflicting new harm and injuries while inhaling his non-consensual pleas and begs. But Deadman ruled against me, claiming I wasn't bringing that trash into his mother's house.

And in fairness, I conceded quickly. That's the house we're going to make memories in while honoring Lily's legacy. It doesn't deserve to be tarnished. But that doesn't mean this scumbag gets to walk free.

I promised Avery in the beginning that I would hunt him down. If her father was still alive, I'd be tempted to re-enact Theo's sister's tribute in some twisted fashion. They both deserve to suffer but her father already got his karma. As much as I wished it was at my hands, I'm secretly pleased that his life was cut short by Avery. It's symbolic—trauma aside.

"I got no time for you, kid. Fuck the move away," Martin slurs again, and my nose wrinkles at the visible beer dribbled down his shirt. This is essentially a public service—a community blessing. There's no way this man needs to be alive, he's a disgrace to human beings everywhere.

At this point I realize he hasn't spotted my clearly visible shiv. It's my favorite one, barely away from me at any given time. I made it just for Avery in Lilydale, and I couldn't think of a more fitting item to end dear Martin's life with.

I step closer, resisting the urge to gag when his body odor hits me. It smells as if he hasn't showered in weeks, other than in cheap liquor.

Cars pass by on the main street, unable to see us down here but close enough that I'll have to be quick. Once again, I hate that idea. I want to draw it out and make him suffer—but beggars can't be choosers.

Finally, his eyes scan my body, stopping on the shiny blade in my hand. "What's that thing?"

I offer him a tight smile, taking a breath as I get ready to recite my hard prepared speech.

"You were an acquaintance of Joshua White," I start, pausing as I search for recognition in his hazy eyes. He's slow, but it's there, a light in the otherwise empty vessel.

"Joshie White? What 'bout him? He's dead."

"I'm aware of this fact," I comment calmly. "And you're about to join him."

Realization dawns on this flaccid goldfish, eyes darting between myself and the shiv. Instantly, he tenses up, that alcoholic rage getting ready to rear its ugly head. I'm all too familiar with it, having dealt with my fair share of lunatics—substance abusers or otherwise.

Sweaty palms curl into fists, a moment of lucidity falling over him as he sizes me up. Sure, he has the weight advantage, but I have something he never will—the desire to turn my girl's rapist into maggot compost.

He'll never touch Avery again. Never steal moments from her that don't belong to him—or anyone.

I clock him coming at me before he's even moved, tipping the shiv up as he lunges through the damp alleyway. The squelch of tearing flesh is music to my ears, my hand against his potbelly as I wiggle the shiv around.

Where's that bravery now? The one he had when impaling his wrinkled sausage into innocent girls? Not so tough when I've got him impaled on my stick...

There's a gargling sound, followed by choking as I twist the shiv upwards, aiming straight for his ribcage. I hit bone at first, gripping his shoulder to steady him as I jerk it around carelessly until I feel something else—hopefully a lung.

Blood gushes and weeps from the wound, the would-be circular entrance a now jagged line as I use all my strength to carve his flesh.

Withdrawing the dripping blade, I plunge into his throat. I deliberately aim for his thyroid—the right side because I'm a sucker for symmetry and shit—before piercing it through his left shoulder. Balance.

His knees start to buckle but I'm not ready to end this yet. "Oh, no you don't Marty," I tsk, shoving him backwards to push him against the wall. "You need to know *why* I'm doing this so that when you descend to the depths of Hell, it's on your conscience."

I wait for him to speak, realizing that I've probably severed his vocal cords—oops.

Sighing, I get to the point. "Avery White," I say clearly so there's no mistaking who I'm here for. "You took something from her because of your dear old buddy. And now, I'm taking your life from you."

Dark blue eyes widen at me, my grin wide as he lands on the same page. That's it... think of her and all your regrets as you leave this earth.

"I'm going to go home shortly," I tell him, slowly pulling the shiv out of his body. "And while you're here, dying and being put out of your miserable existence, I'm going to fuck her over and over to ensure I erase all traces of you. Then

I'll burn your body with acid so that there's no traces of you physically either. Life's a bitch, pumpkin. And that bitch is Grey."

Delivering the final blow, I slice the shiv straight across his throat, doing a damn job better than my father. The line is somewhat perfect, at least from what I can see as blood pours out and he collapses on the ground.

Wiping the blade on my jeans, I tilt my head back, breathing in that sweet smell of death. It's so good, so satisfying.

A few minutes later, headlights appear at the end of the alleyway, heading my way. I lean against the wall, one foot resting on the newly deceased as the stolen van pulls up next to me.

"I thought we said to keep it clean," Theo grunts, leaning out of the driver's way and surveying the blood on the ground.

"What?" I ask amused. "It *is* clean by my standards. He's in one piece, isn't he?"

Theo sighs, getting out of the van and walking round the side to slide open the door. Together, the two of us lift the sack of shit and toss him onto the pre-prepared plastic tarp. Theo glances around at the ground with a disapproving look.

"You're lucky I brought chemicals with me," he scolds, shoving a container into my arms as he starts dousing the ground with another.

I grin. "I knew I could count on you, brother-in-law. Speaking of which, is Avery with Damon?"

Theo nods. "Yep. Righteous prick organized a *pampering session*—whatever that is meant to be."

Cackling, I just imagine Damon supervising a mani-pedi session, having Avery fawn over what color polish to choose. I wouldn't be surprised if we return and find his nails painted. I've been trying to convince him for years to give it a go. He'd probably give in to her just to spite me.

"Alright done," Theo exclaims, tossing the empty container on top of Martin. "Ready?"

I nod, screwing the lid back on. "Let's go conduct some scientific experiments to see how long it takes Martin to disintegrate into nothing."

Avery looks content and comfortable when we arrive back home. Deadman too—but if I tell him he looks cute with his head resting on her shoulder while she sleeps curled up under his arm on the couch, he may launch a cushion or knife at my head.

Even through the shadows, I can see his warning glare, daring me to call him out on his little romantic love nest. Reflections of flames dance around the room from the fireplace, creating illusions on the newly painted walls, and I take a moment to admire them again. Avery picked the color, of course—a dark scarlet—which I tell myself was for me as a reward for her bedroom color.

"Aw, damn. We missed her," I groan as Theo stops next to me. He puts the cardboard box he's carrying on the floor and slinks out of his hoodie.

Narrowing his eyes at me, he scolds, "Told you not to make a fucking mess."

I shrug lazily. "It was worth it. Besides, we have every day with her for the rest of our lives."

"So, it's done?" Damon asks knowingly.

I nod. "And she still doesn't know?"

Damon smirks. "I told her you were out having a couple's massage."

"For fuck sake," Theo curses under his breath, stalking toward the kitchen. "What did I do to deserve this circus of horrors?"

"Murdered someone!" I call out cheerfully, careful as to not wake little killer.

"And you'll be next," he replies back without missing a beat before disappearing from sight.

When it's just the two of us, plus a sleeping Avery, I glance around, spotting a gift bag on the coffee table. My eyebrows shoot up, piqued with interest. "What's that?"

"Take a look."

I stroll over, opening the top of the gift bag before swinging around to face him, holding back a laugh. "You didn't..."

"Did."

Lifting the brand new blender out of the bag, I grin. "Finally got my blender."

"For smoothies and shit though. No dicks."

"This is just *perfect*," I murmur happily, putting it on the coffee table and heading over to the discarded box on the floor.

Damon groans. "Do I want to know *why*...?"

I reach inside the box, lifting a plastic bag up. "Avery said she was thinking of getting a pet. So, I bought a goldfish on the way home!"

He rubs a hand over his face, shaking his head. I ignore his *obvious* excitement about our new roommate, popping the lid off the top of the blender. Upturning the plastic bag, I dump the water and goldfish through the glass rim.

"You know," I start, stepping back to admire my handiwork as the goldfish swims around, probably wondering where the fuck he is and why he's in a kitchen appliance and not a proper fish tank. "I think I'll call him Sam."

Epilogue 2
Avery

I smile at the lilies blooming by the entrance way, the white and pink petals fully open as they welcome us inside.

Damon has really outdone himself. Stepping inside the foyer, nothing reminds me of before. The new blue marble flooring leads to a large electric fireplace. A reception desk to the side sits where Whitface's office used to be before we bulldozed the whole thing and made it a memorial wall.

Photos hang on the new wall, portraying the smiling faces of the people we've loved and lost.

Lily. Paige. My mom. Theo's sister, Madison. Leighton.

Everyone who played an important role in us arriving to this moment is honored, their memories no longer tarnished by hate and lies.

The walls throughout the building are painted in every bright color imaginable. That was my idea—much to the hesitation of Damon. I think it worked out well though. There's not a shade of gray anywhere, even if the building is a regurgitated rainbow as a whole.

"You made it!" A familiar voice announces, the man walking out of an open side door. "Damon, Grey, Theo."

"Connor," Damon nods, shaking his hand.

Grey grabs my shoulders, giving me a little shake in excitement. "It's looking great."

Connor smiles, reaching out his hand to me in a show of respect. "It's lovely to see you again, Avery."

"Hey, Connor," I greet warmly, smiling at the new facility supervisor. "I heard the first new patients are arriving tomorrow."

"That's right," he confirms. "We're all set up and ready to rock and roll. Chris just finished the onboarding sessions and briefed the staff."

"Did someone say my name?"

Dr. Smith—wait, no, Christopher—emerges from another open door near the fireplace dressed in jeans and a cotton shirt. I'm still struggling to call him by his first name, even though he continues to insist on it.

I guess we're family now so I have to get used to it eventually. He comes over regularly for lunch and has just taken on the new role as the Lily Halfway Home's lead psychiatrist. But with his input, Damon hired a bunch more—some new, ready to be mentored by the senior doctors. Just enough to make sure no one was overworked and patients received detailed care.

We changed the name obviously. Any mention or reference that could be perceived to be tied to Alexander was tossed in the trash. But I hope the asshole is rolling in his grave, rotting away while worms eat his testicles.

"Any chance to jump into a conversation and provide your opinion," Damon grumbles, barging his shoulder into Christopher as he stalks past.

"Nice to see you too, dear cousin," he replies, grinning at me. "Ready for the tour, Avery?"

"As ready as I'll ever be, Chris," I laugh, grabbing Theo's hand and dragging him with me.

I know where we're going first. After all, I helped design these two sections.

The Paige Memorial Garden and Madison Commemoration Room are two of my greatest achievements, dedicated to the most important people in our lives who should have still been with us.

The garden is in the new courtyard, which may or may not look similar to the one that inspired me at Ridgeview Valley. No longer is it cold and closed off with nothing but empty grounds. Now, it's surrounded by large windows, full of lawn activities and a beautiful garden bed in one corner. Paige's favorite flowers are there, blossoming in the sunlight.

Madison's room is one of our new recreational activity rooms—inspired by the four walls that used to hide Theo and I when he'd tattoo me. Except rather than an empty shell, it's a music center where patients can grab a pair of headphones and listen to whatever tunes they like. Apparently, Madi loved music so it felt fitting to honor her this way, just like Theo loves his tattoos.

Passing the staff rooms, I smile at the new medical clinic, complete with stickers all over the ceiling so that when patients are being treated, they can focus on the cartoon figures if they feel nervous. Dr. Markel retired, but we have some amazing physicians working with us now to ensure patients are listened to and treated appropriately.

We kept Tony on, of course. But under the strict guideline that if he was never allowed to serve bland pasta and cold vegetables again. The whole staff were happy to stay on—with a pay increase. Trauma payment, they called it. After working for Whittingham for too long, they insisted on compensation in the form of a raise. Worth it though... even if Theo is still giving me shit about Thursday Pizza Night and how pineapple needs to be banned. Absolutely not.

Charmaine even stayed on as a guidance counselor, still giving Grey shit whenever they cross paths and whacking him in the head with paperwork.

Grey catches up to us just as we reach the dorms. We got rid of the double-access pads, adopting Ridgeview Valley's methods and giving patients roommates. But of course, for the antisocial ones like Theo, they can also go solo. No one will be forced to do anything they don't want. This is about their future—their wellbeing.

We're giving everyone the second chance we should have had to begin with. Victims deserve to be heard, to have their pain acknowledged. And the four of us are living proof that no matter what happens, there's a light at the end of the tunnel. We want to give people that hope, let them sparkle their damn brightest. They might not know it yet, but the future is bright and worth living.

Our monsters don't deserve our pain. And they sure as fuck don't deserve our tears. The greatest revenge is living... and it's a gift we intend to continue sharing in Lily's memory.

Heading back to the foyer, I'm surprised to find Christopher and Damon chatting. As soon as they spot us, Damon crosses his arms, pretending to not be enjoying his cousin bonding time.

"About time," he groans. "I had to listen to this asshole ramble on about his personal life."

I laugh, relieving Damon from his *torture*. I slide my hand into his, resting my head on his shoulder. "How is Margie going?"

"She'll be four months next week," he beams. "We just found out we're having a baby girl."

"And he's going to propose," Damon adds. "So, prepare for more rambling in the next few weeks."

Gasping, I break out into a grin. "Holy shit, that's amazing. Congrats!"

"Thanks, Avery," Chris smiles brightly. "We'll see you for lunch on Sunday still. Meg's making that apple pie you love."

"Ahh, she's the best," I groan. "Hopefully we don't run out of whipped cream again." Shooting a glare toward Grey, his eyebrows shoot up.

"I didn't hear you complaining when I had it on your ti—"

"And that's my cue to leave," Chris groans. "I'll catch up with you before you head off."

Damon waits until he's out of earshot, smirking at Grey. "If I knew the way to get him to shut up was to talk about banging Avery, I would have tried it."

"And then I'd be forced to kill your cousin," Theo interjects. "No one looks or breathes at her, let alone hears about her body."

"Fucking psycho," I mutter quietly.

"What was that?" Theo asks, having fully heard me.

I raise my hands. "Nothing, nothing. Come on—Tony's done a practice run for tomorrow and has prepared lunch for us as a little treat."

Grey leans down, whispering in my ear. "And afterwards, I think we should take a quick trip to the library, little killer. You know... *for dessert*."

Afterword

Thank you for reading the Dance With My Demons series!

That's a wrap on Lilydale... well, *for now anyway.*

Avery, Grey, Theo, and Damon finally got their happy ending but something tells me we might see them again from time to time.

Did you think the asylum madness was over?

Until next time, little killer

xx

Stalk The Author

FB Readers Group - Steph Macca's Asylum for Pectoral Perves

https://www.facebook.com/groups/authorstephmacca

Instagram

https://www.instagram.com/authorstephmacca/

TikTok

https://www.tiktok.com/@authorstephmacca

Facebook

www.facebook.com/authorstephmacca/

Online Store

www.stephmacca.com

Other Books by Steph

DANCE WITH MY DEMONS SERIES

(Unhinged, Echoes, Ravage, Exile)

BOYS OF WILLOWBROOK

(The Devils They Are, The Monster I Am)

ALL TOO WELL

THE LIES WE KEEP SERIES

(Vicious Games, Pretty Savages, Recklessly Damaged, Sweet Anarchy)

THE BLACK SPADES SERIES

(King of Spades, Queen of Fire, Aces and Ashes, The Hunter)

THE CHRONICLES OF MAXWELL DUET

(A Day of Ruin, A Day of Chaos)

MIDNIGHT PSYCHOS

(Ruthless Savages, Ruthless Redemption, Ruthless Reign, Ruthless Fate)

WICKEDLY SWEET

SLEIGH

BEAUTIFUL DECEPTIONS & SWEET MISERIES

ANATOMY OF A KILLER

RAYNE